Crocodile on the Carousel

By

Sally Tissington

First published in the UK in 2012 by G-Press Fiction, an imprint of
Golden Guides Press Ltd.

10 8 6 4 2 1 3 5 7 9

A CIP catalogue record for this book is available from the British Library.

ISBN 978-1-78095-002-0 (Hardback)
ISBN 978-1-78095-010-5 (Trade paperback)
ISBN 978-1-78095-041-9 (Kindle)
ISBN 978-1-78095-042-6 (ePub)

Typeset in 12pt Ehrhardt by Mac Style, Beverley, East Yorkshire.
Cover design by Mousemat Design Ltd.
Printed and bound in the UK.

Golden Guides Press Ltd
P.O. Box 171
Newhaven
E. Sussex
BN9 1AZ
UK

admin@goldenguidespress.com
www.goldenguidespress.com

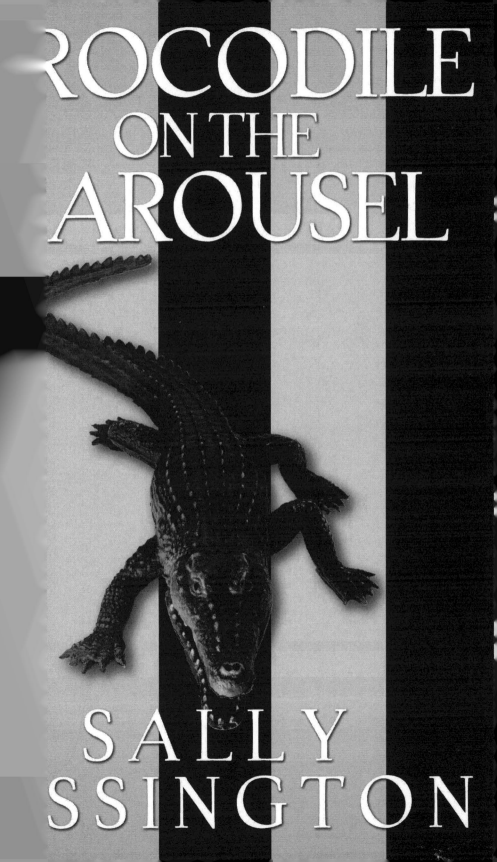

For Alfie Tissington, born 8/02/2001, died 9/02/2001

Contents

I

We Meet my Grandmother

M Y GRANDMOTHER had a dark view of life. If she were eyeing a mouth-watering sponge cake, the sell-by date would loom large at her from the box. From there, her mind would make the small leap to the inevitability of decay for all of us, and the cream, that had tantalised a moment before, would be replaced with the image of a heaving stomach. Similarly, with dog mess on the street, one small piece on an entire road would magnify itself in her head until the smell would reverberate, trapped in the hairs of her nostrils. No matter what other delights presented themselves over the course of the day, the heaving and the stench were the experiences that would stay with her until she fell asleep. What caused such a gloomy outlook? Genetics 60% and life experience 40% – or the other way around? These per centages may vary wildly during the telling of this story.

Our house was no idyllic country cottage. Anyone coming down our road looking for a rose-covered establishment was bound for disappointment when a pebbledashed, white-washed, ex-army hut would loom at them out of the mist. Gran had lived in the house since the 1950s, moving in at the age of two, hours after the building had been erected for the second time. Her father had bought it cheaply after the War and it was eventually transported to the seven-acre plot in panels on the back of an enormous lorry. Originally, it had been built to last 10 years and no more but it had surprised everyone with its robustness; just as Gran had done, a small but wiry child of extraordinary strength. She had a tenuous grip on the idea of owning property and yet had somehow ended up owning a vast portion of land but the house, insubstantial as it was, reflected her real view of life. To reinforce this view in me, she would take me three miles down the road to a section of river she particularly loved. An imposing creek with a derelict pub alongside it. We would sit on the stone jetty.

'As if anybody could own a river,' she would say.

And I would imagine someone desperate, flailing and grasping, trying to hold thousands of gallons of moving water in their hands.

Her father did little to the army hut to transform it into a house, other than put up some plasterboard partitions which had made two good-sized bedrooms, a kitchen, a bathroom and a living area. Ten years later, he added a conservatory and very little had changed from that moment on. Gran took over the place from her parents when she was 19, moving my grandfather, Bill, in two years later.

Although he slipped successfully into Gran's life where many had failed, I often thought that Bill might have regretted his own stealth and high pain threshold.

Gran and Bill were part of a crowd of 20 young people one night, in a pub where a wake was being held. The wake was showing no sign of ending and Gran, then a young girl in a sleeveless shift dress, wanted to move the mourners down to the river, thinking that nature would provide a better send off for the man who had died, rather than the inside of a bar. Nobody else seemed keen to join in with her plan, so my grandmother, who needed to pull the extraordinary out of darkness that evening, carried one of the pub tables and two chairs out into the middle of the river. She intended to sit out there and wait for the tide to come in, before wading, then swimming the last few metres to shore. So she set the table on a mudbank, carrying out candles, food and wine. She thought she was alone, but my grandfather had seen her leave the wake, and followed, seizing a longed for opportunity to talk to her. He waded out to the mudbank and, uninvited, took the spare chair. She sensed he wanted to declare something.

'You have 40 minutes to say what you need to say to me, before the water covers the table,' she said, swigging from a bottle.

While Bill juggled words in his head, she made little boats from foil pie dishes, stuck candlestubs in their hulls and started to float them down the river, one by one. Bill watched the tiny lights sailing away from him but was still unable to speak.

They drew their feet up the rungs of the chairs, knees towards their bodies, as the water rose by increments around them; ending up sitting close together on top of the table. My grandmother delayed his inevitable speech further by pulling at Bill's fraying jumper until she had enough wool to make patterns with her hands. Her fingers moved adeptly through the wool, easily recalling childhood moves to make the pictures of the cat's cradle game.

'The Eiffel Tower,' she said, holding out her hands to him.

'We could go there,' he said.

In the time it took her to raise an eyebrow, she had made another pattern, a cradle.

'We could have a child,' he said.

She snorted, but she still said yes to his proposal, because she had no other options left, and the idea of a sedate, trouble-free existence momentarily appealed, in whatever form it was offered. Even though the events from the previous few weeks of her life had committed her to pessimism, it was incomprehensible to her that things could get worse – and that very night.

Lurking round the corner of the pub, pressed up against the bricks, was a young man not wanting to be seen, which was unusual for him. He had watched my grandparents sit on top of the table, their bodies, faces and hands partially lit by candlelight. Although he had heard nothing, he processed all that had happened between them quicker than they had. My grandmother's treachery overwhelmed him. He didn't blame Bill, he was just another pawn but, as for her, she was something so vile and infectious that, even being a medical student, he struggled to categorise it. Doon was halfway through his studies, undeniably clever and attractive, yet he felt compelled to try and destroy my grandmother, obliterate her place in society. Unexpectedly, his opportunity arose later that night.

* * *

But now, 38 years later and very much alive, she was looking at me, her granddaughter, Amanda, and the box of doughnuts I had just bought: five for 99p.

'How is that possible?' she said.

'Spare me the doughnut/downfall of the world speech,' I replied.

'Who is suffering to enable you to eat doughnuts at 20p a go?'

Suffering was her thing.

I ran my nose around the ring of the doughnut, sniffing exaggeratedly, then I picked off single grains of sugar with my tongue. This would show her that I was in no mood for a lecture. Her eyes left the doughnut box and moved on to my legs.

'Where are those jeans from?' she asked.

'New,' I replied.

'They don't look new.'

'They're distressed.'

'*I* am distressed. As if I needed one final piece of evidence that life is absurd, it's you parading around as a pseudo-peasant.'

I did a provocative wiggle. She threw up her hands half-heartedly, 'So, we live in a society where shortening the life of clothes is not seen as perverse.'

'Call it secondhand without the smelliness.' I said.

'Nothing is without its stench.' Both of us stopped talking because we could hear a car slowly making its way down the narrow lanes.

'What time are you going to start work?' she asked. I worked at the local pub.

'In a bit.'

'The parasols will need putting up. People will burn in this sun.'

'Burn in hell?'

She laughed, and I was glad.

It had taken a while for us to return to this way of addressing one another and I was relieved that Gran had returned to normal after the difficult time we had been through. It felt good to have her back, belligerent as ever.

The car that we had heard moments ago, pulled into the car park, a few metres from us, and a tall man got out. Gran nodded to him. He hesitated about coming closer.

'I hear Bill will be back soon.' She nodded again. 'I'm sorry for what you've been through. I read it in the papers.'

'Extraordinary to be so interested in other people's lives,' said my grandmother when the man was out of earshot.

Regardless of what had happened, Bill was still my grandfather.

* * *

My grandparents married with little fuss other than a final concession from my grandfather. He changed his name to hers, Furnish. Five months after the wedding, on a mean February afternoon, Gran went into labour with her first child. Instead of the home birth she had predicted, events had taken her into unknown territory: the hospital, where the baby was eventually pulled out with forceps and lay motionless with the cord around his neck. A tightly plaited scarf, uniform from the school of non-starters. Three hours later, she discharged herself. She walked out of the hospital with her head rigid. The corridors kept her vision straight and her eyes never moved to the sides. She stepped out into the sun and winced. She refused my grandfather's arm. He called a taxi and they went home.

When they arrived home, she wouldn't go upstairs. A few days later, she became physically unable to get upstairs because of her chosen footwear. She refused normal shoes and, instead, filled two shoeboxes with earth, planting her feet firmly inside them. Wearing these creations, she moved slowly about the kitchen and living room. She made her bed on the sofa. One night when she was settling down, having sprinkled earth over her legs, chest and head, and plugged her orifices with soil, she heard a muffled coughing. It was my grandfather back from the pub. She flicked the earth from one eyelid and opened her eye.

'This had better be good,' she said.

He looked uneasy and hopped from one foot to the other whilst looking at the floor. She was used to the sight of his downcast head. It had become more familiar than his face had ever been. He said that, whilst he had been at the pub, some people had asked about Gran, to see how she was doing. He admitted that he might have mentioned something about her feet. It was a throwaway comment but it had been seized upon.

Gran sighed because she knew what this meant: people crawling up her path. She could smell their imminent arrival on the air. Crunching the gravel, displacing the familiar pattern of the stones with well-made, well-meaning shoes. The closed sign, which she wore around her neck instead of jewellery, would not be enough.

Predictably, the first visitor arrived the next day with a tray full of tempting food, and her head lifted instinctively as the smell led her back to a time when she loved food. Then she remembered. She stuck her feet deeper into the shoeboxes, her toes moved like worms in the soil but her face said nothing. The visitor broke the silence.

'So and so down the road has lost three you know, one after the other, now, that's what I call unlucky.'

The next visitor was better educated and glanced at Gran's feet, pretending not to have seen the boxes.

'By behaving like this, you are creating pathways, neural connections. Every time you go over the events again in your head, you are making it more difficult to move on.'

The third and last visitor came and went. He stared openly at her shoes because he couldn't look in her desolate eyes. He suggested that she make another baby. A replica of the one she had lost. After all, she had the materials available to her. She watched him walk back down the path and engage my grandfather in conversation, a chat about pale imitations.

As soon as she saw him disappear through the gate, she hobbled up to Bill, 'Seven days of being left alone is as much as a person is allowed before they come opening their mouths,' she said.

'Just trying to be helpful,' said Bill.

'Nonsense, they didn't speak to me at all but to their own terror. All too frightened at the thought of their own children dying so they come round here with their disgusting little platitudes. Filthy, inane, simplistic comments. Is that what I have to put up with for the rest of my life? To be surrounded by idiots who can't sit with me in silence for more than a minute without uttering some insipid, ill thought out…'

'They mean well, Cath.'

'Do they? They were at the same wake as I was. Did they stand up for me? Or side with that snake, Doon?'

'There were no other witnesses, they couldn't stand up for you.'

'They knew the kind of person that I was, that I would have had nothing to do with it. And anybody can see through him, see what he is.'

At that Bill, pushed his spade into a clod of earth and broke it in two.

*   *   *

That winter was a cold one, or maybe it was a mild one, but she was cold anyway. She leafed through the small ads of the local paper looking at this and that, gazing at box after box of words that deliberately misrepresented things. Calling items which were battered, 'hardly worn'. Lying about the original cost of objects. She was looking for something to stop her shaking. She found an advert for a heater which took her fancy, so she circled the notice. When she dialled the number, a gruff voice answered and she arranged to go and see the heater. She wanted to interview it, ask if it could bring back the dead and, failing that, take away some of the coldness.

The man selling it talked about the heater with affection, relating its history and pedigree. Little casters enabled it to be moved from room to room quite easily. The roar was ferocious when the match was held close to the grill mouth. Count your eyelashes on the way in and count them on the way out. She handed over her money because she liked a thing with a dual purpose. At least she could be warm whilst deciding whether it was worth living or not. And, if she decided *not*, then the gas from the heater would assist her.

As she got up to go, the man said there would be no trouble for him to bring the heater round in a van; he was always out and about delivering. As he carried on about specifications and safety, and how long a gas bottle would last under normal circumstances, something in his garden caught Gran's eye. On a late-winter afternoon, the sun had made a defiant appearance. Its rays licked something metallic, a twisted golden pole which looked like a vertical umbilical cord. The pole was part of a much larger object which was covered in a patchwork of tarpaulin. But, in the gaps between different-sized sheets, Gran could see glimpses of colour. Like a ride from a fair, a carousel, but much larger than any she had seen before.

She asked why he had such a thing in his garden. The Heater Man had been related to someone who had made carousels. This constructor of merry-go-rounds hadn't made the engines, but he had made everything else – the wooden floors and the figures. The man who made them had been successful, famous among other carousel makers. By his 40th year, he had made 18 of his own and many carvings for others. They were all over the country, mostly in museums now, some dragged out as curiosities for summer fêtes. One had ended up in a ditch after it fell off a trailer. It had been cut up for parts. The horses were used again, given a second life, though still destined to go round in circles.

At Gran's request, they went outside and walked towards the strange mass. The man lifted a corner of the tarpaulin and the water that had pooled over the weeks gushed onto Gran's feet. Her shoeboxes were waterlogged, her feet suspended in a peaty, liquid mess. She had to step out of her boxes. He ran into the house and fetched a pair of Wellington boots similar to cardboard boxes, but more socially acceptable. Her earthy feet touched the cold, unfamiliar rubber. He could see that she was fascinated and, to make up for ruining her shoes, he freed more and more of the carousel from the sheeting. As he did so, he mumbled apologies about the sorry thing they were soon to see.

The figures on the ride were not horses. Her eyes could not make sense of what they saw, so they flickered about and looked desperately for flared nostrils or bright fetlocks. She felt sure she would soon see a carved wooden tail or a mane that appeared as if the wind were blowing through it. Where were the traditional colours? The childlike charm? Not here. Here was a group of animals impossible to categorise. An unwieldy collection of creatures; ranging from the familiar domestic to mysterious hybrids. The only recognisable elements of the ride were the twisted gold poles.

Gran observed an enormous bird, a vulture perched on a steep crag, feeding its two chicks with bloody meat. The man-made rocks that supported the vulture's nest had many different colours running through them, none of them natural. Two gold poles disappeared into the stone and small, seat-shaped ledges had been cut, allowing you to perch uncomfortably by the predator and its offspring and look down on the battlefield with unforgiving eyes as the carousel slowly turned. Moving clockwise, the next animals round were three goats that clambered about on a smoother surface and, again, there were poles for you to hold, so that you could kneel down beside them and share their vulnerability. Following the goats there was an ostrich, a bear and her three cubs, an antelope, an ox, and a hawk in mid-flight.

To the right of the hawk was a prowling lioness whose head shrank cruelly into her shoulders. Her eyes were fixed on some potential prey beyond the carousel, something that didn't stand a chance.

Finally, Gran spotted a horse. So she had been wrong, there had been a horse here all the time. But this was no fairground horse. It reared up from the floor of the carousel, a wounded war horse with a huge head. It was possible to ride it but you would have to hang on precariously, clinging to the animal. Its back hooves thundered into the ground, sensing the nearness of death, yet remaining proud till the end.

On opposite sides of the carousel, as if they were the north and south of the machine, were animals Gran had been avoiding seeing. They were the kind of creatures displayed on maps that are hundreds of years old, at least twice the size of the other animals on the carousel. Beasts glimpsed by an explorer; things too strange to register, so the shortfall had been made up with imagination. The first one was similar to a monstrous, warped hippopotamus, its hulking body dominating the area allotted to it. The carousel maker had carved muscles into its belly and sides. It looked as though it might move at any moment. Gran held her breath in case it showed any signs of life.

The final animal seemed to pull Gran towards the ride and, without asking permission, she bounded up the steps of the carousel. A crocodile monster with a gaping mouth and teeth as large as adult fingers. A powerful thrashing tail, as long as the body. Each scale on its body was uniformly and delicately constructed, yet she could see that the creature had fared badly. Its neck was gashed, the wooden wound open and ugly as though it had been deliberately attacked. Gran knelt by the side of it, placing her hands in the wound and, as she did so, she felt a vibration. She thought for a moment that the Heater Man had started the engine of the carousel but, when she looked, he was just standing there, dumbfounded.

Unselfconsciously, her fingers continued to explore the body of the animal. She removed a huge hook from the creature's mouth and let it dangle on wire from the roof of the ride. She picked at fragments of paint, rich and delicious slivers which hinted at a former, unimaginable brightness. Gran saw no malevolence in the animal's fearsome appearance, nor in the entire carousel as she wandered around, making sense of this piece of work in a way that few ever would. She recognised the two most outrageous animals as God's favourite and most impressive creations: Behemoth, the mutated hippopotamus and Leviathan, the crocodile creature. The creatures of whose potency and grandeur He shamelessly boasted.

In some sections of the carousel, it appeared to be hailing: torrents of tiny white stones hung from tattered strings. On another part of the ride, strips of metal imitating lightning flashes swung from semi-transparent strings. Some of these strings were hopelessly tangled. Bad weather reigned over the ride and ornamental lettering surrounded the roof. To finish, in the centre of the carousel, close to the engine, a colossal star hung over three-metre high, ornate iron gates, complete with giant padlock and key. These were the Gates of Death, delicately engraved with skulls and bones.

The carousel maker had experienced a spiritual crisis late in life. After years of happily adhering to dogma, he had faltered when he came across *The Book of Job* from *The Bible*. It had turned him upside down, rattled his innards and, in response, he felt he had no choice but to make the carousel. He had made it 13 metres in diameter, so that it would dwarf any other carousel in existence – and because 13 was a devilish number. All the pretty horses he had made in the past had been a prostitution of his talent, which was far better suited to making the creatures listed at the end of *The Book of Job*.

The Heater Man started to cover the thing up, looking sideways and mumbling, 'I told you it was ugly.'

'How much do you want for it?' asked Gran.

He had shaken his head. It was a useless thing. Although it was well-made, the figures carved with skill and lightness and the mechanics sound, it frightened children. It was grotesque, who could live with such darkness? Such a message? What sort of man would spend years making such a thing, whilst his family looked on in horror? Why hadn't he turned to church carvings? No one would touch it. No museum wanted it, no fairground wanted it. He had been offered money to take the creatures off and replace them with horses, but he didn't know what to do with the bodies. Logic escaped him in the presence of this thing, and he was normally such a practical man.

There was a mark in the enormous crocodile's wooden flesh where he had once struck it with an axe, intending to chop it up for firewood but had been overcome with remorse. And now he had to suffer the thing in his garden, indefinitely.

'Why did he mess up by not making the crocodile and the hippo to scale? It's those two that make the machine so ugly,' he groused.

He wasn't expecting an answer, just expressing his exasperation.

'I know why he made them like that,' said Gran, astonished that something had interested her enough to make it worthwhile speaking. 'If you were God, the first animals you made would have to be awe-inspiring. Although some of the other animals on the carousel are frightening, they could all be under mankind's control. But the crocodile and the grisly hippo, especially the crocodile, are wild, untameable and inexplicable.'

The Heater Man was barely listening, but Gran carried on as if she were bouncing ideas off another person who were present, 'I'm puzzling it out as I speak, but I think I can see some influence from William Blake in Behemoth the hippo and Leviathan the crocodile. He must have seen Blake's illustrations for *The Book of Job* and been inspired by them, yet the final carvings are more modern with just a hint of the mythological beasts left. Maybe he thought that was best for a modern audience.'

'There is no audience,' said the Heater Man.

'How much?' she asked again.

Three months later, it was in her garden. Thirteen metres in diameter with 18 creatures, oak floors and a collection of the worst weather. The sun rose and set on it. Every morning, she went out to greet those animals, stroked their muzzles and patted them. My grandfather looked on in disgust as she sat on the crocodile and stared back at the house, swinging her legs, now wearing ordinary shoes with her feet barely touching the floor. She watched him in the kitchen, pacing back and forth, trying out different voices, lowering and raising the pitch. Trying to make himself taller. He left the house and came to confront her.

'You sold *what* to buy it?' he demanded.

She replied slowly that the house and grounds were hers, left to her by my great-grandmother.

'But a bloody orchard, Cath, for that monstrosity? After all you've done.'

She leant forward and put her arms around its neck. Her hair fell to one side as she started to pick peeling paint from the creature's teeth.

Bill's tea sloshed as he approached her. He stood several metres from the ride and looked up, lifting both arms in his exasperation. The tea he had just made flew out of the mug, 'They will build on that orchard. I thought you wanted to keep people away from us.'

'That's far enough away,' she said, gesturing to where the barely visible orchard stood.

Frustrated, he changed his attack, 'What's the point of that ride?' he asked.

She couldn't answer because she suspected, rightly, that it might take a lifetime to reply.

Bill's mug hit the ground, where it failed to break, and he marched back to the house. As he reached the conservatory, before going through its door, he turned round, expecting an apology or an explanation from his wife, but she just sat there, smiling.

He shouted, did she want the whole village to think she was mad? She shouted back, 'I've got bloody shoes on, what more do you want, you bastard?'

He was breathing fast in the kitchen and stared out at her, in between piling up the plates in the sink. He sat down and rocked himself. She finally came in when it went dark. He shook his head.

'You can go,' she said, 'no one is holding you here.'

Sorrow gathered in the folds of his face and, for a moment, she instinctively thought about trying to sweep it away.

She glanced down at her crossed legs and moved an ankle in slow circles. She was thinking of the carousel being restored with the rest of the money from the orchard. He was thinking of leaving her. He had been away for several weeks, but something had pulled him back. When Bill was on his own, he thought that he would be able to forgive Cath but, when he was in the pub or walking through the village, he could hear the rustle of raised eyebrows. Judgemental arched doormats over unwelcoming eyes. It appeared that most people believed Doon's adaptation of that luckless night.

*   *   *

During the following weeks, he stayed away from the village and built a shelter around the carousel so that the restoration work could begin. A gritty peace was made between them and she slipped back into Bill's bed. By the end of spring, she was pregnant again.

II

About being Abandoned

MY MOTHER was born the following January. A pale imitation of the previous baby, pink and hairless and, of course, a different gender. She smiled prematurely, not at my grandmother but at a complete stranger. Gran hovered over the cot, frowning. If the world expected my grandmother to be overwhelmed with gratitude for a healthy baby, she was not, she wanted the old one back, and this imposter would never take his place. She tried moving the cot to different parts of the room, and then to different corners of the house, but no matter where it was placed, it didn't look right. The baby stayed nameless. Gran hoped she might disappear if she remained unacknowledged, but my grandfather stepped in and called her Marie.

From the beginning, Marie was indifferent to Gran's moods; she had an autistic disregard for the myriad glares employed by Gran. My grandfather watched this small child with the huge voice and placed all his hopes on her, a faith, that, despite all the evidence placed in front of him, he and my grandmother could live an ordinary married life. He was not a man without his own disappointments. Having trained as an architect and spent years designing an interlocking eco-house in the shape of a hexagon that would attach to its neighbouring house by a single side, he could not find anyone to fund his project. It seemed that nobody wanted to share a communal garden instead of having their own private space, never mind that it was a good use of land. Nobody wanted challenging-looking houses, made of sustainable materials and so, in the end, he took a partnership in a conservative local firm. He never again suggested anything outlandish, or ahead of its time, and, if he had opinions about the clients he worked for whose greatest desire was to enclose themselves with gates and walls, he kept them to himself. He cycled to work, put in the required amount of hours and no more, and scoffed at the figures in his bank statement.

'Imagine being paid for repeating yourself endlessly,' he said.

His eco-house plans remained in his office at home, locked up in a filing cabinet, where no light could get in. He chose to shut down the creative aspect of his brain, any spare energy he might have had was not allocated to family life but to bitterness and regret.

Marie did things as a child to which Gran, with hindsight, gave special significance. When she was three, she danced and Gran was frightened for her. Most people would have given the incident some thought and then paid for ballet or tap lessons. Gran withdrew Marie's collection of bright things, which were obviously warping the child. She took Marie for long walks in the woods near our house until she could recognise the smell of death in rotting animals and mouldering leaves. She tried to make Marie's behaviour reflect the seasons but, every autumn, Marie persisted in kicking leaves in the air. No knowledge of the possibility of dog mess could subdue her. Gran saw an anger in Marie, a simmering, pent-up, turning-the-room-cold fury that Gran recognised as her own. But Marie had decided early on to deny it whenever possible, and so she carried it around on a piece of string and occasionally pinged it in Gran's face, only to snatch it back again and put it out of sight.

One particularly hot summer, Marie had got some green paint from a neighbour and tried to paint Gran's parched grass with it. It was only a small tin but, by the time Gran had looked out of the window, there was a perfectly formed circle where each withered blade had been coated in gloss.

'In denial from the beginning, a cover upper of things,' Gran said, 'like your father, but worse.'

Gran had always thought she would home educate her children, but she walked Marie to school with such speed on the first day of term, that the child was uncharacteristically windswept on arrival at the school gates. Fortunately, Marie had the foresight to have packed a hairbrush. Her straight, fair hair, the opposite of Furnish family hair, was soon returned to its sea anemone status, with individual strands rising and moving of their own accord.

Marie thrived at school, even though she divided the staff between those who wanted to adopt her, and those few who felt the urge to stick out a foot as her particular skippy walk came into view. She wilted at 3.30pm when she had to come home. If my grandfather were there, that made things bearable but, sometimes, his encores were barely audible. The enthusiasm that Marie knew was her birthright, had to be dragged out of some people but, fortunately, she was the child for the job.

Gran was disappointed with the reality of motherhood. She hadn't thought properly about the constant presence of another person who just wouldn't leave.

When Marie was 11, she closed the school's end of term entertainments. She had written most of the sketches and was so heavily involved in every aspect of the event, some members of the audience suspected her of mutating like a shape-shifter. Marie's finale was a song that she sang in a style somewhere between Fado and Karaoke. Most of the other parents cried a little but Gran shuffled uncomfortably in the darkness. Luckily for her, she choked, just as my mother was reaching the end of the song, and had to make a swift exit. Nobody noticed Gran leave the gymnasium, as her footfall was cushioned by the matting that had been dragged in that afternoon by a team of willing helpers, closely supervised by Marie.

My mother's childhood narrative continues with goldfish, a can of Coke, making marks on unpromising surfaces and, of course, the carousel. There is a story that goes with the carousel. No one builds a gaudy, 13-metre creation without being driven. It's a story from *The Bible*, possibly the part of *The Bible* which shows God in the worst light. This is the modern version:

Satan walks into God's office and pokes God in the stomach, just where God's lumberjack shirt is gaping. God spins round on his chair and uses the lever to pump himself up a few inches. Satan pats his own well-honed stomach.

'I wish you wouldn't do that, it's immature and vicious,' says God.

Satan repeats the sentence. He imitates God perfectly, making the pitch a little higher, and catching the tone of despair. He looks over God's shoulder onto his laptop.

'Why are we focusing on that?' says Satan.

'He's a good man, his name is Job.'

'So this is what you do on a Monday morning to save yourself from despair? Search out one half-decent human being from a sea of scum.' Satan rubs his tongue along the point of an incisor.

'This is a good man. One good man can influence others.'

Satan stares at the screen, muscles in and, with lightning speed, flicks through all the archive footage of Job and his life. He reduces it to a few tired expressions, 'Nice car, delightful residence, ahh... twins, double the delight.'

'What do you want?' asks God, wearily.

'We can all be sweet when things are going well for us, but turn the tables on him and then see how much he loves you.'

But God calmly turns away from Satan to breathe in the essence of Job and his decency.

'I'm in the mood for a flutter, you take things from him and I won't mention your *faux pas* at the Winter Solstice office party,' says Satan

'I'm not a gambling man,' says God.

Although God starts out strong, after half an hour of mockery, he caves in. 'Okay, take things from him but don't hurt him.'

Satan doesn't hurt Job. Instead, he ensures that Job's twin boys are vaccine damaged, and all Job's precocious energy is wasted for years, trying to get answers from the NHS. Few people will listen to him. Few people want to know. He loses his position as a management consultant, his house is repossessed and his wife leaves with the other two children.

Satan spits on the floor when he hears Job say to a neighbour, 'I am worn out looking after the boys, I am exasperated with my attempts to communicate with them, enter their world. They are constantly stigmatised and misunderstood, but life is still glorious.'

'Fool,' mutters Satan who leaves God alone for a while.

God hears nothing from Satan for weeks, no reply to texts, nothing. So, in a pro-active moment, heartened by Job's faithfulness, he decides to track down Satan. He finds him sitting in his favourite bar, leaning idly on the counter. Satan smells God from the door and he gives an involuntary shudder but God doesn't notice. God is not quick to pick up little cues that would give him an advantage. All he sees when he looks at Satan is supreme confidence and perfectly regular features, which he supposes adds up to extreme handsomeness. Satan doesn't look round but waits until God is right up close.

'Buy me a drink,' says God.

'One small triumph in an otherwise faithless world doesn't amount to much,' says Satan, pushing a glass of whisky with such force that God dives to stop it flying off the edge of the bar.

Three hours and several rounds later, God has said 15 words. Satan has talked incessantly. God has agreed that Job can be tested further.

'Just don't kill him,' says God, keeping his eyes on his shoes.

Satan leaves, still managing to walk in a perfectly straight line.

Within seconds, Satan has attacked and Job is struck down with a terrible skin disease; a pitiless, crawling infection. He is left sitting in a patch of dirt, alone and with nothing to scratch himself but a piece of old pot. A bit of one of the Wedgwood milk jugs that his mother used to collect.

Job's wife turns up, and she hears him wild and still raving. She can't contain herself, 'For God's sake, give up the campaign with the twins, have them put into care and put yourself in hospital. Stop ranting at a deity that doesn't exist. People will think you are mad.'

Job says that he will not. He continues to rage at God, he begs him to appear and answer why he has put him through all this. But God stays silent. He doesn't have to answer people. It doesn't work like that.

Three of Job's male friends visit him in the hospital: a plastic surgeon, an engineer and a resting actor. They listen for days to Job's fury. At first, they are full of sympathy and say little, but hour after hour of relentless outbursts makes them question whether Job deserves this on some level. They all wonder if they see something in him now that they have never seen before, something unlucky; compatible with a downfall.

The actor, 'Why can't you accept that your twins must have been ill anyway, they were not damaged by the vaccine. It isn't possible, look at the evidence, man.'

The plastic surgeon, 'To be fair, I always had my doubts about your marriage, your wife had a wandering eye.'

The engineer, 'Why are you ranting at God when you never had any faith? You were always the first one to bring up 'The God delusion' at dinner parties. Maybe this is some kind of divine justice.'

God, who was determined not to answer Job, cannot let these comments go unchecked. He appears from out of a whirlwind in the isolation ward. He is taller than Job expected and seems furious. Out of habit, Job points to the hand gel.

God screams, 'Silence, imbecile. Who are *you* to question me? Do you realise who you are dealing with? You and your friends are completely wrong about my nature.'

Job is not scared, he is just glad that God has turned up. God then starts a frenzied speech about all the things that he has made: crocodiles, hippos, lightning, hail, ice, goats, tigers and horses. These images of the natural world seem strangely powerful bounding around the sterile environment.

God continues, 'When you went whale-watching in the Azores you were speechless when that creature rose from the water, you fell on your knees. You said to your wife that it was the most profound moment in your life, you were awe-struck and you couldn't even raise your camera. And yet, the moment you got off the boat, you reduced the experience to an embellished tale for dinner parties. You flattened it out because it was too powerful in 3D. You sanitised it, made it palatable for yourself.

'Similarly with lightning, when you were seven and stuck in that thunderstorm, you felt in touch with something elemental but now, every time you see lightning and your children flinch, you repeat statistics about the unlikelihood of death by a bolt of electricity. You walk up mountains at the weekends, but you wait like a spider for someone to mention that they go to the gym; then you tell them in metres how high you have gone, how far you reached as you trampled the earth beneath your feet, whilst they sweated meaninglessly, with no sense of adventure, in an air-conditioned room.'

Job smiles, 'Whenever I see a bad shirt and tie combination, I know my innate sense of style would never let me make that mistake. I speak three languages fluently. I can fill in my own tax return with ease and can talk about novels, wine, art, all manner of inconsequential rubbish without making a fool of myself. I have always applauded myself for being able to watch the news whilst retaining a sense of detachment. But now you are here, and I know that everything I value is worthless and that I understand nothing. What I mean is, I had just heard about you secondhand, but now I have seen you.'

'There is no other way to watch the news,' sighs God.

And, with that parting comment, he replaces some of the things that he has taken from Job. His wife and children return, but the children are not the same. The vaccine-damaged twins have been replaced with robust, hard-looking youngsters who will float through life with the minimum of anguish. Job feels no affinity for them, they are characterless and will not affect the lives of others. They do not belong to him and, no matter how hard he searches, he feels no love for them. When the new children are in bed, he holds photographs of his damaged twins close to his eyes, hoping to be invited back into their world again, whilst knowing that he is stuck in this one for another 30 years, if he is unlucky. Desolate, in a bigger house, on a more prestigious street.

*   *   *

Gran was a firm believer in the pot-scraping moment coming to us all and tried to instil this in my mother. She tried to prepare her for her own day when she, too, would be sitting alone in a patch of dirt, covered in filthy sores, with nothing but a sliver of crockery. My mother was having none of it; she didn't believe it would happen. As she didn't believe in pot scraping, and felt no affinity for Job's story, so she didn't believe in the visual manifestation of God's ranting reply about the power of nature – the carousel. And, to incense my grandmother and reduce the carousel in status, she referred to it as 'the merry-go-round'.

Marie initially put the carousel down to a visual disturbance. She found that, if one eye were covered and she kept the carousel on the same side as that eye, she could play in the garden quite happily, without that assortment of creatures censoring her fun. As she became older and more determined, she progressed to an eye patch. She kept it on a hook by the front door and refused to go outside without it on.

Those early years gave Marie an aversion to gardens, where she always expected to see something huge, ornate, bloody and spinning. However, she did see the people who came to mend the carousel over the years; men who replaced iron gears and crankshafts with precision-cut steel, people with certificates promising museum standards of paint specification. Then later, the painters themselves, a group of three who stayed all summer, applying vibrant colours to peculiar beasts. The animals were hollow inside whilst Behemoth the hippo and Leviathan the crocodile, being twice the size of the other animals, were each made of five pieces but, once they were painted, it was impossible to see the joins. The only thing that Gran changed from the original machine that she had first seen in the Heater Man's garden, was to refuse to put the hook back in Leviathan's mouth. No human being was ever supposed to be able to do it, only God, so the hook remained dangling half a metre above the crocodile's head.

Red and silver paint gave life to the ornate lettering that circled the roof of the carousel. Each letter was half a metre tall, allowing the unpalatable phrase, 'The price of wisdom is above rubies' to be repeated twice. An enormous tarpaulin coat was made for the machine so that it could be tucked safely away for the winter. It was created in sections and each piece was numbered so that it fitted neatly with no flapping. Finally, it was the turn of the photographer who would document the finished product for *Carousel Monthly*, together with the Editor of the magazine herself, a woman with scruffy shoes called Sarah Chimes. My mother recognised in Sarah Chimes something akin to her own feelings towards the carousel, a deep revulsion, coupled with curiosity. They both wanted to reduce status of the machine, with its grand ideas about there being a place where questions wouldn't matter.

'Why have we got that thing in the garden anyway?' my mother asked.

Sarah Chimes laughed.

'It's a vision,' Gran said frostily. 'What human beings think of as terrifying: lightning, the primordial sea, a lioness on the prowl. Everything we deny about life and try to avoid in our sanitised, TV

27

saturated world...' She was beginning to warm to her subject, 'a ferocious war horse, the vulture feeding its chicks the meat of the slain. It's all represented here.'

'It's the stupidest thing I've ever seen,' my mother said.

'It's difficult for a child, don't you think?' said Sarah Chimes.

'The truth is always difficult,' replied Gran, keen to wind up the conversation and evict Ms Chimes. 'Nature seen from a human perspective is disturbing. Beauty and terror go hand in hand.'

'No, they don't,' said my mother, pirouetting.

'It was remarkably brave of you to buy it,' said Sarah.

Gran ignored her and her lips said that it had been a pleasure to meet Ms Chimes, whilst her arm said, 'Leave now.' This put Sarah Chimes in an awkward position, a woman who was not keen on getting to the point was forced to say what she wanted, 'If you ever want to sell...'

'Never.'

Gran's guiding arm went rigid and the fingers showed the way out. She had secretly enjoyed the first five minutes of this woman's visit and the rightful attention the carousel had received, but now she didn't want Ms Chimes to touch the machine again with those intellectual, long, elegant fingers that remained unshaken by contact with the carousel's surface. She didn't pick up the pot-scraping vibe. She saw this 13-metre piece literally and tapped and stroked its surfaces as if measuring the value of each piece with her fingertips. Her hands had run over the bloody meat with the same indifference that they had touched the lioness' head. Gran asked herself, 'Why would you want to buy something so unsettling and extraordinary when you had reduced it in your head to a mere curio?'

Sarah Chimes' revenge was sweet and Gran paid a price for ushering her out of the garden when, two months later, a photograph of the carousel appeared in the magazine on page 39 in black and white. There was just a line of script describing the machine as a novel departure from a traditional form but it didn't work. It was unsavoury, with no artistic merit.

During those five years of restoration, Marie fine-tuned her charms on others involved in the repairs, but only when Gran wasn't around. Whether you thought the end product was beautiful or not depended on your outlook. It was the simplest personality test of its day. Most people hated it, and the more generous ones thought it was truly strange. Gran wanted too much from people, she wanted the same commitment to the carousel that she felt, the same mixture of awe and fury. But who wants to make a lifetime's study of suffering? One or two over the years felt the vibrations, but one of them was later found hanging. When it was completed, Gran would sit and stare at it going round and round, and feel soothed.

Every year, before autumn was in full swing, Gran would dive on falling leaves to stop their skeletons brushing against the carousel. When there were too many leaves for her to catch, it was time for the machine to be covered up for the winter. The elaborate waterproof coat which Gran had commissioned for the carousel was unfolded. It needed at least two people to help cover up the ride and Marie and Bill were enthusiastic volunteers. Gran would hear them every autumn, muttering random numbers and sniggering, counting down the days until the great cover-up, when they would be able to relax in the garden together on deckchairs, looking forward to a gilt-free winter. They sang, 'Happy days are here again', and Gran ignored them.

Marie tried to get Gran's attention twice in her life. The second time was far more successful than the first and had further-reaching consequences, but both times involved cylindrical objects. The first occasion was when Marie was seven and bored at the end of the school holidays. It involved something orange and fishy in a jam jar. Gran had always refused pets. The mention of their existence resulted in lengthy monologues which would have bored most children out of the idea of ever encouraging an animal into the house.

One sunny afternoon, after Gran had found Marie particularly irksome because of her immaturity, she had taken refuge down at the carousel and was polishing the vulture's claws when Marie began to circle the carousel at a distance. Marie held a jam jar in her hand, with an orange thing in it. Gran glanced and saw the tiny bit of orange, watching as Marie did a slow, deliberate step around the carousel, being careful not to slosh the water.

Gran stopped polishing for a moment and put her head on one side. What the hell was the child up to now? Gran continued to polish and, in the renewed gleam of claw and blood, she thought of a plan. She could launch into a speech about suffering but dress up the responsibility aspect of owning a pet and the wasting of water. She watched Marie for a little longer. The fish would have to live in the bath, which would greatly inconvenience Marie who washed and splashed twice daily.

Marie was often accused of going over the official 7.5-centimetre line, which was clearly marked on the side of the bath and, a far worse crime, the unlawful addition of bubbles. Once, Marie had even forgotten to rig up the irrigation system which collected all the waste water. It was an elaborate system of pipes, tubes and rainwater butts which successfully watered the entire garden.

As soon as Gran had finished her bit of polishing, Marie would find herself caught up in a week's work because of this prank. It would start with the initial design of a pond and end with the final laying down of the environmentally-friendly liner. Gran saw herself in her mind's eye, sat at the kitchen table with Marie, a book of squared paper in front of them. A pile of screwed-up pieces of paper, covered in pond plans scattered over the floor. These drawings would be the ones that Gran rejected due to space considerations, the wilful waste of stone or even an aesthetic pond design whim. The educational possibilities seemed endless.

Gran estimated about 110 buckets of water should fill the pond. She thought of the child's arms stretched like a rubber doll. The pipes from the irrigation system would be out of bounds for this project. Pleased with her plan, she put down her cloth and started to walk slowly towards Marie, the epitome of reasonable parenting in overalls. As she walked forward, Marie began to back away.

'Do you have any idea of what that fish is feeling?' asked Gran. She was just elaborating on fish and their potential to feel terror when Marie took the segment of orange that was the fish out of the jam jar and popped in her mouth. For a moment, it was like Communion. Was the orange a fish or was it not? As Gran stood there enraged, Marie chewed slowly and then removed a piece of cotton from her mouth. Like dental floss, she pulled it through the tiny gaps in her teeth. This was the stuff that had been threaded through the segment of orange and whose gentle twitching had given the orange life.

The second cylindrical incident was many years later when Marie was 17 and in the first year of her A'levels at the local sixth-form college. A stranger appeared at the school. An exotic creature, amongst all the familiar people with whom Marie had grown up. He was a doctor's son who had recently been expelled from his private school, 60 miles away. His father, Dr Doon, was the man who had tried to destroy Gran outside The Tide pub 18 years ago. Following his son's exclusion from education, Dr Doon decided to return to his childhood home and enrol his son in the local college. This would allow his child to shine amongst all those dullards and wouldn't cost him a penny.

But the real attraction of returning was to stir up the past. He wondered how long it would be before Gran heard that he was back and ran his tongue around his lips as he considered Cath and Bill Furnish's last few days of peace. The agitation they would feel at an old story resurfacing would overwhelm them. Admittedly, it was an old-fashioned yarn of malign goings on, set one evening at a wake in a pub, and seemed nebulous in comparison to modern tales of death from needles and pills, but a woman's downfall is always worthy of re-examination.

The son was smart and funny, with surprisingly long eyelashes. The weight of his lashes meant it took him several seconds to lower and lift his lids whilst a gentle breeze accompanied him wherever he went. His father had taken exception to his son's lashes, considering them effeminate, and had managed to have them cut short until now. But the boy was beginning to rebel and had deliberately grown them long before agreeing to go back to any kind of school.

Although he was the doctor's child, something had cracked in him genetically. All the questions his father denied or refused to answer flew round the boy, weighed him down when they settled on him. John and my mother noticed one another immediately. It was an attraction based on genetics. Subconsciously, they recognised their potential to create the person with the most extraordinary eyelashes in the world. A child who would have the eyelash equivalent of a peacock's tail. The two teenagers circled each other shyly for weeks.

Every time John tried to approach my mother, he would hear the roar of his father's voice and remember the bargain he had made. He could grow his eyelashes if he promised to stay out of trouble and concentrate on his studies. Dr Doon gave no thought to Marie Furnish who would be walking the same corridors as his son and eating from the same café. Had he known that she was there, no amount of disinfectant or cleaning of the college could ever remove the revulsion he felt for her. Loathing by association. She was a Furnish. She had done nothing to anger him, but Cath Furnish had.

* * *

John's parents had filled his head with their logic. If he failed at school and wasn't able to earn enough, then he wouldn't be able to purchase labour-saving devices such as robotic vacuum cleaners and remote-controlled blinds. Without them, he would have to live in squalor, supported by other people's pity. One day, the pity would be removed and John would fall into a dusty corner of his own making. His parents were not very imaginative.

Marie was entranced with John, she watched him breezing along. She noticed the way his hair always stuck out slightly and thought about him sleeping on his back, his limbs extended. One day, when he had finished a Coke in the local café and was leaving with a group of students from college, she loitered behind and picked up the can from which he had been drinking. Marie took it home, carrying it carefully, making sure not to dent it. She made a small shrine for it on her dressing table, using an old cardboard box and some shells.

He had dropped a cigarette in the bottom of the can which bobbed in the remaining Coke, and his fingers had left slight marks on the can's surface. She looked at her own skin and thought about his fingers again. She took the can out of its shrine and ran it slowly along her arm, up to her shoulder. Some of the sweet, ashy liquid dripped onto her wrist.

One morning before college, my mother was loitering by the fruit bowl, thinking of John when she saw the bananas. She picked one up and held it. Also lurking in the bowl was a pen, which she grasped in her hand. She began to write on the skin of the fruit. The biro moved seductively over the banana. Was there ever a better material for a love letter? The peel seemed to invite words, coaxing more and more out of her until it was covered with details of what she and John could do to one another if they ever got close enough. When she saw him at college the next day, she slipped the banana into his canvas bag. It was a Friday and she thought she might have to wait several days for his reply, but he turned up on the doorstep on Sunday, having slyly managed to escape a family trip to The Ideal Home Exhibition where his parents were currently rubbing up against food mixers.

John stood on Gran's doorstep, blinking nervously. His eyelashes moved so fast that they could not hear one another speak for the storm he was generating. My mother managed to gesture for him to come inside. From then on, he was a regular visitor, welcomed by Bill, and approved of by Gran, in as much as she didn't shrivel him with her glares. Naturally, she had no idea that he was Doon's son, all she saw was a young man whose inner battles weighed him down and she wondered what he could possibly see in Marie who was such a depthless creature. What he saw in her was a potentially transformative lightness, a cheerful, fun-loving demeanour so alien to him that he was drawn to it.

Suddenly, after a couple of months, his visits stopped as abruptly as they had begun. Shortly after he left for the last time, a gap appeared in Marie's previously closed bedroom door. A small gap, just big enough to glimpse the dressing table. Every time Gran walked past Marie's room, something pulled her towards that opening. It was the can. Gran must have smelt the aluminium; either that or brightness caught the can and flashed through the crack. Gran stopped outside the door to take a look.

She remembered the fish incident, thinking she would keep her mouth shut, but, day after day, she saw the silver and red letters of the can blaze. That night, Gran asked Marie if she had anything in her room that needed recycling because she was going to make a special journey to the tip on her bike with the small trailer attached. Marie shook her head. The next day, Gran passed Marie's room and looked through the gap, seeing the silver ring pull sticking out like an impudent tongue.

She spoke again at dinner that night, addressing both Bill and Marie, 'Do either of you have anything for the recycling bin, any aluminium for instance?'

My grandfather stared dumbly back, wondering who would dare to bring a banned substance into the house but Marie shouted, 'Why don't you piss off back to your merry-go-round and leave us alone? You have never wanted me, only that other child.'

Bill sat in silence and Gran crept quietly out to the carousel, to the animals that understood her.

The following morning, when Marie had gone to college, Gran slipped through the small gap into Marie's room without increasing it at all. Stealthily, she approached the dressing table, picked up the can and gazed into its depths. The first thing she saw on the flickering screen of the flat Coke was John and Marie on the bed. Gran fast-forwarded through tangled limbs and was just about to put the can down when she saw something else, someone else: Dr Doon. She shuddered, wondering how he had managed to slip into a vision after years of successful blocking and negating. She peered and checked, holding the can to the light. There was something else, so small it was barely there. It was me. She poured the contents of the can onto the dressing table and, in the dregs of ash and sugar, she saw me more clearly. She read that I would be like her and that the gifts hadn't skipped two generations. She put two and two together and, with that, she shouted for Bill.

'Why didn't you tell me he was Doon's son?'

Bill shrunk into himself, recoiling at the mention of the name.

'Well?' she said.

'What do you mean?'

'That boy we have been welcoming into our house for the last few weeks.'

Bill refused to take in the information, just stood there, shaking his head. He had heard no mention of Doon for years and wanted it to stay that way.

'I don't believe it,' my grandmother said. 'Of all the boys she could have picked.'

My grandfather stiffened and his face went scarlet. His perfect teeth came together with such force that his jaw jutted forward.

'You're the one with the bloody powers, why didn't you see this one coming?' he said. My grandmother's eyes rolled towards the ceiling. She had explained to Bill endlessly that it didn't work like that.

As soon as Doon realised that his son was involved with the Furnish girl, he cut off his son's eyelashes with a kitchen knife. Getting too close to the eyelid with the blade, he slipped and cut out a portion of eyelid. John could never relax again after that and, whenever he dreamt, a bit of reality always interfered. Doon marched John to the local provincial museum. He held his son's nose against the dusty display cabinets where tiny typed notices lay beside dinosaur bones and flint axes.

'This is the life to which you should aspire, where all can be understood chronologically. There is an order to things, a slow, painstaking order that cannot be questioned. Similarly with life: a successful education will lead to a career which must then lead to a measured, almost ponderous decision to marry – after ensuring that all of the requisite boxes have been ticked. Anything other than these calculated decisions leads to failure and madness.'

John went to smash the cabinet with his fist but the glass proved tougher than he expected. He sat down on the floor and hugged his knees to his chest.

'Get up now, pull yourself together,' Doon murmured. 'This isn't the end of everything for you, it's just the beginning.'

*　*　*

The affair between their son and the Furnish girl had come to light due to the Doons' extraordinary kitchen. Clearing up her son's bedroom, John's mother had come across an old banana skin and popped it into the waste disposal unit. Instead of making its customary gurgle, the machine had begun to recite the words on the banana, in low, lust-filled tones. Dr and Mrs Doon, who happened to be in the kitchen at the time, froze momentarily. The Doctor leapt up and tried to stuff the dishcloth down the waste disposal unit to shut the damn thing up, to gag and muffle it. But it was no use; the machine had discovered a side of itself that it never knew existed and it continued in a slow, sensuous cadence to read to the tip of the skin.

When the filth was finally over, Mrs Doon looked flushed. At that point, the Doons' relationship could have gone in a different direction but Dr Doon gave one of his looks and Mrs Doon was brought back to reality, to her hand-finished, pristine oak kitchen. Dr Doon often congratulated himself on how infrequently Cath Furnish popped into his head uninvited. If she stole or snuck her way into a dream, with the winding hair of her youth, he dismissed it. If a smell or a look from a young woman reminded him of her, he rationalised it. Sometimes, people thought unpleasant thoughts, and she was one of his. He never doubted that he had done the right thing and, with that thought paramount, he brushed invisible bits of fluff from his jacket, as though decontaminating himself from Cath's unwholesome influence.

Doon's relentless carping at his son finally worked and John was overpowered; his spirit was crushed and he swore that he wouldn't marry the girl. After all, they only wanted the best for him – a girl who could write inoffensive postcards to elderly relatives and be wheeled out for family parties where she would neither shine nor offend.

Doon had no choice but to visit the Furnish house in person, but he dropped a note through the door several days before, setting out his terms quite clearly. Having given them time to digest his proposal, he found himself in their kitchen looking in disgust at the draining board where a lone fly was crawling around the rim of a cup. Not that he had anything to worry about, the chance of my grandmother offering him a drink was negligible. He had never met another woman like her, one unafraid of silence.

Struggling with the quietness, his mind flew spitefully about the kitchen, making an itinerary of the little jobs that needed doing; broken tiles, re-grouting, curtains to be washed. He looked at my grandmother again, waiting for her to speak. She looked back. Damn woman! What the hell was wrong with her? Didn't she understand the mechanics of these situations? A minute later, he was relieved to be ushered out into the garden, at least he wouldn't catch anything there. That was before he saw the carousel.

He had heard about it from the people they'd kept in touch with after they left the village. It convinced him that my grandmother was mad and had caused all that had happened to her. The carousel was the last in a long series of justifications he had built up over the years. It underlined the rightness of his own position in getting the police involved on the night of the wake. He would not acknowledge the carousel, he would not refer to it but would keep looking straight ahead. The sunlight, catching a twisted gold pole, made a flash appear in his left eye. He jumped.

'What in God's name is that?'

'Homage to *The Book of Job*.'

'Ah yes, the patience of Job.'

Gran spoke with quiet menace, 'I see you still open your mouth when you know nothing. That's a complete misnomer, Job had no patience. He shook his fist at God and demanded an answer to human suffering.'

Doon shuddered, typical of Cath Furnish to try to make him feel uneasy, she had brought him out here to make him squirm. Well, he had done nothing wrong. If he were guilty of anything, it was not checking carefully enough with whom his son was fraternising at college. There had been a time when his son was completely under his control, he needn't have done anything. Back then, there was no possibility that he would find someone like the Furnish girl attractive. He was kept in line by friends of a similar socio-economic background, by peer pressure. But, since his son's expulsion and subsequent disgrace, the boy had appeared weighed down, and that had left him vulnerable to attack. From the Furnishs.

'And was an answer forthcoming?' Doon demanded.

'Not a palatable one.'

Doon wanted to strike Cath Furnish for descending into that tone, the one he hated, it was dripping with permissiveness and, yet, still managed to be sneering.

'One could almost imagine that you had set up this whole thing between my son and your daughter. What a coup for you!'

My grandmother's laughter ricocheted off the carousel and bounced back to Doon. She said, with all the bitterness and invective she could muster, 'I thought that, by now, you might have taken some responsibility for the turn of events at The Tide that evening but you're still completely delusional, despite having all these years to reflect.'

'I haven't been reflecting, but working hard to attain a position in society that my son could honour and follow if he saw fit. That was, until *your* daughter came along and entangled him.'

'Entangled him? Fucked him you mean. Your words are still as far from the truth as ever.'

'And you remain unchanged. Defiant and vulgar.'

Dr Doon was sweating so he stepped out of the fierce heat, attempting to take shelter under the carousel, although the last thing he wanted to do was to get nearer to the vile contraption. The machine was both illogical and gaudy, both of which he found intolerable in people or objects. Worse still, he felt sure the animals were mocking him.

'I hope that you have had time to consider my proposal and find my idea acceptable,' he said.

'Was there an idea couched in your note?' She slowly unfolded a piece of personal headed stationery and quickly pretended to read it again, before continuing, 'I only remember the death of the baby and abandonment for my daughter as the options.'

'Melodramatic to the last. What I am suggesting is the removal of a cluster of cells which would mean this unfortunate incident would have the least impact on us all. We could all return to the things that engage us, me to medicine, you to... this.'

'What you have suggested is that my grandchild would never see the carousel and know the truth about suffering. And *that* is not possible.'

Doon stamped, if a six-foot tall man could stamp. His face was raw.

'Expect no help from me,' he hissed, 'expect nothing from my family if you go ahead with this ludicrous plan.'

'You arrogant fool. This *ludicrous plan*, as you call it, is going ahead without us. The baby is the size of my fist, cells are multiplying as we speak, this is one of the many things you can't control or manipulate as you have done in the past.'

'I did what I did out of a sense of moral duty.'

'You have no moral compass, just a tattered bag of other people's beliefs that you haul out when it suits you.'

*   *   *

Cath turned her back on him and walked slowly inside. Dr Doon was parched and his tongue felt brittle. Her continual silences and staring had made him so uncomfortable that, although he had vowed he wouldn't touch the unsanitary crockery, he scurried after her, lunged towards the draining board, turned on the tap, snatched the cup, filled it up and drank. He stomped out of the house, got back into his car and turned to his wife, who had waited patiently, not wishing to see Cath Furnish just in case she had any remnants of beauty left. Fortunately, Dr Doon made no mention of Cath Furnish's appearance but remarked that, although he had looked carefully around the kitchen, he swore he hadn't seen so much as a toaster.

'And, more importantly, we have absolutely no evidence that the child is John's,' said Mrs Doon.

It was at that moment that my mother, huddled alone in her bedroom, felt me move for the first time as my eyelashes swept the darkness within her.

Over the next few days, Marie suggested to Gran that, if they had matching dishes and wallpaper that met at the seams, things wouldn't have turned out like this. Her line of argument continued, 'If we were connected to the mains, John would still be here with me. You've never wanted me, only that dead boy. I watch you all the time, though his name is never mentioned, he dominates this place.'

Gran knew that much of what my mother had said was the truth. The 'dead boy' took all the oxygen in the house. For someone who had been gone so long, he had his possessions scattered in every room, waiting to trip people up. Gran also understood that Marie and John Doon had been in love, encased for several weeks in a bubble so huge and intense that they would both be touched by it for ever. She also knew that it was a love that could last a lifetime if necessary and survive minor dramas, possibly tragedy, disappointment, greed, boredom and even envy.

But neither she nor Doon could let it, and so she spoke, 'Even if we had a direct connection to the National Grid and you had tightroped home on the cable single-handedly, he still wouldn't be with you.'

Marie took a running kick at Gran, unable to deny her anger a moment longer.

* * *

That evening, Gran, whose many skills didn't stop at forgery, wrote a terse note to my mother in the hand of John Doon. She had taken a letter from my mother's bedroom and gazed at the handwriting for hours before recreating it perfectly the first time.

The point was to get into the head of the person who wrote it, to infiltrate them. To feel their every step and thought and allow those feeling to transmute down the pen. She felt the boy's sensitivity and gentleness but, if she had any doubts about what she was doing, she justified it all by thinking it was inevitable anyway. There could be no alliance between Doons and Furnishs.

The boy's writing was easy to copy in all its innocent loopiness and slanting to the right. A common black Biro was all that was needed and Bill had enough in his office. I'm not sure exactly what she wrote, but know it was harsh enough to convince my mother that it was over. My mother broke down when she had fully digested the note, which Gran swore had been hand-delivered half an hour earlier. Gran then whispered golden things in my mother's ear, but each phrase had waited so long to emerge that they all came out tarnished.

Then, Marie herself began to turn green and retch. Gran held her cupped hands under Marie's mouth. Soon they overflowed with vomit, fountain-like, as it trickled slowly down the sides of Gran's hands and pooled onto the floor. Still, Gran kept her hands together as if holding something precious. She went to bed that night with the faint smell of sick still under her nails and a piece of useless information which she could share with no one. John Doon would be back, two divorces and a broken engagement later.

III

A Stranger Arrives

A S MY mother's skin stretched and pulled and I had finished growing, my lashes began to beat on the womb door. Gently at first, growing more and more insistent until the door gave way and I surfed out on a wave of amniotic fluid, surrounded by the bits of wall that had supported me. During the months building up to my birth, whilst Gran had been waiting for me, she had been knitting in her head. Not cardigans, but baby-sized sandwich boards out of black wool with tiny white writing around the edge, naturally, from *The Book of Job*, '*Man that is born of woman – how few and harsh are his days.*'

Her idea was that I would wear these garments proudly and show that upstart of a daughter of hers our true family destiny. We were miserable. We could not be steered towards optimism, we were stronger than that. If there had been portraits of our family, going back hundreds of years, there would be galleries full of pictures of people chewing their nails. Long corridors of youthful faces whose foreheads were prematurely covered in lines. Our coat of arms would have been crow's feet.

Gran sometimes blamed herself for Marie turning out the way she did. She used to tell a tale of how, when she was pregnant with Marie, something cheerful crossed her path. Instead of looking the other way, she looked it in the eye. Marie stood no chance from that moment. Gran did everything she could to alleviate the curse of seeing the cheerful entity but it didn't work.

Several months after I was born, Marie started back at college. My arrival had sharpened her ambition, and Gran encouraged her to study every spare moment she had and leave the childcare to her. I was just a reminder of John Doon and her subsequent abandonment. When I was a year old, she got a place at a far off university, studying psychology. She came back at weekends for the first few months but, once she had found her feet, made friends and begun to establish herself, the visits lessened.

Marie thrived and stayed in education for seven years, eventually gaining a PhD. Her research involved the effects of relentless enthusiasm on health. She chose this subject deliberately. Having been completely destroyed when John left her, but not knowing how to grieve, she could only return and cling to the natural exuberance of her childhood. But she wasn't a child any longer and the high spirits she adopted as an adult were just a veneer, which she fought tirelessly to maintain.

By the time I was seven, the contact with my mother had dwindled to two or three visits a year. Despite this, Marie wanted to exert some influence, so she sent happy books through the post. These books tried to ingratiate themselves with our literature but, at night, our heavy, philosophical books would band together and push the newcomers off the shelves. In the morning, I would find Marie's books on the floor with their spines broken. Eventually, the happy books set up in a different corner of the house where they lived fearfully and spoke in whispers.

My childhood was quite ordinary. I would stand on the carousel and give speeches. One of Gran's favourite debating topics was arguing in favour of the reintroduction of wolves into the environment. I learnt to speak passionately about whether or not we could live with reintroduced large carnivores in the U.K. Gran would mark me out of 10 and we would sit and discuss the points I might express more forcefully next time. We talked about risk and learning to think as an individual. Gran spoke disparagingly of people who drove around at speed, encased in tonnes of metal and yet wouldn't countenance a few wild dogs in the woods. Sometimes, she would ask me specific questions to test my knowledge.

'What about the recent incident of a wolf grabbing an 11-year-old boy by the face from his sleeping bag in Ontario, Canada?'

And I would reply, 'The most likely explanation is that the wolf was after the sleeping bag and not the child. There are many reports of wolves running off with sleeping bags being attracted to soft, fluffy and fur-like items with which they like to play and rip apart.'

Sometimes, I played in my treehouse which Gran had built from reclaimed bits of wood. It was an elaborate structure of three storeys, with chimneys lined with stone, and miniature iron grates that sat in the hearths. I was allowed to light them as I saw fit and often cooked my own food. The treehouse was carpeted throughout and warmer than our own house. I would emerge after a long day's playing, covered in soot and reeking of smoke. I pretended that I lived up there with another eco-warrior and we were going to save the world and then get married. When Gran brought my juice into the garden, she shouted up to me to come down and get it. When I got to the ground she said it was a great game that I was playing but there was no need to marry my imaginary friend. And so we exchanged invented vows and continued to live amicably.

My heart leapt when Gran came home with a kitten from the local rescue centre, an animal that had been returned to the centre twice: Once by a family, then by a single man.

'Abandon any ideas of befriending that cat,' said Gran several weeks later when my arms were covered in scabby railway tracks.

'Why didn't you get a sweet cat?' I asked.

'Just leave the cat to be what the cat is and we will all be happy,' she said.

Oddly enough, the cat liked my grandfather and would sometimes follow him into his office. He named the cat Huff. My grandfather played little part in my childhood and I always naturally referred to him as Bill. He was never sharp or unkind, but somewhat vacant. If he did ever express an opinion about my upbringing, he was soon trounced by Gran.

Once, he asked Gran if she thought I were missing out on anything by not going to school. She replied, 'Certainly, she is missing monotony, cowardly opinions and self-doubt. There is nothing she can't learn from me and a handful of classics – *Evelina* and *The Bride Price* for growing up, *Robinson Crusoe* for the struggles of life, and Schumacher's *Small is Beautiful* is still pertinent for the way forward politically.' And, with his doubt securely answered, he ambled back into his office.

I wasn't spared the 'one day you'll have to sit alone with nothing but a piece of old pot with which to scrape your scabs' speech, just as my mother hadn't been before me, but I put up little resistant to it, knowing that, if it did happen, I would survive.

Gran and I walked a lot, we were out for hours on a weekly basis. Mostly, we would end up three miles away from our house, by the river where the now abandoned pub, The Tide, stood, familiar from Gran's childhood and youth. The place had been empty since the last landlord, James Arlet, had drunk himself to death. Gran said that his family must still want to hang on to the place, treat it like some sort of memorial to him and, like a headstone, it was crumbling. The hand-painted sign flaked and cracked a little more each year until the moon over the water was not recognisable. The pub building had been fenced off and the windows boarded up. Gran took no notice of the signs threatening trespassers and swore to me there was no dog, regardless of a curled lipped drawing of a canine head attached to the fence with garden wire. She would lead me straight through a gap in the fence and down to the river's edge.

'How do you know there is no dog?' I asked every time.

'Amanda, there is no dog.'

What insight did she have that I lacked? What experiences in life had convinced her that there was no dog? Once she got so cross with me, that I tore the dog picture off the fence and was about to stamp on it.

'Don't destroy that picture, get off it!' she shouted.

'If there is no dog, we don't need this do we?' I yelled back.

I was shocked. Although notoriously bad-tempered, she rarely had any compunction about my taking things apart. She carefully placed the drawing of a Rottweiler back on the fence, laminated to protect it from the weather.

'There's no dog here,' she spoke kindly.

Temporarily appeased, I managed to suppress the image of 13 stone of muscle rushing towards me uninvited, and we would sit on the battered old quay and watch birds or the occasional boat going by. Once or twice, we saw a kingfisher; crazy darting little thing. I thought if I opened my mouth wide enough, I could swallow it and keep that sprinting streak of blue for myself; from a distance, it looked small enough to swallow. When the tide was out and there was no chance of anything passing by, we would just stare at the mud.

One of the rare days I had with my mother and grandmother together was down by the river when I was a very small child. Gran was always distracted when we were at The Tide and she made no exception just because my mother was there, treating her like an unwanted guest. When Gran and I were alone, I would trail behind her on the river path. Gran rarely looked round and, although I was not afraid of the water, I kept sensibly to the middle of the path. The time Marie was with us, I was sandwiched between them, uncomfortable, my usual freedom squashed. I could feel Marie's tension behind me, her flapping and occasional lurching towards me. I fell in the river. Gran casually pulled me out.

'It's not safe for a small child down here, people drown,' my mother's face was white.

'Careless people have come to a sticky end in this water,' Gran replied with venom.

My mother was silent for a few moments, not wanting to take the conversation further, but then she gathered herself together, 'She's three, how can she swim?'

There was a faint hiss to my mother's voice and the two of them stood apart for a while. Eventually, my grandmother suggested we go to the moors in my mother's car where she would be able to see my swimming. I manipulated the tension between them in order to get an ice cream and I let the unfamiliar goo lie on my teeth until they felt strangely furry. I got into one of the pools on the moors that were made by people damming the river with stones, and began to swim a width across the brackish water.

I heard my mother shout, 'She's drowning!'

'That's just her style.'

I kept on going as Gran had taught me until I reached the bank.

Marie withdrew from us after the swimming incident, only visiting every six months, but I still remember that afternoon and the redness of my mother's face, her blotched neck and stiff walk back to the car, saving her anger for another day.

My other childhood game was deconstructing next door. I say next door, but the nearest house to us was a quarter of a mile away and had been empty for 15 years. It was a house built on the orchard that Gran had sold in order to buy the carousel. It had never been completed, as bad luck had stalked the man who had attempted to build the house single-handedly. In the end, after numerous financial setbacks, he just abandoned the place. Gran said that nobody else would buy the property; it was a mile and a half from the nearest village, down a track unfit for cars and with no mains electricity. Extreme dampness was the least of its problems. Nature, with a little help from me, was slowly but surely pulling the house down. I choreographed the lightning, told it exactly where to strike the roof. And then I would call the wind, pointing out the small gaps in the tiles which could be rattled and worked loose. The rain followed the work of the wind, dripping down the walls, making it easier for me to tear off the strips of wallpaper with my insistent fingers.

It was a slow process but I viewed it as a long-term project, knowing that, one day, there would be nothing left. I pulled up some of the parquet tiles in the living room with a mallet and a chisel, making a little gap in the floor close to the window, into which I placed an oak sapling and wondered if the little tree would feel a sense of triumph, or one of unease, being surrounded by hundreds of tiny rectangles of oak. Perhaps it was like being in a graveyard. The tree needed more light so I picked at the putty in the window frame. Day after day, I removed a little more until all it took was a gentle push and the glass fell stiffly to the floor. In a hundred years' time, the tree would push through what was left of the roof.

When I went upstairs to look at the wilderness of the garden from above, I kicked every second step with my boot. After weeks of kicking, a stair would give way unexpectedly. From upstairs, I was just able to make out where the last inhabitant had tried to bring order. All that was left were overgrown flowerbeds and the vague shape of a path. Inevitably, it would all slowly disappear.

* * *

I grew, my wolf speeches improved and, at the age of 12, I became too big for my treehouse, which meant I had more free time for dismantling. Letters arrived weekly from my mother, sometimes with photographs, often with a cheque inside the envelope. Her world seemed far away from ours and, although we had a vague idea that she was doing very well and had been on the television, it didn't seem relevant. Marie was never keen to come back to our house so, when we did meet, she and Gran would take turns to decide on the place. Marie would choose a lively café and Gran would choose somewhere bleak, like the moors or the local tip. I don't remember being lonely in my childhood, that is, not until Mrs Susan Rink arrived.

One summer's day, Gran, Bill and I were in the garden when Gran's nose went up. Someone was approaching from next door, crossing the border. Susan Rink's perfume arrived a good two minutes before she did. When her body caught up, she gushed at us from behind long grass. She said she was looking at next door and considering putting in an offer to buy the place, but she wanted to meet the neighbours first. She pointed to the carousel.

'Doesn't that thing give you nightmares?' she asked, addressing me and, moving closer, stepped over the boundary to examine us in better light.

'Why would a response to a great and powerful work of literature give the child nightmares?' asked Gran.

Susan ignored her. She was delighted with us. She wanted skin like ours, our vegetable-induced complexions, the whites of her eyes to shine. She was ready to lay aside her face powder and embrace the great outdoors. Susan held out a tiny brown hand. My grandfather took it with enough enthusiasm for the three of us. She hopped up and down on the spot. The stripes in his shirt went several shades deeper; he came alive under her gaze. Suddenly, Mrs Rink went all shy. She wanted… to ask us something but didn't know if she dared. She looked younger than ever, gazing up from under her fringe, her hair full of light and different shades. She was the most exciting grown-up that I had ever seen. Jangly music rose up from skinny, tanned wrists as she mentioned that she had heard rumours in the village and wanted to ask our surname.

'It's Furnish,' Bill said.

Our name tripped off her tongue. She almost squealed. She didn't suppose it was possible that we were related to Marie Furnish, the Happy Lady on the television? Gran's eyes narrowed.

'We are.'

There was more hopping, then she made a strange little movement in the air with a finger as if she were drawing a triangle. 'Stop that thought,' she said.

We all looked back at her blankly.

'Don't tell me you are not gathered round the television with the rest of the country at eight on a Friday morning to watch the Happy Lady?' She declared it extraordinary and typical of our modesty that we had no television and had not seen Marie in action. More people should be like us.

'They're not.'

Susan bought the property and I was told by Gran to keep away from next door from now on.

An avalanche of workers slipped down the lane as the piece of road leading to Susan's house was restored. I pardoned her house from its death sentence. It took a while to persuade the wind and the rain that this was the right course of action but, slowly, the house was restored. Mrs Rink had her husband's money. He was an actuary, 'a glorified risk assessor', Gran had said, who worked on different projects around the country and wouldn't be appearing until the house was finished. He didn't like mess, only numbers and order. As he was a predictor of things, too, I hoped when he arrived that he would be amenable and get on well with Gran. Mrs Rink had a successful cake-making business which she was relocating to the nearest town, where the premises and labour were cheaper than her previous location.

After several months, the condemned house ceased to look like its old self. Not that I saw it up close but, from a distance, it looked just like one of Susan's perfectly iced cakes. She was a professional smoother of things and I admired her. She had taken a natural talent and had aligned it to a suitable profession, just as my mother had done. I began to wonder if there was anything out there for me.

Susan made us a weekly present of one of her cakes. She used the huge white box as a shield as she stepped into our garden, the matching ribbon flapping in the wind, declaring that she came in peace. Gran left Susan's cake out in the porch where the cat dragged muddy prints over its surface, but still it stayed perfect and free from mould. We weren't allowed to eat it, nor feed it to the birds.

'It'll kill the blighters.'

More cakes arrived weekly and, soon, we had boxes piled up in the kitchen as tall as me. I rooted through the boxes, taking away the little plaster columns, watching jam and sponge fall in on itself, and soon had quite a collection, so I built houses from mud in the garden and gave them Greek columns.

Some of Susan's cake was eaten. Bill took tiny, almost unnoticeable slivers of cake, so thin you could see daylight through them. He ate them at the bottom of the garden and, afterwards, he chewed parsley so that Gran wouldn't smell the sweetness on his breath. She noticed the missing parsley though and so, next time Susan made an appearance in our garden, Gran, uncharacteristically, invited her to come and see the carrots which were growing close to the compost heap. This was careless of Gran because, if Susan had chanced to look into the heap, she may have recognised parts of her own company logo from her cake boxes. She might have spotted lumps of Victoria sandwich shouldering up to grass cuttings, egg shells and tea bags. But Susan wasn't the kind of woman who looked in compost heaps, and the cakes continued to arrive.

One day, the noise stopped; no more distant drilling or banging from next door. A week later, a removal lorry struggled down the lane. They could only get so far and a human chain carried the contents of the lorry the rest of the way. I watched from a tree at a discreet distance. The first thing to come out of one of the vans was a bed with light tubes on it. Susan's high voice carried down the lane to me as she ordered the furniture into different rooms. The strange, plastic-covered bed with fluorescent tubes inside seemed to get priority and was taken into the conservatory. That night, I heard Gran and Bill arguing about her. I didn't see the problem; she was fun and friendly, different from the few other people we knew. Gran said that she didn't want her hanging around us and that she was a bad influence on me. I was glad when Bill got the last word in, 'Forget it, Cath, she's harmless.'

Every night at about seven, a strange, blue, ethereal light could be seen coming from Susan's conservatory. It lasted for 20 minutes. I would walk as close to the house as I dared, to bathe in the light.

'It's mystical, Gran,' I said, 'otherworldly.'

'She'll have rhino-hide by the time she's 50 if she carries on like that.'

Susan would pop up unexpectedly in our garden, all glittery-green eye shadow and news of the outside world. Sometimes, she had clippings from the papers with photographs of Marie; she repeated Marie's catchphrase at every opportunity. I was never quite sure what to do with the grainy images of my mother or the nonsensical words she allegedly spoke, so I kept them to myself. Occasionally, I chanted the words under my breath, '*Stop that thought.*' Susan never stayed for long as she was always dashing off to supervise her workers covering things in icing, but there came a day when Gran could no longer hold us back from going to see exactly what Marie did for a living.

On a wet Friday morning, Gran, Bill and I trooped across the border to Susan's house. Our mouths fell open with respect; she was such a small person to have tamed nature. Her grass was softer than ours – and greener. Her orchard was idyllic, like something from a Van Gogh painting. Her fruit trees were subdued with wire. Not a single piece of fruit lay on the ground and she had banned cloud from the bit of sky over her acre of land. She was in love with the country and had never been happier. We took our shoes off in her kitchen without being asked and moved gingerly amongst her pale possessions, trying not to get dirt on anything. The three of us huddled together in her spacious living room.

There were no longer any holes in the ceiling and my gaze jerked over immaculate white plaster. There was no resting place, no scratches, no dirt, not a single mark. I had to look at my rough hands because her house was making my head spin. We waited patiently for Marie to appear. It seemed the whole country was waiting for my mother, according to the man and woman who ran the breakfast show. Suddenly, there she was. The three of us jumped a little. Bill and I leant forward on the sofa whose leather creaked as if to affirm it really was her. Marie looked like the person that I saw twice a year, but glossier. She seemed to take over the whole screen but there was a manic quality to her movements and I thought about a dog chasing its tail. Marie spoke at speed, smiling and gesturing continually. She stood in front of a large yellow triangle, on each side of which was a different word: thought, feeling and behaviour.

'My methods are simple but effective. They are, in fact, so simple that we have to go over and over them using a different language. If you stop the negative thought, you stop the accompanying feeling and behaviour. Just stop the thought. You are in control, nobody else. Stop that negative thought. We have been taught to believe that life is complicated and painful, and this is an untruth. Stay with me today and let me show you a new way of being that is as simple as ABC. I am here to hold your hand every step of the way.'

The camera panned to an unhappy-looking woman who was taking up three-quarters of the sofa.

'I'm 22 stone and I just sit on the sofa eating chocolate.'

My mother took the tips of three of the woman's sausage-like fingers and reclaimed a little of the sofa. Her bony knees, with the scapula quite visible, pointed accusingly at the woman's soft thighs.

Looking into the woman's eyes she spoke, 'We could complicate this situation by asking you what has happened in your past that has led to a sofa-bound life where your drug of choice is chocolate, but I know from your speaking to the programme-makers that you have had endless unsuccessful interventions, including slimming pills, counselling and fat farms and yet none of them have worked. You are taking a brave step today and we applaud you Margaret Bowers from Nuneaton. Now, let's not waste another moment. Let's step out of the mire of negativity.'

My mother then span round, confronting every one of Margaret's negative beliefs, holding them by the throat until they writhed no more. Positive affirmations flashed onto the screen. I think we were all supposed to repeat them. Susan started off chanting but stopped to save our embarrassment when she realised we didn't understand popular culture.

'My method is frighteningly simple and you can see the results on my programme every week when we revisit old friends.' What happened next was a whistle-stop tour of old contributors who seemed remarkably lucid and trouble-free. Their chains of crack and alcohol, over-eating and violent relationships all appeared to have scurried off to destroy other people's lives. It was all over so fast that we were soon staring at the credits and my mother waving a chunky paperback in front of the screen.

'What a remarkably thick book,' Gran finally spoke. Her eyes were mere slits and she was motionless as though she were about to fall asleep. Despite her apparent torpor, she leapt up and left the house, leaving Bill and I to thank Susan for her hospitality.

Bill and I caught up with Gran. She turned on her heel just as I was making a large triangle shape in the air. I did it again, this time a tiny triangle in front of her nose, whereupon she pushed me, a little too firmly, out of her way.

* * *

Susan's visits to our garden continued. She had no children of her own.

'Where's her husband?' I asked.

'Keeping a sensible distance,' said Gran.

Over the months that followed, she brought more than glamour into our garden. She couldn't believe that I was not at school and wanted to take me on an educational trip. She suggested the zoo to Gran who, politely but firmly, explained that we had no truck with such things. But Susan persisted. She painted an enticing picture of the zoo. She told me that, far from being places of imprisonment for animals, they were educational nowadays and preserved species that would otherwise be extinct. She always seemed to be about, muttering the zoo word. She knew that my favourite animals were polar bears and, when Gran was within earshot, she told me of the award-winning, architect-designed environment in which the bears lived in perfect comfort. Free from predators and the intolerable cold. Gran stuck her spade in the soil and came up to us.

'They walk 3,000 miles a season in the wild,' Gran snapped.

'Well, I'm sure they could soon clock that up with the amount of pacing they were doing the last time I was there,' Susan responded.

Gran went back to her digging and I squashed myself into my old treehouse. Soon, Susan was back at the border again, armed with new artillery. This time, it was the butterfly farm. It wasn't far and she could drive, what could possibly be the objection?

Still, Gran managed to delay the trip for a few months. But, one cold November morning, Gran and I hopped into Susan's car and headed for town. As we entered the butterfly farm, I began to notice other people and what they were wearing. I couldn't put my finger on it but something began to turn in my head. A question arose, one that I would never have considered had it not been for the trip. We were wearing different clothes from other people, duller, baggier. Gran seemed uncomfortable; she flinched as though there were a huge crowd when there was only a school party and a handful of people. She seemed to draw her bones in; could pull her ribs in like a corset, taking at least several centimetres from her waist. Susan paid for us and we walked through two doors, both of which had thick strips of clear plastic hanging from the door frame to stop the butterflies escaping.

We went straight into the main area, a huge aviary-like structure. The warmth and humidity hit us. It relaxed me. I took off my jumper and felt my shoulders fall. Gran was soon engaged reading the information boards and looking at the butterflies. Susan stood triumphant on a little concrete bridge.

We all wound down some more. A combination of the heat and beauty of the butterflies soothed any tensions between the three of us. Gran was almost civil. We wandered around, carefully stepping over butterflies who were drinking from the floor. The butterflies brushed past our hair and faces and yet they never bumped into us.

As we ambled through the different rooms, devoted to the various stages of development, from caterpillar to butterfly, we came across a party of schoolchildren about my age, nine or ten. They were half-heartedly filling in questionnaires, scraping their feet along the concrete and sighing. Nothing seemed to be of interest to them, not the waterfalls, nor the pond, nor even the butterflies themselves. None of the children had taken off their school jumpers, as though they were hoping not to stay for long. We got caught behind them, there were too many of them to push past and they were being given an official lecture from one of the butterfly experts. Pencils dropped and hit the concrete and eyes wandered up to the ceiling in boredom.

Susan whispered a little too loudly, 'Don't you wish you were at school, with lots of little friends?'

I said that I didn't and Gran sniffed. We slowed down but the children were moving even slower, cocooned in the monotonous tones of the expert. We prepared to walk through another plastic curtain, close behind the children. They jostled one another irritably. Pushing closer and closer, they became one mass and a bottleneck occurred at the doorway. Suddenly, the curtain fell down and there was a mini stampede as 15 children poured into the next room. There was a commotion, crying and accusations. The children were cleared out of the way. When we got through, we could see that many of the butterflies who had been drinking from the floor had been trodden on. Some of their wings were ripped and a handful had been squashed into the floor like bits of old food. A couple of the damaged ones had made it to the safety of a wall or plant but they looked hideous, torn in half.

Susan guided us round the insect bodies being scraped up from the floor by assistants and swept into a dustpan. I saw little bits of colourful wing caught between the hairs of the broom. Gran was victorious, her vision of suffering made manifest. If it didn't qualify as a pot-scraping moment, it was an omen of one. When we got home, she headed straight for the carousel and the machine spoke to her with its slow-turning engine. The animals acknowledged her just as she accepted their message that, where there is beauty, there is also destruction.

* * *

The seasons lined up behind one another as they always had, some taller and some shorter than expected, but the rest of my childhood was punctuated by my increasing knowledge of the outside world, courtesy of Susan. When I was 15, she came with a magazine. She said that it had all the latest fashions in it and that I might be interested. I kept it hidden from Gran and looked at it in my bedroom late at night. One article stuck in my mind. It was about

Anna Suede, the actress, who had just had an operation, a cosmetic one. She had had her elbows sharpened. She was quoted as saying that, although acting work had been sporadic for her in the past, since she had had the elbow-sharpening operation, great roles were pouring in. America beckoned for her but she wasn't about to forget her roots. I looked at my own elbows in the light. I started to wear long-sleeved tops, even on hot days. I started saving my money.

I told Susan about Anna Suede and she kindly started to collect all the clippings she could find about Anna's career. In some, opinion was divided, were her elbows too sharp or were they just gorgeous? She couldn't stand in queues anymore like ordinary mortals, for fear of stabbing people. Not that she needed ever to queue again, she had so much work that people would drive her anywhere she wanted to go, or wait in line on her behalf. I had an Anna Suede file, £11.50 towards the operation and the name of the surgeon whom I dreamt would save me.

Between Susan's informative visits, things went on pretty much as normal and, only occasionally, did I think about the bluntness of my elbows but, somehow, our garden seemed smaller. The carousel weighed heavily on me. It was not normal. I had witnessed normal and I wanted some of it. I thought about the people in Susan's magazines, dressed in white, eating takeaways from cartons on cream carpets. They looked careless, they were not weighed down by ominous thoughts and I wanted a bit of that ease of mind. I was weary of Gran's severity and I had been given access to a world where there didn't seem to be any – in magazines. Or, if the people in magazines were aware of Gran's carousel truth, they were doing a damn good job of ignoring it. That night, I rubbed the rough skin on my feet on the only piece of carpet in our house, a small, nylon square by the side of my bed, which had been rescued from the tip. I cursed the fact that our house had no soft floorcoverings and that, at my age, I had imperfect feet.

At 17, I added regular television-watching to my weekly routine of gardening, cooking, reading and swimming. I was introduced to *Midlanders* at Susan's house. It was a long-running soap opera where some of the characters had lived in the street for 20 years. I was about to be influenced by someone who was just making her debut, fresh from stage school, her first proper job. The character's name was Maya. Her presence on the screen was the equivalent of a warm, shaken bottle of pop whose top was just holding out under the pressure. She filled the screen with sex and venom in equal measure. Maya lit up a cigarette and became a dormant volcano which didn't need to explode but just smoke a little to let you know how potentially dangerous it was. Long-limbed and dark of hair, she had her own fashion rules.

'She's a little tramp,' said Susan.

'She's magnificent,' I whispered, hardly aware that I had spoken out loud.

'Don't get too attached to her, I've read in the papers that it's all going to end horribly for her. The writers for the series are just debating the different ways she could die before the watershed, hoping to pick the most gruesome and fitting ending. It's gone to court apparently.'

'Fitting?' I said, wondering what Maya had done that could deserve decapitation or worse.

'She's a troublemaker through and through, causes a current of unease in the street.'

'It's a TV series,' I said.

'It's only popular because it reflects reality, she's a nasty piece of work and needs eliminating.'

The fact that she was for the chop only served to increase my obsession with her, making each word she spoke more poignant. She was unashamedly drunk in the local pub, sitting with her legs apart, behaving like a man. When one of the male characters tried to take advantage of her drunken state, she vomited down his back. Everything that came out of Maya's mouth was funny or cutting. She had no compunction about being rude to anyone. She worked as a nail technician but was doing A'levels at night school. She was indifferent to the reactions of the street, truly individual and independent.

'I'd love to dress like that,' I said.

'Like a slapper!' Susan retorted.

I winced at the word. Women used words like that about other women as a way of oppressing them, Gran had said, and men encouraged it because it kept women down. Instead of saying what I thought, I became all mealy-mouthed.

'I don't suppose I could get past Gran in that outfit.'

'Oh, I don't know, I've heard that your grandmother had a vast array of admirers when she worked in The Tide, before it was left to rot. Ask her about James Arlet, the landlord who died of alcoholism, and Dr Charles Doon.'

She must have seen that she had gone too far.

'Arnold Split mentioned it,' she said, naming an older man from the village. 'Of course, that was long before Bill arrived on the scene and captured your grandmother's heart.'

I wondered what part of Gran's anatomy Bill had got hold of, her spleen maybe or her lower intestine, but certainly not her heart. When I got home, I made myself a snack and went to find Gran, she was welding a chair in the garden. It was dusk and the sparks filled the air. I stood and watched her for a while, wondering about what Susan had said.

'Susan said you had lots of admirers when you were young.'

'There's no one left around here anymore who can remember those days clearly.'

'Arnold Split?' I asked.

'A hanger-on who likes nothing better than to open his mouth and watch other people's eyes widen, instead of living himself; because living would be too frightening for him.' she said, turning to face me, flicking up her mask.

'Did you spend a lot of time at The Tide?'

'I worked there.'

'For how long?'

'Until it shut down.'

Her face said that she had had enough of my questioning but I blurted out, 'I want to work in a pub. Susan says there's a job going at The Waggon and Horses.'

'You do not want to work in a pub, you have no idea what it involves, it is completely the wrong place for you and you are too young. There is absolutely no need for you ever to consider it again, this land and our enterprises provide us with enough.'

'Bill provides for us.'

'No one makes him work. We could all pull together and live self-sufficiently.'

I had a horrible vision of what us pulling together would involve. Working the land from dawn till dusk, having no comforts whatsoever and even less to do with the outside world.

'I want a job in a pub.'

'Don't you understand that you wouldn't fit in? Mixing with people, ordinary people, you lose something of yourself. People in groups are unable to think independently, they become cowardly. Everything that I have brought you up to be and to believe would have no standing in the outside world, no value.'

I looked at her, unconvinced, until she shouted, 'You would be brought down!'

I walked away. She wouldn't be able to stop me doing what I liked when the time came. She came in from the garden, her nose full of earth and wholesomeness, to find that a peculiar smell had invaded her kitchen. She sniffed and turned a small circle on the spot with her nose in the air, searching for the source of the offending aroma. Her eyes alighted on my Pot Noodle. The stiff noodles and dried powder sank below the waterline, bubbling. She brought it close to her face and adjusted her glasses so that she could read the tiny script which said exactly what was in the plastic pot. Her head moved from side to side as she absorbed the information. She looked almost desperate as she searched for some health-giving ingredient. Her puckered brow became more pronounced, eyebrows lowering with each tiny line of text until they almost engulfed her eyes and she was left squinting, speechless.

She saw me and put down the pot.

'Extraordinary!' she said.

'No one's asking you to eat it.'

'No,' she said quietly, pushing her glasses back into position again and heading back outside into the garden.

She had ruined my tea. I had looked forward to that pot for days, having saved my longing until the last possible moment. How could I eat it now that it had been condemned by a woman who had revealed the salt content and pointed out each additive's effect on my body?

In temper, I stormed back to Susan's house. I had come to enjoy sitting in her pristine house, doling out colourful examples of my childhood. I knew what she was doing, storing them up to pass on to other people. I could almost see her filing away bits in her head, in a box marked 'Amanda's calamitous upbringing.' Every now and then, I felt a bit bad about what I was doing, but she was showing me so much fun that I felt I had to pay for it in some way and all I had that interested her were horror stories about Gran.

Susan came to the door with a cocktail in one hand. I thought at the time that only she could mix something so magical and sophisticated from alcohol. Whatever was in the glass lay in three bands of colour like traffic lights. She was unsure whether to let me in and I looked down at her feet to see a pair of high heels; not apple, nor lime, nor kiwi – just a particular shade of green. She looked irritated, a little bored of me, I thought, and I began to panic. What if she were to lose interest, stop her education just as I had got started?

So, I said the first thing on my mind. I didn't self-censor, 'The colour of those shoes reminds me of the poison cupboard,' I laughed, pushing my way into her house.

'What?'

'Gran had a cupboard with poison in it.'

'I can't imagine her using weedkiller,' she said, flicking her hair into shape and closing the kitchen door with her foot.

I went red. She noticed. I was changing colour like her cocktail. It was starting at the bottom of my neck and slowly rising up my face, replacing my natural skin tone. I waited for it to settle.

'So if it wasn't weedkiller, what was it? Surely not rat poison? I expect she'd rather catch them and walk them somewhere else.'

She still hadn't invited me to sit down.

'Is it time for the omnibus edition?' I asked, making use of my never wearing a watch.

'What poisons?'

'Since 1974, she's had a poison cupboard.'

'For what?'

'In case there should be a nuclear war, then she could dispatch herself and Bill cleanly and painlessly.'

I'm not quite sure why I used the word dispatched. I never would have used that word in front of Gran. Something about Susan was making me introduce a whole new vocabulary of softening words.

'Kill themselves?'

'Yes, except Bill wanted no part in it, said he would take his chances, thank you very much. They used to argue about it.'

'What did they say?'

'Bill said it was ludicrous, crazy to dwell on such things.'

'And Gran? I mean, Cath?'

'She read a lot about what would happen in the event of a nuclear war and she thought it was sensible, in the face of such horror, to have a way out.'

'And how do you feel about this?'

I shrugged.

'There was a possibility of nuclear war in the 80s. The Cold War wasn't over until a couple of years before I was born. There are hundreds of recorded incidents of near disaster before that. The problem was that she kept the cupboard until I was six.'

I could see by her face that she was incredulous. Although I firmly believed in what I was saying, her frown indicated a great gulf between us. She had adopted the sensible stance and left me no other role than the fanatic.

I started to gabble, 'It doesn't mean that your quality of life is damaged. An awareness of death makes for a sharper life. No one will admit it, but we were close to the end all the time.' I had turned into Gran, but my voice belied my true feelings. I had hated that cupboard, that particular shade of green and had lain awake for several months one winter waiting for the sirens. I lived with only mild anxiety in the day but, at night, the fear took over. In the end, she had repainted the cupboard and said that the direct threat to us was over.

'I don't know what to say, I can't quite make sense of it. Nuclear weapons have kept us safe for decades and continue to do so.'

With those words, the gap between Susan and me became an abyss and the insubstantial items upon which I thought we could build a friendship tumbled down into it – beautifully cut dresses, overpriced handbags and glossy magazines.

Gran had always told me that there were people in life, many of them, with whom it was pointless arguing. These people had something missing inside them. They were mired in delusion. They were not idiots, they were far worse than that, chronically lazy people whose brains had atrophied because they were addicted to being spoon-fed comfort. They would never let in a chink of light or truth because the enormity of it would burn them up.

Susan moved through into her living room where she sunk deep into plush cushions. We were five minutes into the omnibus edition of *Midlanders*, but still, the television screen remained dark.

'So,' said Susan recapping the last few weeks' stories, having squeezed out every ounce of loving from my tales. 'She started showing you skulls at the age of five so that you could be aware of what was supporting your own skin, and she brainwashed you from before you could speak, with that horrible tale of suffering?'

She meant *The Book of Job*. I was glad I hadn't mentioned *The Tibetan Book of the Dead*, Walt Whitman's *Song of Myself* or numerous other texts.

'That's overly simplistic,' I replied calmly.

Again, the image of Job came back to me. Susan's floor seemed hard and cold. Would there come a day when, having lost everything, I would be sat alone with nothing but a piece of china to scrape at my sores? I had begun to anticipate it. It was doing more than cramping my style. Without that image, I could move on freely, consume all I wanted. Laugh, be light-hearted, frivolous even. I could replace that image of suffering with one of Maya, all dripping and tough and seductive at once. But, at this moment, Maya seemed further away from me than ever. And who was to blame for this? Rather than confront Gran, I fixated on the root of all this. That 13-metre spinning thing that represented Gran in all her entirety. Thirteen was supposed to be a magical number which was why the machine was so colossal, but that 13 metres of whirling metal had been nothing but a blight on my life. I left Susan's that night with my first thoughts of attacking Gran's philosophy at its core, but it was to be another three months, just days after my 18th birthday, until my hostility solidified into a plan.

IV

I Confront my Grandmother's Philosophy

IT WAS spring, the season for tearing up telephone directories. We all stood in the kitchen, Bill, Gran and I, ripping, wrenching and tugging at the phone books. Gran always made paper from last year's *Yellow Pages* and she needed us to pull the directories apart before she could start making the pulp. Spring is the season for anger and, normally, I would engage in this family activity with enthusiasm but, at nearly 18, I was having difficulty with the phone books. I wasn't really putting in much effort and Gran noticed my alienation. I'm sure she wished she could erase Susan and her weekly magazines from my mind, then we could all get back to our Utopian vision and leave gloss and nonsense where it belonged – with lesser people.

Gran needed more directories for this year's papermaking enterprise and the man from the tip shop had been saving them for her. She made a suggestion, 'Phone your mother and ask her if she wants to meet us there next Saturday.'

'She hates the tip. Why can't you phone her?'

'She's more likely to come if you phone, if she can forgo spreading sunshine for the afternoon.'

One of Gran's favourite places was the tip shop where she could pick up other people's unwanted items and reuse them. I knew what she was thinking. What better place to meet Marie, and what better excuse than my birthday? Gran always thought the tip had a slightly sobering effect on Marie and had taken her there regularly as a child in an attempt to subdue her, to take away some of her shine.

The wilderness aspect of the place made Marie look a little lost – and Marie never looked lost. Instead, she looked shiny and efficient; confident that she could make a difference to society. That's what Gran hated most about her. Gran knew that her own view of the world was the right one, so she recycled and lived frugally while maintaining a 'we are all doomed' outlook. She couldn't bear Marie's philosophy that everything in life could be sorted out; unsightly loose ends could be tied together or burnt, if necessary, to stop them from fraying. If Gran could get Marie to the tip and make her stand in front of all that grime and profligacy, she would have achieved the equivalent of a thousand heartfelt speeches.

She also wanted something from Marie, other than the opportunity to reduce her high spirits. Gran needed Marie to drive to our home with 65 old copies of the *Yellow Pages* in her sports car. Her little car, not built for acts of altruism, would struggle down our lane, catching its exhaust pipe in the potholes. Marie's only consolation would be that, every time she glanced in the rear-view mirror, her eyes would be full of garish yellow surfaces, succour to someone who liked to look on the bright side. Marie would not refuse to deliver the directories because she knew that, on some level, what Gran was doing was right. Gran and I would walk back from the tip; Marie would drop the telephone directories at our gate and be saved the charade of being asked in, followed by her reply that she must get back. Light-heartedness was waiting for her.

Gran's papermaking enterprise had expanded over the years. She began to make her paper in the spring when she could dry sheets of it on the washing line. Until I was an adult, I wasn't aware that paper is generally white and smooth – we never had any of that type in the house. Gran's earliest paper was lumpy. She would sandwich flower heads and strands of grass between the fibres. She would then try to type on the surface of this paper using a typewriter which she had saved from extinction.

Gran would suddenly leap up, often during a meal, when she thought of a political situation that particularly angered her. Shoving her plate aside and creating a space just large enough for the typewriter to sit, she would continue picking at her food with one hand, whilst keeping her eyes on the typewriter. A French bean might find its way onto the keyboard. God knows what else was trapped under those keys, what lay rotting in the dark heart of the machine. Bill and I would carry on eating in defiance, even though her getting the typewriter out was a sure sign that she had declared family togetherness over.

The keys Gran prodded with one hand would produce blurry letters, due to the bumps in the homemade paper. The carriage on the typewriter would mangle the rough-terrain sheets. This meant that Gran's political letters were largely illegible. And, if they managed to arrive at their destination at all (the glue in her homemade envelopes being ineffectual in the early days), the recipient would probably not give Gran's ideas much time. In between struggling to make out the words, pulling some fibre out of the paper and asking a suited colleague if they, too, thought it was a piece of grass, Gran's message would be lost. I tried to explain this to her.

'If you want to change Government policy you might do better to approach them using ordinary paper and their own language.'

'They must listen to reason, Amanda, and appearances are not important.'

Bill raised his eyebrows, 'I think you know to your cost that they are,' he muttered.

I quietly carried the plates through to the kitchen. Bill would make endless unnecessary trips, carrying one plate at a time, shuffling across the lino, smacking the narrow doorway which led through to the galley kitchen, or letting his shadow loom over Gran and her typing. All these things would infuriate her further; each one adding more anger to her typed letter; making it less likely that anyone would ever read it.

The first day she produced the magic paper, she ran into the garden waving it triumphantly. Paper with shards of silver just below the surface. I took it from her. It was too precious to use and I still have it. She'd stuck to that recipe ever since. Gran began papermaking in a small way on the kitchen table, using a pestle and mortar, but she could only produce a tiny quantity and it was time-consuming.

When the food mixer first appeared in the kitchen, Bill felt quite hopeful for a few moments. 'Do you think that cake might be coming our way?' he asked.

Sometimes, I wondered at his insistent naïvety, but his little face looked quite downcast so I answered, 'Lump-free soup, maybe?'

Gran overheard, 'You two only think about your stomachs.'

She seized the food mixer and didn't even bother cleaning the thing. Instead, she had us lined up in the kitchen, tearing up directories until our hands and muscles ached. I had forearms like a hod carrier. Bit by bit, she fed the food mixer with pages from the directories. She added rain water, mixing it all up to form strange mulch, which she pushed into a specially-made frame with a sieve on the back. I liked watching her moving the pulp along the screen until the surface levelled. Over the years, she became more skilful, sponging excess water, pushing fabric over the back of the mould and deftly removing the material with the wet paper sticking to it. The paper then dried on the line outside our house and was gently peeled from the cloth when it was ready.

From spring onwards, our washing line flapped with metres of strange, silver- infused paper. Our clothes never got near the washing line because Gran had commandeered it for a purpose greater than cleanliness. The silver bits that caught the light and batted them back to the sun were scales from mackerel skin. Every week, she sent me down to the fishmongers to collect the skin. I used tweezers to pick off the scales and line them up on tissue paper to dry. When they were dry, I counted them into little piles of 189; that was the right number to make the paper shine, but not too much.

Gran's final touch with her paper was embossing it with a tiny image of a carousel. That strange fairground ride dominated our lives; the thinking behind it in our house and the actuality of it in the garden. In winter, when it was covered up with specially made sheeting, it still loomed large and threatening and, in summer, when it turned slowly in all its 13-metre glory, we were often lost for words, and that's after 18 years of living with it. Gran had certainly stamped the image of the carousel and the ideas from *The Book of Job* through us. We were like sticks of rock, if you snapped a Furnish in half, you would find an image of the carousel through the middle. I asked Bill if he still found it strange.

'It's as much a part of your grandmother as her nose, I just see it as an extension of her, the way it dominates everything.'

'But do you believe what she says about it?'

'This is where your grandmother and I fundamentally differ. I don't believe in dwelling on things, or pondering questions that have no answers.'

'What if there is an answer but it takes a lifetime to work it out?'

'How can there be an answer to suffering?' he said with unusual exasperation, and then more softly, 'Circular conversations are your grandmother's preoccupation, but they don't interest me. I can't focus on unpleasant things or whimsy.'

'Gran wouldn't call *The Book of Job* whimsy.'

'I'd never say that to her face.'

'Why did you marry her?'

Bill smiled warmly, 'Marrying your grandmother taught me a valuable lesson. Unfortunately, it's one of those extraordinarily cruel and pointless lessons.'

'What do you mean?'

'It was as though she existed behind glass before we were married. In agreeing to marry me, she became exposed to air. I don't and never did have what it takes to make her shine. No charisma if you like. Being with me has tarnished her.'

'That's not true, you rescued her.'

'Beware of what you rescue,' he said, glancing at Huff the cat. 'All things come with a history which will eventually be revealed in their behaviour.' He gave the mean cat a gentle stroke. You could see the creature decide in a moment whether to strike out at him or not. For once, Huff did nothing.

*   *   *

Gran sold her paper through a local co-operative which then sold it on to markets for the tourists in summer. People couldn't get enough of it and, every year, a hopeful manufacturer phoned to ask Gran if she would consider a commercial enterprise, 'Mrs Furnish, we are sure that people would be interested in writing on paper from old phone books with fish scales as a finishing touch. You have a unique selling point.'

But Gran left them in no doubt, 'In my experience most people prefer uniformity and lines.'

Local people left their old telephone directories at our door. Most days, there were one or two on the doorstep. We took in these abandoned books of numbers.

There was a lot of waiting in between the various stages of producing paper and I divided the time between activities and thinking. The physical aspect involved piling up copies of *Yellow Pages* to make a staircase, each edition slightly overlapping the next as the stack grew higher. I could walk up a flight of 23 phone directories without slipping. When I got to the top, my head almost touched the kitchen ceiling. I did this barefoot because the slippery phonebook covers could be quite treacherous. The thinking incorporated how I could get this made into an Olympic sport.

It had everything going for it. It was politically correct because it consisted of recycling, and the need for fitness, dexterity and continual practice made it a sport. It also involved a minimal outlay and was something you could try for yourself at home. I saw potential problems though – on the downside, you had to have small feet which meant that most of the competitors would be women or children. Therefore, it was unlikely that the sport would ever receive worldwide coverage, or be taken seriously. Also, it takes years to get a sport that starts on the street officially established. It would have to remain underground, but, if the glorious day ever arose, I would be happy to be the ambassador.

The truth was that I would never make the Olympics. I would never do anything special or be admired by anyone. Raised on a diet of unsettling questions, I had nothing to which I could look forward. Bored with building straight staircases (they offered me no challenge), I started to experiment with spiral ones. Using a broom handle as a surrogate handrail, I went round in a corkscrew shape. Once, my straight stairways would have been enough for me. It is legitimate to spend a lifetime practising one thing over and over but now I knew there were other people out there doing different things. There was a restlessness in me. I couldn't sit still for long and found it impossible to focus.

'Amanda, I have just found a piece of paper with 185 fish scales in it, you are not concentrating.'

I just shrugged. Gran's eyes were attuned to just the right amount of luminosity, so one scale too many, or too few, never escaped her notice. She looked at me for an apology.

'So what?'

I couldn't bring myself to say sorry or offer to make amends. I carried on with my spiral staircase, but, as my foot touched the 25th directory, I fell, landing on my wrist. Gran rushed into the garden, collecting herbs to make a poultice. I watched her through the grubby window as I held my throbbing wrist. She darted about the large rectangle of earth, dedicated to medicinal herbs, that lay closest to the house. She didn't hesitate, knowing exactly which plants to gather. As she pulled the herbs, their scent was released into the air and came to me through the window. I sat slumped at the kitchen table when she came in, slithering further down my chair until my head and shoulders were all that was visible. She tried to catch hold of my wrist to apply the dressing but I snatched my hand away.

'That stinks, what the hell is it?'

'Borage, garlic and sage, mostly.'

'There's something in it that you are not telling me about, something vile and malodorous. And, anyway, a simple paracetamol would suffice,' I said snidely.

She looked at me with her head on one side. 'Go out and get some, then.'

'How can I walk miles to the chemist's in this condition?'

'I am offering what I have always offered and that's that.' She left the poultice on the table and I applied it awkwardly. The pain soon eased, but I was still angry. I don't know how much longer I could live with this earthiness.

At night, I had nightmares. I was lying in a landfill and, above me, were flying telephone directories, their great covers flapping. They dive-bombed me, inflicting paper cuts on my hands as I tried to sweep them off. Suddenly, I could hear the hundreds of thousands of conversations that had taken place in the last year since those directories had been replaced. All the desperate calls for help, the weeping, the hanging on. The inane calls, the duty calls, the nagging, the monosyllabic responses.

When the dreams began, I could make out individual voices and laughter, but now, there was just conversation on top of conversation, and not a word of sense in any of them. I needed a voice I could trust or hear clearly but things became more muddled, with more crossed lines. I woke up and thought about all the strangers in those directories I might never meet. I was filled with panic. What if one of them, sandwiched between Partridge, J, and Partridge, K.S., was the love of my life?

The Saturday of my birthday arrived, the day we were meeting Marie at the tip. An extraordinary letter had come for me that morning and it gave me a great sense of hope. It was to be my ticket out. I knew it was from my father because it had the stamp of the office where he worked. I had written to him three weeks ago, asking him to introduce me to normality. And I was sure that, nestling comfortably inside this franked envelope, lay the invitation for which I had been longing. There was never any secret about him and I had often walked past the Doons' old house and wondered where they were living now. Gran told me that I could contact him when I was 17, and I had waited beyond the deadline, mostly for fear of hurting Gran. I kept the letter in my pocket, I had plans for it.

It was a bright day when we arrived at the tip and Gran was annoyed that some of the impact of the place was lost. She would have preferred an electric storm, any kind of freak weather which might unsettle Marie's cheerfulness. She secretly hoped that, on the way here, Marie might be first on the scene of a hideous accident; the kind of accident where someone's head was hanging on by a sinew, and yet the victim was still able to communicate. She said she'd like to see Marie doing her little triangle business then. Still, this place should suppress Marie a little. When she arrived, smiling and brightly dressed, she was either oblivious to the accident Gran had hoped she'd see or triumphant from making the victim grateful. Gran stood on the railings, perfectly still, looking down on the desecration. She barely acknowledged Marie but stayed where she was, above the rubbish, hair flying. Hair that had never seen ribbons, or dye or clips. Hair even unfamiliar with scissors.

I led Marie to Gran and the three of us stood on the railings watching the scene below us for a full 10 minutes – Gran like some Old Testament figure, all righteous and full of wrath above the scene of dust and despondency. A JCB tore back and forth with its mouth full of unwanted items and dirt. It was moving one pile of debris to another; using the smaller pile of rubbish to fortify the foothills of what was fast becoming a colossal heap, 30-metres high and 90-metres wide. Each scooped up bucket of refuse sent dust flying into the air. The whole area became covered in ash.

As the dust settled, we saw that an old iron was caught at the back of the machine with its plug still attached. It rattled noisily behind the JCB, swishing back and forth like the tail of some mythical beast.

Even Marie had to agree that we throw out too much and it was a waste. Marie had been throwing out bits of herself for years, ever since she'd left us. There wasn't a bone in her body that she hadn't broken and reset to her own specifications. I moved closer to her, hoping to bathe in her yellowness, near enough to breathe in some of her inane carbon dioxide. Gran's apocalyptic vision was beginning to wear me down and I needed an antidote.

I looked back at Gran who was still standing there, transfixed and full of fire. Sometimes, I forgot that she was such a small person. She must have practised tricks with the light or hovered a few inches above the ground, given lift by her own ferocity. Marie tried to engage Gran in conversation.

'I'm running a one-off workshop where people who have suffered a tragedy will have a chance to look at their lives and see what good might have come from it. I could reserve you a place, if you're interested.'

Gran gave her a look which I can only describe as incredulous, 'Suffering is profoundly felt and deeply personal, you can't offer me a cheap philosophical line.' Gran's despair was not going to be patted on the head and sent away.

'People suffer extraordinary things and yet go on to live happy and fulfilled lives,' said my mother, determined to stick to the script.

'For every one you name, I'll show you 10 who kill themselves.'

Gran walked away from Marie, placed one hand on the tip wall and appeared to leap over into the chasm, a 30-metre drop that ended in concrete, where the JCB was working. Alarmed, we rushed forward and saw that she hadn't fallen, but had just stepped out onto the mountain of rubbish lying packed against the wall, almost reaching the top. She was scaling down a heap of waste which had different strata every few metres. Three metres down was the first layer; a huge piece of sodden beige carpet like a layer of sandstone. The next seam was made up of newspapers and magazines with a bright red lampshade sticking out, waiting to be mined like a ruby.

Further down, I could see bags bursting their skins, the sharpness of the contents piercing the plastic and revealing bits of bushes, trees, leaves and soil. A stray bag of ill-sorted household goods, toys, buckets and a clock were visible. Gran was moving down the mountain with the speed and sturdiness of a goat. Sometimes, she would clamber towards the edge of the rubbish cliff and look down. She made it to the foothills and then began the ascent with something in her hand. The grace and speed of her movements were fluid as she rose up the unstable mass, the red lampshade in her hand.

Marie muttered to me, 'I could buy you any amount of lampshades. My latest book and series of tours have been a great success.'

'I don't think that's the point,' I whispered.

'She can't be angry at the world for ever, you know.'

'She's doing pretty well so far.'

'That merry-go-round.'

'What about it?'

'It justifies her philosophy of suffering. Do you understand that it represents her first baby? Because it dominates the garden, she can never move on. You ought to try to persuade her to get rid of it, or at least put it into storage. I'll pay for it if you get a quote.'

I didn't provide any encouragement.

'I've been on prime time television 11 times in the last month.'

'I didn't see you, Gran is still adamant about no TV.'

I never mentioned how much I had been watching at Susan's. Marie shook her head. Even the way she did that was controlled. She had probably learnt it on one of her courses – the appropriate way to shake your head when you meet people who wilfully refuse to turn their insides out for all to see.

Now seemed the right time for me to open my letter. That would put an end to their bickering and mean that I could move into my father's tasteful world. Hopefully, his letter would contain the bus number and I could be on my way.

But, at that moment, Gran ordered Marie to bring her car round to the tip shop where we could begin loading the *Yellow Pages*. Marie protested feebly.

'It's very dusty by the shop and dust can be so corrosive on cars' paintwork.'

'Life's corrosive,' said Gran.

She then repeated her previous instructions in a firmer voice. Marie was weakening, as if her power were diminishing faced with this place – Gran's personal manifesto brought to life.

Marie dutifully brought round the car and Gran wasted no time in piling in the directories.

'I was thinking about 20,' said Marie, as Gran stacked at least 30 onto the passenger seat before we had begun to help. She was soon up to 80 and the soft roof of the car bulged and buckled. Marie was grimacing and twisting her hands, whilst Gran was now searching for crevices in the car that were as yet unexploited. She was tearing out 20 pages at a time and forcing them into the glove box.

'I won't be able to see out of the back,' protested Marie.

'Well, think how that might advantage you,' said Gran. 'What might you learn from not seeing?'

'It's illegal,' squeaked Marie.

'I wish you had a pick-up,' said Gran, ignoring her and tearing out individual pages, dangerously wrapping them around the handbrake and then continuing to pad the dashboard.

'I don't think a pick-up would send out appropriate messages for me, it could be construed as being a little aggressive...'

I couldn't stand it any longer. I produced the letter from my pocket with a flourish. It turned gold on contact with the air and I fingered it like a television presenter at an awards ceremony. I teasingly ran my thumb under the flap. Now I had their attention, this was more like it. I played with them a little more. After all, the results were a foregone conclusion. Soon, I would be safely ensconced on neutral territory, and they would have a lifetime to reconsider their extremist behaviour.

Gran stood on one side with her arms tightly folded and Marie on the other as I slowly withdrew the letter from the envelope. In my mind, I was wearing a fabulous frock and stood behind the podium of *Yellow Pages* that wouldn't fit in the car. I gave a little cough before speaking and began to read:

Ms Furnish,
    If it's money you are after, I have accrued considerable amounts. Unfortunately, if it's anything else, I find myself unable to oblige,

pp Anthea Fitzackerly on behalf of John Doon.

My mother leapt into counselling mode; with a single twirl she was spaniel-eyed, soft-voiced and menacingly maternal, 'Come and stay with me darling. I know a super Dr Stevens, a specialist in parent-child relationships. And, after he's finished with you, we could set two chairs in an empty room and you could run from one to the other. On one you would be yourself and, on the other, you could pretend to be your father.'

She suggested that I carry on a conversation with myself, but she didn't say for how long it would last.

'Does it involve a sprint or a stroll between the chairs?' I asked miserably.

I needed to work out appropriate footwear. That was irrelevant; the facts were that this was a much-loved professional tool called 'the empty chair technique', which could be very effective and, no, it was not necessary to dress up as my father in between each dash.

The main problem I foresaw, if his letter were anything to go by, was that I couldn't imagine him saying anything of interest, even with me as his channel. Marie's plans went further. She wouldn't stop talking. As if all the talking in the world might soothe this situation. For our evenings, she suggested that we delve into books which might shed light on my father's fear, and the awful consequences of his own childhood. In this way, we could embrace forgiveness and employ understanding. Tears ran down my face. My teeth were gritted and I knew my skin was blotchy. Gran sprang into action.

She snatched the letter off me.

'Give me that. In complete contrast to your mother, I suggest that we kick forgiveness in the throat and torture understanding.'

She took me by the arm and began to march me the two miles home. She shouted instructions to my mother about the delivering of the directories. All the way home, we were silent. My mother overtook us minutes later, driving slowly with her hazard lights on; the car looking as if it had been lowered by teenage enthusiasts. A mile further up the road we found one of the directories by the ditch. It must have slipped out of the window.

'Babbling half-wit,' Gran muttered. 'Imagine choosing an occupation where you lie to other people about how great life is. If you repeat your nonsense regularly, with enough ferocity you get to believe it yourself, and those saps you charge are eternally grateful, thus reinforcing the whole outrageous cycle of claptrap. And nobody has to face the truth.'

She picked up the directory and, gripping my arm and the letter tighter than ever, we stumbled down our potholed road, me sobbing and Gran holding me up. When we reached our front door, Marie had left the directories in neat piles outside the house. Gran marched me straight past them and into her bedroom. She took a rifle out of her wardrobe, led me outside by the hand and, at three in the afternoon, she shot a crow. She proceeded to tear my father's letter into tiny bits and stuff them down the dead bird's throat.

The creature, still glossy in death, was allowed to rot close to the house till the stench rose and would head straight for my father. Two weeks later, when the maggots had done their trick, Gran poured paraffin over the carcass and the bird went up in flames. She swore she could hear the bird cawing for forgiveness from my father. Only a bird so dark could carry such a message. The message would be more powerful than any amount of words.

'What if he doesn't understand the message?' I asked.

'Everyone understands that kind of message.'

A week after that, I was supposed to be making paper with Gran but, instead, was looking through a magazine which Susan had passed over the fence. I had lost all hope. My father was no good. He was not coming for me. Beige World only ever existed in my head. My 18th birthday had come and gone with a cheque from my mother and Gran providing an already half-empty bottle of homemade parsnip wine. No Champagne for me, just fermented root vegetables. My foul mood had reached a climax. I had ceased to speak and spent all my time gazing at Susan's celebrity magazines. Bored with the one I was reading, I went to my stash on the bookshelves. They were gone and, in their place, was *The Bible*. What kind of joke was this? It fell open on the familiar, well-thumbed *The Book of Job*, the only bit of *The Bible* Gran considered of any interest. I looked at the poetry at the end. I used to be inexplicably moved by these lines but, now, they were just the conceited rantings of a tyrant.

I stormed down to the carousel and, for the first time in my life, turned on the engine without asking permission. I had *The Bible* in my hand. Clouds gathered and the light in the garden was dimmed. Even the grass changed from a bright, lush emerald to a dense forest-green. The bonfire, which Gran had lit hours earlier, found something unexpected in its core and briefly flared again. Or perhaps it was speaking to me, egging me on.

'If she doesn't respect your magazines why should you give her viewpoint any space?'

I tore out the whole of *The Book of Job* in one lump, with my fingers tough from phone directories. The thin, crepey pages were like old skin. Tiny bits of ash went up into the air. The fire smouldered, recognising my intent. I rolled page after page into tiny balls and threw them on the fire, pathetic snacks to a great beast. When there was nothing left, and all the poetry, astonishing imagery and conceptual questions had been swallowed by the fire without chewing, I climbed onto the moving carousel and sat high up on the crag next to the vulture, waiting for it to speak. I looked down at all the animals who had given me comfort and whose existence I had never questioned. They didn't have the answers any more. They were just murderers and opportunists, all of them.

The war horse looked more eager to go into battle than it had ever done before. The hippopotamus was just a lumpen brute. The meat the vulture fed to its chicks, which had been so gorily repainted, turned my stomach. I jabbed the bird in the eye with my index finger. Further angered by its lack of response, I jumped down from the jagged rocks and landed heavily on the hand-carved wooden floor which flexed under my weight.

I headed straight for Gran's favourite creature, Leviathan the crocodile. At that moment, it represented everything I hated about my life, Gran's constant harshness and her insistence on concentrating on the darker aspects of existence. Smug reptile. I spat in his face and my saliva ran down his intricately carved scales. The darker the sky became, the madder I got. I made a wild lunge at the hook that hung two metres above Leviathan's head. I intended to pull it down and stick it back in the creature's mouth, so that he would be subdued and God's boast about being the only one who could ever do this would no longer be true. But it was hopeless, even if I could reach it, I would never detach it from the roof of the carousel. To think that I was stuck in this ridiculous place with these monsters for company; the years were disappearing while I festered.

Suddenly, it was just the crocodile and me in the ring. I took hold of *The Bible* and rammed it into his mouth with full force. Three of his teeth were gone in one blow and the sockets where the teeth had been were stained black. The soft black leather from *The Bible* had transferred itself onto the wooden gums of the beast. Unexpectedly, he looked vicious again, menacing. I shrank and he grew. Those fat reptilian feet, which had looked so comical moments ago, seemed to tense. The innate brooding power of the beast became apparent.

Stepping slowly backwards, I crept down from the carousel and turned off the engine. My heart raced and my mouth was completely dry. I started to walk backwards with my eye still on the crocodile. Stumbling, making slow progress, I moved breathlessly towards the house. I had the three teeth in my pocket; burrowing slowly into my flesh, millimetre by millimetre, as sharp as needles.

I was horrified that things had come to this, that I had committed this crime instead of having the courage to say I wanted to leave. That I had layer upon layer of anger and resentment, decaying until it had gained so much power that it rose to the surface. A bubbling, stinking mess.

Gran came in looking strangely cheerful.

'There's a job going at the pub for which you are eminently qualified,' she said, 'What with your debating skills and ability to stoke fires.'

Choking, I felt for the teeth in my pocket. If I hadn't done this thing, I could have gone to work at the pub with Gran's blessing.

'Why have you changed your mind? And what about me being brought down?'

'Maybe you'll fare better than I did,' she said

Crocodile tears trickled down my face. I was just about to speak when she smiled, 'Hand over the crocodile's teeth, Amanda.'

V

I Escape

THE DARK thoughts stopped, no more colossal, lurid, numerate birds haunted me, and I had a job in the local pub. Gran gave me some guidance for the future. Her advice was not, 'always use a condom' or 'don't slouch'. Neither was it 'never stroke a dog with different coloured eyes' nor 'drink eight glasses of water a day'. It was… 'lick gold'. Should you find yourself in a place where you see beams and think instantly of a noose, or when you see grass and think of worms and decay, then lick gold. When a wide expanse of blue sky seems proof to you that there is nothing meaningful, and life rolls on like the mouth of a thoughtless person, then lick gold. Any source of gold will do, a watch or wedding ring for instance.

Gran wrapped up a 10-centimetre square of gold leaf for me as a present. It was the most delicate thing I had ever seen. It undulated a little, like a magic carpet, before it came to rest on the tissue paper. Even in the still of the kitchen, at the height of summer, with no air moving, there was enough of a draught for the gold leaf to float upon. It must have been riding on the invisible current that Gran's words created; trusting them, knowing she spoke the truth.

But I had little or no interest in the truth so, for the rest of that summer, in between helping Gran around the place, I watched soap operas at Susan's house. I was worried about not fitting in at the pub and felt I had a lot to learn. I needed access to anything that might give me clues as to what went on in the real world. Susan continued to help me, she gave me a key and I just let myself in and out. I must have seen a hundred soap episodes. Each one was educational. It seemed as appropriate as going to Spain and getting a language tape. I was going to work in a pub and life in soap operas always centred on the pub.

I felt sure that I was in for an exciting time if these programmes were anything to go by. *Midlanders* was my favourite soap and the character I really sympathised with was Maya Watts. She had had six partners in the last month. She had a wandering eye and a wondering mind. She needed thrills like most people need food. Only lots of sex with different people could satisfy her. Her body glistened and called to people even when she was just popping out to get a pint of milk. She was always surrounded by hopeful lovers and every lover she had, wanted her to stop seeing the others. The way she moved fascinated me most of all, and the power that she had to make people stand and stare. But, mostly, I loved her shamelessness. I asked Gran about it.

'Do you think Maya is a tart?'

'Don't use that ridiculous word, Amanda. Women who behave wildly and spontaneously will pay an enormous price for fighting convention. It has always been the way of the world and I see no evidence for future optimism.'

'What sort of price?'

'Public censure, dismissal, crude categorisation – and that's if they're lucky. Oh, and people like your mother telling them they are incomplete and need fixing.'

'Maya has no choice,' I said, 'she's driven by something, pulled. She has passion. Can you really cause mayhem like that?'

'She has a choice. The key is to know yourself, to be honest about how much you are prepared to pay.'

'Like what?'

'If you take things far enough, you will inevitably face a pot-scraping moment.'

The last thing I wanted was for things to be brought back to the carousel. Why did every conversation with Gran have to lead us back there? My silence seemed to annoy her.

'I don't want a conversation about a fictitious woman where everything is neatly glossed over and life's complexities remain unaddressed.'

Trouble is, that was just the conversation I wanted.

'I wish you would stop watching that rot. Don't live through other people, celebrities or characters from television shows, it's cowardly and destructive. You know enough about things that matter, Amanda.'

I ignored her and vaulted the little ornamental hedge that had recently been planted to separate our land from Susan's. I was off to watch the omnibus edition of *Midlanders*. Gran pushed the hedge aggressively with her foot.

'Ineffectual little hedge. Why didn't she get a beech, a proper hedge? One that would genuinely separate us?'

There was a chill in the air an hour later when I headed back to our house. As I stepped over Susan's immaculate lawn, the grass sprang back after each footfall, as if clearing up after itself. Only Susan could have grass like that, perky grass. Autumn was approaching, shoving summer carelessly out of the way. Gran was in the garden, turning over the soil. She saw me and smiled, picking up some earth and crumbling it.

'Bury me in this, Amanda,' she laughed, 'under this beautiful soil duvet.'

'It's illegal to bury people in your back garden.'

'Ridiculous,' she retorted. To lighten the mood, I picked up a handful of the soil and sprinkled it over her head.

'Lovely,' she said, rubbing it into her scalp.

She walked over to an apple tree, picked two and handed one to me.

'The thought of bodies in the garden has put me off apples,' I mumbled.

She tutted and went on to tell me a tale. An ancient version of *Little Red Riding Hood*, like the ones she used to tell me as a child. The unsanitised versions, from a time before they were written down and made respectable. This variation involved the granddaughter eating the grandmother.

'That's disgusting!' I stropped.

'It's not. It's both symbolic and literally about ingesting the grandmother's knowledge. One woman handing over power to the next but one generation. All this will be yours,' she said, making an expansive gesture which took in the septic tank and the carousel in one sweep.

I wanted to discourage her from going down that familiar path so I said nothing. But I took a handful of soil myself and held it close to my face, breathing it in. I wanted to eat it. I wanted to eat everything; I was full of longing.

I lay in bed that night, listening to Huff the cat clicking his toenails against the lino in the hallway with his own little Morse Code of satisfaction, as he toyed with a mouse before killing it. At night, I heard Gran and Bill's voices, drifting to me through thin partition walls, as they had done for 18 years. Ten words from him and one from her was the usual recipe. They whispered after eleven o'clock without thinking, and they would probably continue to do so long after I'd left. Gran interpreted the cat's cruel message and, scolding it, came to rescue the mouse.

At night, our garden and the lane were spectacularly dark. The night set itself out on the ground like a picnic blanket and the rescued mouse ran over it, wrinkling the material with its tiny terrified feet, only to be picked up, moments later, by an owl. But that was okay, that was the way things were, Gran had taught me these things. I had grown up beside them, unsheltered and grudgingly accepting.

* * *

The day before I began my new job, Gran and I took a walk down to The Tide. I went straight up to the Rottweiler drawing to make sure it was still there, guarding the abandoned pub with its fading ink lines. Would a day come when the drawing would disappear completely and the guard dog slink off, leaving the pub open to attack? I smiled at each carefully constructed mark. Since it had ceased to frighten me, I had become more interested in it. Looking vigilantly at the artwork, I was struck by the idea that the drawing was full of fear and the dog itself represented that fear.

'It's a beautiful drawing,' I said, fascinated.

'It's technically competent and no more,' said Gran.

'It must have taken hours, why do you think they didn't buy one of those plastic Rottweiler signs from the pet shop for £5?'

'You can't buy everything,' she snapped.

Not wishing to antagonise her further, I moved away from the drawing, towards the river.

* * *

Finally, the Saturday night that I had been longing for arrived – the night I would begin working at the The Waggon and Horses. I was tense as I cycled the three miles to the village pub, down narrow lanes where all the colourful hedge flowers of summer were dying back. The hedgerows hadn't been cut back since I had last been past for my interview. My face was plastered in tiny flies when I arrived at the pub. I had always moaned about having to cycle everywhere but, when I looked down at my athletic body, I was proud.

It was a typical enough black and white pub that had no front garden but backed directly onto one of the lanes. There was a large, flat, gravelled car park to the left of the pub. The building itself was dark with few windows. Late-summer's hanging baskets sulked and lichen was taking hold randomly across the whitewashed building. Splashes of dirt and mud had started to appear on the front of last year's paintwork. The front door of the pub was still left open. It was just warm enough to do that. Before I walked in, I let my tongue touch the gold hinges on my watch strap; sure enough, I felt calm surge through me. I walked up to the bar and felt the air brushing over the beer cloths. The glasses that hung upside down from the bar shone in the late-August light.

The girl behind the bar looked up and introduced herself. Her name was Ali and she was going to show me what to do. Harry, the owner, approached us. He extended a thin, wiry arm, not to me, but to the glasses. He had found the one glass with a faint trace of lipstick on it.

One of the locals piped up, 'Don't take the lipstick off, gives us something romantic to think about when autumn arrives now that Ali has rejected all our advances.'

Harry seemed an anxious man. His thoughts must have been full of germs, disorder and other things that might threaten the end of the tourist season. His hair had been heavily bleached by the sun and was just starting to grow back at the roots, a duller shade of blond. He looked about 32, was very handsome but did nothing for me, and I could tell when he looked me up and down, that the feeling was mutual.

I couldn't hear any music or thumping of slot machines but a small games room was available, leading off a dark corridor on the way to the toilets. Everything was clean but slightly shabby. Ali led me out the back, through the corridor and past the toilets to the back door. Dark and heavy, with an old-fashioned latch, it finally gave way and the garden was revealed, the pub's best feature. The lawn gently sloped down to the river which babbled merrily. At one place, the river was crossable via stepping stones.

Just three miles down the river, it was a different story altogether. The river turned into a muddy creek at certain times of the day and The Tide, that old, abandoned pub, sat patiently, close enough to the mud to smell it. But the river here was tame and photogenic. On the other side of the water lay fields. Overgrown trees and bushes made their way down to the bank and almost kissed across the narrowest parts of the little river. It was a safe piece of water, ideal for paddling. There were a few benches and umbrellas dotted about the garden.

The umbrellas were old, advertising drink brands not seen since the 1970s. Painstakingly patched and stored each winter, they added an air of nostalgia and faded gentility to the place. The seating area was paved and seven sad hanging baskets swung from the pub wall.

It was peaceful. Everything moved slowly, including Ali. She was unashamedly lazy and advised me to be the same. She sat down and a tiny bit of tanned belly rose over the waistband of her jeans, like brown dough, warm and inviting. The backs of her calves were so smooth that they looked almost artificial, doll-like. I was also tanned, with scratches on my legs and muscular in comparison. She stayed seated whilst a couple of the locals served themselves and left the right change on the bar. She looked up to thank them.

'If there's only a couple in, I let them serve themselves.'

It turned eight and a few others wandered in sporadically. Ali sighed, got up and took over her post. Her painted toes and elegant feet mesmerised the pub as she padded towards the bar. She showed me how to serve the beer. No one was in a rush. A couple of people asked after me and, when they realised I was related to Cath Furnish, they gave me a second look and nodded in approval. Ali looked at me differently, sizing me up.

We had something in common – Susan Rink. Ali had worked at Susan's cake factory for six months before being sacked. I asked her how it happened, thinking that she must have done something unforgivable, like falling drunk into one of the huge vats where the cakes were mixed, or gone round the supermarkets where they sold Susan's cakes, injecting them with poison. But it wasn't like that.

'Three verbal warnings,' she said. '13th January, piece of hair sticking out of hat. 18th April, sliver of nail varnish on ring finger of left hand. 25th July, open-toed shoes on the factory floor. I was only giving Julie Harp my Lottery money.'

'That doesn't sound like much,' I said.

I was trying to balance what I knew of Susan with this new information. Apparently, it was all clearly laid out in the staff manual, which was updated monthly and weighed seven pounds. Ali interested me. She had mascara clumped unevenly on her eyelashes and there was so much of it, it sometimes appeared to be too much of an effort for her even to open both eyes. There was nothing that she considered worthy of opening her eyes for in this pub.

Ali had a way of starting sentences that were often not really addressed to anyone in particular. But people would listen, as I did, avidly.

'I love romance, that's why I liked working in Susan's cake factory.'

She had only been on cheap fairy cakes, which sold in some supermarkets at 99p for 12, but she had ambition. She was planning to be promoted to wedding cakes in Susan's emporium. Only the most glamorous girls worked in the wedding cake section and they had their own entrance at the side of the factory where they also had a shopfront and a little counter.

'They even have their own tea room.'

'Away from the rest of the staff?'

'Yes. Occasionally, Susan joins them but she doesn't eat much.' Ali was warming to her subject. She looked nostalgic and sad, she clearly missed it. 'Susan even teaches them to speak.'

'They can't speak?'

'No, stupid, on the phone and that.'

Apparently, there were different ways of speaking: on the phone and to customers. Susan trained her spongy elite with the use of a video camera and scripts.

'Like film stars, they are.'

Ali had had plans to be in front of that camera before the avarice of wanting to win The Lottery had caused her open-toed downfall. Since her career in the wedding cake industry appeared to be temporarily shelved, she had taken to obsessing over wedding magazines for her fix. *World of Weddings*, *Dreams in White*, and *Bride Beautiful*, were delivered to the pub each month. The latter had a pull-out cake section that she couldn't bear to look at. As soon as all three copies had been safely delivered, and added to Harry's bills under miscellaneous, she would sit down at a table for two and start cutting things out. It took her a week to cut out 150 dresses. The scissors moved around the intricate sleeves and hems whilst Ali's tongue lolled out of the corner of her mouth, only to be retracted quickly and sulkily when she was required to serve at the bar.

When the snipping was complete, she would sit down and begin to sort the dresses into three piles. A 'no way' pile, a 'possibly' one and a 'yes, definitely, I-certainly-see-myself-waltzing-down-the-aisle-in-that-creation' pile. I thought about what Gran would say about her playing this game.

'To think I marched for women like that.'

But Gran wasn't here and serving behind the bar was easier than I thought it would be. The place wasn't very busy and so, after two nights, I started to join in the game. We had long discussions about whether choosing fabric-covered buttons this year might place the dress too firmly in the 2010s and date the life of the wedding album. She liked my input. She appreciated my attention to detail, and my grasp of the changing world of wedding food.

'I wouldn't have known that canapés were the new vol-au-vents, Amanda.'

I only knew that myself because I had just read an article on it, all 1,500 words of it. Even though Ali said she loved the idea of romance, she was not interested in the reality of it. I watched her constantly rebuff all advances from the locals and pre-empt ones from Harry.

'I'm just holding out till the end of the season to see if I can do better.'

From Harry, I heard the following, 'She's gorgeous to look at but I'm not sure how much there is up top.' I didn't say anything to either of them.

I had worked at the pub for two weeks. The last tourist, like the last wasp was seen 11 days ago and I was confident and happy with the changes in my life. Gran said that she would pop in and turned up early one Friday night. She hesitated at the door. I could see that she had put water on her hands and attempted to smooth her hair down, I smiled. This nod to convention always made her look wilder. I was surprised that she was greeted by several of the locals with courtesy. Some stood up and nodded towards her but no one encroached upon her space. She arrived at the bar and sat down with half a pint of cider. I wasn't expecting any conversation from her but I watched her eyes follow Ali on her way back and forth to the toilets to brush her hair.

'What do you find to talk about with that young woman?'

'Plenty,' I was not going to let her upset my new-found confidence or rubbish my friendships.

'What sort of plenty? I am genuinely fascinated, come on, share the emotional riches of your conversation, the lush vegetation of your exchanges.'

'Clothes.'

'That's a five-minute conversation at most, even if you exhausted your own personal knowledge of the clothing industry as supplied to you by the ever-willing Susan Rink.'

'Boys.'

'What about the rest of the time?'

'Are you jealous that I'm having fun?'

'No, no, it's just that she reminds me of a young woman I used to work with at The Tide, same vacant expression. Idiot girl died, entirely her own fault.'

At that moment, Ali was spared further character assassination because Gran began to choke on her cider.

'Divine justice,' I said, 'For being so spiteful.' But I also patted her on the back. I felt ribs through a green cardigan, she looked quite shaken.

'Sometimes, I don't know my own power.'

'What?' I asked.

'That idiot in the corner. He's heard the crow.'

She pointed to the darkest corner of the pub where a man sat with his back to us. A man in his 30s whom I had seen and served a few times before. There was little remarkable about him.

'What about him?'

'That's your father.'

She whisked me out of the pub, commanding the sullen Ali to take over and leave her three piles of off-white wedding dresses. Gran marched me along the corridor and out into the garden. She put her hands on my arms, as if she were holding me together, and I waited whilst she looked at me intently. I waited for two minutes. Finally, she spoke, explaining that she may have been a little bit hasty with the crow-burning incident. It was strong magic and she hadn't really thought through the consequences of John Doon turning up now. She said that it wasn't entirely her fault and that he would have come anyway, it's just that she might have speeded things up a little.

I was expecting an elaborate plan to emerge from her lips but, instead, all she said was, 'Block him.'

'What?'

'That technique I taught you years ago to avoid people.'

It slowly started to come back to me. You imagined the person wrapped in the covering of your choice from head to toe, then they would cease to be a nuisance to you. If you did it really effectively, they could almost become invisible.

'What material should I use?'

'A prison blanket,' she said far too quickly. 'Something austere, dark and preferably prickly.'

I couldn't think of anything like that. The only thing my mind would come up with was a huge sheet of bubble wrap. So I wrapped him in hundreds of tiny pockets of air. I swathed my erstwhile father in a double layer of protective packaging.

'Have you done it?' she asked.

I was about to explain my problems with the prison blanket when she kissed me roughly and said, 'Right, I'm off.'

No heartwarming chat, no clues about what to say if he approached me. No rational advice. Nothing. I would have to rely on my own resources again. Instantly, and without flinching, I made a decision – I would completely ignore him. He had no right to turn up now at the beginning of my career. I felt stupid, I should have guessed. It was the eyelashes that gave him away. They were not insanely long but had obviously just been trimmed with scissors. They were too blunt. Only I had eyelashes like that. Most people's eyelashes have gradations but his had been cut straight across very recently. I had no idea what he wanted and no intention of taking any notice of him. His letter had made things seem final and I had put away any ideas of him ever being involved in my life.

I told myself that biological was nothing and reliability was everything. Gran had brought me up with a minor input from Bill and they were the only relatives I had who were worth anything. Gran had rumbled him. I guessed I had several months to play with until he revealed his identity to me and I hoped Gran's blocking technique would work. Gran had used this technique on Susan and had been so successful, she had once tripped over Susan in the lane.

I gathered my thoughts and headed back into the pub. He was still there, sitting alone in the corner with another pint, his back to everybody. I carried on serving and surprised myself with my air of nonchalance. I just wish I hadn't chosen the bubble wrap as my material because I could still see him. He wasn't clear but it was still unmistakably him through a plastic screen. Worse than that was the noise he was making. He kept on cracking as if tiny bubbles of air were popping between his joints. Every time he did this, I jumped because it sounded like a balloon bursting.

I should have listened to Gran. I remember her saying that he cracked his fingers continually as a young man. I wish I had used the prison blanket. He left the bar half an hour later and, over the next few days, I practised the visualisation with the bubble wrap intently. He started to come into the pub weekly and stay for the same amount of time. If someone were sitting in his usual seat by the window, he would only have half a pint and stay for 10 minutes, standing as close to the door as possible. I could make out the shape of his body, tall and gangly, and I could see how dark his hair was through the plastic, almost black – like mine. I stopped that way of thinking immediately. Lots of people have very dark hair. Ali and I always worked together so, when he came in, I could disappear to the cellar until he left. I was determined not to get worked up about his appearances. He was, after all, a stranger.

When he was gone, Ali and I went back to frock sorting. I had been there for several weeks when October came round and we were still fully involved in the wedding game. Each week, we fought over new dresses to cut out. I had a whole new vocabulary, a friend my own age and an insight into a world I hadn't known existed, and Gran wasn't there to spoil things. I think that's what I liked best, talking about things that she despised.

Suddenly, we had less time for pondering, 'Are leg of mutton sleeves inevitably a mistake?' Discuss. Harry, the owner, became very angry when Ali asked his opinion about a dress. My theory was that the sight of the gown had exacerbated his own sense of loneliness. He woke up like some lumbering beast and said we had to prepare for the tourist season, even though it was seven months away. There was much moaning and dragging of feet from staff and regulars alike. He put a swear box on the bar which made £85 in the first week. He went round the regulars and suggested subtle changes to their wardrobes. He even concocted opening lines we could use on tourists to make them feel welcome and wrote them down on little cards for us.

We weren't changing fast enough for his liking and, in the end, he stood in the middle of the pub and shouted, 'If you can't make yourselves ingratiating, find somewhere else to drink.'

Then he settled down at the bar and made Ali and I keep his glass topped up. After several hours, he burst into tears. His huge blond head was bowed, and mucus ran freely down his face. He sighed and wiped it away with the back of his hand.

'I'm sorry, this place is all I've got.'

Harry offered us cash in hand if we would come in and help paint the main room. He said that we would stay open but all the regulars would have to congregate in the middle with no furniture.

'Just keep them off the walls.'

I had been painting for several hours and stepped outside the pub for a breath of fresh air when I heard a strange crackling sound. A blurry figure approached, a smudge of a man, who got within two metres of me before I stepped smartly in front of him with a paintbrush in my hand.

'We're closed for redecoration.'

'How long are you closed for?'

'Six months.'

'Six months?'

'There are plenty of other pubs around here that would be glad to take your money.'

I rushed back inside and watched his distorted body retreating towards the car park, making popping sounds every few steps and taking his vague impression with him.

Harry employed two other girls and took us all aside separately, giving the same speech, word for word. To paraphrase, it went something like this, 'You are the only bit of class in this joint and I am relying on you to bring the others up to speed.'

Ali was the only one who didn't realise what he'd done and she started to walk differently now that such status had been conferred on her. She leapt on patches of dirt and handed out beer mats, which gave me more time to sort dresses. By November, the place was unrecognisable. Bright but still quaint. Not cold and damp but airy and unpretentious. In the middle of the month, Ali came in to work, she hovered in the door frame looking small and deflated. Her jaunty walk had been taken away from her.

'What's the matter?'

'This bloke has been staying in a B&B next to my flat. He's gorgeous, got the lot: car, money, looks. He's buying that pub, three miles down the road.'

'The one with the muddy creek?'

I knew she meant The Tide, but I couldn't bring myself to call the pub by its real name. It suddenly occurred to me that I felt the place belonged to me and Gran, just because we had walked uninterrupted down there for so long. It was difficult to access, only approachable by narrow lanes or boats, which is why there were so few visitors. And half the time, when the tide was out, the view from the terrace was pure mud and even boats couldn't get anywhere near the pub. But there was something magnificent about the place and Gran and I loved it down there.

'What happened to him?'

'He was all friendly and nice, charming... We were chatting for days. I thought it was all going really well.'

'And?'

'He's not interested.'

'Blimey!'

I pumped Ali for all the information she had and then passed it on. Rumour had it that this man had come from London with all his money and was going to turn The Tide into a gastropub. I thought he would have his work cut out for him because, the last time Gran and I had walked down to that pub together, the building looked more decrepit than ever. But still, when Harry heard about the possible plans, he looked uneasy. The locals curled their lips and, collectively, we set about to demonise the stranger who thought he could resurrect The Tide. We leapt on the facts that arrived daily from different local people: Monday, he was twice-divorced; Tuesday, one daughter; Wednesday, shifty-looking. By Friday, he was ruthless, somewhere between five-foot eight and six-foot two, between 30 and 50 with indiscriminate coloured hair. Each passing day added a nought to his fortune and a greater arrogance to his gait. Everyone agreed he must be something special to have rejected Ali. Her long fingers were idle; no longer leafing through frocks.

I asked Gran what she thought. 'It's time for The Tide to move on.'

The conversations in The Waggon and Horses continued. 'He may have all the money in the world but what's he going to do about the stinking mud? Perfume it?' asked Harry.

'And those lanes, no tourists will drive down there and take the chance of getting stuck,' added a regular.

With Ali incapacitated and talk of tiny plates of food swimming in clashing sauces, served beside a scented creek, distracting the regulars, there was nothing else for it, I had to take over. It was easier than I thought and I proved a popular and efficient manager. We never ran short of pickled eggs. There was no bulk buying of Christmas-flavoured crisps that had to have the label scribbled over with a permanent marker to make them saleable after the festive season had finished.

I employed a chef. I say chef, although Barry had been thrown out of catering college for his foul temper and filthy mouth. I knew how to handle him because he reminded me of Gran, apart from the cold sores. Under my guiding hand, he flourished. His scabs disappeared and, slowly, we started to introduce more adventurous food onto the menu. Harry was delighted and relaxed about the invisible threat of the gastropub.

We added one new ingredient at a time and, if there were complaints, we both shouted in unison, 'It's only a bloody carrot,' when it was obviously a sweet potato.

We wore them down and were soon awash with poncy dishes, but we called them by plain names. They were like the sons and daughters of the famous, except we had exchanged celebrity-style names like Portia for Paula.

The place was full on weekend nights and, one day, Harry took me aside, 'I can confirm that you are the new manager, but I'd rather it stays unofficial, industrial tribunals and all.' As he said this, we both looked at the shadow that was once Ali.

Strangely enough, a pay rise didn't come with my new unofficial status and the locals still cowed under Ali's tongue at closing time, when she could be bothered.

One day, a purple silk cushion appeared on one of the benches. The next day, another two appeared. It was like a rash and, by the end of the week, you couldn't see wood for cushions. The locals muttered and grumbled. They took a vote on it and Mark Bailey, a local builder, was put forth to deal with the invasion. He came in from outside with a cigarette, took hold of one of the cushions in his gnarled hands and stubbed his fag out on it. There was a strange smell and a perfect hole that would never fray. The next day, Harry lovingly gathered up the cushions and took them upstairs in black bin bags.

'I haven't given up on my dream, I just realise I might be pushing people a bit faster than they can cope.'

I nodded.

'I'll bring them out again in the beer garden when we have the summer barbeques and a more refined clientele,' said Harry.

Harry had fattened up over the autumn, had his hair cut and was looking almost attractive. Ali, who had witnessed the purple cushion side of his personality, started to perk up. She flicked forlornly through the magazines I had brought her and cast surreptitious glances in Harry's direction. It started subtly between them but she was seen to be writing her first name and his surname on beer mats. She practised hundreds of times and the pub was awash with them. Every night at closing time, Harry threw them all out in a frenzy of hygiene, not willing to stop and look at stains but, after 11 days, he finally noticed. He held one close to his face, to make sure he had read it correctly, and smiled.

The possibility of romance came my way, too. He was pretty and persistent, so I agreed to a date. He drove me seven miles to the nearest town and we went to a pizza restaurant. We sat down at a table decked with a red and white cloth like a chessboard. He talked about potholing. The starters came. He talked about white-water rafting. I watched his mouth open and shut as my soup cooled. This was nothing like Maya's dates, where was the thrill in the air? Why wasn't he entranced with me? Gran suddenly appeared in my head and made a move on the tablecloth with the pepper grinder. She moved it two steps forwards. It caught me by surprise.

'What are you doing here with this boy, behaving like this?'

'This is what 18-year-olds do.'

I spoke to her politely but firmly, moving the salt three squares towards her end of the board. She came back with an incredibly aggressive move involving several little packets of sugar.

'Wasting your time, with nothing,' she hissed.

She waved at my date, as though to dismiss him, wiping out 20 years with one swipe, as if every thought and action during his lifetime had been without merit. I thought for a while and then suddenly moved the ashtray sideways, so quickly and deftly, that all her sugar bags were mine.

'You just want everyone to suffer because you have. To lie awake, writhing in misery. To endlessly question everything and struggle with ideas...What normal person is obsessed with *The Book of Job*?'

I had forgotten the empty alcopop and she thumped it down on the table, grabbing half the sugar back.

'It asks the only important question there is. Is the universe benign?'

I snatched a menu from a neighbouring table and swept all the pieces to the side, and Gran with them. Determined to make my universe benevolent, I caught the waiter's eye.

'Another Bacardi Breezer please.'

I downed it in a couple of minutes and ordered my fifth. My date was talking about the rules of fencing. I began to feel remorse, maybe she had a point. What the hell was I doing here? I wasn't enjoying myself. I wasn't engaging in conversation, or exchanging ideas with another human being. I was playing at something and playing it badly. The boy had gone back to potholing. Gran was right. I pretended to go to the toilet and, instead, walked home in the dark, kicking the decaying leaves.

VI

Finally, I Get a Pet

ONE QUIET night, we were all in the pub, distracting ourselves. Some of us were pretending that there was an order to life by clicking dominoes together to make patterns. Others were avoiding dealing with life's awkward questions by dishing out beer mats; plonking them down on tables, hesitating, then moving the mats a couple of centimetres to the right. Trying to anticipate impending spillages. Which way would the liquid fall and what kind of stain would it leave? Pretending it's possible to protect the shine of life for ever, that no one ends up like an old, tarnished table. Gran would scoff at such lunacy. She acknowledged more than most that you could never guess what was going to happen to you in life. She just hoped it wouldn't be too smooth and mundane because she could never cope with that. Gran used to throw sugar over her left shoulder instead of salt, to keep God away.

'Never mind hardship, it's sweetness that should be kept at bay,' she would say.

Likewise, she thought that a glossy appearance was a curse. Before I had gone out that night, I had asked her what she thought of my latest look. I had remade myself with the help of *Sophisticated* magazine's Christmas edition. My hair was courtesy of page 47, and my face was laid out, step-by-step, on page 83. My entire outfit was copied from an article entitled, 'Make it look like you haven't tried too hard'.

'Gran, how do I look?'

'Unapproachable and your mouth looks too big.'

'Gran!'

'Smooth and hard… and that's as close as I can go towards saying what you want to hear, Amanda.'

'That's not very close.'

Sometimes, the strangest things make her cross, but I decided not to take any notice of her and, later on in the pub, I continued to look idly at my own body in the mirror behind the bar. I could only see bits of myself in isolation in such a small piece of glass, but each part satisfied me and I moved languorously onto the next, as if admiring a stranger. I was looking at my arse, which involved twisting awkwardly while looking over my left shoulder, when Susan walked into the pub – with a man who was not her husband. I knew without moving my eyes from my bottom that it wasn't her husband, because he had never registered as male on my radar, not that I had seen Mr Rink for months. He seemed to be spending more and more time away from her.

I couldn't remember what he looked like. In fact, one time we were in the pub, we had a conversation about people having sex and his name was mentioned, we were all suddenly reminded of mundane tasks that we had been putting off, ringing the brewery or watering the hanging baskets. I saw a few bits of crisps on the floor and it suddenly seemed imperative to pick them up.

Susan spun round this stranger as they headed together towards the bar, looking up at him for approval, making sure she had his attention. Virtually rubbing up against him like a cat. Two regulars glanced up briefly. One of them grunted but none of us muttered exclamations of outrage because the man she was with was nothing like the demonised figure that rumour had created. Here he was in our midst, but the pretentious, Ali-rejecting creature before us did not match our expectations. He smiled a lot, wide and gentle. He laughed loudly and managed to get in several gentlemanly gestures towards Susan between the door and the bar. He was a strange animal, a new breed with graceful, generous movements and I sniffed and peered at him, reddening when he addressed me.

'You must be Amanda of the famous mother and infamous grandmother with the crazy fairground ride.'

'I've been telling him all about you,' said Susan, slurring slightly. 'Amanda, this is Michael Packs.'

She interpreted my gawping wrongly and added, 'He's bought The Tide.'

'Leased The Tide,' he corrected.

'I thought Arlet's family were keeping it as a kind of memorial to him,' I said.

'They have decided to move on and have sold it to a group of entrepreneurs who want no part in the running of the business, which is where I come in,' he said.

Smiling politely, I moved away from him and he turned round to look at the pub. We both watched Susan as she tottered off to the toilet, struggling with the door and catching her heel on the step. She was not a regular here; there were too many uneven surfaces for her. I couldn't think of anything to say in the face of such magnificence, so I swallowed and busied myself at the bar, staying just close enough. I wanted him.

Ali came up from the cellar, with the Christmas decorations in a cardboard box and saw him. Her facial muscles betrayed her for a second, they collapsed momentarily, but were soon pulled back. She had been waiting to decorate the pub for weeks and had finally got permission from Harry but she carefully placed the unopened box behind the bar and disappeared down the cellar steps again. I wondered why she bothered acting, why she couldn't just let him see how much she liked him. What would be wrong with that?

People performed well, that was one of the main things I had noticed since I started working in the pub. They said one thing but their hands said something else entirely. Or their feet told on them by twitching, or their eyes became informers through the slightest of narrowings. I was not used to this and I had to study other people carefully to work out how it was done. Ali quickly found Harry, who was looking more attractive by the moment because he was in love, and she draped herself around him, exaggeratedly, a most fetching accessory.

I looked at Michael to see if his face would give anything away, but it remained placid. I waited for him to say something about the Ali incident, 'She's not my type,' or 'Beautiful women do nothing for me.' But, instead, he looked at the floor, then at his watch and, finally, up at me, smiling. I was angry that I, too, yearned for a complete stranger. And so I decided to be cocky and a little aggressive, the things I do best. I knew the pub he was going to take over very well, I knew every inch of it from my endless walks with Gran but I thought I would pretend not to be impressed with his purchase.

'What are you going to do with that muddy pub then?'

'Modernise it, keep it simple and friendly.'

'Like yourself?'

'Simple and friendly works everywhere.'

'Are you going to single-handedly remove the mud, scoop by scoop?'

'I'm happy with the mud. It's the flip side of owning a pub on an estuary.'

'What about the treacherous roads, with no passing places?'

'It's a beautiful place, worth making the effort to get there. People will see that by the time I've finished with it.'

'It must be in a state inside, why's it been languishing so long?'

'It had a bad reputation in its day, people round here are slow to forget, and it's difficult to get to.'

It was only what I'd heard from Gran over the years, nothing new.

'How are you going to do it up? We've all heard gastropub.'

'It's what people want, food they can't cook at home and comfortable surroundings in which to eat it. They don't want the clutter they have in their own living rooms. They want white sofas, impracticality. It makes people feel special.'

'That wouldn't work with me.'

'What would work with you?'

He made my heart stop for a moment and, when it started again, it had definitely rebooted between my legs. I was scared, so I decided to say something stupid.

'Eels, mash and a pint, works every time.'

I wasn't sure why I was being so hostile but it seemed to be working. For the moment, I had his interest and I intended to maintain it. I was not my grandmother's granddaughter for nothing. When we saw what we wanted, we would get it. The conversation had given me time to look at him closely. He narrowed his eyes when talking and they were startling. Not in their colour, they were just grey, but there was something unusually intense about them. His hair was flecked with grey, short and spiky. It was essential that I lick him, obligatory that I smell him immediately, close up. He needed me to undo the buttons of his shirt sleeves, and gaze up them to see his arms. His feet needed to be freed from the constraints of those shoes. He spoke – and money and first-class tickets flew out of his mouth.

'What's it like working here?'

'It's fine.'

There were pauses between our sentences when we would stare at one another. I could feel my breathing getting shallower. I half tried to deny it to myself. Like talking myself down from the ledge of a very high building.

'Would someone like yourself consider working in a different pub, one not too far away, under new management?'

His brown skin glowed, I could smell how clean he was from across the bar, his teeth squeaky, all washed and brushed. I had to address my other self sharply, she was still undecided on the ledge, 'Get down here now onto solid ground.'

I thought about what Gran said about Maya in *Midlanders*, 'If you went with your feelings, there was a price to pay, just be sure you are prepared to pay it.' I needed to protect myself.

He asked me what I would do with a barely accessible, rundown pub, miles from anywhere.

'Ask me out and I'll tell you.'

He laughed, longer than necessary. Susan came back.

'Share the joke.'

'Amanda's maligning the plans for my new business.'

'Amanda has connections with The Tide, her grandmother used to work there.'

Susan always knew much more than she let on but I had obviously upset her enough to come out with this snippet so I stayed in triumphant mode.

Seeing that her comments had little effect on me she carried on, 'When are you going to come and see my new business?' Susan pulled a sulky little girl's face. That was all wrong and I was delighted. That would never work with a man like Michael. She was unsettled by him, too, and had no better idea of how to behave with him than I did, even though she was much older. One of Susan's false nails had broken off and she nursed it in her left hand, thinking no one would notice. Her generosity to me seemed to be waning with each passing month. She had loved me as a child when I had not challenged her in any way but my grown-up self constantly seemed to disappoint her.

The conversation began to dry up between the three of us. Awkward chasms appeared in the air where weak, ill-shod little sentences fell to their deaths. Michael's lines were better prepared. He must have had a thousand ready to go at any moment. All able to cope with unexpected situations. That's what charm was, having that store in your head that you could call on at any given moment. I wondered if he spent a lot of time rehearsing. Gran said people like that had practised for years, that's how you got to be so good at it.

Susan and Michael left together about 10 minutes later and Michael took my insides with him. I had only heard him say a few hundred words but I imbued each one with wisdom. I retraced his steps to the bar, did numerous re-enactments of his time in the pub, his leaning on the bar, signalling for crisps for Susan. I breathed in the air where he had stood, drawing tiny particles of his body into mine. I had something of him inside me and I would hold it and use it to conjure up his image when I was alone in bed, until I saw him again.

I was just about to keep the glass he drank out of when I remembered how Marie had felt about John Doon, my father. How she had built a shrine for a Coke can from which he had drunk. I flinched and put Michael's glass in the dishwasher, on a heavy duty wash.

I had heard about Susan's new business. It had been in the paper and Susan had been there too, nestling between the newsprint; the face I knew so well, flattened and reproduced in black and white fibres, as if she had been ironed. She was frozen in that picture, her teeth as bright as doves. It was the face of someone who had smiled for show thousands of times, so many times that the face just fell into position on command, and yet it was joyless and frigid. She had called her new business Doves of Love.

Gran had renamed it Pigeons of Acrimony.

It was another wedding-related business. She would take her doves to the wedding venue and release them from wicker baskets at the appropriate moment. She had a foldaway arbour which fitted into the back of her Volvo and a selection of artificial flowers which she would twine around the arches meticulously. The bride and groom would be assembled into a ridiculous embrace whilst still managing to look at the camera. They were told to look at one another with an expression that would have Gran seething. Then the photographer would click and another digitally enhanced, mid-flight snapshot would find its way onto another mantelpiece. The picture would delight friends for years. Who could fail to be delighted by this piece of theatre? The birds would be a white blur but the bride's phoney delight and surprise would be in perfect focus, captured for ever.

'Why is it making you so cross?' I had asked Gran when she screwed up the newspaper into twisted tubes that she would use to light the fire.

'It's dishonest.'

'Why?'

'Those sorts of pictures gather dust and remain unchallenged. Discontent with one another sets in and that picture still represents a day that never was. With each passing year, the truth becomes more elusive.'

'It's romantic.'

'Complete rubbish, it's not what a marriage is like and, if it ever comes to fighting over the Labrador, then that picture with the doves will be the one to haunt them for ever.'

I thought about it. A symbol of peace, fidelity and fecundity frozen above the happy couple.

Gran had the last word, 'Susan Rink's going to cause sorrow.'

* * *

A date was arranged for me to go and see the doves. I thought about phoning and cancelling as snow threatened, but I set off on my bike, wearing my new denim jacket whose sleeves were slightly too long. I had bought it from the market with some of last week's wages. Its nipped-in waist suited me.

A mile away from Susan's new business premises and the sky blackened further. I decided to take a road that was very steep and narrow. Very few people ever used it, because there were no passing places. It had a line of grass, green and tipped with frost running along the middle of it. I got off my bike about a quarter of the way up. The hedges were six-metres high and maze-like. I heard a rumble of thunder and thought I heard a car too. Clouds gathered and bashed angrily together. Suddenly, the rain started falling in huge, semi-frozen droplets. It bounced off the road in front of me but I wasn't bothered about being caught in the rain.

The engine noise grew louder and I stayed in the middle of the road so that they would see me clearly. It was Michael's car. I recognised the BMW immediately because I had memorised the number plate and colour. He pulled over, skidding slightly on the wet surface.

'Do you want a lift? We could put the bike in the boot.'

'No,' I said, pushing a wet piece of hair behind my ear. I moved the bike closer to the car and he wound his window right down. The droplets fell down the inside of his door, little tongues on the leather. I could see down the neck of his jumper and, being high above him, I saw the computer that had allowed him to find this road.

'Why won't you accept a lift? It's freezing.'

'I can't get any wetter. Get out and feel the rain on your face.'

I pushed my hair back from my forehead, glad that I was wearing no make-up. I knew that my face was glowing and mischievous and, at that moment, I was lovely. He said no half-heartedly and glanced down at my leg. I moved in closer to his car and began tracing my finger along the condensation on the window.

The rain dripped down his face and he was laughing. I threw my head back, stuck out my tongue and then spoke quietly, 'When's our date?'

'I didn't ask you.'

I smiled my best smile. I had a gap in my tooth, about a quarter of a centimetre, I let my lips open and show it for several seconds.

'You are delicious, but I'm not divorced – and I can't go out with an 18-year-old.'

'You really are a man with a beige vision. You should be grateful that I'm interested in you at all.'

I walked off slowly, wheeling the bike and leaving Michael sitting there. I knew that I had made him uneasy, got to him at some level. He didn't move the car for about 30 seconds and I could feel him twitching and resisting. Thinking he might follow me, I walked slowly and the wheel of the bike clicked in satisfaction each time it made a full circle. He drove on, a little too fast.

Susan was cross with me when I walked into her new premises, an industrial unit on the edge of town, 40 minutes later. I wondered how many buildings had sprung up in my lifetime about which I knew nothing. But now it was different, working in the pub, I was out and about and would miss nothing, I had finally connected with the outside world.

There were 15 boxy buildings on the industrial estate, all with corrugated roofs. They were not dissimilar to our house in design, although each had a path of concrete slabs and several cars parked right outside. It could have been a perfect housing estate for obsessive people who hated dust and disorder. There would be no need to bother with flowers or a pretence at relationships with neighbours. All that concrete to keep you focused on the tougher things in life.

Susan barely acknowledged my presence in her office but kept talking on the phone. I wondered if she could smell that I had spoken to Michael. She could sense it. Susan had made a mistake, still seeing me as a child. She needed to make herself feel important so made no attempt to end the conversation.

She carried on, 'You wouldn't believe the demand for doves. Once I'm fully operational with three vans, I'll sell the business as fast as I can. Yes, I've already had an offer. Of course, I would remain involved in an advisory role but I wouldn't have to smell the damn things.'

She laughed too loudly and I worried for her acquaintance on the end of the phone, flinching from that squawk. I smiled at her, hoping this would encourage her to wind up the conversation, but she spun round on a leopard print heel so that all I could see was her skinny back under cashmere and her overly-exercised bottom in a pencil skirt. She wouldn't shut up, saying that doves had distracted her from her true passion which was cakes. I sniggered and thought about those chilly monuments of smoothness whose production she oversaw but whose cloying texture surely never slipped down her own throat.

Waving me away, she mouthed that she would be five minutes. I flicked my hair and a few drops of water hit some of her paperwork. Somehow she saw me do it. She sighed, crossed the room and blotted them with a tissue, all the time keeping the conversation going with a series of 'Mmmms.'

Annoyed by her ignoring me, I wandered next door where I assumed the doves would be. A white door connected her office to a barn-like structure with cages covering one side of the wall. There was no evidence of the bad smell she had reported, just straw and warmth. The cages were clean and spacious and the birds had plenty of light. They could see the sky through three huge skylights. It was all typically Susan, the brightness of the white walls hurt my eyes where she had painted over the breeze blocks. And I could see those floaters you get in your eyes when your vision is assaulted by a vast expanse of white; little snaky dust patterns that look as if they are projected onto the wall but really exist as jelly in your own eyes.

The birds made gentle noises. The warmth of the room and the thought of Michael made me want to take one of the doves out of its cage. I needed to touch something that was warm and had a heartbeat. I would have preferred him but, if a bird was all that was available, it would have to do. Everywhere I looked, I saw Michael, as though a film of him were playing constantly in my head. I needn't give the pictures of him my full attention but I could never turn it off because it ran in a loop. I undid the latch of one of the cages and picked out a bird. Feeling its tiny heartbeat and vulnerability threw me but I calmed myself and held it close. Overcoming my reluctance, I nestled it closer; still thinking of Michael. I put a maternal arm around it and sniffed its head.

Susan came in. I held the dove tighter. Something about her efficiency and suppressed fury combined made me nervous, but also keen to provoke her.

'I just saw Michael.'

'Dressed like that?' She was looking at my skirt which clung to my thighs. I pretended not to understand but wanted to continue annoying her and twisted my waist so that the material rose higher.

'What did he say?' she asked.

'Nothing much.'

'Don't go getting any ideas about him.'

'What's it to you?' I asked.

'You'll get hurt, that's what it is to me, young lady.'

As I loosened my grip on the dove I saw that the denim dye from my jacket had stained the bird quite badly. Susan saw the discoloured patch all over the feathers and quickly walked up to me.

110

'Why did you handle them when I wasn't here?' she asked.

'Can we wash it?' I asked meekly.

'Cheap denim stains everything,' she said angrily. 'Just put it back, I'll put it on the insurance.'

'What?' I demanded, chilled.

A look came over her. She had seen something in my appearance, a weakness and was about to exploit it. She was going to mine my appearance for emotion. Gran was right, why didn't I listen?

But I was a reasonable actress. There was no need for this to go badly for me. I just had to stay cool and make her think that she had been mistaken in seeing helplessness in my face, and I needed to define exactly what she meant by claiming on the insurance.

'What are you going to do with it?' I asked coolly.

I had to choose my words carefully, knowing the use of the word 'it' might throw her off the scent a little. But she tested my resolve.

'Wring its little neck, of course, and pop its corpse in the freezer.'

She waited for another response from me but I was going to prove to her that she was wrong. She had dug out one emotion successfully, but that didn't mean that she could always read my face and all its expressions. It was a complete fluke that she had spotted one and tried to claim it as her own. She was getting no more from me, not a thing. If I were going to save the dove, I needed to be cunning.

'I have to keep the bodies as evidence in the freezer over there.' She pointed to an old-fashioned chest freezer.

'Are there many in there?' My voice remained casual.

'One that got its leg caught in the rose-covered arbour, last week. They can be stupid things – ruined the photograph. Fortunately, digital photography allows you to eliminate the things you don't want in life.'

'That's a lot of electricity to freeze one small bird; you could keep your ice cream in there, too, for the sake of economy.' I thought a bit of frivolity might throw her off the scent but she continued with her unforgiving stare.

'There is a lot of bureaucracy surrounding the use of animals in business and I am a great one for adhering to the rules,' she said self-righteously.

'I understand. You must want this business to be as successful as your cake one,' I softened my tone and looked her in the eye.

She frowned and examined my face to see if I was being sarcastic but, seeing no trace of mockery, she swiftly turned the conversation back to herself and her own entrepreneurial skills. I breathed in. I began to understand precisely why Gran didn't like her. I hadn't seen it quite so clearly before. I had been naïve, taken in by the surface gloss of the woman, enraptured by the clicking of those long nails on all sorts of surfaces.

The phone rang again. She waltzed off importantly, leaving me with the denim-stained dove. I thought about wringing its neck or poisoning it myself and then realised I wasn't up to it. Gassing it at home in the oven might be a possibility but, under no circumstances, would I let her do it. These brave thoughts led to images of a frail white thing, peering through the smoke-coloured glass of our oven door and tapping its little beak frantically. Gradually, the tapping would be less insistent and, soon, there would be silence.

I waited until Susan was properly engaged in a conversation. It sounded like a serious enquiry that might go on for several minutes, so I pushed the bar down on the emergency exit of the building, stuffed the bird into my jacket and did up all the buttons. It didn't struggle. As I cycled home, it began to snow. Gran was in the kitchen.

'I've stolen something.'

She looked at me, half smiling.

'Something of Susan's, a dove.'

At that moment, I heard Susan's car pull up outside our house. She must have been moments behind me on the cycle home. Obviously, she hadn't rushed here but had lingered cruelly in her office. She had never brought her car this far down our lane before for fear of potholes, and the gleaming navy paintwork looked strange covered with a dusting of snow. Bill had been making a cup of tea in the kitchen, doing his normal painfully slow dance between the recycling bin and the cupboard with a steaming teabag balanced precariously on the spoon. Frequently, he dropped it and this usually caused me great amusement but, this time, he stood still, close to the bin and lifted his head. He abandoned his mug, spoon and bag on the sideboard and fled back to his office, probably barricading himself in.

From the window, I could see Susan checking her face in the rear view mirror. She sat in her car for a minute or more before turning off the diesel engine. Suddenly, everything was horribly quiet. The 30 seconds it took for her to travel between our gate and front door was time enough for my stomach to constrict. She tapped on the door and Gran moved slowly towards it whilst I stayed out of view behind the kitchen door, but could hear everything quite clearly.

'Susan,' Gran said brightly, not inviting her in.

'I don't know how to put this...' Susan began.

'Amanda has stolen one of your pigeons.'

'It's a dove.'

'Same family, *Columbidae.*'

'I need the body of the animal for insurance purposes.'

'I've got a well-hung wood pigeon in the pantry, will that do?'

'Unfortunately not, everything has to be above board with a new business,' Susan answered smoothly.

I could imagine Gran nodding slowly and then she said, 'Like your extension plans?'

I peered through the crack in the door and saw Susan step back and her neck redden.

'Nothing has been finalised, Cath,' she snapped.

'How much do you want for the dove?' Gran asked, sounding bored.

Susan thought for a while and replied, 'For the loss of a bird, a replacement that will need training...'

Gran interrupted, 'Teaching birds to fly, is there no end to your talent, Susan?'

'There seems to be an end to your parenting skills,' Susan snapped back. 'That girl is going the same way as you.'

'And what way is that, Susan?'

'Off the rails. Sexually.'

Gran stifled a yawn and walked deliberately slowly into the kitchen, allowing the snow to settle further on Susan's head as she waited on the doorstep. Gran took the cash out of the drawer, counted out every last penny and handed precisely £58.76 to Susan, the figure she had demanded, plus VAT. Susan could barely hold so much small change in her hands.

There was no further discussion about the rights and wrongs of the case. Gran didn't seem interested in my motives or apologies. All she cared about was finding enough spare wood to begin making an aviary. I kissed Denim on her tiny white head and Bill made a rare appearance before teatime, emerging from his office with the cat behind him, clutching a drawing which he handed to Gran. He walked away as if indifferent to her response.

'That's the first thing he's drawn for us for years, I'd better do it justice,' she said, surprised.

I looked down at the beautifully executed pencil drawing. It was an aviary, simple, functional but elegant. Gran and I went outside, dressed in hats and gloves, and I helped her begin to pile the wood and fetch the screws and tools she would need. We worked in silence, only our frozen breath mingled, but, after an hour or so had elapsed, I was weary of being contrite and spoke to her.

'How did you know about Susan's extension?'

'I don't know anything about any extension but it stands to reason. A woman like that, never satisfied, always acquiring things. She'd soon run out of space to put them. No space will ever be big enough for her. I heard her business was expanding and doing well, so it was logical what her next move would be. Even though a person can only be in one room at a time, eight rooms would not be enough for her. Eight rooms could not contain her. A house stuffed to the rafters would not be enough to demonstrate who she is to people.'

'What did she mean about off the rails?'

'She is referring to a two-year period in my life when I worked at The Tide, even though she wasn't around at the time. It seems she has gained her knowledge from Arnold Split, that famous regurgitator of events.'

'What is she referring to exactly?' I was determined to pin Gran down.

'My having sex with several young men, some of whom worked there and others who were regulars.'

I dropped my hammer.

'Don't worry,' she said wearily. 'I've no more desire to rake over those days than you do. All I can say is that I did what I wanted for a while, unhindered by society's expectations or nonsense about reputation. Think of it as an experiment.'

'Was it a success?'

'No, not entirely. In fact, it caused me great suffering.'

'Is this something to do with your buying the carousel?'

'It's so tedious to be caught up in the minutiae of your own life, much better to try to see your tiny part on a larger scale.'

She frowned and waved away my compliments and thanks, then suddenly grabbed my face and tilted it towards the light.

'Who's making your eyes shine?'

I thought about lying for a moment but I wanted to say his name out loud, I needed to speak it, 'Michael Packs.'

'Oh, God.' She saw my face and softened, 'I never thought for a moment that he would be your type,' she said begrudgingly. 'Let's get on with the bird cage.'

After what she had told me, I made a decision. I would seduce Michael at the earliest opportunity. After all, it was in my blood.

We began tacking the wire to the frame and I wondered if it needed to be quite so big. When I put the little dove in her new home at the end of the afternoon, she stayed in her nesting box initially. Huff the cat looked on from a distance with his head on one side.

'I'm going to let her out daily,' I said, thinking this would appease Gran and her usual objection to anything caged.

'I don't rate its chances around here with all the sparrowhawks but the least we can do is make its final days more pleasant,' Gran said.

'I won't let her out, then,' I said.

'You have to let it out, everything must take its chances in life. Better to have your guts ripped out by a sparrowhawk or Huff, than to live caged and fearful.'

Bill came out and silently walked around Gran's interpretation of his drawing, making further tracks in the snow. He seemed pleased with the smoothness of the edges and the general look of the cage but Gran didn't hang around for compliments and, instead, cut off the conversation in mid-flow as she always did, disappearing into the house. I followed her in and went to warm my hands by the kitchen fire, when she appeared with a dress.

'Your mother always wanted this dress but I would never let her have it,' she said, her eyes sparkling maliciously.

'Between the ages of 14 and 17, she searched for it when I was out. Always looking for the wrong thing, your mother, in the wrong place. I'd watch her rifling through my wardrobe looking for something carefully encased in a dress bag, not exposed to the air. That's the way you should treat an heirloom, when all the time it was stuffed in a plastic bag in the coal hole,' she laughed.

'Don't you think that was a bit cruel?' I asked.

'Not at all, there's not a natural fibre in this dress, it could have stayed screwed up in the darkness for years and still be wearable. It was made in the Twenties, when some fool thought we could do without cotton for ever.'

I shot her a look.

'Oh, your mother, you mean. It's just that I knew she would never do it justice, that she would try too hard. That she would flounce about in it, wearing too much make-up, adding garish jewellery and that its folds would never hang right. Your mother, always striving, struggling, clawing. Never able to sit with herself for a second. Always with the radio on or some other damned distraction. No one with a dress like this needs to try too hard.' She threw it to me. 'It was mine, but I didn't have very long to wear it.' Her mouth went thin for a moment.

'But then you came along and things were better,' she added.

I knew I hadn't made things better, although I might have eased them a little. It was him she wanted, that baby. I'm surprised she hadn't dug him up and stuffed him with sawdust. She could have made him into a puppet and out of his mouth would only come the words she wanted to hear. She would never have had to deal with the reality of having a child that was not like her. I sometimes thought she was self-pitying and should have drawn a line under him by now. I wondered what purpose he was serving for her, hanging on to him like she did.

'Where did you get this dress?' I asked.

She hesitated for a moment, 'From an encounter that was cut short.'

I looked at her but she had turned away from me.

I went to work in the dress, thinking about Gran with a man other than Bill. Just as I was leaving the house, Bill came out of his office.

'Where did you get that dress?'

'Gran gave it to me.'

'Just when you think the past has released you, some vicious memory is triggered and you are back, immersed in pain from years ago'.

I was shocked by this melodrama, he was normally so indifferent to life, 'Why, what is it?' I asked.

'Nothing to do with you, love. It's just, sometimes, I wonder why I stay with your grandmother. Every day, she lets me know how little I mean to her. Go on, go and enjoy yourself. You look magnificent, just like she did,' he sighed and shut the door, leaving me standing on the step. I felt a wave of grief for Bill but his life had been his own choice. I had to agree with him, nobody should have married Gran, no one in their right mind, at least.

Just as Gran advised, the dress and I kept quietly in the background. The pub was covered in tinsel and, in comparison, I was minimalist. I wore trainers with the dress; an incongruous look but I knew it worked. It was a little ugly but the dress needed to sulk to become fully glorious. It needed a kick. I was Maya Watts in that dress, totally in control and congruous. It was almost as though it had been made for me, an extension of my own skin in material form. Arnold Split, who usually ignored me, came up to the bar. He was so tight, he rarely bought his own drink, although he had plenty of money.

'That's some dress.'

'It was Gran's.'

'Are you going to be spreading your favours generously, like she did?' I couldn't work out the tone of his voice, there was certainly malice in the recipe but something else there as well. I remembered what Gran had said about him but was soon distracted as the door creaked open and Michael came in, amidst a shower of stars.

I wanted to shout at him, 'You just look wrong in here, what the hell are you doing in this pub?'

I couldn't put my finger on it. Ali was glamorous and she fitted, but Michael's appearance was somehow jarring. It was as though he clashed with all the fixtures and fittings in the pub. I looked at his clothes, was it the quality of them that made him stand out? No, Susan had expensive clothes and she managed to force herself to fit in anywhere. It was something else.

We swapped some inanities about the locally-brewed beer. I moved away from him and started to empty ashtrays and collect glasses. I was glad of something to do whilst I tried to identify the strange way I felt when he was around, the most overwhelming need to wrap myself around him. He drank his half pint and then tried to get my attention. I wandered over, smiling in the same way that I would to anybody else.

'You look remarkable, even better dry than wet and I wouldn't have thought that was possible,' he said. 'About that date?' Almost whispering.

'Just a minute,' I said dismissing him with a wave as I went to serve someone else. I took my time and even chatted with the people at the bar, asking some woman how her dog was and feigning interest. I slowed down my every gesture. I relaxed my whole body and every movement became languid. When I walked, it was as though I had been choreographed. I knew with absolute certainty that I would not trip and that things would go my way. He was watching. When I came back, he was smiling, his pupils dilated.

'What time do you finish here?'

He was waiting for me outside when my shift ended. I was delighted with everything about him, how well he stood by the pub wall, the turned up collar of his navy pea coat. Overwhelmed by his attractiveness, I panicked for a moment and wondered whether I was good enough to be seen with him. The dress was not enough to elevate me into his world, and I only had my old coat on top of it. My heart was beating and my whole body was tense as I climbed into his warm car. Michael was fiddling with the mirrors, not looking at me.

'It's too late to go to any of the local pubs,' he said.

'The Cross is open in Fiton.'

'We'd only get there in time for one,' he spoke flatly, with a hint of despondency.

I wondered if he didn't want to be seen with me. He was searching for a cloth to wipe some invisible mark off the windscreen. It was as though he could go so far with me and then the reality of my age made him uncomfortable.

'Let's go onto the moor, then,' I said, smiling.

I thought, even though it was a cold evening, that we could swim in one of the natural pools. Knowing exactly where they all were and how deep each one was comforted me and, hopefully, would impress him. But, mostly, I thought it would be a way to get our clothes off quickly. Being a strong swimmer and at home on the moor, I wondered if the pools would frighten him a little; dark water with stones, and who knew what else, underfoot. Wanting to see what he was made of seemed a good idea at the time. We had several beers in the car that I had brought from behind the bar and I opened one of them with the gap between my teeth. He flinched but took the beer and I vowed to be a little more ladylike. I wasn't used to watching my own behaviour.

The awareness that had been between us in the pub had disappeared and I wanted to get it back. I tried with funny anecdotes that would have had Ali roaring with laughter but Michael only laughed a little. He looked at his watch three times in the 10 minutes it took to drive onto the moor. I instructed him exactly where to park. The flat bleak landscape spread out before us and I was comforted by the familiarity of the place, keen to show off as well as reclaim some of that earlier spark, so I leapt out of the car, not needing light but waiting for my eyes to adjust to the darkness. As my trainers landed on the hard ground, I thought about all the different shoes from childhood to adulthood that I had worn here. Had I imperceptibly affected the landscape, instigated a tiny change immeasurable to the human eye? I felt the ground measure me and deliver a faint shake of recognition.

But, as I stepped away from the car, the wind was wild and Michael and I could hardly hear one another. The landscape and the weather made it clear that they were in charge, and didn't care about the hundreds of picnics and games of football that Gran and I had played. Still, I remained optimistic. The wind whipped me up; I was flying, hysterical, full of fun and anticipation. I wondered whether, if I let go, the wind would support me above the ground. I led Michael by the hand towards the pool. I had chosen this one because it was the closest and not too steep to get down to in the dark. It measured five metres by twenty, a long and thin streak of clear water where, in the light, you could see each stone at the bottom.

Conversation was pointless because of the roaring wind. His hand, although it held mine, seemed flat and passionless. The landscape and weather were having the opposite effect on him that they were on me. Instead of opening up to the bleakness, he was closing in, hugging himself and looking uncomfortable. I sensed he didn't want to be here with me and I felt myself losing control of the situation.

We stood together on the edge. The last time I had been here, I was the only visitor until Mrs King had turned up with her Labrador with its bad teeth. The animal insisted on picking up very heavy rocks from the bottom of the pool and bringing them to her and had lost many teeth from the effort and the weight of the stones it was determined to carry.

'Shall we go in the water?' I shouted hopelessly.

'No, let's not.'

'Chicken.'

'Possibly.'

'Come on, swimming in December is one of those things that seems strange but, once you've done it, you will be invigorated and remember this for ever.'

He just stared at me.

'It's a magical thing to do; you could become part of the landscape. The silence in the water. It's like being a rock or a blade of grass and there's a quarter of a moon too. That will look brighter than you can imagine once we are in the water. It's like the water makes way for you, out of a strange kind of respect because you have chosen to swim when nobody else would, letting you in on its secrets.'

'We've got no towels.'

'We can run around in the wind, like kids.'

He flinched.

I started to unbutton my dress slowly, he must have got a glimpse of my smooth belly but he leant forward and pulled my dress together again. Gentle but patronising, as though dressing an errant child. With that one move, he had hammered me into the ground, all my courage and sexiness had gone in a gesture. My fun had sloped off with barely a backward glance and I felt somehow shamed; not a feeling I was used to. He must have seen my discomfort and tried to placate me.

'I'm not going in there, Amanda. This is an expensive shirt, I'm not leaving it in the dirt and I don't have time to go to the dry cleaners.'

The expensive shirt had triumphed. Somehow, a shirt with fold-back cuffs had more power than the moon or the water or the austerity of the place. I knew when it was time to give up. The determined dog's teeth rose to the surface of the pool and arranged themselves in a triumphant leer. All thoughts of slippery bodies wrapped around one another disappeared and I was desperate to go to the toilet.

'You go back to the car, I'll see you in a minute.'

He had turned down all that I knew and all that I had to offer. Even though I thought he was wonderful, he was rejecting everything I presented to him and there was no point trying to change his mind. If the beauty here couldn't sell this place, couldn't tempt him into the water, then I didn't know what else to do. He didn't want any contributions from me and I was sad, but not sad enough to try to be something that I was not.

I watched him walk back to the car with the same kind of walk he would have used in an important meeting, as though he was born with innate confidence and unquestionable rights. I consoled myself thinking about how he would struggle out here in this landscape if left alone for long, counting the hours before that suit of his would start to look ridiculous. His shoes, built for the street, were inflexible and too heavy. But he was not walking like a man who knew this about himself. He had erected an office-like space around him, even up here. A temporary corridor between the water and the car.

I waited until I saw the light of the car go off and knew he had shut the door. I knew he couldn't possibly see me but I found a bush and squatted down to pee. I couldn't hear my own heart because the wind was so strong.

Relieved, I stood up and began to walk back but, as I took my first step, my foot squelched. The evening was well and truly over. The spiteful wind had blown some urine into my trainer. I got back to the car and forced the door open; surprising the wind with a show of strength.

'Take me home, my shoe is full of pee.'

'What?' he asked, peering at me.

'I'm sure there are women queuing up for you who don't piss in their shoes, so take me home!'

* * *

We got back to the house. I made Michael drop me off at the top of the lane.

'Amanda, in a relationship with an age disparity, it's up to the man to introduce sophistication into the woman's life and not for the woman to try to make the man re-experience his youth. I have a diving qualification. I wasn't scared of the water in that pool. I didn't want to swim in December after an exhausting day. Does that make me unreasonable?'

'I thought it was the suit that didn't want to swim and, anyway, it's not the swimming, I was just wondering how someone could go to a spectacular place and not be moved by it. I've made a mistake,' I said dejectedly.

'What are you talking about mistakes for? We've only just met.'

He was smiling and talking gently, as if to an idiot. He reached out to touch my cheek but I moved away just in time. Michael kept his arm out straight and his fingers dangled in the air. Persistently, he reached out again, as though he thought I might come back, but I shut the car door wearily.

He spoke to me through the window, 'I've just moved here and you are acting like we're married.' He said this spiteful sentence with great softness.

I walked very slowly down the lane without looking back. He stayed sitting in the car until the dark wrapped me and I disappeared to him.

That was when I knew I should leave him alone because he was one of those game-playing people, maybe he didn't even know he was doing it. It had all been obvious from the Ali incident, he must have given her considerable encouragement and yet, when she pounced, he stood back with his hands in the air, swearing he no more saw this coming than his great-aunt trying to seduce him.

Before I got the job at The Waggon and Horses, I would have seen this kind of situation and understood it quickly and clearly. I would have made a mental note to avoid such a person, but something about mixing with other people, so many different types of people, was clouding my judgement. As though I were picking up little bits of personality all the time, breathing them in. Or perhaps other skin was settling on mine and giving me another layer that I had never had before. A layer of stupidity.

There was a time when I would have seen clearly that Michael was a man who drew out feelings in people, and then ran in the other direction denying everything. Making others feel that they had done something wrong or, worse still, invented the whole situation. He was the kind of person who would make you think you were mad. How long had he been doing it and what was it all about?

VII

My Grandmother Finds a Job

I DIDN'T go straight home but, instead, was drawn towards Susan's elegant ambient lighting. I walked up her path and thrills shot through the soles of my feet, similar to slipping a little but managing to retain your balance. She didn't have her blinds down. They were remote-controlled and I could see the device on the windowsill. Logically, I knew that there was no way she could see me outside in all this darkness and that I could look in on her for as long as I wanted but I still couldn't quite believe it. What if she had special powers and was toying with me only to suddenly reveal her cat-like night vision? No, she was just a woman, a confident woman who didn't give much thought to things lurking in the darkness.

As I crept up to her lounge window, I could see she was on the phone, very animated, with a glass of wine in her left hand. She moved around her oak-sprung wooden floors, periodically looking down at her shoes, lifting a foot to admire it before placing it back carefully. I could see she was laughing, almost hysterically, but I couldn't hear a thing because of the triple glazing. She really should draw her blinds, after all, you never know who is creeping about in the dark. Suddenly, she looked my way with an artificial movement like a puppet, I jumped, then froze, but she was just checking her hair in the window. Finding it deficient, she moved towards her big mirror and smoothed an eyebrow. She put her Susan face on as she looked at herself, the one she had cultivated for years.

Coming off the phone after a volley of goodbyes, she sat at her desk with a mound of paperwork surrounding her. Her face was now completely different than when she had been talking, all hard and unforgiving, no movement to give it life. I wandered back down to our house; it was just after midnight. Gran was still up.

'Good time, love?' she asked.

'Terrible.'

'Did anything happen?'

'Nothing happened, it was just him. He makes me question everything I have ever loved. Every word that comes out of my mouth seems wrong. I've never thought that before.'

I told her everything about the night, every disappointing detail.

'Have nothing more to do with him,' she almost hissed.

'But I like him.'

'So?'

'He's fun. Sometimes.'

'Have nothing more to do with him,' she repeated, less aggressively.

'Are you going to help me out or just say things over and over again? Some things aren't as simple as you make out.'

'Everything is as simple as I make out; people choose to complicate things for their own crazy purposes. If someone makes you feel uncomfortable, avoid them.'

'You always say that, you've been saying it for years,' I said in a jaded voice.

But it didn't shut her up. 'Warning signals are wired into us. If someone sets off alarms for you, avoid them. If you ignore the alarms, your life will be messy.'

She was not about to stop so I thought I would be nasty, to make up for all the things that had gone wrong for me that evening, 'Your alarm must be going off all the time, then. I'm surprised you can hear yourself think.'

'He reminds me of Doon. There's something about the way he looks at you. It's a combination of that dog-like drooling but letting you fall, then jerking you back like a yo-yo.'

And, with that, she turned off the light and left me standing in the dark, thinking I would follow her to bed. Instead, I slumped down in the armchair and began picking at the horsehair stuffing inside, allowing my fingers to wriggle inside the ripped, faded material, making the tear slightly bigger. I thought, this is what Michael is doing to me. Pulling my insides out and trying to stuff them back in, in a different order, one that suits his own particular view of how women should behave. Then I thought of something worse as the hair bulged out of the ripped material. Maybe he was doing it for the hell of it.

The next morning, Gran came into my room and shook me awake. She said we should go for a walk. We started out in the direction of Ivybridge and, pretty soon, I guessed that we were going to what was now Michael's pub. I stood still in the road, refusing to go any further until I remembered that he had said something about going down to London for the weekend to see his daughter.

'We have walked on that section of the river since you could first toddle, what is the difference now?' asked Gran, knowing the answer already.

'He owns it.'

'He is merely leasing. Anyone could lease it,' she said patiently.

I started walking again. She had convinced me. The place had been empty for 37 years and we had gone there together, at least weekly, for as long as I could remember, until I had started at The Waggon and Horses. I was not sure why Gran liked that particular stretch of river but I assumed it was because very few people went down there. The 'No Trespassing' signs kept most people away. I felt more and more belligerent the closer I got to the pub. Why should

I be banned from a place where Gran and I had spent many hours walking, just because it had changed hands?

It took us just under an hour to get there. Even though Gran had set off at a cracking pace and, although conversation was awkward between us, I knew better than to try to fill it with inanities. Gran was sweating; in December. She was getting older and I had missed it, it had happened so stealthily. Her face, even in the winter light, had started to fall in a little. It horrified me how people's faces disintegrated differently – some fall in on themselves, like canvas gone slack on the frame – and others end up with puff pastry faces, all swollen and flaky. Gran was still only finely lined at 59, but some of her usual glow seemed to have diminished. I hardly dared to look at her face because I couldn't bear to see the change. I had always thought of her as invincible, even though she had always told me differently.

'I know what you are looking at,' she said, unwrapping her scarf.

I stayed silent.

'I see the revulsion in your face, Amanda.' She laughed so hard she had to stop and support herself on a wall. She was right and I hated her for it.

'Ageing, none of us can avoid it. I don't look so good any more and I'm glad of it.'

'How can you say that?'

'Because I always knew it would happen and I was ready for it. And you'll be ready for it because I have brought you up properly. With an emphasis on more than your physical appearance.'

That was true, she had always been sparing with compliments about my looks and I had been indifferent to her lack of praise. That was before I started at The Waggon and Horses, though. Now, those things suddenly seemed to matter more and I gained scant comfort from all the attributes of which she did speak well. Sometimes, she seemed to admire things that other people would consider faults: temper, stubbornness and ruthless honesty.

I was grateful when we arrived at the pub. We walked down the concrete slope towards the water. The overhanging trees on the other side were bare. The river looked huge in winter with the tide out. Gran looked at her watch.

'It'll be back in to cover up the mud soon.'

The unwelcoming signs had been taken down and put in a skip. I looked in forlornly to see if I could see the Rottweiler drawing but there was so much debris and wire in there that, even if I had got into the skip and lifted all the wood, the chances of finding an old piece of laminated paper were minimal.

'What are you doing?' asked Gran.

'Looking for that dog drawing.'

'Oh, that,' she said, walking away from me. 'Get Bill to draw you one.'

'He only draws buildings,' I said.

'Mmmm,' she replied.

Within seconds, a change had come over her as it always did in this place. She was inaccessible by nature but, here, she was completely withdrawn. I trailed behind her towards the river and, looking back, saw that the fencing had gone, too, and the windowless pub hadn't fallen over but stood like a staggering drunk with its eyes shut.

We came to the jetty and I stared miserably at the miles of mud and wondered what was beneath it all.

'Why do you think they let it after all these years to Michael?' I asked.

'Time for the place to move on,' she answered distractedly.

'I'm not sure I want it to come alive, it won't be the same.'

She laughed loudly. At least *she* was enjoying herself with her riddles. At that moment, a BMW slowly came down the slope with two men inside. Michael and a stranger.

'Hell, now what am I going to do?'

I just wanted to disappear or only appear in front of him if I were totally in control, with rehearsed words ready to trip off my tongue and full make-up that looked completely natural. I looked to Gran for help. She snapped out of her other-worldly mood instantly.

'Stand calm,' Gran ordered.

I tried to be calm. I looked out at the flat surface of the mud and tried to replicate that flatness, that smoothness, within myself. But it was no good. I felt myself going red and shuffling, I pulled my hat further down my head.

Michael approached with the stranger and introduced us to the pub designer who had been specially drafted in to help with the renovations. Gran seemed disinterested in him and his credentials and she embarked on an educational discourse about kingfishers on this particular stretch of the river. About how she had watched them for years, and how, this morning, she had insisted that I accompany her to see if we could see them together. Winter was a good time to see kingfishers on estuaries. The authority and seriousness in her voice made the men listen and the pressure was off me. Surprisingly, she had their attention completely by talking about a blue, darting bird.

By the time Michael turned to me, my staring at the mud had done its trick and I spoke unhurriedly, as Gran had done, 'They're much smaller than you think when you're up close to them,' I said.

'I've only seen a stuffed one,' said Michael.

'Unfortunately, the luminosity of the feathers is completely lost once they become detached from the bird,' said Gran. 'People could never understand what happened when they plucked a single feather and put it on a hat and the feather looked so ordinary. And yet they didn't stop trying for hundreds of years. That's humanity for you.'

As if to prove Gran wrong, in a token of friendship and decency, Michael drew attention to a folder in his hand and addressed Gran, 'Do you want to have a look at the plans?'

Why did people always want to share things with her when she offered such little encouragement or interest? Perhaps that was it, like children, we always wanted attention from the people least likely to give it. Calm surged through me and I walked slowly to the end of the algae-covered jetty. Gran was right. I looked at Michael objectively from the last plank of the jetty. It was as though I were far enough away from him for his charisma to be failing. He was an extremely handsome man who had money and manners but, here in the biting cold, surrounded by mud and the oppressive building, he was small. The world was full of Michaels, in every nationality and colour.

I moved closer, scuffing the broken boards with the toe of my trainer. Michael was unfolding plans and talking quickly, 'One of the ideas is to have the jetty replaced with matchsticks. Obviously, the matchsticks will be reinforced with steel. It would take six months for seven million matchsticks to be assembled by a team of 11, and here is a model of what it would look like. It would be an extraordinary talking point.'

He pulled a tiny model of a jetty out of his pocket. It has been laboriously made with miniature matchsticks. The designer smiled but didn't look at Gran. Michael continued talking about sculptures and lights strung across the river, costing thousands of pounds.

'You don't need a matchstick quay or any of these fripperies,' said Gran.

'A marble quay is the other possibility,' said Michael, obviously wounded. 'I want it to be spectacular.'

'Money won't buy spectacular,' Gran sounded bored.

'I think it will,' the architect spoke. His smile was slightly too wide and lasted a moment too long. 'In fact, if you wanted, I could give you a tour of sites that I have managed myself where, contrary to your opinion, money has in fact bought spectacular, superlative, exceptional and unparallelled.'

His teeth said the last sentence was a joke but his eyes longed to see Gran drowning in the mud.

'I could project manage this for a 10th of what he's charging and, what's more, it could be open and successful within four months,' Gran said, turning her back on the designer and addressing Michael.

Oh my God, this time, she had gone too far. I thought of walking back down to the end of the jetty, just keep on walking until I fell off the edge into the mud and was buried. I had a ridiculous grandmother who insisted on embarrassing me in public. The designer looked pityingly at Michael, waiting for him to dismiss the ludicrous, elderly lady.

'What do you know about project management?' Michael asked.

The designer shifted on the spot, examined his little fingernail as if to suggest that that amount of space would be large enough in which to fit Gran's knowledge of project management. He looked at his watch and said he would call for a taxi and see Michael tomorrow. As he walked slowly away, he sniffed slightly, very slightly but, somehow, the direction of the wind or the isolation of the place magnified the sound. It ricocheted about us. Michael and Gran seemed unaffected but I barely managed not to cover my ears.

'Yes. See you tomorrow, and thanks,' said Michael over his shoulder.

Michael was just being polite. He was a good man. He wasn't about to embarrass an old woman in public. The designer and Michael had obviously exchanged a secret signal. But Gran was not to be silenced so easily.

'I know skilled craftspeople, artisans. People who owe me favours. I have connections at the salvage yard, and not a novelty-monger in sight.'

'Quality costs. I want to win at this game, I've got the lease on this place and I have the budget to make it extraordinary,' he spoke passionately.

'You have the money to make it ghastly,' she pulled his passion out of his mouth, dropped it neatly and extinguished it with the ball of her foot, leaving it in the mud.

I knew better than to interfere but I just wanted the conversation to end. I turned round with a tear in my eye, ready to guide Gran home where she could take up her place on the sofa and look through her sweet pea catalogues. But she was being guided in a different direction. Michael had his arm almost around her shoulder and was leading her towards the pub door. Furious, I scurried after them and I was slightly out of breath by the time I caught up with them. Michael unlocked the door with a flourish.

'Come and look round, Cath. I am genuinely interested in what you have to say and we could continue chatting while you take in the general devastation.'

It was as though I weren't there, but I was determined not to be left out. I pulled my hat off and straightened my hair. My humiliation had been replaced with anger and, if Gran was having a tour of the pub, I should accompany her but I would not let her get all of his attention.

As you entered the pub from the riverside, you went straight up two short flights of wooden stairs with a landing between before you could get into the main room. At the bottom of the stairs, a small corridor went off to the left and that was where we all trooped first to see what would become Michael's office, a long thin room with eight windows overlooking the quay. It was a bit like a greenhouse but it felt colder than being outside. You could also access the pub from the road, avoid the stairs and walk straight into the big room. This was the winter entrance and anyone wanting to see the river or sit outside in the summer would go down the concrete slope and use the bottom door. The stairs were rickety and the place was dark except for one bare bulb on the landing. To the left of the landing was the kitchen, directly above Michael's office. The inside of the kitchen door was coated in dust and grease, and the ovens looked more domestic than commercial. Appearing disinterested in kitchens, Michael marched us back across the landing and into the main room.

The first thing to greet us when we walked in was the carpet. The room was about 12 metres by six and the carpet shrank from the edges of the walls in shame. But when it saw us, invading after years of peace, it rose up, monster-like, proclaiming Axminster credentials but, being so filthy and downtrodden, I knew it was lying. I wondered what had brought it down so low. Drink presumably. The second thing I noticed was a vole from the river. A tiny pointy thing, lost in what was left of the great swirling pattern, taking ages to become visible on the red patches of carpet before disappearing again on the brown.

'What the hell's that?' asked Michael, who had followed where I was looking.

'It's a tiny, harmless vole,' I replied.

'It must have got in somehow, though I don't know how it managed the stairs,' Gran said.

I went to scoop it up and the minute creature was lost in my hand. I walked back down the stairs with it and took it back down to the river. It stayed on the quay for a while, as if it might die from fright. Finally, it became reoriented and disappeared into the folds of the bank. I wondered about it catching a tiny foot between the gaps if Michael went ahead with the matchstick quay. It could be a magnet for trapped vermin. Then I imagined it sliding across a marble surface, its tiny feet unable to get any purchase on that funereal surface.

Little did it know when it had left the safety of the river and climbed two mountains that it would encounter the Leviathan of the carpet world. More swirls and loudness, more vulgarity and stench than the little creature had ever seen. When it trotted home, it was for ever elevated in the vole kingdom for its story-telling ability and remembered as the vole who had experienced the carpet-induced trip.

I walked slowly back towards the pub. The whole place had an abandoned, unloved air about it. It was quite a grand stone building, with three huge windows on the first and second floors. Michael's office was a homely-looking garden office, attached to the left of the building, wearing fragments of blue paint. Its existence softened the otherwise austere appearance of the pub. To the left of his office were the remnants of an outside bar with its windows boarded up. The pub's boundary was marked by a long fence that ran down to the river. From the road, the pub looked unprepossessing and small. That was because, like an iceberg, 75% of it was below the level of the road and accessed by the sloping concrete drive. Once down the slope and in front of the building, the stone gave the place a sombre aspect, and, with no customers and no cars parked by the quay, it appeared less than welcoming. Looking at such an expanse of stone, I wondered how Michael was going to make the place look inviting.

Although I was very familiar with the building, my recognition of the place was based on it being an abandoned thing with no hope of re-opening or ever enticing the public within its walls. Gran and Michael were just heading through a fire door to the left when I walked back into the abandoned bar. He was directing her but she didn't seem to need guiding, she must have remembered the place clearly from working there.

Without Gran and Michael, I had a moment to take in the surroundings by myself. It was ugly, spacious and unsightly. The lights didn't appear to be working in some sections of the pub and, where they did, the fluorescent tubes flickered and clicked irritatingly. Although the room was basically a rectangle, there was a smaller, L-shaped piece at the bottom where filthy old wallpaper clung to the walls. The place smelt damp and, with its cloths still in place and the optics all drained, the bar was ghostly. The glasses and drink were all gone but odd things remained like 30 black plastic ashtrays piled up in the centre of the room. Michael could have them cast in brass and made into a centrepiece.

Mustard yellow curtains that were half-falling off their rails looked as though they had been swung on, the fabric was freezing to the touch. There was some furniture piled up in one corner, 15 tables and twice as many chairs, all made from the cheapest materials. The overall effect was one of tiredness, cold and degradation.

The two of them reappeared downstairs. Michael shook Gran's hand and said that he would be in touch. I was impressed that he was so skilled at rejecting people but surprised that she had fallen for his charm and that she looked pleased with herself.

We walked home in silence. Michael had offered us a lift but Gran had refused. I was grateful. I didn't think I wanted to see all those plush fittings and hear the way the stereo sounded so smooth and calming, as if the presenters were in the car with us. I didn't want to touch his perfect upholstery or smell that odour of nothingness that permeated his car. In fact, it permeated his entire life. His existence was odourless in its self-contained perfection.

I was determined to stay completely silent on the way home. After half a mile, I could feel my lips sealing up permanently, a game I used to play as a child. If you purse your lips together tightly for a minute or more, your body secretes something that makes them stick together. Then, if you try to move them just slightly, you can pretend it's too late and you will never have to speak again. What a relief that would be at this moment; no need to explain or whine ever again. Shrugging could replace speech. To me, it seemed to be the only answer as none of this made sense. I wondered if it had been shrewd for me to try and break away from home. It wasn't like people had said. Opportunities had come – but at such a price. The endless questions about life were making my head spin. The constant guessing of other people's motives and thoughts was exhausting me.

Gran spoke, 'I take it that you are very angry with me.' No answer, although several poisonous lines of sarcasm began to take form. 'This place has special significance to me and I fancy doing something away from home,' she said.

Silence.

'Michael wants me to project manage the pub, he is paying me generously, all the money will come to you in the end.'

I could hold out no longer, 'I thought you said I was to keep away from him!' I shouted.

'I did tell *you* to keep away from him. But now I have realised he is harmless.'

'What do you mean 'harmless'?'

'I mean unlike Doon.'

'What's he got to do with it?'

'Doon tried to destroy me on this very spot. He was a regular at the pub for two years.'

'Did Bill work here?'

'No, he was a customer, too.'

'How did Doon try to destroy you?'

'He turned people against me.'

'Why would he do that?'

'He didn't like the way I behaved. He thought everything was available to him, as it had been throughout his life: his exclusive upbringing, his academic success, his face.'

'Was he handsome?'

'Everybody thought so.'

'But not you?'

'There's something jarring about such a well-ordered face, no room for the imagination.'

'What's all this got to do with Michael?'

135

'Standing here for a moment, seeing you here, alarmed me. But then I realised that Michael Packs is non-toxic.'

'You know that I like him and that's all you can say about him?'

'That's all there is to say about him.'

'In your humble opinion,' I said and, with that, we walked home in silence.

*   *   *

Before I knew what was happening, Gran had started to galvanise things at Michael's pub. She seemed less self-contained than I had ever seen her before. She was always charging about between the salvage yard and various builders' merchants. Behaving out of character became an everyday occurrence, including phoning my mother and asking favours of her. Asking for lifts instead of walking everywhere. She still walked around the village and into town but, once, I even saw her coming back in a taxi which dropped her discreetly at the top of our lane. She had hoped that Bill and I wouldn't see her.

'Well, Michael's paying and he wants everything done yesterday.'

But it was more as though she were the one who desperately wanted the place open again.

I wondered if the renovation project were too much for her, if she regretted her involvement with other people and was finding it exhausting, so I watched her closely. At her insistence, I walked to Michael's pub with her when I wasn't working, and she introduced me to all the men and women who would be under her command. She carried the air of great confidence that she always had at home in the garden with her onto the building site. She never once appeared to be fazed by doing things she didn't normally do: talking at length on the phone, giving instructions to other people, calling meetings. She was in full-on bossy mode but it was never with ill-feeling and the people she dealt with seemed to appreciate her straight talking. She had finally found her vocation.

I had thought healing was her thing, but it seemed that the building trade was. I had never seen her so frantic, her whole face often contorted with effort. Although she sometimes looked tired and occasionally sat down when no one else was looking, she had a kind of radiance. She adopted a builder's hard hat and, with a dress and work boots, I don't think I had ever seen her look so beautiful. She strode around the pub grounds with a measuring tape and a pencil. Her hair was white with plaster dust or sawdust, her face grubby.

She and Michael maintained a dignified distance from one another and, when he turned up, she became slightly defensive. He could see from his quick visits that she had the whole thing under control. She was marshalling all the local tradespeople, comparing quotes and calling in favours. She had a diary in which she set up people to work alongside one another or to follow straight on from the previous workmen and ensure that no days were lost.

Surprisingly, the old pub was quite sound and there were no walls to be knocked down. First, came electricians to rip out the fluorescent lights from three decades ago. We were not going to be dazzled over our pints but gently illuminated with recessed spotlights. Gran insisted on plugs everywhere, especially in the dark corners where additional lamps would go. A week or so later, the carpet was dragged out, kicking and screaming. It took three men to hold it down and its shouting and swearing echoed across the creek. It was as though exposure to the air gave it a new lease of life and all the stench of beer and smoke trapped within its fibres was released. Its bare patch wounds, with cigarette ash rubbed into them, were exposed to daylight as the injured carpet was dumped in a skip.

As spring progressed, the ugly brickwork from the old bar was knocked down and removed and all the floor tiles were lifted, most of them cracked. Layers of wallpaper were stripped, each newly revealed pattern telling a different story about the pub and the dreams the previous owners had had about the place. I popped down from The Waggon and Horses most days to see how things were developing. Sometimes, nothing had moved and, from where I stood at the top of the concrete slope, although I saw bodies shifting and carrying, lifting and dumping, it was as though they were all working in vain.

Even though I still felt manic whenever I saw Michael, there was something about Gran being around the place which allowed me to control my feelings a little. It was as though she took some of the gloss off him. My immediacy to her meant some of his layers were removed and he looked less god-like and more human. I realised that was what she did to everybody: peeled them.

True to his word, Michael offered me a job. It was casually done with no fuss and no contract but I assumed he was trustworthy because, otherwise, why would Gran be working for him? She had said that the pub would be ready to open in another four months. I accepted the job, only hesitating for a moment. I would stay silent for eight weeks, then give a month's notice at The Waggon and Horses. By doing this, I wasn't leaving them in the lurch because it wasn't the busy season and they had time to advertise. When I told Gran, she seemed pleased but not surprised.

Michael walked past and said, 'It's a Furnish family affair this pub now, isn't it?' I beamed but Gran gave him an odd look.

With Gran around, able to reduce him to a normal stature, I knew I was taking the job for the right reasons, needing to move on to a better position. Although no situation was perfect, and sometimes I was still open-mouthed at his loveliness, I hoped the more that I could concentrate on his faults and ordinariness, the less I would be obsessed by him.

That attitude didn't last the week. By Friday, I could no longer deny that he was staring at me. I wanted to hurry the work along at the pub, wanted to start up with him where we had once left off. All these people around and I wished they would finish twiddling with their wires or flaunting their emulsion, or whatever other trade they plied, and leave. He always acknowledged me immediately when I turned up, I could see him looking at me. I could *feel* him looking at me and I wanted to kiss him.

I surprised him once by coming on an afternoon when he wasn't expecting me. He saw me from the quay and waved. The welcome sun hugged me and I walked deliberately slowly down the slope towards him. I felt as if I owned the world and I were the most beautiful thing in it. In the few minutes it took me to walk towards him, he never once stopped looking at me.

That Friday afternoon, I felt a change had occurred to the place as I walked down the slope. Then I saw it – half the building had been painted. It brightened the whole place. It was a creamy white and had been Gran's idea, she had even sourced ecologically-sound paint. For someone who clung on to things and didn't like items replaced that were still workable, she seemed to take great delight in ripping out the insides of The Tide and plastering its face with so much make-up that it was unrecognisable.

I was heading towards Michael, when Gran popped out of the pub. 'I have never explained to you my connection with this place,' she said.

'You worked here for a while and this is where you met Bill.'

'I fell in love here.'

I could see Michael still standing and waiting to speak to me as I looked over Gran's head. This could have been my moment to work things out with him but she had decided to unburden herself now. She couldn't have meant that she fell in love with Bill here.

'With this place?' I asked, still glancing in Michael's direction and avoiding her eyes.

'There's nothing much to say, go to him,' she smiled.

I took her advice and walked to Michael. We sat on the jetty. The plain jetty, unaltered apart from the algae and dirt being removed with a power hose, and the broken slats replaced. We dangled our feet over the mud. The sly, shifting, secretive mud. Michael was wearing jeans and a long-sleeved T-shirt, he looked better than ever in more casual clothes. Somehow, he looked slightly too perfect in a suit, a bit pompous, but, in jeans, he looked generous.

'Cath says it'll be ready to open in another four months.'

'Amazing,' I said, although that wasn't soon enough for me.

'You're not having second thoughts about becoming the manager are you?' He seemed genuinely concerned. 'Everyone I have spoken to at The Waggon and Horses praises you. They say you turned the place round and are universally popular with staff and locals alike, so don't tell me you're not going to do it.'

'Of course not,' I said.

'I'm relieved, I don't want to start looking for somebody else.'

We sorted out a preliminary starting date and he said he wanted to pay me for the hours I had already put in assisting Gran as a goodwill gesture. He got a notebook out and we talked of table numbers and restaurant suppliers. We talked of table decorations and limited menus. Of napkins and whether we should have crisps. We talked of wine and who could supply it. We talked of early evening specials that might lure people in. With each new sentence, I hoped he would mention something about us. I saw him looking at me and knew he wanted me. With each small page turned and filled in, I expected him to suggest that we could start over and everything would be all right.

But his neat, efficient writing just continued to cover the page. Line after line. We talked about buying cutlery and whether white plates would be the best. At that point, Gran came up and joined in the conversation. She had already commissioned a local potter to make our complete stock of plates and bowls, more than we would ever need.

I needed to be patient, approach him in an entirely different way with the past firmly behind us. I was mature and I took greater care with my appearance than ever. I began to fool Michael when I appeared one day in a black pencil skirt, a white shirt and a waist-cinching belt. To avoid looking like a frump, I also wore pink shoes.

I had the afternoon off and, rather than go home and spend it alone, I decided to stay and help where I could. I was coming out of the pub, with a large sheet of plasterboard that left only the bottom of my feet and my arms showing, when Susan's car came down the slope and parked in front of the quay.

'Michael said I could come and have a look,' she said defensively.

There was a huge piece of board between us and I felt both safe and protected. It also looked like I was very busy and she was the interloper. Confidently, she stepped closer until she was a metre away from me.

'Amanda, let's forget the dove business and start again,' she held out a skinny, vein-covered, tanned hand.

How could I forget the dove business when I had to let Denim out every day and rattle her in with a tin of bird food at night? As for Susan, she was the last person with whom I wanted to start again. I could have cried. I longed to hear those very words but from a different mouth. Still, I took a deep breath, leant my huge board against the side of the as yet unpainted pub, stepped forward and took her hand.

'Aren't you the stylish one,' she said.

I brushed a little dust off my skirt and stayed quiet, as if my style were a given, a permanent fixture, instead of being scaffolding that could be taken down at any moment. Michael sprung out of the pub as if he had been watching us. He took over the conversation, making it light and airy, unnecessary small talk. Honest words were too brutal. I had started to see the benefits of small talk and was practising daily, watching people carefully and writing down phrases in a small book. The idea seemed to be not to let any silence get in the way. It didn't seem necessary to listen in detail to the other person because you always needed to be ready to get your bit in at the appropriate moment. You had to understand the signs and leap in when needed with your bag of banalities open.

Susan left after five minutes, giving Michael a cursory kiss on the cheek. For some reason, I felt furious. I wanted to stick out my foot and trip her up on the way back to her car. I hated the way she pretended to run everywhere as if she were so important that she always had to rush about.

'That woman is something else,' Michael said.

Those were the words I needed to hear. The meagre sun suddenly felt stronger and I no longer had to waste time thinking malicious things about her silly run. He had seen through her and told me quite clearly that she was no threat to me.

'When all this is sorted out, we'll have to go out again. Maybe we could have a better evening together?' he said, his forehead wrinkling slightly in anticipation.

'Fine,' I said.

Hallelujah, he was still interested. I knew I had kept catching him watching me when I wasn't looking. I felt my attractiveness return, my power rose. I went home and let Denim fly.

VIII

An Insidious Word is Used

I MUST learn to drive; Gran had spoken. Suddenly, after cursing the car for years, and after numerous incidents involving rows with people in the town while I shuffled shamefaced on the pavement, I must learn to drive. Did I mention the legendary clash when Gran took the tread off a man's tyre with a mini hacksaw she happened to have about her person and he threatened to hit her? Or other occasions which were similar, but where motorists' faces had morphed in my head and some have probably changed gender? However, what each scene had in common was that they arose due to Gran's overwhelming loathing of cars. Despite this, I was to learn to drive.

Never mind the impact on the environment or what would happen to my muscles if I didn't use them (she always used to wave flaccid dough about to illustrate slack muscle tone), I must move with the times and learn to drive. It was not relevant whether I drove or not after the test, but I must possess that piece of paper. Options must be open to me.

Once, home was enough for both of us and Gran had been the Queen of Insularity. She would have advocated staying at your own address and being at peace with yourself to anyone who would listen but, recently, she had sprung forth with her building project and why not? I could give many reasons why not but the chief one was because her presence on the building site meant that my longed-for affair with Michael could never start. She had ceased to be a comfort to me. The last thing I wanted was her being around all the time, that's why I'd got a job away from home in the first place.

I also knew I couldn't control her; had no right to try. If she fancied a change of scene at this stage in life, ideally, I should be encouraging, but I wished she had chosen a different project, somewhere I would never go, for instance. It was the same with the driving. What was the hurry? Perhaps she had plans as yet undisclosed involving me chauffeuring her about the country. We were going to use up all the green points she had accrued in a whistle-stop tour of bizarre English towns aboard a gas-guzzling motor.

'Don't be ridiculous, Amanda, I have no ulterior motive. It's just about you learning to drive. If you are working late at the pub, you can get home quickly after a long shift.'

This was not what I had in mind, but I thought about the advantages of driving. I wouldn't end up all crumpled and fly-splattered at the end of every journey.

'What will happen to my legs?' I asked.

She sniffed in reply.

'Oh well, at least I'll be able to drive 12 miles to the nearest gym to build them up again.'

She bit before she could stop herself but it soon turned into a smile. The only thought that genuinely scared me was what *would* happen to my legs? Years of tone would go out of the window. I would have to develop a fake run like Susan's. I couldn't copy hers directly but would have to put something of myself into it.

The other part of the plan on which I was not keen was that Gran insisted I ring Marie and ask her to teach me. Gran had filled in the form for my test before we had even arranged anything with Marie.

'What if I fail?'

'A monkey could learn to drive in three weeks. Anyway, the waiting list is about five weeks at the moment. I have worked out a timetable for Marie to teach you intensively on a daily basis.'

'You've really got this one worked out, haven't you? Why can't I have lessons from a stranger like everybody else? Is it the money?'

'Not at all. It just so happens that your mother, remarkably untalented as she is in every other respect, happens to be a competent driver.'

'You've never said that before, in fact you've said…'

'What I have said in the past may have been overly harsh. And I will not be around for ever.'

'Why? Where are you going, a pensioners' building convention or similar?'

Suddenly, the over-60s were going to take over the building trade. Cowboys would be obliterated and everything would be done very slowly but meticulously.

She handed me the phone. I was embarrassed as I rarely spoke to my mother these days and just to ring up and ask her to teach me to drive seemed rude. But I was pleasantly surprised. She jumped at the chance and said she would be around the following evening. While we were on the phone, she also spoke a lot about a new boyfriend and I suspected that's what she really wanted to tell me about. Perhaps she were planning to marry. I shuddered. As long as she didn't expect us to get involved.

Gran was right. Driving was easy for me – as soon as the practical aspects were explained, I was off down the road at a steady speed without a single lurch. When I was in the car with Marie, my emotions were level and all my actions were automatic. It made a pleasant change from the endless philosophising and questioning that had overwhelmed me since I had started work at The Waggon and Horses. I was happy in my steel cage. The only disadvantage was Marie's presence but, with any luck, she would voluntarily eject from the passenger seat as soon as I had my driving licence in my hand.

'I've met someone, Amanda. Someone who admires me enormously,' she said on our eighth lesson as we approached the nearest town. I sensed she had spent the previous seven lessons building up to this declaration, because, although she had shown great interest and patience with me, it was obvious she was withholding something.

I thought about enormous admiration. Marie needed it. She was doomed to spend a lifetime in search of it because it didn't come from the one person from whom it should have come as a given.

'He's been a fan of mine for years. He has my TV appearances in date order in a DVD collection. He's a little younger than me.'

Fortunately, I was practising a hill start and made it clear that this was taking all my concentration and speaking would not be possible for me at the moment.

'He has persuaded me to move away from studying happiness and towards anger. He thinks that anger will be more profitable in the long-term. And so, for the last few months, I have been concentrating solely on anger. I have abandoned happiness,' she laughed.

'Gran will be pleased,' I said. Although she ignored this comment, I felt her prick up with interest. I wondered at her sudden change in direction.

'Can you become an expert in another subject in just a few months, then?'

'The skills I have are transferable. In theory, I could teach anything.'

I decided it was best not to question the validity of this but, in my experience, she didn't know a thing about anger as hers was so repressed.

'Zak is about to give me the greatest possible accolade,' she continued.

So, he had a name, and what an unfortunate one. The approach to a tricky roundabout rendered me speechless again.

'He is naming an entire centre after me.' She paused, I indicated left and turned down a little side street, preparing to parallel park. 'The Marie Furnish Centre for Anger Management.'

For some reason, this struck me as being particularly outlandish. If ever there were an angry family, a bad-tempered bunch, it was the Furnishs. Anger was our fuel, our reason for getting up in the morning. Never had a Furnish bypassed the opportunity to smoulder. Even Bill, after living with Gran for so many years, was renowned for his aggressive sulking.

'Can't you call it something else?' I asked.

'What do you mean?'

'Well, if it's as serious as you seem to be saying, maybe you will marry this man and maybe you could use his name instead.' I couldn't bring myself to call him Zak.

'That's very astute of you, Amanda, and it brings me onto another subject entirely. Zak has offered to marry me and he has given his express permission for you to adopt his surname if you wish. It's Veile.'

I managed to mumble something. Why on earth would I want a stranger's name? The name of a man I had never even met. Was Marie finally cracking? I drove sedately back to Gran's and even managed to go through the 'Would you like to come in?' rigmarole.

'Is Cath here?' Marie asked casually.

'No, she's rebuilding Britain from old railway sleepers.'

'I'll just pop in to say 'Hi' to Dad, then.'

While I made the tea, I heard her tell Bill all the stuff that she had told me in the car. He made all the right noises and thumped her encouragingly on the shoulder. They sat close together on the sofa and I watched them and saw how alike they looked. As she was leaving, she said, 'By the way, did Cath tell you your test had come through? It's two weeks on Thursday.'

I kicked the wall as she drove off up the drive. What was happening round here? Firstly, her communicating with Gran without me as a mediator, then my being the last to know things. For all I knew, the wedding with the new boyfriend could already be arranged.

Perhaps, Gran had hired Susan's doves. No, that was going a little too far, even for me.

I passed my theory test at the local test centre. I managed to remember the meanings of strange little black and white drawings encased in red and blue borders. I hoped that I would get the deer sign. I was going to use up one of my mistake points pretending I didn't recognise it. I don't suppose they allow people from around here to be tested on the deer sign; it might get people started on stories and anecdotes. Deer hitting car stories. Flying, headless deer, in a grisly re-enactment of countless children's Christmas songs. Hoof for ever embedded in your walnut dashboard.

I sailed through the hazard perception test. I could see trouble coming, it was a natural talent. The mouse clicked through the multiple choice questions and I left the building elated. I had passed. I now had to pass my practical test within two years. There was no hurry.

I started to hang around Michael's pub more often in my spare time. I still had a months' notice to work at The Waggon and Horses, but I was having almost daily meetings with Michael about the food and wine, plus the clientele for which we were aiming. I ceased to worry about Gran being a hindrance to me because she exercised a strange kind of charm over Michael. He was always lively and kind after talking with her. Quite sensibly, he had given her free rein.

One day, waiting for Marie to come and collect me for a driving lesson, I watched my mother coming down the slope in her car. At that moment, the phone rang in the pub and it was one of Gran's cronies from the salvage yard. Dutifully, I went looking for Gran through rooms that were being renovated. Rooms that had been broken down and stripped of everything they had known and were now being put back together. Their wallpaper had been torn and scraped from them. Patterns with which they had been familiar, like old coats, were just peeled off and dumped.

But, as I walked through one room and then another, I realised we were at a stage when things got worse before they get better. The phase when ceilings and walls were gouged and then filled, ready for sanding, a spell when everything looked much shoddier than it ever did before.

Just before I found Gran, I saw her diary on the floor, large scruffy writing all over the place that ignored the lines as if they were bars, defiantly breaking out. I felt a wave of affection towards her caused by the unseemly scrawl. Glancing again, I saw there was a piece of white paper sticking out from the diary with very different lines. I was sure it was the Rottweiler drawing but, just as I was about to bend down and touch the diary, Gran came through from the next room. I thought I must have imagined it. I handed her the phone and went to meet Marie who had sat in the car for a few minutes, stiff and formal, in case Gran should leap out of some crevice and demean her. But the sun caressing through the window had made her open the door and stick out a leg. A minute later, when it seemed that Gran was not around, she had stepped out of the car and walked towards the jetty. She stood on the edge and looked into the water.

'Sad, old river,' she said.

'Why?'

'Nothing. Let's get going.'

* * *

The day of the test arrived. Marie had suggested a long drive with an added detour. 'We could call in at The Marie Furnish Centre for Anger Management, just for half an hour.'

I wasn't sure and didn't rush to reply.

'Zak is a very calming influence and is very keen to meet you,' she said warmly.

I was keen to be calmed and drove smoothly to where my mother's centre stood. It was a granite building, a rock of pent-up fury and grimness if ever there was one. I was pondering on whether this could seriously upset the clientele as we walked up the stone path. An enormous sign loomed over the door in green and blue. It was too high and involved craning your neck to make out the italic lettering. It was supposed to be soothing but was anything but; not only would you have your own inner turmoil to contend with as you arrived, but also a pain in the neck.

We walked into the reception area where everything was green and blue, the walls, the carpets, the stationery. The logo was everywhere. There were some goldfish in a large tank, my eyes rested on their brightness and sighed.

Zak came in. He was smaller than I expected. Too small for a man who could bestow bountiful compliments and accolades on my mother. Surely she needed a bigger man to do that? He was charming and gentle, but there was something about his manner that was so smarmy, I couldn't resist interrupting him. He listened calmly to me and then carried on saying what he had been saying before I'd cut him off. He was obviously in client mode all the time.

He and Marie danced around one another, carefully waiting for the other one to speak. So much mutual respect, it was nauseating. He was handsome in a rounded sort of way, his face was chubby and boyish and his ears neat and small. He was accomplished and clearly loved my mother, but I couldn't let go of the idea of her needing a fatter, larger man who oozed generosity instead of offering it in carefully packaged doses with added sweetener. It was as though he had rehearsed everything he said. Perhaps he had spent so much time practising speeches in his life that this was now his only way of being.

I began to feel sick with all the blue and green, the sea-like quality of the place. Like a sailor who couldn't cope with smooth water, I longed for a little rough sea or a change in the weather of the conversation. A little sarcasm wouldn't go amiss, or a little less eye contact from him when he was speaking to me. I was glad to leave but I still hoped that Gran would not be mean to Zak, that she would welcome him into our lives. But it was unlikely.

We headed back and, on the way to the test centre, I distracted myself by telling Marie how nice Zak was. What an asset to the family he would be with his gentility and fine calves. God knows, our family could do with some delicacy. I ended up gushing over him because, as usual, Marie, under the surface, was desperate for reassurance and, as

I spoke my compliments out loud, the real Zak disappeared and was replaced by a stranger. A stranger who deserved all the respect I was so freely giving. Enjoying the sound of my own voice and insincerity, I began to understand life better. How being false makes other people happy – and is damn good fun to boot. Maybe I had held the quality of honesty in too high a regard in the past.

As I complimented the lack of grey in his hair, I thought that even my voice began to change a little and something of a Susan Rink trait began to creep in. I wondered why my mother was soaking it all up and I thought about my situation with Michael. All we had were a few flirty moments, exchanged glances and overly long stares, things that were impossible to quantify. Whereas my mother had a bloody great granite building named after her, and she was still insecure. I hoped that, one day, a man might name a building after me: an outhouse or a store cupboard, knowing my luck. Enough, I must stop immediately. It was fun while it lasted, but now I needed to return to reality. Zak was, in fact, an odious creature.

Marie kissed me good luck with great affection and I found myself welcoming it and hoping that our relationship could continue in this vein. There was a cheerful simplicity about her which I found refreshing. She stayed inside the driving test centre as I sat alone in her car, waiting for the examiner to come out of the building. I was seated and he walked round to the passenger side. Could a man walk more slowly? I didn't think so. Formalities were exchanged although he made no attempt to make me feel comfortable but, as soon as my foot hit the pedal, I was in control. He just sat there and let me drive him around. It was as though the instructions came from nowhere and I moved swiftly but safely to fulfil them. I passed. I flew. I could now officially hurtle around the countryside in my very own metal box. The world lay at my feet or, rather, the bits of it that were accessible by road. I was empowered. I hadn't wanted to do this driving lark, but I had done it. I was to be congratulated – I had a licence to maim people.

I didn't have a car but Marie said I could borrow hers for the next few months until I had earnt enough working at Michael's pub to buy my own. She said she was almost always with Zak and, if she weren't, he was on his way to fetch or carry her, his bandy little legs weighed down with yet another accolade to give her.

Gran was less than effusive about my success, 'I told you you'd do it easily.'

I was given little chance to revel in my accomplishment as I had been given the task of fetching Gran from Michael's pub at nine o'clock that night. Why she needed to work such long hours, I didn't know. So, my first trip alone was in the twilight, around roads that were familiar to me on foot or my bike but which, as a driver, now, seemed strange. Somehow, in the car, the hedges felt more oppressive, as if they were closing in like a maze, and the roads came to abrupt T-junctions with little warning.

I reached the pub and committed my first misdemeanour against all the driving instruction I had received. I turned off the engine and lights and rolled down the concrete slope, my excuse being that the moon was full and acting as headlights. It seemed an insult to the environment to keep my headlights on when the moon was so loud. The pub looked shut down for the night. The tide was in and the water still.

Then, I saw Michael sitting with two other men under an umbrella with a portable patio heater, barricaded with empty bottles and glasses. I hadn't planned to run into him, just to grab Gran and run. I wasn't prepared to see him. Normally, when I was at the pub, I was on constant alert for a possible appearance but, tonight, I felt sure I could quickly slip in and slip away. I had no choice other than getting out of the car but I had an uneasy feeling about the whole situation. He whispered me over. Or, I should say, slurred me over.

'Hey, gorgeous.'

'I've come to get Gran.'

'When did you pass your test?'

'This morning.'

'You'd pass my test for being fuckable, any time,' said Nick Deal, the eldest of the other two men and the head of the carpentry team.

I calmly ignored him, 'Is she here?'

'The project manager left 10 minutes ago in a taxi,' said Michael.

I was furious with her. She told me she would wait for me at the bottom of the slope.

'I can give her a message tomorrow,' he said.

'I'll see her tonight myself when I get back. I do live with her, unless the last 18 years have been a horrible dream.'

'Come and live with me – here,' said Michael.

Nick Deal guffawed, the younger man remained silent. I had seen him at the pub, hanging doors.

I stepped back. The mud rumbled underneath the water and even the moon pricked up her ears. I saw the shadows of another two bottles under the table. My heart was in a metal bucket going slowly round in one of those fairground rides where you get to the top and look over. It went over the edge and was slowly coming down the other side. But there was something else in the bucket with my heart; my spleen, traditional home of bile. I was so angry with Michael and his stupid game playing. More angry than he could ever know but, foolishly, he wouldn't shut up. Throwing careless comments in my direction.

'The place is big enough for the both of us and, when my daughter comes to visit, you can move out of my room and into your own and we can pretend we hardly know one another,' he slurred.

'We don't,' I said, firmly enough to shut him up. 'If Gran's gone, I'll catch up with her.'

'What's the rush?' Nick asked. 'Stay here and show us your tits.'

'I speak to your wife most days when she brings your sandwiches, shall I pass on your compliments?' I asked.

'Who do you think you're talking to, missy? Don't think I haven't seen you, prancing about the building site, barely dressed.'

'If, by prancing, you mean going about my own business, then I'm sure you have been lucky enough to see me on numerous occasions, Neanderthal!'

'You should watch it, you foul-mouthed little piece or you'll end up like your grandmother, up the duff and stuck with the last bloke who will have you.'

Michael muttered as if trying to stop the conversation but it was too late. I stood firm and spoke slowly, as if to an imbecile, 'I do love to meet erudite men.'

'Shut it, you little slut!'

* * *

I flicked the keys into my palm and made myself get slowly into the car. I hoped the car would start and it did, first time. I drove slowly and carefully away from the river and back up the slope. I got home and stormed into the house. Gran was washing jam jars for some of her foul concoctions.

'Why weren't you there?'

'Because I am here.'

'I've just been called a slut by Nick Deal.'

She looked up at me from the sink.

'Did you hear me?' I asked.

She nodded.

'The one time in my life when I was hoping for one of your hour-long rants about language and the historical mistreatment of women, you are silent. I'm going over the words that he said in my head and, individually, none of them seem so bad, so why do I feel like this?' I was crying.

'Perhaps you misheard or misunderstood?' said Gran.

'You're a useless guardian, grandmother, whatever it is you're supposed to be. What the hell are you doing at that pub anyway, what's it to you how it's bloody well decorated?'

'It's everything to me. I had an affair with James Arlet.'

My rage was hijacked. I had no choice but to leave behind my own humiliation and focus on Gran.

'It was James who gave me the dress, instead of an engagement ring. He was dying and I didn't want to be left with a lumpen bit of metal but, rather, something beautiful that wouldn't last.'

'Does Bill know?'

'Of course, he was there.'

'So how did you get together with Bill?'

'The night of the wake. Hours after James had been buried, Bill asked me to marry him.'

'Be careful of what you rescue,' I said spitefully, paraphrasing Bill's words to me about Gran.

'Oh, there was much worse to come than that,' she said.

IX

Nature's Warning Colours

IN A STROKE of genius, I poured my hunger over Michael into nature programmes. I bought a boxed set of *Wild Planet* programmes on DVD and I watched them at The Waggon and Horses during quiet times. I only had two weeks left, so what did I care? I rewound the gory bits, including the scene when the lion leaps, that moment before it hits the zebra's neck. I watched endless pieces of film of things being torn apart, great fleshy chunks coming away from bone, and blood lingering around mouths.

We could have a free lunch at The Waggon and Horses and I had never taken advantage of it before, but now I started having steak. I liked the feeling of the grease and meat juices on my lips after I had finished eating. Never had my lips been so soft, my clothes and hair smelt meaty and, trapped between each hair on my head, was an animal smell. My fork was poised in front of my mouth, quivering with a piece of fillet steak as I wanted to coincide the exact moment

of the lion's first mouthful with my own, when Ali came into the bar
and saw my elbows resting on the beer cloths, my face inches away
from the small television.

'Will you turn that gore off?' she asked.

'Just watch this next bit where the hyenas fight and shriek over the
last pieces of flesh on this unrecognisable skeleton.'

'It's disgusting, I can't look.'

'I haven't got anywhere else to watch it,' I said rudely.

'Get a TV like any normal person and watch it at home,' she said,
only half-joking.

I started watching tiny snippets of it when she was in the toilet
doing her hair. Sometimes, the same scene again and again, then I
would go down to Michael's pub rubbing my lips together with the
grease that still remained on them. Although I had the fat on my
lips, I didn't dress in an oily way but wore cold clothes – narrow
skirts and spiky shoes. I was determined to behave the way that I
wanted, regardless of the incident with Nick Deal. I had nothing of
which to be ashamed and, every day, I expected to bump into him
and receive an apology. But I never saw him.

There were still a lot of men around and I loved it, it deflected
from Michael. Many of them were lovely to look at and even those
that weren't had something of interest about them. I looked at a lot
of men's bodies, the differences between hands and necks and hair
and feet. I feasted on them.

* * *

Michael and I were to start interviewing for staff, I was uneasy and
didn't really want to do it.

'Choose the ones you would want if it were your place,' Gran said.

'How can I do that?' I asked, exasperated.

'Michael may not be around for ever.'

'What have you heard?' I asked crossly.

'Nothing.'

'None of us will be around for ever. Bloody hell, I'm turning into you.'

She gave me a rare kiss and hug. I clung to her and lifted her off her feet. I put her back down on the ground as if I were far stronger, but we were quite alike physically.

'You smell of cooking, yes, it's meat, a meaty smell is all around you. A meaty aura,' she said.

'Better than a cakey one like Susan's,' I joked.

'Oh yes, much stronger than that, but strength and rawness don't always get you what you want.'

During the next few weeks, we appointed bar staff, a bookkeeper and cleaners. I watched Michael dealing with other people and I noticed there was little difference between the way he spoke to strangers than to me. Always the same jokey warmth, that never got any hotter or colder.

Even though I had a day off from The Waggon and Horses, I called in there at lunchtime and ordered the biggest steak they had on the menu.

I watched 10 minutes of an antelope being stalked by a lion as I tucked into the sirloin with mushroom sauce. I had asked for it medium-rare and could smell the juices. But then, something occurred to me that made me put down my knife and fork. In many ways, apart from my eating habits, I was still behaving like the antelope, flitting about looking tantalisingly tasty and vulnerable. That would never do. I would do the stalking if there was any to be done. So I started to flirt, unsubtly and not just with Michael, but I kept something of myself back. Like Ali's, it was a hard kind of flirting that didn't invite any serious attention and said, quite clearly, that it was just a game and, if you attempted to come anywhere near me, I would, in fact, rip off your head.

Michael went for it big time. I was surprised. How could he be so stupid? It was straight from the magazines I had read, heavy-handed and unoriginal. To make up for the lack of variety in innuendo and hip wiggling, I wore long, floaty clothes; tubular, stretchy ones;

small, skimpy outfits; tight, restricting material – and he appeared to notice them all. I sat by the side of the quay wearing my jeans and a white shirt and stretched out my legs to admire the tone and the softness of the denim.

Still, when he appeared, it was as though I had taken a bite from a lemon. My whole body jolted with shock.

Gran watched me growing more confident and oozing sexuality. 'You are causing havoc at the pub, like Maya,' she said.

'Sorry?'

Then I remembered the conversation I had had with Gran months earlier about Maya from *Midlanders*. A woman who was sweeping and sleeping her way through entire populations. A woman who could sexualise buying toothpaste.

'Your little entourage at the pub, growing day by day,' Gran said, nodding towards a group of young men who were setting up scaffolding in between gawping at me.

'Is that a criticism or an observation?'

'I'm just waiting for someone to push you off course, to attempt to destabilise you.'

'Why would someone do that?'

'Out of spite or fear.'

Finally, she was going to talk about her past. I was going to get all the juicy details and learn from her experience. I must tread carefully and not appear to be desperately interested. But she held out the pub's phone to me, 'Your mother has called, she seemed very keen to speak to you.'

'Damn, does she want her car back?' But Gran had walked away. I rang my mother and got through immediately. This in itself should have been sufficient warning.

'This is difficult, Amanda, but your grandmother has asked me to speak to you.'

I laughed.

'Consider the message of your clothing,' she said.

'They are material, they have no voice.'

'Don't pretend not to know what I mean.'

'Be explicit then,' I retorted, angrily.

'Clothing that reveals so much of the body invites intense reaction.'

'Ah, Gran told you about the slut incident.'

'I am just saying that a stronger position for you as a woman might be achieved if you exercised a little more caution regarding the length and the tightness of your garments.'

'Bollocks, I can wear what I like. I am more than this body and these clothes, and if the world is full of idiots who interpret clothing with such little intelligence, is it my fault? I consider that I am waging war on such misogynist rubbish.'

'It's a war you can never win, as your grandmother will testify.'

I put the phone down and went straight to find Gran. She wouldn't turn round and look at me.

'Why?'

She sighed and sat down on the floor with her head in her hands, 'I'm sorry, Amanda, I knew she'd do it all wrong.'

I was so shocked to receive an apology and to see her sitting on the floor that I took her by the arm and hauled her up.

'You still believe everything you've ever told me, don't you?'

'Yes, it's just that, sometimes, the world doesn't believe what I believe and that cancels out my views.'

'No,' I said, vehemently, 'The truth is the truth and the world will have to catch up.'

*   *   *

At Michael's pub, things were coming to a head. I was licking my fingers after a bag of crisps when he appeared from his office and we just stood there, a corridor's distance between us, poring over one another. Messages flashed between us, faster than our minds could process, and yet he did nothing, just turned around and walked away. His left hand scraped through his hair as he disappeared at speed. I didn't want to wait any longer and, fortunately, I didn't have to.

One of the decorators asked me out. He was lovely, much lovelier than Michael would ever be. The whites of his eyes were emulsion – shiny and liquid. We sat talking over beers that Michael had provided for the workforce as things were coming to an end. The day was unusually warm for April, and the beer went down our throats like the river that day, all slow and soothing. As I was collecting the empties, I looked at the back of the decorator's neck and my tongue nearly licked him. I sniffed him.

'Hey,' he said. He grabbed hold of my wrist and pulled me towards the table. 'I felt you do something then, what was it?'

'I just sniffed you, is it a crime to sniff a decorator now?'

'As long as I can sniff you back.'

He stroked my wrist, then sniffed and kissed up my arm until he got to the cap sleeve of my T-shirt.

I thought about the simplicity of it. A sweet man, a lovely man, sensuous available – and interested in me. I couldn't hold out any longer. At the end of the evening, his workmates left and we stayed sitting together. Our faces came closer and closer together. I was just about to kiss him when I heard a shout.

'Amanda, we've got to get this place tidied up. Are you employed here or not?'

I could see Michael by the pub door. I waved nonchalantly. I could see that he was furious by the way he walked into the pub. I was triumphant. I gave the boy my home phone number, picked up the last of the bottles and sauntered in.

I loaded the dishwasher with the coffee and teacups from the day, picked up cigarette butts from outside and went to turn out the lights in the bar. But Michael had slipped into the room.

'All done, boss. I'm off now.' He stayed on the other side of the room, glaring at me. 'See you tomorrow, Mr Joyful.' I said. I couldn't resist it. The words just slipped out and I laughed.

'Amanda…'

'What?'

'Stay and have a drink, I want to talk to you.'

I poured the drinks, taking my time, so that I could work out a number of alternative endings to the evening and my reaction to them. Our chairs scraped the floor in unison as we sat together. Telling myself to be calm, whatever the outcome, I looked coolly at Michael. I had seen another man that I fancied and I was going to be fine.

'I don't like you talking to that boy.'

This was not one of my imagined scenarios.

'Michael, you move two steps towards me and then you withdraw. Well, you can relax now because I've backed off you, for good.'

'I don't want you to back off.'

I stayed quiet so I could hear more of what I wanted to hear.

'I just wish you weren't 18.'

I was right. I should have trusted my instincts and gone with the decorator.

'I wish you weren't a greying git, but there we are.'

As I got up to leave, I put my hand on his shoulder and kissed him on the forehead in a conciliatory gesture. He put his hands around my waist and I moved towards him. A glass fell off the table. We were pressed close together with the top of my head awkwardly under his chin. He kissed my hair and my ear and we folded down together onto the floor, as though our bones had left us. We lay together on the tiles, looking at each other; I never thought lying on cold flooring could feel so magical.

'Let's draw the curtains or go upstairs,' he whispered.

That was him all over, always worrying what other people would think, even in the middle of nowhere.

'No, let's stay here.'

We finally got to touch one another, after so much waiting. It wasn't what I expected. It wasn't disappointing but it was clumsy and rushed. He rolled off me. He seemed really edgy again. We'd used a condom which he just happened to have about his person. I knew the machines in the pub were full of them but he hadn't just bought one spontaneously. He must have thought he could make this happen and I didn't like that.

I'd had enough of him. There was no affection or fun afterwards, he just flicked the dust off his trousers and coughed. His hands went to his sides in a flappy penguin sort of motion. I got up and walked out.

I drove home. I was a bit drunk. Very drunk. Fortunately, there was no one else on the road.

That was it. I'd had it with him. I intended to wait for the decorator to phone me. Michael was nothing.

I didn't know what to expect when I turned up to work the next morning. I dressed extra smartly and organised people quietly and efficiently. I was not going to go all moony and desperate when I saw him. Only, I didn't see him. He had gone to Bristol, which was two hours away, and wouldn't be back until late that night. He left me a polite and kind note. The type of note that an employer would leave to their trusty staff member.

I hadn't lost my job and was glad of it, this would all blow over. If he didn't want to make reference to it again that was fair enough. I wouldn't do a Gran, carrying on about someone for years. Yes, I was massively attracted to Michael. I wanted him. I wanted to devour him, but these were just chemical feelings, inconvenient and inexplicable. Nothing more. I would not deny them and, therefore, give them extra power. They were just states of mind that would pass. Gran was right about that.

There were still lots of men around at the pub. Plasterers, decorators, electricians. Men that Gran knew from the salvage yard, including Vince, a lanky, long-haired, clever creature with whom I am sure Gran would have loved to have set me up. While I had all these other men around me, it was fine. I still got the jolting sensation when I saw Michael, but I managed to talk myself round a lot. I had two days left at The Waggon and Horses and, in the eight months that I had been there, my hair had grown past my shoulders and my confidence had soared but, even so, I was not looking forward to the leaving party they had organised for me.

It was Ali who'd insisted that I had a party. The whole thing was a bit embarrassing. Everyone knew that I was going to work at Michael's for a decent wage. But I suppose they also knew that he was in a different market and was not really a threat to them. Three miles down country lanes was far enough.

Ali had made a banner wishing me luck. She gave me back my DVD collection. The evening was awkward because, after I'd finished work, I didn't really want to stay for a drink at all, but was forced to have one for the sake of politeness. Conversation between Ali and I was awkward, whilst Harry had never really tried to talk to me, but most of the customers who came in that night bought me a drink and filled me with compliments. After a decent amount of time had elapsed and I'd successfully poured several drinks down the drain, I walked towards the door surrounded by shouts and cheers. I reached desperately for the door but someone was coming through from the other side – Michael. I sidestepped him and carried on heading out but it seemed that he had come for me.

'I don't think you'd be too popular in there tonight,' I said.

He followed me out with his head hanging a little. 'Come back to the pub with me, come and see what's arrived today. Some crazy things that Cath has ordered. The place is going to look bizarre.'

'Bizarre?'

'It's not bad, I can't describe it. There are all these strange things everywhere, objects with odd, clashing colours.' He hesitated. Seemed genuinely worried.

'She has a strong vision for the place and you have encouraged her to run with it,' I said.

'I know that, I just need some reassurance.'

'She isn't selling you a matchstick quay is she?'

He took my arm and we laughed our way back to his car. People arriving in the car park saw us linked up. Our conversation was easy and fun, he relaxed and so did I. Happiness flooded through me with no thought for the future.

We walked into Michael's pub and our eyes were drawn to the left-hand wall. It was yellow. A kind of yellow I hadn't seen before, really bright but somehow natural. It must have been one of Gran's ethically-sourced paints, probably made from dandelions or something. There was the intensity of the yellow, a singing yellow, a heart-lifting, foot-tapping colour – and there was so much of it. The wall was eight-metres long and the wall adjoining the yellow was painted black. The rest of the room was still lining paper over plaster. The bar had been put in and I recognised what it was from the smell – green oak, Gran's favourite wood. It was irregular looking and yet each piece interlocked seamlessly. It looked effortlessly crafted, big and bold, solid and present in every way, but, contrasting with the yellow wall, looked amazing.

Gran appeared from giving orders upstairs. 'What do you think then?' She spoke to Michael.

'I love it but I was expecting something more neutral.'

'Neutral?'

'Yes, you know, natural beiges or creams.'

I flinched because I knew the speech that was coming.

'There's nothing natural about beige or cream. Show me a beige thing in nature. Go out and fetch me something…'

She waved him away but he just stood there, perplexed.

'Neutral colours are an abomination and there is nothing natural about them. They simply represent what we have been fed by the media, to what we should all aspire. They package these banal colours and sell them to us as grown up and sophisticated when, in reality, it's got nothing to do with being mature and is just another excuse to let a handful of wasters dictate to us over another area of our lives. Bleach the individuality out of us so that every public house, living room and hotel in the entire British Isles looks the same. Can we avoid mistakes in life by choosing insipid colours? Will surrounding yourself with a dull, lifeless colour protect you from vulnerability?'

'Calm down, Cath, I love it. It's just different, that's all.'

We all stood back and were silent for a moment.

'It's magnificent, Gran.'

She calmed down a little.

'I was inspired by nature, Michael. I thought of black and yellow together in nature. A warning.'

'Who are you warning?' he laughed.

'I'm off, I've called a taxi,' she said.

She left. I could see she wasn't cross. As usual, she was so sure of herself that nobody else's opinion mattered.

'Have I upset her?' Michael asked.

'No.'

'Nature's warning colours?'

'I know,' I said. 'But it works.'

Somehow, she had pulled off something really strange but wonderful. It was warm and dramatic at the same time. She had saved Michael from an amorphous gastropub makeover. This was to be the last outpost of originality.

There were boxes and sacks by the door; boxes as tall as me, stuffed with objects. We began to get some of them out. A huge white cuckoo clock emerged from under shredded newspaper, then a set of Russian dolls with fairy tale illustrations on them. We sat on the floor together and set the dolls in a row, trying to work out the story. The decoration on them was exquisite, lurid and fantastical and it went strangely with what Gran had already done. The illustrations were of a girl dressed in a donkey skin. I tried to think back about what the story was about but was distracted by another box that Michael was rooting in. He pulled out a 30-centimetre long, clear glass polar bear.

'Feel the weight of that,' he said, passing it to me by its neck. The shape of the animal was so simple, as though the least amount of bumps and curves had been used to portray the bear. The ears were almost negligible but still perfect. I looked up to see Michael delving into another huge canvas sack, one full of metres and metres of yellow velvet. We pulled it out of the bags and laid it on the floor, then sat in the middle of the pub in this great pool of yellow. It was delightful. Our eyes filled up with yellow as though we were in a field of sunflowers. I stroked the nap of the fabric, it was quality material and I loved the way it changed in the light.

'What do you think she is going to do with this?' Michael asked.

'I don't know.'

We just sat there spellbound and mesmerised by this vast expanse of yellow. We looked at each other shyly. He crawled towards me and held my head. We started to kiss. We heard a cough. It was Gran. The taxi hadn't turned up. She was unembarrassed and so we remained sat where we were, on the material.

'Where did you get this from?' I asked.

'Istanbul, I had it shipped over.'

There was nothing more to say, really. She helped us to fold it up and put it back, then Michael drove us home. Gran sat in the front and I sat in the back. I was able to watch all his movements and angle my head to gaze at the nape of his neck. I could see down the back of his T-shirt where the skin changed colour in gradations from pale to tanned. I stopped asking what it was about him for a moment; just deciding that it must be an extraordinary combination of features. Thick forearms, long fingers, neat feet, pale eyes. None of these features were very interesting in themselves but, together, they produced a cocktail of a person who had intoxicated me.

'What's the story behind the Russian dolls?' Michael asked.

Gran didn't speak.

'The girl with the animal skin on, what's it about?' I prompted.

'A young woman dresses herself in a stinking skin to avoid the attentions of her father.'

We travelled the rest of the distance home in silence. Gran got out, thanked Michael and headed towards the house.

'She hates me.'

'I don't think so,' I said, unconvinced.

'She's saying I'm old enough to be your father.'

I couldn't work it out. It was completely out of character for her to do something so underhand, she wasn't frightened of giving offence. I wasn't going to let her get away with that, so I sought her out in the kitchen.

'What's the meaning of those dolls, did you put them there on purpose?'

'What are you saying, Amanda?'

'Why is trying to humiliate Michael your new game?'

'Sometimes, objects come to people and it's up to individuals to work out their significance.'

'Are you saying that Michael screwing me is like him having sex with his own daughter?'

'They wouldn't have come to his pub if it weren't something for him to sort out. You saw for yourself, the pictures were very clear.'

'But you must have bought them from somewhere. Chosen them. Seen and handled them and said, 'Oh yes, I'll have those'.'

'No, I've never seen them before. Although they sound quite magnificent and, if he doesn't want them, I'll buy them off him.'

'But they came out of a box of things that you chose for the pub.'

'Extraordinary coincidence?' With that, she snapped her book shut and left the room.

*　　*　　*

By the end of the following week, 11 sofas of differing sizes and 16 non-matching armchairs were covered with the same yellow velvet. The floor stayed grey but was barely visible as it was covered with thick black rugs. The huge yellow wall suddenly grew great thick planks of green oak shelving that smelt heavenly. Onto these shelves went the glass polar bear, a family of resin koalas and five candelabras in various states of tarnish, but not the Russian dolls. The huge cuckoo clock hung majestically on the wall over the top of the highest shelf.

Michael handled the objects that went onto the shelves, touching them as if he were frightened of them. 'Won't people steal these things, Cath?'

'Nobody will take them.'

'But they look like collectors' items and this is a pub.'

'They are safe, Michael,' and, with that, she wandered over to the shelves and adjusted the polar bear, moving it dangerously close to the edge of the shelf, as though the animal were looking over a cliff.

'Moving your self-portrait?' I asked.

'Hmmm?' she answered.

'You're a polar bear: solitary, tenacious, terrifying.'

'They certainly survive under the harshest of circumstances,' she replied.

An enormous chandelier arrived, one-metre across, and was hoisted above the yellow furniture. Despite its size, it produced a delicate glow. I squinted up at it and my head was filled with tiny, twinkling lights. Gran had divided the pub between eating and drinking. The eating area was twelve metres by eight, and held seven tables, none of which matched but they had all been painted black.

Mirrors had been hung all over the walls, each one a different shape and size, but all similar in that they were tarnished and battered gilt. Yellow napkins arrived and were set out on the tables. I folded them into thin tall triangles and put them in glasses. From the hundreds of reflections that bounced back at me from the mirrored wall, the napkins looked like a flock of strange yellow birds nesting in the mirrors.

When all was finished, we just stood back and shook our heads. I had never seen anything like it, so friendly and yet so unusual. Gran made the electricians come back and fussed over tiny recessed lights in the wall. She ran her hand over the yellow wall, tutting, and examined the underneath of the chairs and tables in the dining area in minute detail.

The menus arrived. They were black and yellow striped on Gran's homemade paper. There were three starters and six main courses. The food would change seasonally and there would never be more than six choices. No food was to be bought from more than a 15-mile radius of the pub. People came to see us before we opened. Typically of Gran, we still had another few days left before the official opening but the pub was triumphantly and undeniably finished. Harry and Ali came, Bill popped down with Marie when

Gran was at the salvage yard. Everybody was impressed. Who wouldn't be? Even if you didn't care a thing about colour, she had pulled off something so idiosyncratic that no one had seen anything like it before.

Susan came to see it. Michael told me she was coming, so at least I was prepared to see her again. She had bought a red setter puppy and asked if she could bring it in. It struggled in her arms and messed on the floor, sliding manically over metres of roughly cut slate flooring and, finally, it landed in a corner of the dining room. It was a stupid dog and a typical impulse buy. I knew she would never put the time in to train it properly. I was glad of its presence, though, as a distraction when Gran came back unexpectedly.

'Cath, what can I say? The place is a triumph, I never had you down as an interior decorator,' said Susan.

'I just wanted to put something a bit different together and I think I've achieved it,' said Gran.

'You came quite close to owning this place yourself...'

Gran glared.

Susan faltered but she had started to say something and couldn't stop, 'Well, if things had worked out differently between you and James Arlet. If he hadn't died so tragically.' There was more glaring, still Susan continued, 'So, now you bravely tackled the past by taking on this place and putting your own stamp on it. And you are deservedly confident.'

'No one can afford to be too confident these days.'

'What do you mean? This place is going to go down a storm,' Susan smiled at me.

'I mean there is too much grief and suffering in the world which leads me to believe that the overconfident and those who sleep soundly 365 nights a year are, in fact, idiots.'

I offered Susan a drink in an attempt to move her away from Gran. Why could Gran never accept a compliment? There was nothing wrong with what Susan had said. She had delivered a generous sentence or two, why couldn't Gran just shut up and revel for a moment in the yellowness and curiosities that she had brought together?

But Susan didn't seem keen to accept my offer of being airlifted away from the voice of bitterness. She declined my olive branch and her body movements told me she was up for a fight with Gran. She wasn't prepared to let this one go. I thought I would stand around for a little longer and, if it all became too much, I could walk away or play with the dog. They were both grown-ups, after all.

'Cath, what you have just said sounds almost religious. I never had you down as a religious woman, even though you have *The Book of Job* carousel in your garden.'

'Call it what you like, but I call it awareness of the fragility of life, our relationships, our status, all comes and goes quickly. It's always good to keep that at the forefront of your mind and you won't go far wrong.'

I shuffled and looked down. Where was that dog?

'But Cath, with that argument you are making Amanda's life a misery, how is she ever going to live for the moment, be spontaneous and happy?'

'Spontaneity is overrated. Happiness nonsense.'

Michael, with one deft and beautiful movement, came between them as though he had thrown the remnants of the yellow velvet over their cages to stop them from twittering. Somehow, it worked and an uneasy silence replaced the bickering.

'Let me show you upstairs, Susan. There are three guest rooms and rooms for the staff,' I said.

She shot me a look and glared at what I was wearing before smiling. 'Delightful, Amanda, and then let's have that drink.'

She wanted to ask me something, I could sense it. We stopped halfway up the stairs and looked out of the window to the quay. The tide was out and the mud lay flat and waiting.

'It's an extraordinary place, you have done so well, Amanda, to end up as the manager here with no formal qualifications. I'm afraid I wouldn't be able to employ you in my factory without the appropriate NVQs.'

'Cake-making really wouldn't interest me.'

'No, it requires a delicate touch.'

I let that one pass. I could see her looking at the heels on my shoes. I could feel her eyes all over me as I walked up the stairs. It seemed as though the kindness I had received from her as a child was unquestionably over now that I had grown up and become competition. Any hopes of us returning to the past were futile and no good would come from my dwelling on this. I swiftly showed her the guest rooms with en-suites. I showed her Michael's flat and the two rooms that were set aside for staff to stay in or unexpected guests. She lingered in Michael's flat, although there was little to see. He didn't want Gran to decorate it and said he couldn't care less as long as it had a bed and a sink. It was white and pristine, waiting for Michael to stamp his personality on it. Although there was no bed in his room, Susan came over all coy when we went in there, averting her eyes as though she had seen something unsavoury. But I couldn't get her out of the living room, nor his spare room.

'What's this room going to be, a dining room?'

'A guest bedroom, I think.'

'For whom?'

'His daughter, I suppose.' I felt like being rude but I had to make up for the dove incident.

'Does he see much of her?'

'Not much, she's grown up, he mostly goes down to London to see her.'

'She's only 18, isn't she, or have I got that wrong? That's hardly grown up.'

I wanted Susan out of my territory. 'The tour is complete, you've seen all there is to see, let's go downstairs and drink to good times for the pub and success for all of us.'

'Why not?' she asked begrudgingly.

Finally, Susan left, Gran left, and Michael and I were alone. He put his arms around me, 'This is some place we've got here.'

'It looks fabulous.'

He saw a puddle on the floor. 'That dog of Susan's is a baby substitute if ever I saw one.'

We went upstairs to bed, leaving the urine to evaporate.

* * *

I started to stay at the pub. I only popped home every few days to get more clothes and to pretend to be polite to Gran and Bill. But my mind was elsewhere. I loved that place before it opened and we had 12 idyllic days together. On the seventh day, I was potting up sunflowers in great white stone planters that would go in front of the pub when I saw a man coming down the concrete slope. A father-shaped man, a man free from bubble wrap. During the last few months, he must have disentangled himself. I had stopped doing the visualisation last time I was rude to him, so that would explain things.

I wiped the soil on my trousers before I held out my hand to him. He looked haggard and was so much taller than I was that he had to do a little curtsey to reach my fingers.

'That's kind of you, Amanda. I know I don't deserve civilities.'

'I don't know what to say to you or how to start this conversation. We are strangers. All I know about you is what Gran has told me about the Doons.'

'My father hates your grandmother. I'm not entirely sure why, it doesn't make any sense.'

'They knew each other here. Do you think something happened between them?'

'This place has seen some sad times, James Arlet dying and that girl drowning, all within the space of a month.'

'What girl drowning?'

'One of the bar staff, Josephine Flower. She died after a night of heavy drinking.'

'Gran's never mentioned that.'

I moved the conversation away from this news because I didn't know this man at all and wanted to hear the truth from Gran.

'Your mother and I were very young when we met. When she became pregnant, I sent one letter, but then I allowed myself to be influenced by my father. I took his advice, which was to leave her alone. I waited for months for her to contact me. I kidded myself that, if she did, I would have the strength to stand up to him, but she never did get in touch.'

He spoke so quietly and firmly that I felt the first glow of warmth towards him. I couldn't believe that he was my father, apart from some obvious physical similarities, our hair colour and eyelashes. He had not had anything to do with my upbringing but was now showing persistence in seeking me out again, and I would try to be polite to him. I didn't care that he hadn't been around all the time. It didn't matter. I was here with Michael and I could afford to be generous to stragglers.

I got two chairs from the pub and we sat on the quay. He didn't say much for a while, just circled his ankle, 'I always thought that I would have other children and that I could put the knowledge of you in a cupboard and largely ignore it.'

'And?'

'And I've realised that I will not have any more children. I've just left my almost third wife.'

'Why was she your almost-wife?'

'Because I have left with half the build-up to a wedding – dresses and suits ordered, food piling high, cream invitations. A vicar standing by, a man my father had in his pocket who agreed to give us a church blessing. What do you call that? Profound belief in humanity or just a man battered by my father's gruesome charm?'

'What about the feelings of the almost-wife? You haven't mentioned her.'

'Oh, I'm doing her a favour. She didn't know the man she was going to marry. *I* don't know him.' He looked agitated and in need of a few good meals. I felt well-fed and relaxed in contrast. He asked if we could meet on a regular basis.

I wasn't offended by what he had said about the 'other children'. I was struck by his honesty. And, anyway, he was here now wasn't he? Trying to make amends.

'I never thought for a moment that Cath would know where I was, let alone allow you to contact me.' He spoke gently, almost hopefully, and I was moved by something in him; an unexpected straightforwardness, coupled with sensitivity.

'Why now?' I asked.

'Oh, you'll think this is mad, but I had a recurrent dream about a blackbird calling your name.'

I gave him my mobile number. We arranged to meet in three days for an hour. He would come down here again. The next time he turned up, things were a little easier. In the course of our conversation, he even managed a few jokes. I thought we had plenty of time on our hands and that ours would be a slow getting to know one another.

I timed our meetings for when Gran wasn't here. We decided that, if she were to arrive unexpectedly, he would just get up, walk away from me and drive off. There were so many people milling around that she would never notice him.

Looking at his face outside in the bright sunlight on our second formal meeting, I tried to work out how old he was; he looked a little older than my mother. He had taken three weeks off work and, each time he appeared, he seemed a little more relaxed. His hair was growing at great speed and, sometimes, he even had a little stubble. He was pointy-faced and quite good-looking, I supposed. His best feature was his hair, washed or unwashed and, regardless of length, it fell in a perfect sweep as though each individual hair was choreographed. One of his eyelids had a big scar on it. The ugliness suited him and gave him something of a pirate quality, especially as he was getting more relaxed in his dress sense with each meeting.

'I'll have to go back to work next week. I work for my father as a production manager in one of his businesses. He abandoned medicine years ago but still likes to be known as Doctor. Maybe we could meet in the evenings?'

'Why do you have to go back to work?' I knew he wasn't short of money, so there was no sense to what he was saying. He shrugged and looked shocked.

'What would I do?' he asked. Quite how he thought I could give careers advice to a man in his late-thirties was bizarre but I was touched by his asking me.

'There must be people who can do your job and you said you had enough money,' I said.

'Will you ever forgive me for that letter?'

I ignored him and went to fetch us a couple of beers. When I came back, I carried on with my plans for him, I hadn't meant to refer to the letter at all.

'Travel the world. Grow your hair long. Gran told me how beautiful your hair was and what a free spirit you were when you were about my age.'

'And look what's become of me, in my father's sway for almost 40 years. I don't suppose your grandmother will ever forgive me.'

'For leaving Marie?' I asked.

'For leaving both of you.'

'Marie's done all right.'

'Yes, I know.'

I started to tell him about The Marie Furnish Centre for Anger Management and Zak but stopped mid-sentence. There was something vulnerable about him today, I had been right to wrap him in bubble wrap in the first place. No wonder that specific material had come to mind.

'I bumped into her,' he said with some hesitation.

'You've seen Marie?'

He didn't answer, just hung his head.

'Did you think she had changed?' I asked, genuinely curious to know what he would make of my mother after 19 years. I began to make little triangle shapes in a pool of spilt beer whilst nervously waiting for an answer. Change that thought.

176

'No.'

'Oh, come on, she must have done; 19 years is a long time.'

'She looked just the same to me. Marie Furnish, sharp as a knife.'

Seeing me talking to another man, Michael blew me a kiss from the pub door. I stood up to give my father the hint to leave but, seeing his face, I agreed to meet again next week, texting him when the coast was clear. He said that he would take another month off. It was his life and he could do what he liked. I was amused to think of him taking advice about his future from a virtual stranger.

X

An Unexpected Friendship

IDECIDED that moving one piece of clothing at a time into Michael's pub hardly constituted moving in and I had a question for Gran, so I popped back home to fetch a lime green trainer.

'Here's your other shoe,' she said.

'Oh, thanks, but I'll just take the one with me today.'

'Keeping a foot in both camps?'

'Funny, you should join the circus! Why stop at interior decorating?' Then I remembered what my father had said. 'I heard about a girl drowning at The Tide when you worked there.'

'She was a complete sap. Another of Doon's stooges. The cold killed her.'

'A common cold?'

'Don't be ludicrous, Amanda, she was drunk and waded into the water in November. I assume she submerged herself for some time, without swimming to warm up so, when she did try to swim, she went under, breathed in water and drowned.'

'That must have been awful.'

'Absolutely not. I never liked her, head full of sawdust. She reminds me of that girl you used to work with.'

'Ali?'

She made no reply.

'How can you be so heartless about someone's death? You worked with her didn't you?'

'Our acquaintance was casual, just like having to see Doon in the course of my work, but they were nothing to me.'

I stared at her.

'What?' she asked, 'What do you want from me? Remorse? She was a grown woman, entirely responsible for her own demise.'

'What about Arlet? He drank himself to death, he also caused his own demise.'

'That's different. He struggled with life.'

'We all struggle.'

'It's incremental.'

'So, the girl, Josephine, was full of sawdust and not worth anyone's pity, whereas a socially dysfunctional landlord is?'

'He was never socially dysfunctional. Quite the opposite.'

'More details, please.'

'The devil's in the detail. Now, here is your other shoe, take it.'

I could cope with being away from her because I still got to see her in the day as she gave orders to the final few people and signed for packages and parcels. She quibbled over the cost of things and continued to check the workmanship, although the main room in the pub was completely finished and looked extraordinary. But there was a feeling that things wouldn't go on like this for ever, she was certainly winding down, like a clockwork animal.

'Are we going to have any curtains or blinds?' Michael asked Gran.

'No, nothing, I want people to see that particular stretch of the river when the moon is full. You could even set up a table and chairs and serve people on a mudbank.'

'We'd never get past health and safety with that,' said Michael.

I questioned what was behind Gran's idea of making something inviting for the public. She was, after all, a woman who had spent a lifetime trying to create a force field around herself and her home in order to keep out other people. She must have accessed a part of herself that she had kept hidden up to this point and I questioned why she had really decided to renovate the pub. I guessed that this was a way of letting go of the past but something else must have motivated her. She had managed the project of Michael's pub brilliantly; coming in just under budget and seeming to have enjoyed herself at the same time. Admittedly, it might not have looked to other people like she was having the time of her life, but I could tell that she was.

While Michael was still dithering about the name of the pub, a sign had arrived, simply saying The Tide in blue neon, the name it had always had. My eyes widened and I wondered if Gran had finally gone too far but Michael just shrugged and it was put up over the outside bar. The other sign on the road entrance to the pub would stay the same but the paint would be touched up by another of Gran's cronies. I was looking up at the neon sign, feeling hopeful for the future and wishing the day away, wanting the evening light to show those illuminated letters to their best effect when Gran came downstairs from talking to the electrician.

'Your mother is at the police station.'

My first thought was that she must be delivering anger management training and, if that were the case, what was the meaning of the scary face?

'She has hit your father.'

'How hard?' I don't know why I said that but it just came out. 'Was it a tap, a flick, a brush?' I needed details for some unfathomable reason, probably to make it real.

'Hard enough to break a bone,' she said.

I didn't say a thing, just stared at her. We were both in shock. Next thing I knew, Gran had begun her own monologue which was not really addressed to me.

'All the times I have stared at your mother's scrawny little arms and known she would never do anything physical for a living and there she was, harbouring astonishing strength.'

'Marie is at the police station?'

'Yes.'

'We must go down there. Now!' I said.

'No.'

'What?'

'She's fine. We have to go to the hospital.'

'Why?'

'Your father. Damage limitation. Amanda, please, get in the car and drive.'

'I've got to go to Marie.'

Her voice dropped an octave, 'Come with me if you want to help your mother.'

We got into Marie's car and, after eight minutes of winding lanes, we reached a B-road. Ten minutes later, we passed a junction which would take us to the town where my mother lived or straight to the police station where she was incarcerated. Before I could drive, I never thought about how isolated we were and how difficult it was to get away from where we lived. My thoughts turned to my mother and how it was hard to imagine anyone less likely to be in custody. She must be holding herself in and trying to avoid touching the stains on the walls; checking any seat she was offered before she sat on it.

Under Gran's command, I drove past the sign, missing the turning and treacherously headed on towards the hospital. The car felt sluggish and unresponsive as if appalled by this latest act of disloyalty towards Marie. Gran had her lunchbox with her and she clutched at the recycled plastic like a talisman. It was only half past 10 in the morning. How long did she think all this was going to take? We drove silently most of the way to the hospital and were approaching the outskirts of the town and heading up the steep hill to the hospital when I slowed down, as we were entering an urban area.

'Get a move on, Amanda.'

'There's a 30 speed limit.'

'I need to speak to him before he goes to theatre.'

'Theatre?'

'To assess the damage to his brow bone.'

We turned into the street close to the hospital and she directed me vigorously into the emergency spaces outside A & E.

'I don't think we should be parking here. These spaces are for ambulances. I'd better just drive us to the official car park.'

'Stay where you are and put on the air conditioning,' she said.

Taking up a space reserved for ambulances was one thing but air conditioning? I paraphrased her speech about it in my head like a mantra to keep me calm, 'Another devilish device to disconnect us from the rhythm of the seasons; invented for scented, sweatless, sugar-filled layabouts with no human smell left to them.'

I looked at her to see if I had misheard or if she had gone completely mad. My lips started to form words of opposition about turning on the air conditioning but, one glare later, I had forgotten what I was going to say and swiftly turned the dial to max.

She sat there for three minutes, cooling down, putting her face close to the vent. Stray strands of hair blew out past her ears like one of those scary fans with pretty-coloured ribbons that stream out, warning you not to poke your fingers through the mesh. Then, without a word, she entered the hospital building and was gone for 25 minutes. She came back with her arms full of sweets and crisps and fizzy drinks that she must have got from a machine and, saying nothing, she got back into the car and started eating the crisps, slowly, delicately. After three single crisps, she turned the packet over, looked at the ingredients and sighed, dropping the bag on the floor. Her falafel salad reeking of garlic languished on the back seat of the car.

Then she said, 'Let's go home, I've seen him and told him what I think.'

'What do you think? Because I'm not sure I know any more. You're behaving so out of character.' I forgot to ask how my father was.

'I told your father I'd be back tomorrow,' she said, completely ignoring my question. I don't know why I had momentarily forgotten that she was above being asked to supply reasons for her actions.

Every day, I drove her to the hospital. I didn't go in and see him, I was not allowed to do that. Only she could go in. She went every day for five days at the same time in the afternoon. Michael had been supportive and encouraged both of us to go to the hospital. It didn't make any difference to Gran because she had finally finished at the pub but I needed to be there. Gran gave me the bare information about my father, saying he couldn't speak because of the pain and swelling going from his left eye all the way down his face, but that he could write quite quickly.

'What does he write?' I asked.

'"She must pay".'

'Oh.'

I wished that I had never asked. I wondered if he were going to do anything crazy like press charges against my mother. I had already spoken to her briefly on the phone where she sounded calm but drugged. There had been no enthusiasm in her voice. She didn't talk about what she had done, didn't even refer to it, even though I had arranged to meet her at her flat the day after the event. She hadn't mentioned anything about the police station except that they didn't keep her long and a friend had turned up to get her out. Not Zak, but a friend.

Gran continued speaking about my father, 'He writes his letters like an attacked man. His writing is the equivalent of hands put up to protect the face, with venomous spikes on the Ts and Fs.'

'Is he going to destroy Marie's career at The Marie Furnish Centre for Anger Management?'

'What was it like in there, by the way?' she asked.

'Is he really going to try and destroy Marie? Is that what he means by "She must pay"?'

Gran looked indifferent and repeated her question, 'What was the Centre for Anger Management like?'

'It made me feel seasick. All blue and green and supposedly soothing but, just like a doctor's surgery, it had the opposite effect. It was the institutional equivalent of trying too hard to be cheerful at Christmas.'

'You've never been in to doctor's surgery.'

I didn't tell her that I had recently visited one to go on The Pill. 'It's like I'd imagine one to look. If this gets out, I suppose Marie's reputation is at stake,' I added quickly.

'It's out, Amanda.'

Gran continued to give me the minimal information about my father's condition and two nights running, after dropping her off, I went back to The Tide and Michael where we spent our evenings tidying, drinking or having sex. And, in those day-to-day activities, I managed to forget what was happening to my parents. But not for long. I spoke to my mother on the phone.

'Zak has taken the sign down. It is no longer to be The Marie Furnish Centre for Anger Management. He is going to use his own name.'

'Oh.'

'Everything is over for me.'

'Maybe you weren't supposed to walk into that building,' I spoke without thinking.

'You sound like Cath, from whom I haven't heard by the way. Although, why I should expect her to come up trumps at this stage in my life, I can't imagine. That's the thing with parents, though. You never stop hoping.'

I invited her down to the pub, thinking she would never accept but would prefer to stay at home for a few days, licking her wounds. Half an hour later, she arrived. I guided her into the pub. She looked at the décor with a frown. I sat her down on one of the yellow sofas, it emphasised the unusual sallowness of her skin. All those times when she had pretended that she was not angry or sought a logical explanation for something that was annoying her, the muscles in her arms must have twitched. And, with years of involuntary twitching, hundreds of times a day, she had developed muscles of immense power. The very same muscles which had allowed her to hit my father so hard whilst claiming to be a peacemaker.

'After nearly 19 years, he just walked up to me and began a conversation, as if those years had never taken place. All that I have struggled to become, all my qualifications.' Tears dripped down her face, 'And he asked me to interpret a dream.' She laughed bitterly.

'What kind of dream?'

'What does it matter what kind of dream?' she snapped. The whole world had gone mad and was turning against her. I stood up and put a hand on her shoulder. She smiled and shook her head, 'Something to do with a bird – a crow or similar.'

'How outrageous,' I said.

The day John (I could no longer see a point in the future when I would call him Dad) was due to come out of hospital, I drove Gran through streets of grey houses as usual, some of them set back on steep hills and all with tiered gardens to make them safer, to the hospital at the top of the hill.

'Why are you visiting on the day he is coming out?' I asked, uninterested. My mind was still on Michael and being in bed with him. I smiled to myself in anticipation of much more sex to come.

'He's coming home with us,' she said.

'Thank God, I'm living at the pub!' I spluttered.

'There's still a place for you at home.'

'Don't you think it's a bit disloyal to Marie?'

'On the contrary, this was inevitable. You must never set yourself up as something, it's just inviting fate to take a swipe at you.'

'What if you are an expert in some area, like she is?'

'Being an expert is one thing, but pretending you have the answers is another. People never learn.'

'Learn what?'

'To stop moralising.'

I stared at her, shaking my head. I was grateful that I was returning to Michael and some level of normality. Soon, I would be wrapped around him, drowning in his smell, up close to his flat belly and muscular chest and none of this would matter.

My father came out of the hospital door. Head cast down, eye patch on, a carrier bag in each hand, expensive coat betraying him by looking like it belonged to another man. Hair bedraggled and the unpatched eye black from the impact of the blow. Gran leapt out of the car and scurried him into the front seat, taking his bags from him.

He hardly said a word during the journey back but stared straight ahead, his eye fixed on the road. We stopped off at a garage along the way to fill up with fuel. After I had paid the surly fat woman and stepped back outside, I passed the plastic newspaper stall with scratched see-through covers to protect the papers and allow everyone to make their choice. Then I saw it. My mother on the front page of one of the tabloids.

'Anger management specialist breaks ex-lover's brow.' 'Former TV star, Marie Furnish...' The word 'former' went round and round in my head and started forming into a song. The wind, bitter and edgy, whizzed round the wind tunnel that was the garage and tried to shake the papers in my hand, encouraging me to read on. But I had seen enough.

For want of anything better to do, and from a sense of loyalty to my mother and grievance towards my father, I started to tear the front pages carefully from the seven or so papers that remained in the holder. No one came to stop me but Gran and John could see what I was doing from the car. John watched me for a few moments with his mouth open and then slumped down in the car so I couldn't see his face. It was futile. I screwed them all up and stuffed them into an empty space where the more popular papers had all been sold. Still, no one said a thing. The woman inside the petrol station glanced up but even she cared nothing for the papers' destruction. She wasn't going to step outside in this vicious wind in a nylon uniform with a great gap between her trouser band and the end of her tunic. Life was harsh enough without unnecessary draughts down your back. Gran was stony silent and John just looked ahead. He must have grassed on Marie. The rat.

I stopped calling him John. He didn't deserve it. Neither could he be referred to as my father so, for simplicity's sake, I called him Biological. That about summed up his involvement in my life, his usefulness was over years ago. I dropped them off at home and didn't wait to see Gran guide him safely into the house but sped off up the lane. Twenty minutes later, I could breathe again and was sitting by the river, just watching the trees and the water plod by. Michael came up to me with a cup of tea. I was thinking out loud.

'Biological has ruined my mother's career.'

186

Michael nuzzled up to me and slipped a hand under my jumper. 'She can get another job.'

'She is the Happy Lady and she's just punched somebody in the face, what openings do you think might be available to her?' I hadn't finished at all but was just getting a taste for catastrophe. 'What if this place is cursed? You know what happened to Arlet. Yes, it's beautiful but what if that isn't enough? I'm starting to think it's creepy here. Why wasn't it let for almost 38 years? What about that girl drowning?'

'Every stretch of water in the country will have had someone drown in it and Arlet was just another landlord who couldn't keep his hands off the bottles.'

He guided my hand to his crotch and I laughed.

* * *

The next day, I was restless at the pub. My mother's car keys dug into my thigh through my jeans pocket. I was itching to go and see Gran and needed her reassurance. She always put things right, however harshly she did it. She always managed to resolve a situation and move forward. So I went home on the pretext of fetching a sock. The door was open, so I let myself in. I walked along the corridor into my bedroom, thinking that I would go and find Gran in a minute and have a cup of tea with her.

My bedroom door was shut. I didn't give it much thought but just opened it. Biological was in my bed staring up at the ceiling with his unpatched eye. I rattled my chest of drawers to make a point, startling him and, grabbing what I wanted, headed off to find Gran. She was in the garden, turning over the compost. I didn't get too close because, being at the pub, I'd got used to different smells and conditions than I'd had at home. I had to shout a little to make her stop doing what she was doing. She had a rhythm going, graceful and strong.

'What's he doing in my room?' I demanded.

'You tell me. I assume you've just been in there.'

'Why can't he recuperate in the kitchen or, better still, in his own home?'

She stuck the fork in the compost and came towards me. 'He won't be here for long.'

'How can you be sure?'

She stared at me.

'Maybe he'll take a fancy to staring at the ceiling and doing nothing all day,' I said.

'I know this is your house and that you are not happy with him being here, but you must trust me on this one.'

Everything was moving just a little too fast for me. I stropped back to the pub, Michael was there to comfort me and I helped out in the kitchen. The whole place had a different feel to it. All the temporary workers who had been around for months were gradually pulling out. The painters and decorators, electricians and carpenters, kitchen fitters all started to disappear, even Gran. She had stopped coming down so much, even before the Biological incident. She'd finished, but I felt her there in the yellow walls and I bathed in the yellowness, breathed it in and it comforted me.

Permanent people replaced the ones who had recently travelled in and out of my life. Bar staff, including the twins, Jake and Dan, two lanky 20-year-olds who would pull in a younger crowd. They were show-offs and would work well behind the bar, as well as being easy on the eye. One was much better-looking than the other and I wondered why they stayed together so slavishly.

Michael had employed a female chef called Dawn. She was motherly in a predictable way and I took advantage of what she offered because it was not what I was used to. She was plump and reassuringly cheerful.

There were only nine dishes on offer when we first opened and they were liable to change at any moment, depending on what was seasonal and readily available from a radius of 15 miles. I wondered whether people were ready to have some of their choices limited but Gran had persuaded Michael that they were and he, in turn, had persuaded Dawn. It was odd to hear them reiterating Gran's arguments. It made me think that she should have come out into the world sooner and influenced more people. Dawn and Michael were almost evangelical.

'People can only eat what's available. They'll have to get used to the idea,' said Michael.

'Gone are the days when we can fly tomatoes in from Spain,' Dawn chipped in.

We would start with four meat, two fish and three vegetarian dishes. In order to make myself indispensable, and keep the pub going no matter what, I worked in the kitchen alongside Dawn and learnt to cook the dishes myself. The food that she produced under Michael's guidance was, like her, no frills. All the permanent people wanted to know about us, especially Dawn. She questioned me in the kitchen about my relationship with Michael and, sometimes, I felt odd answering. But, most of the time, I was so happy, I just blurted things out and Dawn nodded and smiled.

'As long as you're both happy it's nobody's business but your own.'

She sniffed. She always sniffed after a pronouncement. I had the feeling that Gran might say she was interfering but I liked the warmth she gave off and her physical closeness, she was a great hugger and toucher of people.

Those idyllic days when Michael and I did what we wanted were over. If we wanted to have sex, we had to go upstairs discreetly. Anything else would have been unprofessional. He was the owner and I was his partner. People, apart from Dawn, kept a discreet distance from me but remained friendly.

I practised for hours in the kitchen with Dawn to see how the pub would run. I made notes and rehearsed every last detail. Like Michael, my clothes clung to me. I smelt of cooking. It was in my hair and on my skin. I was brown, slightly plump and oily. I gleamed. Relaxing a little after the week's events, I stopped looking in the mirror so much because I was too busy. I was truly engrossed and largely distracted from the chaos between my parents. When Michael and I walked upstairs at night, I was heavy with contentment. Sometimes, I had to drag myself up the stairs but it was a good tiredness. A sense of achievement went with it and I knew that Michael was pleased with my efforts. Occasionally, we ate alone in the kitchen, finishing off something Dawn and I had made in the day. But, mostly, there were other people around, getting used to the idea of us opening. I didn't always want them around.

'Why can't we have our meals upstairs?'

'No way, I can't create an environment of them and us,' Michael replied.

The truth was, he loved having other people around, the more the merrier. He hadn't made a big thing in the press about the opening. We wanted to open quietly and build up slowly. He said there was no rush. It was early June and we could take a month before the holiday season would be on us. Then, it would be our busiest time and we would be working flat out until the end of August. He thought we had enough time to prepare.

I went to see my mother again. All my fears for her were allayed. Her flat was pristine and her face contorted slightly as a few of my biscuit crumbs hit the floor. She glanced quickly between the crumbs and the kitchen bin, wishing for a sudden eddy of air which might swoop up the offending bits and carry them triumphantly to their destiny. But then she remembered that she didn't do annoyed and concentrated on me again to distract herself. She seemed positive again and I marvelled at how quickly she had turned the situation involving my father to her own advantage.

'What are you going to do?' I asked her.

'I'm in negotiations with a television production company.'

'Wow, will it be similar to the *Happy Lady* show?'

'Not exactly.'

'What is it, then?'

'Initially, I'm going to put forth my side of the story and then, after several days have elapsed, attempt to make a comeback.'

'Days?'

'I must take advantage of the publicity.'

She amazed me. She was one of those creatures that, no matter what happened to them, could morph into something else, as though the evolutionary process would happen faster to her than it could to any of the rest of us. Her ability to move on and make the best of a situation was astounding. I was grateful.

'What will your comeback involve?'

'Being filmed going through my own anger management programme alongside the other clients.'

Speechless, I continued my visiting schedule by calling in on Gran and Biological. I wanted to let Gran know that Marie would be okay. Seeing my mother normal again had made me feel slightly less aggrieved towards Biological. She *had* smacked him in the face after all. I told Gran what Marie had said to me about a potential comeback.

'She has what it takes to bend the public's opinion to her own advantage,' said Gran.

'What do you mean?'

'She's conniving and has no sense of privacy.'

'Don't you think she's doing well to get up and start again?' I implored.

'Some people will always rise from excrement smelling floral, whilst those of us unwilling to manipulate the community will for ever flounder in muck.'

I frowned, unable to make sense of her last words but could tell she was in no mood to explain herself.

I visited again two days later. John (I had stopped calling him Biological) was polishing the carousel and Gran was bottling something in the kitchen but kept glancing out of the window to check on the shine of her beloved machine. I walked up to the carousel. This would be easy. This machine was my territory and not his. I put a hand on the crocodile's head for protection and started up a conversation with him.

'Marie's going to be all right,' I said sharply.

'Cath said that but hearing it from you is confirmation. I can't tell you how sorry I am for what I did.'

'How long do you think you'll stay?' I blurted out. We seemed to be done with the niceties that had been the basis of our relationship back when we started meeting at the pub.

'Quite a while,' he answered.

He saw my face.

'Any time you want your room back, you can have it. I will sleep in the garden if necessary but I just need to be around your grandmother for a little longer. Did you know I refused to see her when she first came to the hospital? I could barely see but I scrawled stupid little notes to the hospital staff, saying that "She must pay".'

'*Gran* must pay?'

'Yes, she confessed to me about forging that letter to your mother when we were both 18.'

Gran had always been entirely open to me about forging the letter. She had sworn that Doons and Furnishs were utterly incompatible and that she was doing Marie a tremendous favour, for which my mother would thank her in the future.

John continued, 'Now I see it doesn't matter that she wrote the letter. I would never have had the courage to move in with your mother and raise you. I didn't have the spine to stand up to my father then, but I do now.'

'Why do you need to stand up to him now? Over your near-miss marriage?'

'Everything: my job, my choice of lifestyle, his version of the truth.'

'What's that then?'

'I'll tell you when I finally winkle it all out of your grandmother.'

He would be here for some time, then.

Climbing onto the carousel, I moved clockwise around the animals, slowly taking my time to say hello to all of them. The vultures, the goats, the ostrich, the bear and her cubs, Behemoth the hippo, the antelope, the ox, the hawk, the lioness, the war horse and, lastly, Leviathan the crocodile. I stood by the heavy iron gates which were supposed to represent The Gates of Death and ran my fingers comfortably along the hundreds of tiny engraved skulls and bones. I thought I saw John flinch.

Gran had turned on the carousel from the house and was heading down towards us with a tray on which were glasses and some of her wine. But John left us to it. Gran and I watched his gangly walk up the slope towards the house.

'He didn't do it,' she said.

'What?'

'Grass on your mother.'

'Who did, then?'

XI

Susan Rink is No Longer 'That Woman'

THE GRAND opening. The day arrived, as all things do. The new people and the temporary staff that we had hired for the day congregated in awkward little groups, whispering or talking too loudly. Michael was the worst offender of all as he rushed back and forth through the bar, creating his own mini hurricane; spinning around the people who had arrived with the sandwiches and canapés, nodding at their superior knowledge about how many nibbles one person might eat in a two-hour stretch. It all sounded spurious to me. Who was this networking, twice-round-the-room, six-small-sandwich-eating creature?

I needed to get away from everyone as I was picking up on their anxiety and anticipation and I had enough of my own, so I went upstairs slowly and walked into the guest bedrooms looking for comfort. I stroked the towels in the rooms, fluffy, pale and untouched by bodies. Lying on the double beds, I thought of all the people who would sleep in those beds and leave some kind of imprint. I hoped that all the people who slept there would have reasonable dreams.

Abruptly, a more Gran-like voice took over. 'Don't be so puerile, of course people will suffer in these beds. Since when did being able to stay in a place like this protect you from disease or grief? There will be no warning when it comes. Creeping up your path, slipping into bed with you, gazing unmoved out of the window whilst running a cold professional hand over your throat. Or, worse still, slipping noiselessly away, allowing you to think you've got away with it, until you see it is clutching the pitiful thing that was once your health – or your child – in its arms. No one will escape a visit.' I told the Gran-like voice to be silent. I started to feel panicky, hopped off the bed and stared accusingly at the comfortable mattress and fluffy towels. They would offer no substantial relief. In fact, their newness and softness might just serve to taunt.

The room became darker and smaller like an enclosing tomb and I sat there hopelessly, waiting for the next volley of vile thoughts. Then, Michael came bounding up the stairs and into the guest bedroom where I sat. His appearance in the room grounded me and I grabbed him, throwing my arms around him and pulling him down on the bed, wanting more of his life-affirming smell and taste. But, as I buried my head in his neck, he sat up, then pulled me up.

He looked relaxed, a man who was not questioning the possible success of his project. Whose mind didn't stray into areas that were off limits, areas of pain and suffering.

'I've nearly done it,' he said.

'Yes?'

'It's just about to kick off.' And, with that, he was gone, taking the last word of his sentence with him.

I stayed in the room, looking out of the window and watched Michael greeting the musicians. He waited until they were set up on the quay, then he started to walk back to the pub, picking up a piece of compost from one of the sunflower-filled pots and crumbling it in his hand. He looked up and waved me down with exaggerated arm movements. I decided not to mention how I felt responsible for the dreams of complete strangers who were yet to set foot in these rooms, especially as we weren't going to start offering the B & B until the pub was up and running. I left the fluffy towels to their own devices and went back downstairs.

We were to open at twelve o'clock: lunchtime. Both doors were open so that people could come in from the road if they chose. Giving away free snacks was a predictable way to encourage stray folk to wander down to us, but it worked. The band had started before anyone arrived. I thought it was good that they had begun and relaxed a little. I was supposed to be showing interested parties upstairs, local business people who were looking for places to entertain their clients. We expected about a hundred people and had six bar staff and five waiters all ready to go. Half an hour before it opened, we all stood about, staring at one another, our nerves on edge. I was fiddling with my hands. Michael was distracted.

Then Gran turned up, walking slowly down the concrete slope, wearing shoes that I had never seen before and one of Bill's jackets pulled in at the waist with my brown belt. It was one of the many things of mine that were still at home. She looked perfect, brown with just the right amount of lines and, suddenly, I noticed the sky was blue and there was just a slight breeze, a perfect day. She was 30 minutes early, magnificently, admirably, brilliantly early. We could have kissed her. Both Michael and I leapt on her. She was lost in the crush of people attempting to ram canapés and drinks down her throat. Her presence calmed us and she stayed until the first of the other guests turned up and then she disappeared. The last I saw of her, until later that day, was her staring out over the mud. I was just about to go up to her and see if she was all right when at least 15 people arrived together in close clusters.

More and more people arrived. What had we started? The reality of it dawned on me, my privacy was now largely gone. I was tied to this place and would be known by these people whether I liked it or not. The chat that flew around the room was nonsense but necessary nonsense, I supposed.

At first, I was tempted to flick it off in irritation but then I thought about Gran's views on polite conversation, 'Making noise to drown out the sound of death's boots.'

She would always laugh raucously after a pronouncement like that and I sniggered to myself at the idea of her being there at the pub on that afternoon, being forced into conversation. Except she wouldn't be coerced, she would simply walk away. I thought about people jangling their tongues, just letting them go for no apparent reason. I had recently learnt to do it myself quite successfully and would take no notice of Gran. I would have to be proficient at it to work at the pub and not everyone could be as self-contained as Cath Furnish. Most people are terrified of silence.

I had discovered another reason why people rattled their tongues – you had to in order to keep people at bay. You needed to offer a fictional self that people could latch on to, like laying down a false scent, otherwise you would find yourself exposed and vulnerable to attack.

Once I had counted 26 people, I was busy enough to stop counting. As I showed local business people the bedrooms, I was grateful for the speech I had rehearsed, complete with inane grinning at appropriate moments, and launched into it with enthusiasm. As the words slipped out, they began to lose their meaning and I could have been speaking any language. I hung around whilst prospective clients took their turn running hands along the fluffy towels and inspecting the quality of the shower fittings.

I felt grown up. I *was* grown up. I had a strong sense of my own abilities and had forgiven myself for minor crimes in the past. I felt tough and invincible and no longer responsible for the happiness or otherwise of the world. Those thoughts that had plagued me moments ago no longer made sense. What sort of person would think up something like that? It had just been a passing bit of darkness, cloudlike in its intensity. I was not to make too much of it, it was merely the result of living with Gran.

She had taught me many good things but there was no need for me to inherit her gloom-mongering when I could cast it off, hand it back to her, saying, 'Thanks, but, after careful consideration, I have chosen a life free from oppressive dark thoughts and ruthless honesty. Although I admire your relentless and fruitless questioning, I'm afraid that I don't have the disposition for it and would rather live happily.'

Susan arrived with a group of friends to whom I had probably been introduced over the years. Some of them looked vaguely familiar. The women had a certain look about them, as if they were holding back time, and the effort of this was causing great strain on their faces, unnatural tautness in some cases. Two of them were very brown for the time of year but, unlike my own cack-handed applications of fake tan, theirs were seamless. I went behind the bar to observe them better, taking a tray of dirty glasses with me.

I had gulped down a glass of Champagne and now I was able to watch Susan and her acquaintances from behind this beautiful barricade that Gran had sourced and organised to be placed here, specifically to protect me. The group of three women were talking, but looking around to see who was coming through both doors, heads twisting like owls. One woman would comment on an item of clothing or watch that the other had bought, it would then be held out so the other friends could see it properly. Then, the conversation would be about scarves or watches for about five minutes until something else caught their eye. Often, the something else was Michael. Susan held out her foot to pretend to trip Michael up as he went past.

'The lengths I have to go to, Michael, to get your attention.'

'You always have my full attention, Susan.'

'These are my friends, Olivia, we call her Ovy, and Mags.'

'Delighted to see you here and I hope that we'll be seeing lots of you in the future,' he said with a complimentary smile so wide that his side teeth were revealed, straight and magnificent.

I watched Michael. He could certainly be charming and make you think that he was genuinely interested, spreading his warmth like a blanket. Susan's friends behaved as though Michael had slipped a hand up each of their skirts and the attention was welcome, each of them sat up a little straighter and they vied with one another for his interest. There was much laughing in the little group but I couldn't tell why because nothing funny had been said. I stayed, emptying the bar dishwasher so that I could watch. The squeaky hot glasses were slowly replaced on the shelf. I made perfect lines with them and, if one were slightly out, I stopped and adjusted it. I held up one of the new glasses and looked at Susan and her friends through it as I pretended to look for smears. I heard Michael deliver the same line that he'd already spoken to other people outside on the quay.

'I'm so pleased you could be here and I would love to sit down with you later but, right now, I need to deliver a bottle of sparkling water to the saxophonist before he falls in the mud and is engulfed. He has managed to neck two bottles of wine in an hour and a half, despite playing. I do have professional liability insurance but I'd rather not use it on the first day!'

Paroxysms of laughter from the table and all the women's eyes watched him as he walked out of the door. For a few moments, all their heads moved in together. Susan's silk shirt was tucked neatly into the waistband of her skirt but she fiddled with it, tucking it back in and then pulling it out a little again. I hadn't realised before how fine the skin on her face was. It was delicate and stretched like canvas over the bones of her face. It was the kind of skin that probably wouldn't wrinkle or sag too much.

'I think we should have Champagne. Call that girl over, Susan,' said Ovy, speaking loudly enough for me to hear, but I stayed behind the bar, lining up my glasses.

'I've got to drive,' answered Susan, lacking in conviction.

'Nonsense, when do we three get a chance to meet up? Who knows when the next opportunity will be? Get that tarty girl's attention, Susan. You're far better with the minions than I am.'

I continued to order my glasses into neat rows and breathed deeply. Each little glass stem at a perfect distance from the previous one.

'Amanda, come and meet my friends,' Susan shouted.

I walked over, a little quickly and a little too smiley. As I was doing it, I wondered why I was bothering, they barely acknowledged me and interrupted Susan when she said, 'Girls, this is Amanda...'

'There's no time for niceties when Champagne needs drinking. Could you be a darling and bring us the list?' Ovy smiled.

'We only have one kind,' I replied.

I spoke very slowly with a low voice. They didn't appear to understand me and were frowning, so I added, 'We didn't anticipate a demand for Champagne.'

'No, I can see that,' said Ovy. 'Who on earth chose that ghastly colour?' She waved in the direction of Gran's magnificent wall and I waited for Susan to come to my defence. After all, she had complimented Gran on her décor just days before. No help was forthcoming and I decided not to worry about these women as they would never be regulars. They were only here because it was our opening day and they were the type to be first at everything, especially if it were free.

I brought over the Champagne and was opening it carefully when Ovy grabbed the bottle from me.

'That's not how they do it. For God's sake, hand it over or it won't be worth drinking!'

I left them to it. I regained my composure by speaking and moving amongst other people I vaguely knew. I served efficiently behind the bar for over an hour until I realised that I had not been doing the wrong thing with the Champagne.

The free drink had gone and we were steadily busy with four of us behind the bar. The next time I looked over at Susan's table, I saw Michael taking away an empty bottle. He had replaced it. I hadn't noticed him come behind the bar and get more Champagne. I supposed this was the way it would be in the future for us, we would have to be less time to be together.

Susan's table was becoming louder but, again, I was distracted by customers and, when the queue slacked off for a moment, I slipped to the Ladies. I recognised Ovy's precise way of speaking as she came in to the toilets, and, in a moment of cowardice, decided to stay in my cubicle until she had gone.

'That Furnish girl, Michael's piece, is it serious?' Mags asked.

I froze and, although my mouth opened, nothing came out. I could have walked out and confronted them but, instead, I stood there, desolate.

'It won't be if Susan has her way.'

'Ovy!' said Susan.

I shivered at Susan's mock horror.

'She's living with him, isn't she?' asked Ovy.

'Lodging,' said Susan. 'I don't think he has had much say in the matter. It all has a sense of history repeating itself, living with the landlord like her grandmother before her.'

'What? Does Michael piss himself and walk about plastered in vomit like James Arlet used to?'

'Very funny, Ovy. I meant the grandmother's illustrious past. That girl plays games with all the men who work here, with anyone who will have her.'

There are many moments in life when, if you don't move quickly with your mouth or your feet, you have missed your chance. And, having missed your chance, you become invisible and trapped, but still I waited in my coffin of a cubicle.

'Did you see Marie Furnish in the papers?' Ovy asked, changing the conversation.

'Naturally,' said Susan.

'What a joke. To think I used to be a fan of the Happy Lady.'

The mention of my mother's name broke the spell. If I could not stand up for myself, it would be easier to defend someone else. I pushed open the cubicle door and confronted them.

I addressed Ovy, 'What does Ovy stand for? Overbearing? Overweight? Overindulged?' She wasn't at all overweight but I had seen her picking at her food and stored the image away. I did not know it would be so useful so soon.

'Little freak!' she muttered, as I barged past her to wash my hands before leaving the room.

I was unsettled and didn't know how to deal with such behaviour. I went to find Michael. He was collecting glasses, making another table of people laugh; he moved on smoothly, saying he had to get more drinks for the musicians. If he were telling the truth, he would have been on his 10th trip to the saxophonist with sparkling water. The poor man would drown, his lungs full of carbonated mineral water. I reached out and touched Michael's wrist, quietly calling his name. He didn't hear me or notice me. I really was becoming invisible. I spotted Gran and my father on the quay, their legs dangling over the side. I rushed towards them. Gran saw my face and made a space in between the middle of them.

'I've just been called a freak,' I said.

'I should think you have. The highest accolade a dull person could bestow on you,' said Gran lazily.

'How do you know they were dull?' I demanded.

'The need to categorise those who are different from you is fundamentally dull.'

'It was one of Susan's friends.'

'Who else would it be?'

'Show me where they are and I'll sort them out,' my father spoke.

I cried. Tears fell over the edge of the quay, dropping straight into the water, tiny worthless crystals of self-pity. His offer was well-intentioned but 19 years too late.

'This isn't the playground,' I said.

'How do you know?' said Gran. 'You've never set foot in a playground.'

'I wish I had. I might know better how to deal with those Champagne-swilling morons.'

'The Champagne is not relevant to them being moronic. Let's have a bottle,' Gran said.

'Gran, are you serious?'

'I want Champagne, go and get me some,' she said.

My father pulled some notes out of his pocket and thrust them in my hand. Gran looked impatient and my distress was diffused. She always did this to me, pushing me on when I wanted to stop. I just wanted a moment of sympathy while I was waiting for my feelings of self-loathing to stop. But, as always, action worked, the stumbling up from the quay and the first few hesitant steps were the worst. A few steps later, I was restored and would just get on with things.

On the way back with the bottle and glasses, I shouted across to Michael, 'I'm taking half an hour off.'

The three of us sat by the water, waiting for the mud to be revealed, and sipping Champagne. I looked at my father's face. Gran saw me examining him.

'Handsome devil, isn't he?'

* * *

The rest of the afternoon and early evening passed without incident. The last guests dwindled away at seven and we were left with the clearing up. I had some clearing up of another kind to sort out, too.

'Those women insulted me,' I said to Michael.

'They were drunk.'

'You were all over them.'

'An element of charm is necessary for a landlord to be successful.'

'Even at the price of me being treated like dirt.'

'Look, Amanda, they probably won't come here again. You know what women like that are like. Don't take things so personally. Let it wash over you or you'll never be able to cope here.' He put his arm around my back for a few moments and then we went our separate ways, tidying up.

I still can't pinpoint the exact time when Susan stopped being 'that woman' in Michael's eyes. It could have been on the opening day, or it could have been any of the Friday or Saturday nights shortly after when she arrived at the same time, 8.30, with her friends. Sometimes, there was a gang of 11 of them, other times, as few as three. It was never the same three as that opening night, thankfully, and I was normally in the kitchen until 10 o'clock. The group was always lively but without those three personalities together, there was restraint.

From July onwards, it was warm for weeks and, if Susan's gang ate at our pub, they ate outside, for which I was grateful. As I was mostly busy in the kitchen, I didn't spend all of my evenings running around after her. I began to notice something – if my confidence were up, she was more than civil, sometimes genuinely friendly, but this was only fleeting. Still, I found myself holding out for a generous glance or smile from her, even though I hated myself for it. One Saturday night when she was very drunk, she even slipped an arm around my waist and I stayed by her side longer than I might have done. My logical side was screaming at me to stay away from her but the side that needed affection stayed for whatever scraps she was doling out that night.

Susan was definitely the leader in her little gang. Sometimes, she was quieter than usual and let one of the others emerge from the position of understudy but, mostly, she would control the conversation. Various people hung around with her: lawyers, shopkeepers and a teacher from the local secondary school, Stephen Whit. He seemed to take the same approach to socialising with Susan and her friends that he used for teaching. He was mildly amused by his charges, gave them time and often found them genuinely diverting, however, he was always glad to get home at night. He was always the generous one from that group at the pub, often on the outside but only by choice. He was decent to me and, if I saw him in the group, arriving late as he often did, my mood lifted. Stephen flirted with me, too, which annoyed Susan intensely and undermined her.

Why should I fixate on one person in a busy pub? Why couldn't I just let her do whatever it was she needed to do to get through life? The answer was that I didn't know. It wasn't logical. There was a hardness to her that I was always trying to crack. I hoped that she would show me the same type of kindness that she had done when I was a child. Or maybe she had always been manipulative and I had been too young to notice what she was doing. Had she only ever been interested in attacking Gran through me? And, now that I had turned out more in the mould of Gran than her, she could no longer contain her distaste. I don't think that anything she did was without motive. No word came out of her mouth that wasn't carefully considered for its impact.

'Amanda, darling, would you be so good as to go and get me an extra shot in this gin? That disloyal Michael has obviously forgotten that I have a triple in a long glass on a Friday night, even though I have been coming here for months.'

Stephen spoke, 'You'd better watch it, Susan, you are on the slippery slope.' He smiled at me. But I knew she was on no slippery slope at all. She had probably calculated the calories she'd expended all week at the gym and worked it out exactly. No deficit. The perfect energy accountant.

Michael started to sit with them for an hour before closing time on a Saturday, whilst the rest of the staff cleaned up.

'I've earnt it and Stephen's a nice, interesting guy,' he said.

But I wasn't interested in Stephen. 'She's after you.'

'Who?' he asked casually.

'You know who. Susan.'

He reassured me. Said all the right things in the right order but he had too jaunty a walk that evening. I watched him as if he were a stranger. He did it so well, always appearing good-natured and even-tempered. Always willing to have a drink with his guests.

Susan's only topic of conversation was sex. That was why she was so popular, titillating in word and deed. Sometimes, she pretended she talked about other things apart from sex; she dressed it up with interest in other people's marriages, relationships in general, jobs and families but, if you removed all the packaging, sex inevitably lay at the bottom of the box. She was talking about one of the girls in her cake factory.

'She deteriorates by the week, gets fatter and fatter by the moment. She must be helping herself to the imperfect cakes from the production line. And, still, her handsome husband does not stray. Why would that be?'

'Some men are interested in more than appearances?' Stephen suggested.

'Precisely my point,' said Susan. 'Her hair's lank and the heel's wobbling off one of her shoes. Still, he collects her on time every night and doesn't so much as look at another woman.'

'At you, you mean,' said Mags.

'Then, one day, I see her laughing. She doesn't laugh much. She has no teeth. Her mouth a great gaping red hole whose incisors and molars were extracted long ago.'

'What's he staying for, then?' asked Mags.

'Extraordinary oral sex, apparently.'

Susan was finished and sat back a little on her seat, the better to hear the raucous laughter from a distance. Better to sit back and see the effect she had on her loyal crowd. I was furious, couldn't she think of anything more original to say? And, if her only topic of interest was sex, why wasn't she more upfront about it?

'Are you saying that because a woman has nice teeth she can't give a good blow job?' I asked.

It was Susan's turn to shiver. 'Amanda, lowering the tone as usual.'

'She was simply taking the argument to its logical conclusion,' Stephen said.

Susan looked at me with distaste and started talking about selling Doves of Love, 'Thankfully, I got rid of those stinking birds at the top of the market.'

I was grateful for Stephen again as I picked up the glasses and headed back to the bar. For the rest of the night, I tried to make the twins serve her as much as possible but they wriggled out of it, turning the whole thing into an argument about which of them would 'do' Susan if given the chance.

Jake punched Dan on the arm, 'Leave off, she's such an old tart.'

'She's gorgeous for her age,' Dan argued.

'How old is she?' Jake asked.

This was a sore point with me. She was approaching 50 and had mentioned to Michael that she would like to have her party at the pub. I filled the tray from the outside bar for her group of friends and headed down to the quay with it. Susan's latest bid to stop time in its miserable little tracks was to work less at the cake factory and spend more and more time at the gym, and didn't we hear all about it.

'My personal trainer flirts with me incorrigibly,' she looked down at the heel of her shoe.

'Oh, Susan, no!' said Mags.

'Oh, I've seen it coming for months,' said Susan.

'Maybe he's confused by a series of contradictory moves from you,' Stephen suggested. He made beckoning motions with one hand and stop signs with the other.

'Stephen, you are so horrible to me,' she said, 'and that's completely untrue!'

I didn't hang around to listen to how Stephen dealt with Susan's simpering, nor how she dealt with the rogue from the gym.

When I listened to entire conversations dominated by her, I began to realise how she did it; what her trick was, the trick that enabled her to keep her audience hanging on indefinitely. It was to hint repeatedly at salacious things but save the big one until as late as possible in the evening when everyone was really drunk. But, once she had dropped the bombshell or scandalous snippet, she would back-pedal for all she was worth, whilst maintaining an innocent look. Then, when somebody else continued the conversation, wanting to take things further, she would look slightly appalled and let them take the blame.

Although Michael spent a lot of time talking to Susan, Mags, Stephen and the rest, I only sat with them twice, for about 10 minutes both times. The last time I had sat there and Stephen wasn't there, I was left out. I had nothing to contribute to the conversation, so I got up and went to help with the clearing up.

I tried to speak to Gran about it, but, when I turned up at the house on my night off, she was deep in discussion with my father again. The last few visits, they seemed to be getting closer and closer. A couple of times, I had come across them with their heads almost touching, their conversations were so intense.

John retreated when he saw that I needed to speak to Gran and took up his habitual spot on the steamer chair that Gran had made. He often sat outside, alone in the dark.

I started straight in about Susan, 'I feel like she is constantly undermining me, tugging away at my foundations. How can she do that? Can one person do that to another or is it my imagination?'

'We all have to do battle with people in life. She's just one of yours.' Gran saw that I looked alarmed, 'She may be your only one.'

'Really?'

'No,' she sighed. 'And, what's more, I can't imagine why you have picked such a feeble adversary. I would have made mincemeat of that woman at your age.'

She squinted at me and moved closer. She took hold of my face in her hands and moved my head this way and that while staring at me intently. She had always done this and I shut my eyes with the comfort of it. But still, tears fell down my face. Again, I was a fool to expect sympathy.

'Remember when your mother took you to the zoo without my permission and you saw the polar bears and were horrified by them?'

I remembered it all too clearly. The trouble was, Gran was always right but that didn't stop me as a child trying to defy her or prove her wrong, at least once in a while. I had gone to the zoo and seen the bears. They were nothing like I'd imagined. They were sorry and yellow. Crestfallen and stumbling.

'When you behave like this, you remind me of one of those bears.' I cried more. She made no attempt to comfort me but carried on, 'Something removed from its own environment and suffering as a result of it.'

'Are you saying I shouldn't work at the pub but should always stay here with you? Incarcerated in the middle of nowhere, with nothing but a disturbing merry-go-round for company?'

'Not at all. I'm just saying that you must remember what you are and stop being pulled into other people's insubstantial little worlds.'

'I can't help it.'

'Then you will continue to suffer.'

'Do you speak so harshly to him?' I demanded, pointing to the darkness that had enveloped John Doon and the steamer chair.

'Of course I am as hard on him. Harder, if anything. He's just ready to listen.'

Back at the pub, Susan had arrived with her red setter who was now four months old and a regular visitor to the pub. Some of the people who came by boat brought dogs with them. And some of the locals would bring their dogs, too, walk them a mile or two around the lanes and then stop off for a pint. There could be three or four dogs at a time, congregating by the outside bar. Most were well-behaved and lay quietly by empty tables or ran along the quay, fetching balls or sticks thrown to them by any willing visitors.

But Susan's dog was a nuisance, she slipped over the edge of the quay and into the mud when the water was out. She would roll herself thoroughly, stirring up the stink of the mud and then leap back out and go up to people. Often, Susan was too distracted holding court to pay proper attention and locals and visitors alike would be muddied by the red, matted-haired creature. I started to hate the dog. I resented putting water out for it. I transferred my feelings of hatred from Susan to her dog. It was the natural thing to do. Stupid, stinking, hyperactive mutt.

Once, I even had to hose it down. Susan was so drunk and the place was full of new people whom I wanted to encourage to return, so I washed the dog underneath the outside tap behind the fence where we kept the bins. Then I tied it up with string from the kitchen until she came looking for it at closing time. I had seen Susan that night huddled around with seven of her friends buying her drinks. Someone offered her a coat which swamped her tiny frame but she took it.

'What's wrong with her?' I asked Michael.

'She's split with her husband.'

I was not surprised. I had rarely seen her husband and everyone knew it was no marriage, except on paper. Susan seemed to grow smaller as the night drew on, eliciting stiff hugs from her women friends.

'She's milking it for all it's worth,' I said.

'She's deeply hurt,' said Michael defensively, before heading off to join the little band of rescuers who sat by her side until she and the dog were bundled into a taxi at 12.22am precisely. I knew – I was counting the minutes.

It was my 19th birthday in late-July, and it went by with barely a murmur, in contrast to talk about Susan's party. Michael gave me a silver key ring, expensive but impersonal and I sensed a distance in him. I came up behind him and made him jump, instead of laughing, like he usually would have done, he tutted and stormed off. That morning, he'd offered me his bathrobe when I was walking around his room naked.

'Don't stand in front of the window like that, you never know who might see you.'

'It's too early for anyone to be about. I was just looking at the water,' I said in disbelief.

It was seven in the morning.

It was all about appearances with him. He spoke to Dawn about the way she was presenting the food, saying that there had been a complaint, 'Couldn't it be more…?' he started.

I didn't give him the chance to finish his sentence. 'Food–like?'

'Delicate,' he said at last.

Dawn was frowning as she stood in the kitchen between us. I wanted to make him realise that he was being stupid. We had discussed the food endlessly and decided that simplicity was the key. That and generous portions. It wasn't long before I realised who'd made these suggestions. I joined in with Michael that night as he was having his usual few drinks with Susan and her gang. I had invited Stephen Whit who was single-handedly keeping my birthday evening afloat, when Michael's daughter phoned. I hadn't spoken to his daughter before and there was a dismissive tone in her voice which chilled me but, nevertheless, I went to tell him immediately that she'd rung and asked him to call her back sometime that night. I stood at the side of the table by the quay, waiting to speak as Susan and Michael had a serious conversation.

'I'm sorry if I'm speaking out of turn, Michael,' Susan said.

'Go ahead,' he encouraged.

'Well, the food is okay as far as it goes, but I really think, for a place of this calibre, you need a professional chef.'

'Dawn is professional and is working to a brief which has been agreed upon,' I said curtly, before sidestepping her and telling Michael about his daughter.

Susan interrupted again, 'Dawn's all well and good for the moment but, if you have ambitions for this place, she'll hardly do for the future. I know people…'

She did know people. Some evil ones.

'Just a little tweaking, some fashionable sauces, white china,' she carried on, indifferent to my being there.

She was trying to obliterate all that Gran had set in place. I looked at the plates that Gran had commissioned as I carried them back into the kitchen. Each one imperfect and magnificent. The colours of the glaze unusual, they were robust and welcoming. Susan would choose bone china. She would only recognise its delicacy, shine and elegance as she held it up to the light and saw through it. She would never consider the name of the clay, 'bone china'. She wouldn't think of the ground down skeletons that gave the china its transparency and toughness combined. She was the queen of ignoring the distasteful. I was building myself up into a foul temper when Michael came in.

'How many pairs of shoes do you need?' he asked, tripping over a sandal and shoving it into a corner.

'I've only got two pairs of shoes here.'

He apologised and massaged my bare foot, only to wander off moments later, leaving me to go and find comfort elsewhere.

Thinking of sharp-flavoured sauces and tiny portions, I crept up the stairs and turned left at the landing into the kitchen where I heated up a huge plate of mashed potato from the fridge, adding more butter. It was a creamy mountain of richness on an original plate. I imagined Susan siphoning all the fat out of it with a tube and placing the reduced portion on a white plate. Still thinking of Susan and her perfect, see-through china, I was reminded of a childhood game. I found a torch in the kitchen drawer, turned off the lights and just sat there with the torch held up against my clenched fingers. I could see the beautiful colour of the blood, glowing round the edges of my fingers, orange, warm and comforting. Dawn came in.

'What are you doing sitting in the dark, sweetie?'

I looked up and attempted a smile. I shrugged as well, for good measure.

'Come into the bar, everybody is gone. Have a birthday drink,' she said cheerily.

I decided to confide in Dawn as she poured me a glass of Chardonnay, my favourite tipple, 'It's Susan.'

'Yes, sweetheart?'

All of a sudden, I could think of nothing to say. I couldn't repeat what she had said about Dawn's cooking and all her minor crimes against me suddenly seemed intangible, difficult to pin down or explain to someone else.

'She's a lovely looking woman,' Dawn said.

I swilled down the wine and choked on the last drop.

Despite my hostility, Susan started to increase her visits to us but, instead of despairing, I discovered a new weapon that allowed me to stay away from her as far as possible. It was *The Little Book of Tides*. I suddenly realised something when I was wandering down by the river. Susan never came here when the tide was out. I had heard her moaning about the mud and how, if her dog went in it, the animal would mess up her car on the way home. She wasn't worried about a muddy dog bouncing on other people's clothes, which it had done on several occasions. She wouldn't leave the dog at home on its own either, so her only choice was to bring it here when the tide was in because it was frightened of the water and wouldn't jump in. The little book that I kept in my pocket was my weapon of choice. It was small and incredibly detailed. I knew from then on exactly when she would and wouldn't appear. If the water were out, I could relax for a few hours. The dog might be a gift, after all.

XII

I Lose my Dignity and a Tooth

THE SUMMER limped on. The twins argued and were separated at their own request. It were as though they had to be mean to one another for fear of the intensity of their love. Michael decided that a substantial wall between them was the answer, so Jake carried on working in the bar and Dan went to help in the kitchen. That way, they knew that they were still in the same building. There was only room for two people in the kitchen so I had to come out from my place of hiding where I had sheltered for the last 12 weeks. The kitchen cave where the comforting Dawn lived would no longer be my domain. I was being chased out into the daylight.

From now on, Dan would be on the receiving end of all Dawn's gentle mothering and occasional bad-tempered remarks. He took over my job as commis chef and, although I was still involved, knowing exactly what was on the menu and how to make it, that was only an emergency position in case Dan was ill. Unfortunately for me, Dan was robust and couldn't remember the last time he'd had so much as a headache.

'Last year, when Jake and I were surfing, he came at me on his board and deliberately cracked me on the head. I stayed in the water for six hours after that, even though I was bleeding. That showed him.'

It seemed I would have to get used to my position of being more in the hub of things instead of being closeted away for most of the time. To make up for this, I went into town and bought 15 face packs so, at the end of the night, I could relax in the bath with a mask on. I bought one for every kind of skin – although my skin was normal, I needed to be prepared for change. At night, I lay in the bath staring at the ceiling with some self-heating, rainbow-coloured gloop weighing heavily on my face. After 10 minutes, I washed it off and got into bed with Michael.

I got up early one roasting July morning. It was so hot that, by nine o'clock, it was warm enough for shorts. A box from the printers had been left outside the pub, it contained the extra menus. Our food had proved popular and there was nothing worse than food-smeared menus so I had ordered some more but they had taken a suspiciously long time to arrive. Ten minutes later, I began idly to pick away at the brown tape on the box whilst holding my tea in my other hand. The first glimpse of the menus made me spill the liquid on the flagstones in irritation. The design had been changed.

I shouted up to Michael, even though I knew he wouldn't hear me, 'They've sent the wrong ones.'

I took out the invoice to get the printers' phone number to call them and complain, when I saw that there had been a huge mistake. The invoice was addressed to us and we had been charged for replacement artwork. Gone were Gran's black and yellow stripes and, in their place, was dark purple with gold lettering. When I checked inside one of the menus, I saw that three more dishes had been added. I was furious and leapt up the stairs two at a time and sat down on the bed I shared with Michael. He sat up slowly, smiling.

'Since when has asparagus been available in this country in August?' I demanded in disbelief.

'Ahh, I knew there was something I had forgotten to tell you. It's what the clientele wants, Amanda. We must be adaptable in such a competitive business. You can never really tell who your niche market is going to be until you have been open for a few weeks and, for this place to be a success, we need to be catering to people's needs.'

'People's needs? We expressly agreed on a policy of how to run this place. Twelve weeks ago we had principles, ideals even.'

'I knew you'd be upset, which is why I probably forgot to mention it,' he slipped an arm around my shoulder. 'If you think it's a reflection on Cath and her worth to this place, it's not like that, Amanda. It's a financially-based decision. Cath may be fundamentally right but that won't get me in *The Good Pub Guide.*'

I had been a fool. I thought I was involved in the pub and that I had some sway with Michael. That was the moment when I realised that was not the case.

'What else do you have in the pipeline that you haven't told me about?' I asked, accusingly.

He sat up rigid, looking slightly confrontational. His perfectly-shaped head touched the wall with a slight smacking sound, as though he were doing this to himself before I got a chance to do so.

'My daughter is coming to stay.'

'Okay.' I knew that was inevitable. I just kept breathing deeply. Obviously, there would come a day when I would have to meet her.

'It happens to coincide with Susan's birthday weekend,' said Michael, slowly.

'Weekend? Last time I mentioned it, we were talking about a few curly sandwiches and, suddenly, it's 48 hours of the woman.'

The menus had caused me pain, Michael's daughter arriving had left me inoperative, but I was finally broken by the revelations about Susan's party; she had smashed into my territory and was getting ready to replace me.

'Don't exaggerate, Amanda. You knew Susan was getting a quote for here and The Buck's Head. Well, we've won her business.' He said it so glibly. All these things happening and I was unaware of them.

'Were we cheaper?' I asked.

'They couldn't supply the wine she wanted… and they didn't want the staff from the cake factory to be drafted in as extra waiting staff.'

'I should think not. Cheapskate, conniving…' That woman had managed to engineer a situation where she was using her own staff from the cake factory to infiltrate the pub.

'Amanda, really! I can't talk to you when you are like this,' he said in a calm voice.

'Why are the covers of the menus purple?'

'It's regal-looking, stylish.'

'Who says?'

He hesitated for just one moment too long. Purple – pompous colour with a Rink whiff to it.

'I didn't realise just how much experience Susan has in terms of advertising and marketing until we were talking the other night and it all comes down to profit in the end. Her approach may be conservative but it's been consistently successful,' he said.

'So it all comes down to economics in the end? Damn originality and ethics.' I wanted to ask him if I should be looking for another job, but I was not confident enough to call his bluff. Inside, I knew the answer without having to ask.

'You and this place are very important to me, Amanda.'

The words were the right ones to say but it was as though he were reading them from a screen with no rehearsal time. He kissed me and I allowed him to pull me under the covers but, as soon as the sex was over, I had to deal with the reality of my situation, which was sudden, enforced and bitter; cruelly magnified by the oblivion I had experienced moments before.

I shut my eyes and prayed for sleep, any means of escaping consciousness would do. When I awoke, Michael was gone.

I had been an idiot to sleep with him after that menu incident and now I would suffer for not listening to the warning which, after all, was in bright purple. One of the glossy expanded menus lay by the side of the bed, verification that I was being pushed out. What more proof did I need?

I lumbered to the phone to take a call from my father. 'Come over for coffee and watch Cath bottle things up.'

I had seen Gran bottling things on hundreds of occasions but it was the best offer I was going to get on my day off and it would take me away from the pub. When I got there, Gran would be brutally stuffing blackcurrants in jars and throwing in brandy for good measure, this was our Christmas drink. I popped my head into Bill's office as I hadn't seen him for days. He seemed more distant than ever, hunkered down, avoiding John and the unpleasant associations he brought with him.

I looked at my father. He looked like a man who would still be here at Christmas and one who was undergoing a greater transformation through being here with Gran than just the healing of his eye. He was in awe of everything she did and touched. He marvelled at our fruit trees. He slavered over her planning which ensured we would be largely self-sufficient over the winter and she looked as if she were enjoying the attention from him. We talked about mundane things as we watched Gran. I felt strangely affectionate towards him. He loved Gran, which was not an easy thing to do, and that was good enough for me.

I knew I wouldn't be able to sit around for long and, soon, both my father and I were commandeered into the final round of fruit picking. Ignoring the rain that had appeared from nowhere that afternoon, Gran shooed us outside impatiently. It fell in fine but persistent drops and I began to feel annoyed that she had made us move out of the dry house. I wanted to talk to her about Michael, ask her advice.

The rain spitefully found gaps to flow down my neck, between skin and clothing, icy drips, the opposite of the sweat that had pooled on my stomach that morning. I tugged in anger at the bottom of my cheap jacket, this had never happened when I lived at home and wore sensible clothes. Then I remembered that, until recently, I'd been indifferent to being caught in the rain.

The ground remained hard underfoot but a few birds appeared looking for worms and the familiar smell of the soil rose and drifted around us. Most people might associate their grandmothers with warm kitchens and Sunday roasts, whereas I associated mine with the smell of the earth and that exasperating carousel.

Gran suddenly became silent and looked up a tree. My father watched her as though he were learning something extraordinary from a very wise person.

'I can see your mother's fingernails in that tree, like a flock of red birds,' Gran spoke in a whisper. I felt a little cynical and was determined not to play into her hands by looking up but, after a minute, curiosity forced me.

'Ten red birds,' Gran said, chuckling.

Both John and I looked up at the tree.

'They've been here for a few days now, twittering and carrying on. I've been feeding them,' she said. Before I had the chance to ask what you fed to fingernails in a tree, I had my answer. 'Bits of bacon and other flesh.'

I wondered if this would be just a little too eccentric for John who had only stayed with Gran a month, and might now be questioning if he should scurry back to suburbia and his office life. But he stared resolutely up the tree, not giving anything away, as though roosting red fingernails were an everyday occurrence. Or maybe he just understood that she was not literal-minded but given to exaggeration and whimsy. He was smarter than I was. I was just about to sigh audibly to express my disapproval of Gran's nonsense when I remembered the last time I had seen Marie. Everything was in place: her hair, her shoes and clothes, all perfect and pressed, but she was not wearing nail varnish. I don't recall ever seeing her without painted nails before, her signature red nails were definitely missing. I summoned up an image of her staring at her slightly yellowing nail beds and thinking how vulnerable she looked without the colour.

'That's it,' said Gran.

We all looked up again.

'They're getting ready to go.'

'Are they going to fly back to her?' asked my father.

'Definitely, within minutes,' she said.

'Shall we stay and watch them?' he asked.

I looked at him for any sign that he, too, could suddenly see fingernails in trees, but all I saw was a man who wanted to hang around Gran long enough to try, even though he knew it were hopeless.

'No, let's leave them now,' she said.

We wandered in, silenced again, probably all thinking of fat, red fingernails, gorged on flesh, flying back to their rightful owner.

* * *

Horrible events had a way of galloping towards you when you were not looking and Susan's party was no exception. She came down regularly to see how the preparations were going. She was cool with me, so I turned my temperature down 15°C and was full on frosty with her, often barely bothering to speak.

Susan had her own little dance that summer, two steps towards Michael and one step back. She had been practising for several months now and her routine was carefully choreographed to include special ways of touching Michael and looking at him. She even had her own costume which went with the dance. It was purple and made her eyes look bluer than ever. Graceful and enchanting but ill-intentioned. I was not one to waste an opportunity, or look away from a spectacle just because it was about to turn ugly. I witnessed her performance time and time again over that summer; watching her improve, grow more courageous with each passing week, add flourishes and take flourishes away. I knew she was almost done rehearsing. She was ready.

Maybe I should have done something earlier. I could have thought of a dignified speech or merely tripped her up but, all season long, I just watched. Watched her change from making tired movements which were laughable, to becoming so skilled that I could no longer challenge her.

The morning of Susan's party, Michael's daughter turned up in a sports car with matching case and hand luggage. She neatly extracted a tan-coloured suitcase from the tiny boot. How much time did a person have to have on their hands before they considered co-ordinating luggage? Although I knew these things were just fripperies, they were part of the unsettling nature of her appearance. She looked stylish in a way that I would never manage, with light brown hair, a turned-up nose and no trace of make-up. Her diminutive steps allowed her to take in everything on the way, the new umbrellas and the general air of success that the pub had since its overhaul. The reflection from her sunglasses might have played like a little film to all who watched her progress across the cobbles to the door of the pub, had anyone been watching apart from me.

She was early and Michael wasn't downstairs to greet her because he was too busy in his bedroom tidying away all traces of me, a young woman virtually the same age as his offspring. The tide was in and his cold daughter blanked me. She was a young woman with a firm belief that, if you ignored the unpalatable, it would go away. Fortunately, Susan was there, ostensibly checking the details of her party. She expanded herself to 30 times her size, blocking out the sun, and me of course, and engulfed the young Fiona Packs with beaming teeth and outstretched arms.

'Fi, I have been longing to meet you, we hear so much about you.'

Susan made no reference to me. I wondered how much Michael had told Fiona about me because, to an outsider, it looked as if his relationship were with Susan and not me. I just happened to be lurking on the cobbles, dealing ineffectually with Susan's hapless dog and awaiting instruction from its mistress. I had a choice at that moment. No stranger to boldness, I could have leapt in front of Susan, puffed myself up and shaken the daughter's hand vigorously, whilst keeping a stream of conversation so intense and constant that Fiona would have been pulled into my world, left shaking and wondering what had hit her. It wouldn't have been an enjoyable experience for her, but at least I would have made an impression, rather than shrinking.

Why didn't I? Sometimes, you became aware that a situation was going to go a certain way, and I had recognised that some time ago.

Not in the Gran sense of predicting the future and seeing strange things but in an unstoppable, stinking, huge ball-rolling kind of sense. There was no shaking off the knowing. During the rest of the day, each time I was dismissed or passed over by Fiona or, on one occasion, offered a pitying half-glance. My new-found confidence, which had seemed infallible, was being taken from me, piece by piece.

I had begun mourning the loss of Michael within weeks of meeting him. You could say I saw it coming; knowing, despite the slavering and dripping intensity of the physical attraction, that it would go wrong. So why did I hang around? Why didn't I get into Marie's car and drive home to Gran? The truth was that I still felt the pull. It would only take one glimpse of the underside of his forearm or the back of his neck and my resolve went out the window.

Susan's party was quite intimate. Just 96 of her closest friends, some of whom she rarely saw because they worked in her cake factory and she had less time for smoothing surfaces these days, with her desperate, one-woman attempt at stopping time. Even as she was hanging from the hands of her own vast personal clock, trying to stop them from moving forward, she was doing inner thigh exercises. And now, at her party, she was reunited with her dear friends, Ovy and Mags. As if protection from them was not enough, a little posse of wedding cake girls, Susan's elite force, stuck together religiously in case anyone should try to touch them or ruffle their hard-won perfection. Susan bounced, if such a thin, taut body could bounce, between compliments all afternoon.

'I can't believe she's 50,' said a cake-making protégée.

These comments, and more like them, were always made within earshot of Susan and I watched her body stiffen slightly as each one came within reach of her coils of smugness, where she would strangle them and leave them for later when she could digest them in peace. One of Susan's skills was proving particularly useful to her that day: the ability to hear conversations others were having as well as simultaneously take part in a loud, vigorous chat with a different person.

On top of all this, I had Michael's daughter to contend with. She had already been given a clear message from Susan that it was fine to ignore me and, seeing that a mother-figure in Susan was more amenable to her than a potential sister-figure in me, Fiona continued with her disdain. Although his daughter only saw Michael twice a year, she told everyone how close they were. Perhaps they were able to communicate telepathically, although I doubted it because Michael looked a bit sheepish when he was congratulated on his fathering skills.

When I looked closely at Fiona, I decided that she had the worst of Michael with added faults – the falseness without his charm; the haughty looks without his humour and, finally, his ability to gush, without his discretion. Altogether, an unfortunate package – no one else seemed to think so, though.

Finally, my own cavalry arrived in the shape of Stephen, with a huge bunch of flowers. He sidestepped Susan, managing to keep close to the quay as he walked around the guests who were standing round in a little square, before approaching me.

'I'd rather give these flowers to you but I'd never get away with it,' he said disarmingly.

'What do you really think of her?' I asked him, extending a tired flourish in Susan's direction.

'You know what I think of her,' he laughed.

'Please spell it out, I'm feeling overwhelmed by her presence,' I said quietly, close to tears.

'She has a certain something, a boldness I suppose. If I had to choose individual words, they would be cold, contained, taut, even exotic, possibly. But you shouldn't be asking me, I can never get on in a crowd. I'm not going to stay long, don't know how much of this I can stand,' he said, waving towards the jazz band. 'And I've recorded *Midlanders* for later.'

'What do you think of Michael?' I asked. I knew it was unfair, but I had to ask.

'I'm not falling for that one,' he said, 'I'll be damned if I insult him and damned if I don't. You look unhappy, Amanda. You're welcome to come home with me and take refuge for the afternoon.' I shook my head and he looked disappointed. He quickly spotted a colleague in the crowd and made his was over.

Susan's success in bringing her cake factory staff to help in the kitchen and serving the snacks and drinks meant she had surrounded herself with her own troops and everyone in the pub that day would be under her employ in one way or another. Dawn wandered about miserably, knowing that her position was in jeopardy.

The atmosphere between the twins worsened in spite of the kitchen wall and they ended up being frogmarched by Dawn to the quay where they sat down together for peace talks to see if they could spend the next 50 or so years together, or whether they should separate and make a run for it now. The wine and Champagne ran freely and the twins had imbibed enough to make themselves useless but, still, it was good to see them hugging on the quay. From a distance, they looked like the same person. Stephen's teaching colleague had left and we were alone again.

'Imagine being able to hug a version of yourself like that,' I said to Stephen.

'I'd rather hold somebody else.' I could tell he regretted his spontaneous comment, as he looked down at the ground and left for home.

The conversation revolved around Susan's face and taut upper arms. Was there nothing else to talk about? Why couldn't I laugh about it and let it go?

I interrupted a little group of Susan's admirers with more than a tray of drinks, 'She is going to die, to wrinkle and sag eventually, as we all will, regardless of how many hours she spends down the gym or under the knife.'

Mags overheard and stepped up to me, 'I don't think that's a nice conversation to have on somebody's birthday. If you can't control your jealousy at not being the centre of attention, I suggest that you retreat quietly into the pub.'

Michael's daughter glared, too. Soon, the glaring was as infectious as yawning, and 10 pairs of eyes were wishing me elsewhere. I wished that Stephen hadn't gone home. There seemed no point arguing but I knew it was not jealousy. It was far worse than that. It was a daily painful jarring, a deep-seated hatred wrapped up in disbelief. It was the result of being constantly stunned by other people's conversation.

Any attempts to fit in that I had made when I had first started at The Waggon and Horses had fallen apart. I had grown bored with it all. More than bored, I was desperate and lonely. They could sniff out an interloper at a hundred paces. No matter how hard I practised and tried, I could only keep it up for so long, my mask would slip and I would be revealed for what I was: an outsider. I felt my choices in life were painful; I could follow Gran's example, but I knew I could never live up to her reputation, or live a half-and-half life like Stephen, joining up with people when he was desperate for company and then retreating to wash them off. Neither position seemed palatable.

When I looked over to see Michael's daughter smirking and enjoying the spectacle, I saw that she had something on her table. Gran's Russian dolls. How dare she have something of my grandmother's? Those dolls, for a moment, were the equivalent of my grandmother being around. I watched Fiona's cold, horrible, little fingers that she had offered me that morning in a three-fingered shake, move over the painted surfaces of the dolls in turn. I headed towards her. Staying calm, but with my heart pounding and my breath struggling, I spoke quietly. I had no intention of making a scene, I would just take the dolls and go. Once I had them safely in my hands, I would be able to breathe again, collect my things from upstairs and leave.

'Those dolls are my grandmother's,' I said.

She tipped her head on one side and a neatly plucked brow made the shape of a bow; taut and pulled back, ready to fire.

'They have been missing for a while,' I continued.

'Dad has given them to me. I found them upstairs when I was having a look around.'

'I'm afraid they are not his to give and I need them back.'

'That isn't possible, I love them and they have been given to me.'

The controlled sweetness of her voice told me there was no point in arguing, so I reached forward to take them. Quickly, she gathered them up, out of reach, and began slowly placing one inside the other until they were one doll and she had her hand closed round the biggest doll's neck. With one great shove, I pushed her off her chair. She saved face by grabbing the robust table leg just before she hit the cobbles. Her extraordinary power at that moment came from a horror of being seen on the floor. I took what was mine and headed towards the door of the pub. I slipped into the pub, turned left by the stairs and went into Michael's office.

I sat in the narrow, L-shaped room with its swivel chair, filing cabinets and windows that looked out onto the cobbles and the quay. There were blinds in there and, luckily, they were down because Michael never wanted to see the beauty of the place and get distracted from bills and phone calls. I had spent hours in this room helping him set up; phoning the brewery, the printers, the catering suppliers.

I started to do my own dance on Michael's swivel chair. If Susan had a dance, I must have one, too. To warm up, I let the gas in the seat take me up and down to its full height and then the lowest position, several times at speed. The ludicrousness of the chair's action suited the situation well. Then, I started whooshing across the long narrow room, slowly, with a bottle of wine in my hand from a case underneath the desk. I stopped long enough to open it by brutally pushing the cork in with Michael's fountain pen. The nib bent round in a gold circle before collapsing under the pressure. Each part of the nib went a different way like a pair of fat, splayed, gold legs.

I needed to see how fast I could go on the chair while drinking the wine and not splashing it on my clothes. After 15 spins back and forth, I looked like I had wet myself. Fortunately, there were still 11 bottles under the desk that Michael had been going to save until later. The good stuff. I whizzed up and down with another bottle, grabbing papers and files on my way – and setting them free.

When the letters hit the ground, they were just ordinary bits of paper again. I ran over them; crumpling them with my speeding wheels. Soon, the floor was awash with paperwork and I was drunk enough. I opened a second bottle and poured it onto the official documents on the floor.

I scooted towards the wall, waited until my feet touched it and then pushed myself back. I had the bottle in the side of my mouth, on a jaunty angle and, as I hit the wall, I felt one of my teeth break and the rushing taste of blood.

I panicked and sobered up a bit, the pain and shock of what I had done to myself hit me. After a minute, I felt which one it was with my tongue. It didn't matter. It wouldn't show, it was a side one, past the bottom incisor on the right-hand side. Just missed one of my wolf-like teeth. I spat the blood and saliva out onto the floor where it joined with the rest of the mixture, and the tooth must have fallen down there, too.

I let myself out of the office's back door and slipped through the fence that separated the bins from the pub – and me from the party. The fence stretched down to the river. I had a full bottle of wine in one hand and managed to stuff some large sheets of cardboard from behind the bins under the other arm. Leaning against the fence for support, I waddled to the edge of the river, where I sat on the cardboard and drank my wine. I had poured so much down my throat that I had reached a level of numbness that seemed right in the circumstances.

I fell asleep close up to the fence, lying on the cardboard with one large sheet on top of me and woke just before the sun went down. I couldn't believe the evening had come round so fast. The spiteful fingers of dusk were on my shoulder, trying to move me on. It was all well and good behaving like that in the day, but the evening was a different matter. The evening required an altered decorum, slowed down and reflective.

The moon was indifferent to me; she had seen so many like me that she had lost all compassion. She had a job to do and that was to clear the riverbank of stragglers, set them about their business and move them on. They had choices. If they chose to fall in love with the wrong people, then they couldn't just loiter there with their sadness. What she really couldn't stand, though, was people asking for mercy from the stars.

With the remnants of heavy eye make-up spiking my eyelashes, I began to pick off the clods of mascara as I sat by the river, refusing to be ousted. I was shivering with cold and felt filthy, even though I had only been outside for a few hours. My jeans were damp and clung to my legs and my head pounded. I was desperate for a drink but, at the moment, I couldn't face walking over to the outside tap and getting water. I needed to sit for a moment and think, I still had my car keys. I was much too drunk to get in the car but I thought, if I took things slowly, I would be able to drive in half an hour or so.

I attempted to stand up, taking my time before walking to the gate in the fence near the pub. I slipped out quietly, hardly moving the latch, but I needn't have bothered. For the first time since we had opened, the outside of the pub hadn't been cleared up properly and the party was over. The lights were still on in the pub and several cars remained. I saw a packet of cigarettes and found five cigarettes and a lighter inside. I lit up, immediately feeling better as I inhaled. I walked unsteadily towards the car and, with a few jumpy manoeuvres, was soon driving slowly up the concrete slope, back to Gran's. In my drunken state, I had no regard for the hurt I could cause to other people on the road, or to myself.

'What in heaven's name has happened to you?' she demanded.

'I've knocked out one of my teeth.'

'You and teeth,' she said, as she rushed around, fetching the pestle and mortar and grinding herbs into a paste. I let her apply it to the gum. Then she guided me towards the sofa and covered me up with a blanket.

'Don't you want to know what happened?' I asked.

But I was asleep before I could hear her say, 'No.'

I woke several hours later to find her sitting beside me, frowning. John was in the background, looking anxious. Gran waved him away and he went with a backward glance, out into the garden with his hands in his pockets and his head down. His hair was even longer and it fell around his face, dark and wavy. He pushed it back with a gesture that was neither masculine nor feminine but stylish. I saw a glimpse of how he must have looked 20 years ago when my mother first met him, gangly but with a certain charm.

I couldn't resist poking my tongue into the strange gap in my mouth. I couldn't remember what had happened to the tooth itself. I must have left it in the office. I shuddered when I thought about Michael or Susan coming across the mess I had made there, and I went through my list of things I wish I had not done, until they all fused together into overwhelming embarrassment.

Exploring the hole that my tooth had left, felt sexual. I could feel tiny bits of skin flapping as my tongue poked the fleshy hole. I congratulated myself because I had made a sculpture inside my own mouth which would for ever represent this mess with Michael. I thought of all the things I had seen yesterday. All the subtle glances that Michael had exchanged with Susan, how she had touched his chest and he, in turn, had touched her shoulder; a less obvious but still unmistakeable stroke.

But the scene that I could not get out of my head was Ovy arranging a little group to be photographed for Susan's party. Susan was sat on a high-backed wooden chair, one of the non-matching ones that Gran had salvaged for the restaurant. Michael's hands were on the back of the chair and his daughter was looking on smiling, just two metres away, when Ovy shouted, 'Come into the picture, you're family.'

Fiona didn't need to be asked twice and Susan was enthroned and surrounded by loyal subjects, friends and girls from the cake factory.

I was lost in these miserable recollections when Gran cruelly began enlarging on her polar bear speech again, 'What are you doing with your hair all matted and your breath stinking, Amanda?'

I felt in my jeans pocket for the cigarettes. They had been taken out and put on the windowsill. As if anticipating me, Gran passed them to me. 'I'll be in the garden when you've finished,' she said.

I wondered what she might be doing out in the garden at one in the morning but I followed her when my lungs were full of smoke.

The gap in my tooth was now like a burnt-out fire grate and the smoke coiled over the bloody gum. Gran had turned on the carousel and was sitting on the crocodile. All the lights glimmered and the gold on the underside of the canopy shone, making the animals look frightening. I squinted at it because I was still drunk and the brightness seemed astounding. I couldn't make sense of the machine sober but, now, I flinched from its cruelty. The early morning was not cold but I shivered and stood at the bottom of the ride, making no attempt to climb onto the carousel and join her as it rotated. I didn't think I had the energy or the balance. Gran passed me, queenly astride the crocodile, sitting bolt upright.

'I've gathered up all the papers concerning the carousel.'

Her voice was projected perfectly for the time of the morning, with no birds to compete with it, and echoed round the garden as if she were in a theatre. Those were the words I heard when we were face to face for a brief few seconds, before the ride showed me, firstly, the side of her face and, then, the back of her as it took her away temporarily, only to be returned moments later.

'What?' I asked mournfully, when she reappeared.

It was a slow conversation as we could only speak a few words to one another with the constant revolving.

'So that you can sell it if you like, dispose of it one way or another. I have had it valued and it will fetch enough to buy you your own house.'

'Have you lost your mind?' I shouted to her back.

For the next revolution of the carousel I ran alongside her, 'Why would you want to sell it? It's everything to you, always has been.'

'Nothing is useful for ever, not even our most valued objects. Even treasure has its time and place.'

'This is not an object,' I argued, exasperated.

'The papers are all together in a yellow folder, clearly marked on the kitchen bookshelves.' She spoke as if she hadn't heard me, 'I am done with it.'

'How can you be done with it?' I asked, standing still.

'Go back to bed, I don't want to discuss it any more.'

It seemed a year before she came round again.

'Why?' I demanded.

'You will need somewhere to live in the future. The place I had in mind for you may no longer be suitable.'

'Can't I stay here?'

'No, you can't.'

'Are you throwing me out?'

'Stop playing games, Amanda, we both know you are ready to leave.'

She jumped down from the crocodile and I lit up again. We walked around the garden together, I sought out my new hole and it stung as it was touched with a smoky tongue. I could still feel the metallic thrill of the blood.

I looked at each of the animals in turn, I had the chance of my own house, my own place where I could start again. It was a bit of hope in this otherwise ugly situation. The crocodile would be exchanged for a kitchen and hall. The war horse for a washing machine. The machine, engine and all the workings would be sold for a roof to go over my head.

There were so many questions I needed to ask her. How would you go about selling something so strange? How would I advertise it? Why did she want to sell it now? I imagined the wording needed for such an advertisement:

Wanted: Buyer for 13-metre fairground ride with a difference. The whole thing is supposed to be God's crazy answer from The Bible *about why people suffer.*

I could see it being snapped up. I stumbled off to bed and slept surprisingly well for someone who was being abandoned again.

I woke the following morning to Gran shaking me. There was no build up to what she said, no preliminary 'Good morning' or 'Here's a cup of tea' but, instead, she moved seamlessly into the next part of her plan, 'My final tying of the threads is to get your mother and father to meet here again. I need them to be on speaking terms, at least,' she said. She had an amazing ability to restart conversations, which had ended the night or week before, without prior warning.

'Why now?'

'Your mother is due in 10 minutes.'

'Why am I always left out of decisions?' I wailed.

'I'm staying out of it. I thought it would be best if I weren't around.'

'You're leaving me with those two?'

'You'll be fine. Don't try to stop them bickering or fighting. Better to let them openly express any antagonism.'

It was nine o'clock, much too early to get up. Far too soon, the bubble of my house fantasy was burst by my mother's knock on the front door. Neat and efficient. She kissed me effusively. My hair was knotted from the night before and I hadn't bothered to clean my teeth.

'Amanda, you look terrible, what on earth have you been doing?'

'She's all right,' came John's unmistakably gruff voice from behind the living room door. I wondered if they were seriously going to fight over me now, after years of absence. It seemed too ridiculous to be possible. I led my mother to where my father was sitting and kept out of the way, making tea, whilst the awkward greetings were made. What do you say to a man whom you have punched in the brow? By the time I returned, it was all going adequately, a courtroom calm pervaded our house. I wondered if the ghosts of their younger selves were weeping in the corner to see these two, passionless and frosty, both having betrayed one another.

'We need to be civil, for Amanda's sake,' my mother said.

'Yes,' he answered sadly.

'You seem intent on staying in this area, so I suppose we both need to get used to the idea of running into one another,' she continued.

'I can cope with you on the street. It's when you pop up on the television, it scares the hell out of me.' My father was trying to lighten the conversation but Marie was having none of it. In fact, she used this as an opportunity to attack him.

'How much longer do you intend to stay here?'

No answer. She sat back down on the sofa, deflated, so different from her television self where she was always calm and in command. I wondered if I were finally seeing the real her.

'I must say, I am surprised to see you two gel. I would never have guessed it. She has, after all, made it her lifetime's work to keep our families apart.'

'Cath is an extraordinary woman: humane, green, a visionary, an entrepreneur,' said John. A little smugly, I thought.

'Good Lord, John, I always thought you had far more intelligence than that. Let's tackle those one by one shall we? Humane? What you see there is detachment from other people, she loathes people and it's her loathing that helps her appear objective.'

She hopped up from the sofa and looked down in disgust at the imprint she had made in the horsehair cushion. Her face was red and her neck was covered in blotches which seemed to be rising.

'Honestly, John, I would have thought better of you. She is brutal with everybody but herself. Green? She chooses to live in a way to which the majority of society can never aspire, which, in turn, makes her feel superior and gives her another simple way of dividing people into good or bad. Or bad and worse in her case.'

Her voice was getting higher and higher, helium hysterical. She realised this just in time and called on her TV training to lower it a whole octave, until she sounded like she was barking.

'Visionary? Hardly. She is obsessed with one book of *The Bible* which nobody reads because it is an intellectual artwork for the leisured class. A parable for someone with time on their hands. She has never worked for a living, apart from a brief period in a pub where she fell out with your father, demonised him and has successfully used him as a scapegoat for everything that has gone wrong in her life ever since.

'Entrepreneurial? She could have expanded any of her ideas at any time to educate others. For instance, the papermaking. I believe she got 17 offers to start a business. She chose not to, not because she believes in the kitchen table as a business model, but because her aforementioned loathing of people and lack of generosity makes her reluctant to share her talents. What do you call a talented person who holds their gifts to them with a vice-like grip?'

She drew breath. She didn't want an answer and glared at John, just in case he saw fit to supply one. 'And, most importantly, she is vain,' she said, exhausted.

'Yes, she is vain,' I agreed.

There was a small cough from the corridor and Gran wandered into the living room. My mother knew that she had heard everything and yet she stood there firmly, unapologetically. I felt glad, too. I was delighted. I wanted Gran to suffer the way she had made us all suffer. I imagined my mother's words finally breaking through her thick skin. She would be reeling from the truth. Humbled by the facts and have no choice but to look deep inside herself. Meanwhile, my father looked mortified; distraught that his new heroine had been so insulted.

'I must take issue with the vain,' said Gran, brushing a long grey strand behind her ear, wearing a dress that still showed her figure and smiling, revealing her still lovely teeth.

My mother stormed out of the house and Gran shouted after her, 'Everything you have said is true.' Marie stood still. With an immense effort, she turned round slowly to address my grandmother. There were two metres between them: steps and flowerbeds, plants and earth.

'In order for this to be a fair exercise,' said my mother coldly, 'you naturally have the right of reply.'

'You are sharp, focussed, hardworking and ambitious. All this bound up with a remarkable capacity to spring back.'

And, with that, Gran shut the front door.

XIII

Chaos Erupts

THE FOLLOWING day, I managed to ignore the morning, rising at 12.30pm. I took Denim out of her cage and walked around the garden with her. She struggled to be set free but I couldn't let her go that day, sensing the closeness of a sparrowhawk, even though I had seen nothing. I put her back in her cage.

From late-afternoon, Gran, John and I sat around at home with nobody saying much. We all looked at the seams in the wallpaper or the knots in the wooden floor. Bill and Huff poked their heads round the door a couple of times during the course of the evening but both made a hasty retreat when they sensed the atmosphere. After an hour of silence and staring at the floor, I had worked things out.

'I'm going to go and get my stuff back from the pub later tonight.'

'Do you want me to go for you? I could drive you? I could collect your things?' John asked eagerly, desperate to do something useful in the situation. Gran, of course, felt no such compunction, knowing only too well that, as an adult, you had to sort out your own mess.

'No, thanks. I'm going to wait until the pub has closed and just nip down there discreetly, get my things and come away.'

Gran shuffled her foot on the floorboard, running it back and forth repeatedly over a particularly large and dark knot in the wood. I was reminded of my own childhood deconstructing of the abandoned house before Susan bought it. But, just as I had tried to destroy that house, I now wanted my grandmother to grow something magical in our home. If she really concentrated, then the friction of her foot might manifest branches from our own flooring. Stubborn little twigs at first that would suddenly thicken as they grew and sprout little offshoots themselves. Then, thicker branches would move tentatively forward like a hand in the dark. Within minutes, we could be within our own primeval forest so, although Gran was unable to offer traditional comfort, she would have made the state of my mind come to life in an empathic gesture. I was stuck in a forest, unable to find my way out.

Selfishly, she chose not to conjure up the wood at all and her foot was stilled. Several times, she looked as though she were about to speak, going to say something important, but, every time I caught her eye, she stared at me, frowning. In the end, all she said was, 'You don't really need to collect your things.'

'I know that they are replaceable but I want them back. The last thing I want is her gathering all my possessions into a dustbin bag and leaving them outside the pub.'

'No, that's not what I meant,' she said.

I didn't have time to hear what she meant because the clock struck midnight and I leapt up decisively, left the house and headed towards Michael's pub.

I did the same as I had done one summer's night, weeks before, after I had passed my driving test: turned off the engine at the approach to the pub and drifted down the slope. There was mist coming off the river, the sky was cloudy and looked as though it were lowering itself metre by metre, pushing closer to the ground.

It was a Tuesday night, traditionally our quietest night at the pub and there was no trace of any last stragglers, nor any signs of life through the downstairs window. Fiona's car had left, the staff's cars were gone and all had been tidied away for another day.

I thought of not putting the brakes on so the car would reach the edge of the quay and drop into the treacherous mud. But really, I had no intention of dying and the idea of being trapped in a small car, sinking in mud, was not appealing. I was glad that I had thought of that image and dismissed it instantly, though. It told me a lot about my state of mind. I was hurt and humiliated but not suicidal.

I took the keys out of the ignition and crept towards the door of the pub. Although I had looked in the downstairs windows as I arrived, I hadn't been able to bring myself to look upstairs. Long before I saw the landing window, I knew what I would witness. Sometimes, we just knew. It was as though my eyes didn't want me to look up, as I forced my head to glance in the direction of the upstairs window. Ah, there was nothing to see. I exhaled with relief and then, just as my breath mingled with the slight breeze, everything changed. Susan was making her way along the top corridor, presumably going to the bathroom, wearing Michael's dressing gown. With the tide out, the wind suddenly picked up the smell of the river and wafted its salty stench over me. I walked to the pub door, put my key in the lock and crept up the stairs into the main bar.

Now that I had seen her and my worst fears had been confirmed, I found myself without a plan. I wasn't sure why I had let myself in, considering I could hardly collect my things with her there. I could have raged into the bedroom and upset them but I didn't want to see him naked with her. What would be the point of it? Some images, like her in his dressing gown, were just painful truth but others we never needed to see.

As Susan had been walking between the bathroom and the bedroom, the robe was done up tightly. Not like when I used to wear it, leaving the rope hanging like a noose. In the few seconds that I had seen her, she had been walking gingerly with the newness of things, testing out the carpet on the upstairs corridor for fit. Finally performing her new role as Michael's lover after months of slowly trying to make it happen. I wondered if she were disappointed; I suspected not.

I poured myself a couple of drinks in the bar. The place was so familiar to me, I could find my way around in the dark. I reached out for the expensive brandy and knew exactly how many bottles along it was without having to check. I stroked the bar that Gran had commissioned and thought about how much of her there was to leave behind in this place. Never mind expendable clothes, it was all the hours she had spent sourcing extraordinary things. Finding that stunning yellow paint and those peculiar objects on the shelves. It didn't seem right that I wouldn't see them again. I was starting to slip into despair, so I licked the gold on my watch as Gran had told me to do over a year ago if life became unbearable. And, sure enough, as soon as the metal touched my tongue the sense of hopelessness lifted.

It suddenly occurred to me that I didn't know what to say to Susan or Michael if I were to meet them tonight. Despite this, my body moved me forward on autopilot and I found myself creeping silently upstairs.

As I neared the landing, I slowed down even more. I had known that this was going to happen and, now, each new step was laborious. Did I have to put myself through this, the possibility of seeing them in bed together? I could slip out now and send John or Gran to get my things tomorrow. I slunk into the bathroom to consider my best course of action. I could smell Susan's scent and the faint smell of her urine.

I stood there in the dark, mentally recalling what of mine was in the bathroom cupboard and how each was positioned. I thought about my collection of face packs. I had 14 left in that cupboard. My beloved face packs. I switched on the shaving mirror light and the dimness allowed me to go through my collection, reciting their names including Strawberry Smoothing, Clay Refining, Mud Nourishing, Avocado for Softening. One was missing. I checked again, making sure it hadn't dropped down the back of the cupboard or behind the sink, but there was no trace of it. It was the face pack for mature skin. I had bought it thinking that I would grow old with Michael.

I heard a woman's footsteps heading back towards the bathroom and, in an instant, I knew what had happened. In the time it had taken me to let myself in, have two drinks and creep upstairs to check on my belongings, Rink had used my face pack for middle-aged skin. Granted, it wasn't a great deal of use to me but that was not the point. Not content with stealing my man, making me lose my job and entirely undermining my confidence, she'd stolen my face pack. I didn't really care about 99p worth of sea kelp extract, but I did care that she was so sure of her position with Michael that she would wear a face pack in front of him. I winced when I realised they could only have spent three nights together: the night of the party, last night and tonight. And now, she was on her way back to rinse off *my* face pack and all the goodness of the sea.

I switched off the shaving light and ducked behind the washing basket. It wasn't much bigger than me but she was a rational woman and wouldn't be looking for a body behind a wicker basket. If you're not looking for something, you don't see it. Gran's quotes popped up at the most inopportune moments and I wondered if my whole life would be like this, so profoundly affected by her.

Susan looked relaxed and content. I remained crunched up behind the basket, glimpsing her through strands of tightly woven wicker. I was just about to start thinking benign thoughts about her when I remembered that I was the wronged woman.

Suddenly, I leapt out from behind the wicker basket, screaming at Susan. I knew what I wanted to say and the words were formed in my head, but they came out twisted and corrupted. Had she been able translate the jumbled language, she would have heard me accuse her of sickening betrayal, far worse than taking Michael from me. Unexpectedly, clarity returned to me.

'You were supposed to be on my side but, for the last few years, you have tried in every conceivable way to crush me. Why have you, a mature woman, devoted so much energy to making me wretched?'

She shrunk into herself and her eyes moved hastily over my face. I could hear her dog coming along the corridor. Skidding at the bathroom door where the carpet runner ended, it pushed its way into the bathroom. The dog didn't recognise Susan because she was wearing a face pack and, having its sense of smell dulled by too many rollings in the mud, the animal decided to protect me, whom it remembered and needed to repay for numerous benevolences. It leapt at Susan, placing one paw on each shoulder as it bit her on the face. She fell backwards onto the sink, which detached itself from the pedestal but remained attached to the wall by a few strands of silicone and the tiling.

It was all over in an instant but, for a moment, the front of Susan's body had been covered in a red fur coat. A flash of red fur. Fleetingly, it had no longer looked like a stupid red setter but was redeemed, the domesticated mutt became wolf-like and terrifying. It must have been as proud of that instant as I was. We didn't think we had it in us.

Susan's blood mingling with the face pack was interesting and held my attention long enough for Michael to arrive. He provoked the dog into a further frenzy with his dramatic timing. I admired him for a second. It was one thing to be able to look up examples of appropriate behaviour and copy them but it was another to live without a script. He managed to shut the dog in the next room and was instructing me to phone the ambulance.

Susan was sitting on the side of the bath, sobbing, 'Is it bad? I can't look.'

We ignored her.

'Look for me, somebody, please,' she pleaded.

I could see that it was minor and was thinking about the practicalities of the ambulance arriving from 10 miles down the road, twisting and turning down the narrow, winding roads.

'It would be better for you to drive her,' I shouted to Michael. 'It will take too long for an ambulance to get here.'

'I'm drunk, can't drive her. Can you drive her?' he asked.

I looked at her face and made doubly sure it was superficial. 'It's not too bad, you could drive yourself,' I told Susan.

Reassured by my diagnosis, probably because she was still in shock, Susan left the bathroom, cursing that she would drive her bloody self. As she went down the stairs, holding a towel to her face, she screamed at Michael, 'Get that bloody dog put down!'

I sat on the bathroom floor.

'Do you think she's going to be all right?' he asked.

'Yes, it wasn't too serious a bite. I suppose her own dog couldn't smell her through the face pack.'

'I told her not to touch anything of yours.'

He looked at me and knew that he had no right to shout at me but I could see it welling up inside him. 'I'm going to drown that damned animal!'

'Don't be ridiculous!' I said.

He spun out of the bathroom and into the room next door; grabbing the now subdued dog by her scruff and pulled her down the stairs. She whimpered. We were both shouting for some reason, even though the pub was deadly quiet.

'Michael, let me have the dog, it's not her fault.'

'You heard her say have the bloody dog put down so that's what I'm going to do. I'm going to drown the bitch.'

I thought that following and staying calm would be the right thing to do but not before I had gathered the things I wanted: my blue-hooded sweatshirt and my black dress. I wasn't going to let Susan examine them with distaste. I also realised that Michael was no dog killer and, most importantly, I knew that the tide was out because I had smelt the mud, so I watched him from the pub door. All he did was tie the dog to a boat close to the quay. A boat that wouldn't be moving for two hours. Long enough for her to drown. The dog, sensibly having found the firmest patch of mud, just stood there shivering, moving occasionally when the mud rose up to her knuckles.

I stayed in the pub while Michael came back from the quay, looking triumphant. 'At least the damned thing's out of my sight for a moment.'

'I'm not going to let you drown the dog, you know.'

'I know you aren't. I'm relying on your good sense.'

I hadn't shown much good sense in the past few days but I normally did. I was furious at him for playing at drowning the dog. Who was he trying to fool with this macho rubbish? I had a sudden thought and, as Michael was already drunk and in need of calming down, I suggested another drink.

I disconnected the brandy from the optic and kept his glass topped up while he spoke, justifying what he had done to me, 'I got freaked out by the age difference between us, especially with my daughter arriving on the scene. When I saw you with her, it felt completely inappropriate.'

'You must have planned things long before then. I saw the way you started to look at her weeks ago.'

I knew if I goaded him, he would drink more. He hadn't got the courage to tell me to leave and I wanted to see him digging a great hole with his stupid mouth.

'We just have more in common than you and me, Amanda. She's a serious businesswoman, too.'

'I haven't had the chance to be a serious businesswoman. I'm only 19.' The mention of that figure made him cringe again. I no longer needed to help him top up his drink, he was doing an admirable job himself. 'Just tell me when she stopped being "That Woman"? The one we both ridiculed?'

'I don't know. I can't pinpoint an exact moment.'

I knew he was lying. 'She wore you down with her relentless pursuit?' I mocked.

'*You* are wearing me down with your questions,' he slurred.

'You owe me. In case you've forgotten, I've been sleeping with you for the last three months and, now, *she's* here.' I spat out the last words.

Michael shuffled uncomfortably. He was completely unused to facing up to things.

'Am I so easy to dismiss?' I asked.

'Oh, Amanda, it's not like that! I didn't see things turning out this way.'

'Which way?' I was determined to make him say it. I would squeeze and squeeze until a tiny droplet of truth emerged and, finally, it did.

'That Susan and I would end up together.'

There, he'd said it. He was lost to me for ever and, as if in a final act of cruelty, he pushed his shirt sleeve up, exposing his beautiful forearm. I was looking at his body in delight and could still smell his skin from a metre away. But he had no interest in me.

The phone rang and it was Susan. As I headed up the stairs again to fetch the rest of my belongings, I heard him repeat what she must have said to him, 'Superficial puncture wound, requiring three stitches. No lasting scar. Just a tetanus jab.' I stood still to hear the rest of the conversation. 'No, good idea, best not come back tonight. I'll sort all this out and see you tomorrow,' he whispered. 'Yes, everything's okay, it'll all be fine, trust me. Love you.'

I wondered whether human bites were worse than dog bites. I should have bitten her myself, it might have proved fatal. I walked into Michael's bedroom. Susan had left a catalogue on the bedside table. And a wash bag. It looked as though she had been here for at least two nights. I didn't suppose that she would take weeks to move her belongings in and, instead of waiting for him to allocate space for her, she had probably seized it greedily. The clothes catalogue was not a big, thick cheap one with slimy pages full of poorly cut clothes, but a slim volume printed on quality paper. Nothing in the book was too tight, too low-waisted or too baggy, unlike my own wardrobe.

I soon found representations of Michael and Susan in the catalogue. A glamorous older couple, both beginning to grey, cavorting on a British beach. There were no children in the brochure or, if there were, it was by implication. This couple's children were grown up, independent and successful, decent people without nightmares. The clothes were not appropriate for me, they wouldn't allow me in the catalogue with my penchant for bright colours and revealing jeans.

Where was I represented? Because I had never seen a brochure with me in it. It used to be all right when I lived with Gran, I didn't need to see a reflection of myself but, now that I was broken, I needed the affirmation. But I knew that no such book existed and it never would. They didn't make catalogues showing real life: the doubts, the anguish and self-searching. What clothes would go with those emotions? No clothes, that was what, and nakedness couldn't sell much. A tear dropped onto the dancing couple and the paper was so thick and shiny that it repelled the watery droplet.

I put the catalogue down and headed back to Michael with my arms full of clothes. His head in his hands, he was pretending to have passed out at the bar to avoid having to speak to me. In an act of misplaced kindness, I helped him up the stairs to bed and left him there, in the bed he had just rumpled with another woman. But it wasn't to be the last time I went into his bedroom.

Meanwhile, I set out to rescue the dog. She was pleased to see me as only a potentially drowning creature would be. Her fur was matted. I wondered if she were Susan's alter ego. Susan kept herself so tightly under control with everything she ate and drank. All her clothes were so pristine and without creases, everything had to be perfect. I wondered if the dog might represent the untamed side of herself, that's why she wanted Michael to have it killed.

Grateful for all the times I had tried to save the dog's appearance by rinsing her off roughly with the outside tap that lay behind the fence, or combing out the worst of the knots in her fur, she came with me willingly. I scurried her upstairs into one of the en-suites. I showered her, using Susan's products that she had brought with her in the candy-striped wash bag. That peculiar smell of wet dog lingered despite the expensive fragrance of the shampoo. The dog and I watched the mud slither down the drain in lumps and melt to tiny particles that made the water brown-grey.

She scrambled out of the shower, soaking me with her doggy odour, and I dried her, using as many of the pristine, fresh towels as was possible for one large, soaking wet dog. And, when I had used them up, I went out into the corridor and pulled down the neat bale of towels that lay waiting for their first outing from the airing cupboard. There was something good about pulling down that tower of cream fluffiness. There was no sign of Michael in the corridor. I crept towards his bedroom and relaxed when I heard him snoring gently.

When I had dried the dog's hair as much as I could and brushed it neatly, I got Michael's hair clippers, set them on number one and sheared her. She lay, sheep-like, between my legs, looking more interesting without all that hair weighing her down. More dog-like, more heroic. I made a comfortable bed for her with one of the new king-size duvets and fetched her a few biscuits. I took the red hair I had clipped from the dog and gently placed it on Michael's pillow.

Then, I quickly ushered the dog downstairs. She came willingly and I sat her on the car's passenger seat. She seemed as pleased as I was to be leaving the pub. I smiled as I thought of Michael waking to a vision of red.

XIV

Training for War

WHEN I walked into the house, I found John and Gran talking. They finished abruptly when they saw me with the bald dog.

'Should I be expecting a visit from Susan as you seem to be bringing another one of her animals into the house?' asked Gran.

'No, she wants her dead.'

'Then we must embrace her,' said Gran, calling the dog towards her and looking into her eyes. 'As I suspected, an intelligent animal away from Susan.'

'Is it all over between you and Michael, then?' John asked.

'Yes.'

'In that case, I'll leave you in the care of your grandmother and say goodnight.'

'Goodnight, love, we'll start training the dog in the morning,' she said.

I wasn't expecting that. I was expecting one of her lectures, something that she had been rehearsing for weeks, involving polar bears but, for once, she must have realised that I wasn't up to it.

'By the way, what's the dog's name?' she asked.

'Pumpkin,' I said, surprised by the question.

'We'll call her Chagrin, then the animal can have a fresh start with us and won't be confused,' she said.

I hadn't the strength to argue and was left alone with Chagrin, and the familiar sympathetic creaking and squeaking of the house.

The next morning, Gran shook me awake. I had been at her elderflower wine and fallen asleep on the sofa. I shut my eyes again, hoping she would take the hint and leave me alone, or at least make me a cup of tea.

'Time to commence the training.'

'What?'

'You can't have an untrained dog. It's a liability around here with our cat, the wildlife and the deer.'

'You do it and I'll watch you,' I said, almost growling.

'Get up, Amanda, and make the best of a bad situation.'

'Get lost!' Tears rolled down my face and my whole body was wracked with sobs, 'He preferred her.'

'I'm not surprised,' she said.

'What do you mean by that, exactly?' I snapped. I still had enough spirit to defend myself.

'Well, he's a feeble cardboard cut-out of a person. He is not a passionate man.'

I thought about what she had said. Not a passionate man. It was true, he had learnt to turn it off when it suited him.

'Get up, the dog won't train itself,' she said again. 'I have worked out an intensive early-morning training routine for you and the dog. Firstly, it involves you running with Chagrin alongside you on a short leash for half an hour each morning.'

I did what she said. What else was there to do? The dog responded to Gran's plan with a fervour that made me weep. I ran to the top of our road, passing Susan's house and noticed that her car was not there. If Chagrin showed any recollection of the house, she seemed as keen to hurry by as I did. I only got to the top of the road before I was sick in the hedge. The dog tried to eat it, I like to think she was removing the evidence from Gran. Finally making do with sniffing the vomit, Chagrin seemed to make a diagnosis from it and turned to me with a compassionate look. At least someone in the house could do an impression of concern. With me sweating and shaking, we set off back home.

Gran and John were always talking, huddled up neatly together. They stopped every time I came into the room. They needn't have bothered, my misery was so great that they could talk freely about anything and I couldn't care less. John didn't say too much to me, mostly because I cut him off mid-sentence, but he did a good trade in sympathetic glances and he moved out of my room, into the conservatory. The next morning was the same, except Chagrin and I reached further than the end of the road. We ran for half a mile before I was sweating and panting, and my legs felt like they might give way beneath me. This routine carried on for a week. I stopped looking for Susan's car as I passed her place. Each day, I got a little further. I hadn't realised how unfit I had become but, now that I was stronger, John sometimes joined me. It meant that we had time together but we didn't have to speak, we just ran in comfortable silence.

For the rest of the day, I moped about the house and garden, largely ignored by Gran. A week into the training programme and she said that the intensity should increase.

'As long as you just mean the dog.' Naturally, she didn't.

Outside in the garden, she had made a series of cloth tunnels from flour sacks for the dog to run through on command. I had to accompany Chagrin to show her how it was done. This was not the case in reality. The dog flew through the cloth and I shambled on all fours. Huff watched from his usual 10-metre comfort zone; he and the dog barely tolerated one another.

By the second week, Gran had made a sort of seesaw for Chagrin which we had to run up and down together. Each day, she introduced new tricks and she made me run with Chagrin all the time. The dog's zeal was infuriating.

'The dog's a fast learner,' I said.

'Mmm, one of you is.'

Each trick had to be perfected. She nagged and nagged. On many occasions, I sat on the ground and cried and said that I couldn't do it. Gran would just stare up at the sky and speak in a monotonous way, 'Get up, Amanda, and get moving.'

'Gran, this isn't helping.'

'I never said it would.'

'What's the point, then?'

'None whatsoever. All you can grasp from this is that, when spring comes around again, you will be strong.'

I looked up, trying to copy as much of the dog's expression as possible, so that she might treat me with compassion.

'And, when you are really fit, you will be able to outrun your misery.'

'Really?'

'No... well, only temporarily. When it catches up with you, it'll be the equivalent of a polar bear's weight in wretchedness on your back, knocking you to the ground, but at least you'll have had a glimpse of what it was like to leave it behind.'

Regardless of the weather, we were outside for hours every day and I finished the sessions by doing press-ups and lifting homemade weights.

'Do you think she's preparing us for war?' asked John.

She was.

Every night, the dog lay exhausted, as close to Gran's feet as she could. Weeks passed in this manner. Her fur had grown back beautifully and I was sure Gran was feeding Chagrin something to make her coat redder than ever: strawberry jam or beetroot, possibly. She was a magnificent animal and so well trained, she started to pretend to be asleep at night when we all sat reading. When Huff walked enticingly close to Chagrin, the dog looked straight ahead and refused to be drawn into a confrontation, relaxing once the cat had passed by safely.

One morning, when John and I were practising walking along a narrow plank five metres from the ground with no safety nets, Gran came into the garden. She called up to John, 'He's finally come for you. I can't help you, I'm going to The Tide.'

His face sank and, in that moment, he looked like a 15-year-old. When we reached the ground, I rushed to him and put my arms around him, 'You don't have to speak to him you know.'

As Gran had deserted us, I followed John into the house to find his father waiting impatiently.

'I never thought I'd be back here again,' he said.

John stayed quiet.

'I've been to your office to try and find you after we hadn't heard from you for weeks and they told me that you were holed up here.'

'I'm not holed up, I'm taking time to get to know my daughter.'

'When are you going back to work, John?'

Doon ignored the reference to me, just as he had refused to acknowledge my presence.

'I don't know if I am.'

'Don't be a damned fool! All those years to build up the business just to throw it away here...'

'I'm happy here.'

'If you've had some kind of breakdown, I know people. Discreet people.'

'There's been no breakdown.'

'Have you been in touch with the girl's mother?' John didn't answer. 'You're not about to marry her?' Doon Senior looked genuinely concerned.

'No, she'd never have me,' John said.

'Well, at least that's a relief. Why are you dressed like that?'

I hadn't thought much about how we were dressed. Gran had got our kit from the army surplus store and, as I looked between my father and myself, I saw how odd we must have looked, and yet how fit and healthy. We had been running together regularly for a month now.

'We're in training,' I said.

My grandfather turned his back on me. 'John, you're still my son, despite what has happened. You can stop this ridiculous business any time you like.' He softened and wheedled, 'Your mother and I are wondering when you're coming home. We can look after you there.'

'I'm not coming back.'

'John, think what you're throwing away, not just your career. Bella is from a superb family.'

John laughed, 'You never change.'

'What about the girl?' Doon asked. He spoke as if I weren't there. Despite weeks of training, I was still invisible.

'My daughter, you mean?'

'How can you be sure? Consider a DNA test.'

'I don't need any tests and, while I stay here, I'm finding out the truth.'

'There's no truth here, I've told you all that happened.'

'You've told me your version of events, but I have listened to Cath Furnish and the truth has not come together in the way I expected.'

'She's manipulative, John. Don't tell me you've been fool enough to be taken in by that lying bitch?'

'No, you brought me up, presented me with a simple story which I had no cause to question but now I find out that you were lying. And, with your deceitfulness, you've destroyed people's lives.'

'They would have ruined their own lives without me. I acted out of everyone's best interests. I didn't think it fair on Arlet's family. I genuinely believed something untoward was going on at the pub. It was my duty to deal with it.'

'Cath Furnish unsettled you. Who knows, you may even have loved her in your own, strange way but, rather than deal with those feelings, you attacked her.'

'What's all the fuss about, John? She's still here isn't she and it was all a very long time ago. We have all moved on.'

'Some of us were not able to move on,' Bill had appeared, unnoticed, and was standing in the door frame.

'I wondered where she was hiding you,' Doon said contemptuously.

Bill made a clumsy move to hit him but Doon stood his ground and pushed my grandfather to the floor. John went to pick him up.

'Is this her attempt to get me back? To steal my only son? To try to come between us? Well, Bill, you can tell her from me, it won't work. It's only a matter of time before he sees through her like I did. Where is she, by the way? Down at that squalid little pub? I heard she was helping with the refurbishment but I didn't believe it. Is it true?'

'Yes,' said Bill. 'She has every right to be there.'

'I'm surprised, after what happened.'

'Don't ever set foot in that place or I'll kill you!' Bill threatened.

'I'll go where I like with a clear conscience, despite your pitiful threats. What right have you to keep me away from The Tide? Same old Bill, still devoted to Cath and, after all these years, she's still utterly indifferent to you.'

He turned his back on Bill and said to John, 'When you see sense, I'll be waiting for you.' With that, he left, closing the door quietly behind him.

XV

Carousel for Sale

THAT evening, after John and I had come back from our run, we stood bent over the seesaw catching our breath and speaking between gasps.

'What was all that business between you and your father?' I asked.

'After Arlet's death and the girl drowning, my father brought the police in to find out if there were any suspicious circumstances involving your grandmother.'

'And were there?' I asked nervously.

'You'd better ask her yourself.'

I didn't see Gran again that day, for which I was grateful. There was nothing unusual about this, she had always drifted about as she saw fit. I needed time to psych myself up in order to ask her all the questions I had planned. Chagrin suddenly brushed against me and I felt the dog's sleek, muscled body and saw how healthy her coat was. It had grown back significantly in two months. I felt suddenly remorseful about that night, then pictured Michael again. Thinking about the beauty of his body still caused me pain.

John now slept in the conservatory on a Z-bed. He would wake early enough to watch the light come over the garden and illuminate the carousel. If I woke up in time, we would sit huddled together on the floor. As the light washed each animal, it became recognisable: Behemoth the hippo, the vultures, the goats, the other creatures and, lastly, Leviathan the crocodile. I could stare at one tiny detail for minutes at a time, like the bear's claws, until my eyes stopped seeing edges.

'I like the crocodile best, like Cath,' John said.

'And I like the hippopotamus creature with his penis like a pine tree and his bulging testicles,' I laughed.

'What?'

'In modern interpretations of *The Book of Job*, they mention its penis,' I said, sipping my tea innocently.

'Trust you to know that!'

'How could I fail to know that, living with Gran?'

'Do you think you would ever have bought such a thing? She wasn't much older than you when she got it,' he asked.

I didn't like the question because I didn't know if I would have had the courage to buy it, just like that, regardless of other people's opinions. I think the logical side of my brain would have cancelled out my desire for it.

'I'm not going to buy it. I'm going to sell it and buy a house with the proceeds. I have her permission.'

'I know.'

'She has even sorted out all the documents and put them together in a nice, neat little folder for me.'

It was as though he didn't hear me or chose not to. Instead, he carried on in his placid way, 'Do you think you need a licence to drive the carousel?'

'You need a licence to understand it.'

'If this is the visual manifestation of God's answer to suffering and I stare at it enough, I might make sense of it all,' John said.

'You're missing the point, you'll just exhaust yourself with that kind of thinking. There's nothing to make sense of. It's an inadequate answer to the question of misery. In fact, it's a downright insult. Why am I in agony? "Oh, shut up, I'm great and you're not, and by the way, look at all the things I have made,"' I said facetiously.

'If you were God and someone asked you about suffering, why would you give an answer that doesn't make sense?' asked John.

He was very naïve. He hadn't been steeped in this way of thinking since childhood. Voices from the whirlwind were all new, and illogical answers confounded him.

'To shut someone up. It's easy. It's a way of keeping people ignorant, pretending that it's all too complicated and magnificent for a simpleton such as yourself to understand. "How could a simple creature like you possibly grasp my extraordinary scheme?" And, all the time, there is no scheme. It's *The Wizard of Oz* all over again.'

'Do you deign to compare *The Wizard of Oz* with *The Book of Job*?'

'Why not? There are charlatans and people who realise they had-what-it-takes-all-along involved in both books.'

'That's cynical. To me, the meaning of the carousel is an admittance that we know nothing. Job rants and rants and waits patiently for an answer and, when it does come, it's unlike anything he could have expected, so God Himself will be unlike anything we can imagine.'

I could see Gran's influence there and, maybe, they genuinely did think alike. I decided to be sarcastic because I felt a little jealous at the thought of John being emotionally closer to Gran in terms of the way he saw the world than I was.

'Of course it appeals to Gran, because she's got time on her hands to waste on hypothetical matters when the answer from *The Book of Job* is quite clear. It's God saying, "You can ask questions but don't expect any answers because your human logic cannot be applied to my world." How convenient is that for God? What a great excuse. Or, of course, an even more unpalatable way of looking at it: if there is a God, he's half-evil, get used to it. Or, thirdly, you've got the view of most of the population, if you bothered to ask them, that the question is not interesting in the first place. Their answer, if they even had one, would probably be, "As long as it's not me suffering why should I care?"'

John was silent as a glimmer of sunlight bounced underneath the roof of the carousel and the gold leaf sprung into life, looking brightest on the twisted poles.

'You don't give a damn because you are heartbroken and lacking in energy. Ranting and demanding answers would be too much for you.'

He said this tenderly as he wrapped his arm around my shoulder and we stared out of the French windows together. After a minute, I began to feel uncomfortable. I wasn't used to people offering physical affection and calm. I had been reared in the 'pull yourself together' school and, as much as I tried to fight against this, it was too strong for me.

So, I went into my own personal translation of the voice from the whirlwind, where God sounds like a petulant, ranting child. For authenticity, I also added a touch of absurdity, 'Can you hold Leviathan with a delicate rope? Can you walk through the shopping mall with him straining at the leash, terrorising all who witness? Can you stop him from splashing in the local swimming pool?'

'No,' he said smiling, 'I can't do any of those things, and I repent in dust and ashes at your feet.'

'In that case, I will restore all your lands and children.'

'My daughter is restored to me.'

'Oh, he doesn't get his original children back, they all die when a brutal wind comes from the desert and blows the house down on top of them. God replaces them with different ones. From our modern perspective that's one of the bits that seems most jarring. God agrees to this ridiculous wager with the Devil where the outcome is so horrific for one person and there never is a genuine reparation, not one that makes sense, anyway. That's the way life really is.'

I wanted John to feel guilty for missing my childhood, almost as if, because he had only ever known me as an adult, I had been replaced; just like Job's children. But he didn't pick up on it.

'It's not always that bleak. Sometimes, you get a second chance, take it, and turn your life around,' he said.

The next morning, I slept in too late to watch the carousel appear with John. Stretching both arms out together, I admired the tone all through them, from the forearms to where they met my shoulders.

For once, I was keen to get up and on with the training program. The sun came in through the hall window and I dragged my feet along the lino, looking down at my calves, all brown and toned again. At that moment, the flimsiness of the house seemed just right. The boards that protected us from the outside were just the right thickness to let in the early morning warmth.

I touched the wall as if my hand would flow straight through it and I would follow and be outside in my dressing gown. We didn't need 18-centimetre thick walls because we were born with an understanding that life continually hung in the balance. We never made plans that were too far off because we didn't know if we would still be alive then. It always occurred to us that we might not be – and that was the difference between Furnishs and most non-Furnishs: an ever-present sense of mortality.

We never really knew what it was like to be young, and gazed incredulously at other people who thought they were immortal. Occasionally, we envied their freedom and spontaneity but, mostly, we knew what we had. When we woke up and were pleasantly surprised that we were still breathing, we could always find some small thing about which to be pessimistic.

Today was the day I was going to do it. I would ask Gran in detail about Arlet, the drowned girl and the police investigation that John had mentioned. She could no longer worm her way out of answering me. I would be like Job, I would rant and rant until she replied with the truth.

When I went into the lounge, John and Bill were sat together on the sofa, as far away from one another as possible. Barely perched on the cushions, they looked like they were about to leap up. I wondered whether they had argued.

'Relax,' I said, 'You both look really jumpy.'

'She's gone,' said Bill.

It was right that he was the one to tell me. He had earnt it after being married to Gran for so long but the words seemed to drain all the life out of him.

'What?' I asked.

'Early this morning,' he replied, handing me a letter. It was just a few lines saying that she would be back. There was no time limit for Gran's disappearance and no indication of where she had gone.

'I wondered why she let me sleep in,' I said.

'She must have caught a taxi from the end of the road,' said John.

My attention returned to Bill whose small, suffering face was unbearable. I thought of all the selfish things that she had ever done and decided that this was the worst. I tried to comfort my grandfather, but he turned away from me.

He built a fire in the garden and frantically threw papers on it. The designs for his eco-house that had never been accepted.

I stood in the garden long enough for the smoke to cling to my clothes and tried to speak to him, 'Are you sure you want to do this?'

'It's long overdue. Now, if you don't mind, I've got lots of paper to destroy.'

He had been so easy to dismiss over the years with his mild-mannered lack of direction, but now he was doing something so final and so difficult that I felt for him.

The world was truly a miserable place. He'd offered a solution and it had been rejected. I felt deflated and close to despair. I made John help me to put the tarpaulin on the carousel. He stayed on the ground while I clambered all over the sloping roof, carefully fitting the numbered sections together, encasing the crazy machine in its winter coat. It was still autumn but it seemed like an appropriate act of mourning with Gran gone.

'There's no point dragging yourself about. Lick some gold and then listen to me,' John suddenly spoke with authority.

'What do you know about licking gold?'

'It's an antidote to despair,' he said, lifting my watch strap to my mouth. 'I've got a week's worth of things to tell you.'

I thought back to all the times in the last weeks when I had seen Gran's head close to John's. I had thought they were talking about me and had taken some small comfort that I was sustaining so many whispered conversations.

I didn't expect to hear from Gran, thinking that she would instinctively know that we were safe and would get on with whatever it was that she was doing.

'What do you think she *is* doing?' I asked John.

'Making sense of things.'

'Why has it taken her so long to make sense of things?'

He shrugged, 'I suppose it does take a long time.'

'Do you think she'll be away for months?'

Again, he shrugged, and I thought that, knowing her, she would.

Bill wanted nothing to do with us and my time with John was not working out in the way that I thought it would. He was kind but withdrawn, lacking his usual good humour and, as for the information he had promised me, it was not forthcoming. He often looked as though he were going to speak and then, overwhelmed by what he had to say, fell silent. I didn't like his inconsistency, so I spent more and more time in my room with 20 of Gran's carousel magazines for company. I looked in the back of them at the small ads to see if I could find anyone who might be interested in buying a carousel.

I went to the local library and e-mailed 12 tentative enquiries to collectors, museums and international carousel magazines; including one that had been circled by Gran and left in the yellow folder. If she had left that file so readily available, what did she expect? I had to make my own life and the chance of having my own house was enticing. I also had a horrible thought in the back of my mind. Maybe she was never coming back. In that case, I needed to look after myself more than ever.

I was not expecting to hear anything back from my e-mails and spent the time painting my toes and drifting in and out of sleep but, two hours after sending them, I had a phone call from a Sarah Chimes, the very advert that Gran had circled. She was a woman who sourced curious objects for various museums and private collectors around the world. She had been to our house years before when Marie was a small child, and had written an article about the carousel for her magazine. She was very keen to come and see it again and show me the photos she had in her collection from the time when Gran had finished the renovation. She said she never thought she would see the day when such an unusual piece might be available.

John tried to put the dampers on my scheme, 'I wouldn't hold out much hope of selling it… It's very much an acquired taste and I don't expect that woman will turn up anyway. She sounds a bit strange to me. What sort of person does that for a living?'

'I've been given permission to sell it and I must think of my own future. Gran said I could buy a house with the proceeds and that's what I intend to do. If the person who looks after you abandons you, your only choice is to look after yourself,' I added, self-pityingly.

My speech managed to induce considerable guilt in John and he spent the rest of the evening telling me that he would not leave again, although I never doubted that.

I didn't tell him that I had been on the phone again to a very keen-sounding Sarah Chimes who was coming to see the carousel in two days. Beneath her mannered speech was a desperation, a strong desire to own the carousel. I was delighted, who would have thought that it would be so easy?

Two hours before she arrived, I casually mentioned her visit. John stood rigid and leant on the wall for support, 'I don't think Cath really meant for you to sell it, you know.'

'Why did she say that I could, then, and leave all the paperwork in an easy place for me to find?'

'Because she was calling your bluff?'

'She should know me better. Will you help me to get the tarpaulin off it before Sarah Chimes comes, please?' I asked John. It had only been eight days since we had covered the carousel.

'Let's wait until she arrives. It all sounds a bit unlikely and it's a pain to cover up, especially if it's windy.'

I decided to do it by myself if he would not help me; I had done it successfully once before. I moved confidently over the roof of the carousel, the only one who could tackle the tarpaulin single-handedly. The doorbell rang exactly on time and a short, plump, gruff seller of the curious stepped into our living room and took a seat on the sofa. Her shoes were scuffed. I had expected someone slicker, someone more professional-looking. I chatted to Sarah for a few minutes. The kind of nonsense conversation skills I had acquired at the pubs came back to me at just the right time. She was polite, but soon turned the conversation round to the carousel.

'It's an imposing thing to have in the garden. It's taking up a lot of space which you could utilise for other things.'

'There's plenty of garden for it and it's always been there,' I smiled.

'Yes, but I'm sure a young woman like you, with her whole life ahead of her, would hardly wish to be saddled with it. It's very stark.'

She seemed to take buying the carousel completely in her stride, as if it were something that she did on a daily basis.

She pre-empted all the questions that I'd written down. How the money would be transferred to my account. How the carousel would be lifted by a crane with minimal disturbance to both house and garden. I was taking my time. This was such a big item to sell that I didn't want to get it wrong in any way. It had been with us for so long, that there was no hurry for it to go. I felt a little uneasy about selling up, maybe a tiny part of it was revenge against Gran, but I also knew she would never have suggested selling it if she weren't serious. She must be done with it in some way. Something must have worked itself out in her head. It had taken a long time, but maybe things had just gone round and round so endlessly, like the figures themselves, that some kind of conclusion or groove had been reached; or maybe she had just stopped asking.

The only thing that was spoiling my composure was John interrupting us all the time. The first time offering coffee, then biscuits and then more coffee. Then fussing about the temperature in the room, opening and closing windows. He seemed edgy and was really annoying me. As he set the kettle to boil for the third time, I asked Sarah to excuse me and went into the kitchen.

'What are you doing? Trying to spoil the sale? Please keep out and stop interfering.'

I returned to the living room and sat down heavily on the sofa, releasing a cloud of dust which performed a few turns around the room and resettled elsewhere. If Sarah noticed our shortcomings in terms of cleanliness, she didn't show it, but she was not friendly. Instead, she was stonily polite. John came into the room and sat down. I frowned at him but he refused to leave. I took a deep breath and decided to ignore him. I would not be overruled on this, all was going smoothly and the negotiations were coming to an end, we just needed to agree a price. I was thinking about a two-bedroomed town house.

'I can't believe a thing like that has a market,' muttered John.

I sighed audibly to tell her that I was on her side and to warn him to be quiet.

But she seemed unconcerned and gazed at him kindly, the poor ignorant fool who knew nothing of the rare carousel market.

'I'll give you £400,000 for it.'

I was delighted, my imaginary house had just doubled in size.

'Thank you, I accept your offer. I'll put together a folder for you with all the contact details from the people who restored it 15 years ago… If they are still alive,' I added.

'Thank you, Amanda. The Museum of the Curious really looks after its exhibits. Everything we house is pristine. I have noticed a few marks on the war horse which will need touching up, and some teeth missing from the crocodile, but we have our own specialist painters and carpenters who will do the job expertly and, when the Furnish Carousel is inside in a controlled environment, it will be protected from damage and the weather.'

That was her way of rejecting the restorers' details. I had never known such a convoluted way of saying no and was full of admiration.

'A controlled environment?' John asked.

'I don't want people touching it,' she smiled so slowly, it seemed to take a minute for her lips to finish exposing white teeth which were at odds with her unkempt appearance.

'Do you feel a connection with it?' John asked.

'I don't think that's relevant,' I said.

'I admire the workmanship, the bizarre character of the carvings and the uniqueness of the piece. I'm also aware of the theoretical issues it throws up, "Did He who made the lamb make thee?" But, if you are talking about a spiritual connection, I'm afraid not. That's not my thing.'

'If you don't feel a bond with it, why do you want it so much?'

'Perhaps I haven't made myself clear. I do understand the significance it must have had for you and your family over the years. To live in the shadow of something quite so imposing must have affected your growing up enormously. I think a museum environment will dampen some of the cruelty of it. I can transfer the money into your bank account on the day we come to collect it.'

We set a date, it was all ridiculously simple. I could be a homeowner in a few weeks, just before autumn. John closed the door a little too hastily when she left, so she missed my final wave as she walked through the gate.

'She wants to possess it and put it in a museum to reduce it, to take some of its power away,' he said.

'So?' I replied.

'You've lived with it for 19 years, *The Book of Job* is in your blood; injustice, suffering. You *do* care.'

'It's just a story.'

'There's something *underneath* it.'

'So, it's a multi-layered story.'

'There's something underneath it.' He spoke the words slowly, as if to an idiot.

'Is it James Arlet?' I joked, laughing at the relief of having sold the carousel and picturing my new home.

'It's the baby, the Arlet-Furnish baby. It's been there for 38 years.'

'Well, there won't be much left of it, then, will there?'

I began thinking of a story Michael had told me about digging up his pet cat and finding no flesh and little fur seven years later. Then I sat down on the sofa. My humour was deflated and the dust rose triumphantly again to take another turn of the room.

'Are you serious?' I asked. He nodded. 'The dead baby wasn't Bill's?'

'No. Cath took the body from the undertakers 38 years ago.'

'You mean she stole it?'

'It's hardly stealing if it's your own child.'

'Why did she bury it in the garden?' I thought back to the conversations we'd had about bodies in the garden and began to see them all in a new light.

'She had her reasons for taking the body and burying it here.'

'What reasons?'

He told me that, after the baby's death, Gran had chosen the nearest undertakers, thinking they were all the same and the burying of the dead was not something which you negotiate. The closest undertaker was on the outskirts of town who used part of his house as a chapel of rest. From the moment Gran saw him, she hated him. She detested the shininess of his suit, his smell and the way his hair parted. It was a physical hatred. Mostly, she abhorred the language of death. The coffin was called a casket, the hearse that would deliver the body to the graveyard was a hearsette. What were these words supposed to do? Sugarcoat the dead?

Two days after she had left the body at the undertakers, Cath found herself hanging around outside the building. It was tiled white on the outside like an abattoir. Cath rang the bell and was let in. She demanded to see the man who had sold them the coffin. She burst in on him and he was eating a white bread sandwich filled with grated cheese. He spoke with his mouth full, and tiny bits of Red Leicester cheese escaped and were floated on his stinking breath before they fell to the floor. His heavy tread squashed them into the floral carpet, leaving flattened orange strands of cheese crushed into the fibres.

Cath asked to be alone with her baby for a while, saying she wanted to be the last one to touch him and that she wanted to change his clothes. She was told that his appearance might disturb her but she calmly replied that it was fine. She took three bags of sugar, weighing six pounds in total, from a Co-op carrier bag and swapped the sugar for her dead baby, so that, when the undertaker picked up the coffin, he wouldn't notice anything suspicious.

She took her bruised and blackening baby from the coffin and stuffed him into the plastic carrier bag. Then, she walked home with her six-pound baby in a bag. He was odourless, his tiny veins shoved full of preserving liquid like the pickled gherkins she made in her kitchen. As soon as her tiny baby was safely buried in her garden, she changed her footwear to two cardboard boxes filled with earth, mini coffins in themselves. She called them 'the footwear of the living dead'.

'Did she spend the next few weeks looking for something big enough to cover the hole that she had dug?' I asked my father.

'Not really. She was freezing cold all the time, in a way that she had never felt before, as though someone had stolen one of her layers, skinned her alive.'

I winced, finally understanding the bravery of my grandmother and her obsession with everyone having to face a pot-scraping moment. John continued his tale, 'Anyway, she was reading the small ads, because that's what she did all day after the baby died, and they had no television. She could only concentrate on five lines at a time. Cath didn't make visitors feel welcome so they'd stopped coming.'

'That doesn't surprise me,' I said.

'But she was still lonely and needed a connection with the outside world – that's what the small ads gave her.'

'How?'

'A sense of the world continuing, people bartering over small things as they have done for centuries. Trying to make their lives more comfortable...'

'I know the next bit,' I said. 'She couldn't bear the cold any longer so, when she spotted a gas-fired heater in the small ads, she went to buy it. She was just about to hand over the money when something in the man's garden caught her eye. It was an uncovered fragment of the carousel. She bought it that very afternoon. Imagine that, finding the perfect monument when you are out shopping for something mundane.'

'Yes.'

I thought of another question, an important one. 'Does Bill know about the baby?'

'He always knew the baby wasn't his.'

'Does he know it's under the carousel?'

'No, he thought Cath would move on from James but she showed no signs of it. He was working insane hours when she buried the baby, often not returning home before 10 at night. He came home one night to find the carousel.'

'She was never frightened of dead things or digging things up, stinking things and objects that made other people squirm. But now, I will have the body properly exhumed and buried where it should be, in a graveyard,' I told him.

'Why is that the proper place?'

'That's what people do.'

'Why?'

'Well, it's better than burying it under Bill's nose and then erecting a great big fairground ride on top of it. You can see how little she cared about making the marriage work or she would never have done that.'

'It was to stop Bill.'

'Stop what?'

'Sweeping things under the carpet the way he does, going around in that little bubble. Pretending everything is fine. Sitting amongst his architecture books and never thinking about anything unpleasant.'

'Why should he think about unpleasant events?'

'Because he married your grandmother.'

'So?'

'So, he had a choice. He could have married another sweep-under-the-carpet person but, in marrying Cath, he acknowledged that there are uncomfortable questions.'

'Such as?'

'Why he lacked the spine to do something with his own project. Why he didn't try to get his house design out there. He only had one rejection. He could have tried again. And why he never stood up to my father,' said John.

I couldn't comment on Bill's lack of spine. It was always just the way he was. Instead, I thought about Gran and the carousel, specifically her having the audacity to buy something so fierce at a time when most people would have been searching for comfort.

'She said it gave her tremendous peace of mind knowing it was there and that, should they ever discover what she had done, replacing the baby with bags of sugar, it would be very difficult for them to retrieve the body.'

'I bet it did and it gave her even greater satisfaction to rub Bill's nose in it every day. She wanted to have the child remembered. She never gave Bill a chance.'

'Maybe he didn't deserve one.'

'What do you mean?'

'By being so weak all the time. By thinking that he was being so bountiful and decent. She was always completely honest with him about Arlet's baby and the marriage.'

'He *was* bountiful, most men wouldn't have taken her on.'

'Maybe he shouldn't have.'

'She's got to you,' I accused him.

'What do you mean?'

'She's poisoned you against Bill and made you see everything from her point of view.'

'No, it's not like that,' he said gently, 'she tells the truth about people, and herself.'

That evening, I was alone in my room with my evaporating plans for a house. I sat huddled on my bed, wishing we had central heating and despairing at the thought of another winter in this place. With every minute that passed, another detail of my home flew up into the ether. The gleaming handrails, the river position, the little balcony. The eye-level grill and the swinging doors into the kitchen all disappeared. I left a message with Sarah Chimes saying that the carousel was no longer available for sale in the light of recent events, which I didn't enlarge on and, half an hour later, received an ungracious phone call from her. I couldn't blame her; Furnishs had lured her with the carousel twice and then cruelly seized it back.

XVI

My Potential Escape into the Sunset

I HEARD his voice first. He was in our garden. He would never have dared if Gran were here. How quickly news had spread about her departure. John and I were silenced and stood sheepishly in the feeble September sunlight as Michael approached us with his sexed-up walk and easy smile. Why couldn't he give it a rest? Have a day off once in a while? Why couldn't he stumble or at least stop glowing while he was in my company? He was carrying my belongings in bin bags. I reached into one of the bags and retrieved a favourite top. It smelt musty and I wondered where he had been storing my clothes. Perhaps Susan had threatened to throw them away or burn them if he didn't get rid of them.

'I knocked on the door for ages but you couldn't hear me, so I thought I would try the garden,' he said.

Then he just stopped, as though the carousel had suddenly risen from the ground in front of him. Somehow, he had managed to walk into the garden and deny it was there, but now, it was screaming for attention in its own particular way and was not to be overlooked.

'I don't know what to say to you – or about that merry-go-round, Amanda,' he said with a fake laugh, pointing to the carousel.

He *would* have to make a joke about it, Michael would never have the courage to address the carousel. He was wearing his 'I wish circumstances had been different' face. John left us alone.

'If you had been a little bit older, things might have turned out better.'

'Patronising bastard,' I said, flatly.

He laughed. 'Susan had told me all about the carousel but, now I see it for myself, I just can't believe it.'

'That's because you are too shallow.' Then I softened a little bit because he was being so pathetically slimy that I actually felt sorry for him and blurted out, 'I considered selling it and then decided not to.'

But he was not interested in the fate of a disconcerting fairground ride. 'You look really well.' He had his head on one side, his eyes wide and enquiring. At some time in his life, someone had told him that this was a compassionate look. They had lied to him.

'But not as lovely as Susan,' I had to add.

I had thought that I would be dignified when I met him, keeping my pain to myself for pride's sake but, as he was in my garden, I decided not to bother. I felt very angry. Why should I suppress my feelings just because it made *him* feel better? As for dignity, that was overrated. Decorum was never one of my assets. Michael squirmed as though I had said something terrible. What did he expect? He still kept that faux compassionate look on his face. I wanted to madden him so much that he would be forced to drop it and adopt a more honest expression. Boredom, a dread of confrontation or just plain annoyed would do.

'How is the old witch's dog bite?' I asked this just as the dog came bounding into view, and he didn't answer me. I expect Susan's own inner poison would have killed off anything Chagrin might have had in her saliva. I carried on, 'There is something odd about keeping a physical distance from someone you've slept with.'

'Can we keep this friendly? This is hard for me, too, you know.'

'Oh, I remember us being extremely friendly, in great detail.'

'I can't say how sorry I am about all this, Amanda. My daughter forgives you for pushing her over, she wasn't hurt.'

No repentance from me. I'm sure he would prefer it if I broke down and cried but, unfortunately for him, tears were as far away and as unlikely as Susan's tan being natural.

'Tell me, what your plans are now? Can you go back to The Waggon and Horses? I'm sure they'd be pleased to have you back,' he said in an upbeat voice, like a teacher with a sulky pupil.

I thought about Harry and Ali welcoming me back, It was unlikely as we had all moved on.

'I'm spending a few weeks with John, my father.'

It was the first time I had openly acknowledged John in front of Michael. Even though Michael had seen John several times at the pub, I had always played it down, just in case my father ran off again, I supposed. John appeared at the French windows, as though he had heard the words for which he longed. He gazed out at us anxiously. At least one of us was hearing what they wanted to in the garden that day.

Chagrin bolted past Michael again and he flinched but she showed no interest in him whatsoever and appeared not to remember who he was.

'It was quite a shock waking up to that red hair but I understand why you did it.'

'I doubt that.'

'I know it's tricky, Amanda, but we plan to stay at the pub for some time. You and I are going to run into one another and I think it's best for us all to be grown up.'

It was the 'we' that deflated me. How could they be 'we' after a few weeks? That was not long enough to become a couple. I suppose they didn't have much time on their hands as they were both getting on. I had no alternative but to accept it. They were together, in the ball and chain sense of the word. Having sniffed one another out and recognised a kindred spirit, there was nothing I could do about them.

'Have you got an extension on the lease, then?' I asked, imagining the rest of my adult life stuck in a remote area, close to my tormentors. Every time the wound would be healing a bit, I would bump into one or other of them and my skin would split apart as though scar tissue were being re-opened.

'No, but there's no reason to expect we won't. The place is doing very well and only an idiot wouldn't give us another tenancy after the improvements your grandmother and I have made.'

'I don't think you should be so sure about that,' John had crept over while Michael and I had been taking turns to stare at the parched grass. Michael looked at John with a pitying stare, he had heard about the supposed breakdown that John had suffered, and had little time for mental illness.

'Susan and I are very hopeful.'

'Well, you can hope as much as you like but you can't change the facts,' John shouted at him.

Both Michael and I stepped back at this outburst. Michael recovered first, nodded at me and started to leave the garden, walking slowly. As if to say that he was unafraid of having ventured into this crazy garden but was now choosing to leave, quietly and without a fuss, but John shouted after him.

I didn't say anything and Michael stopped, keeping his back to us, his right foot close to the little hedge that Susan had planted 12 years ago. The hedge which was now barely alive, having been slowly strangled by a slow-growing but stronger group of bushes that Gran had planted just in front of it. Michael turned round slowly, finally beginning to lose patience with the Furnish-Doon stand-up routine that was John and I.

Patiently, in a monotone voice, he explained to John, 'The Tide is held in trust by a limited company called Grenvelt. I have a 12-month lease with them…'

'Probationary,' shouted John.

'A 12-month lease…' he repeated calmly, 'Which will be reviewed shortly and, more than likely, be extended for three years. And, from then on, it will be a rolling tenancy.'

'Who do you think is behind Grenvelt, you fool?' replied John.

Michael spoke gently, as if to contain his anger, delivering a sales pitch he had repeated too many times, 'Grenvelt are five businessmen who have done well and wish to invest in a public house, without having any direct connections with the business. They purchased the pub, surrounding land and moorings from the Arlet family 11 months ago.'

'There is only one woman behind Grenvelt,' said John.

Michael was silent, shaking his head and walking out of the garden. He turned sideways to slip through the iron gate, even though he had no need to do so.

'Cath bloody Furnish,' bellowed John.

Michael paused sideways between the bars of the gate, shaking with distaste when he heard that my grandmother owned The Tide. I stood by John, looking at his face to see why he would have said something so stupid. Michael realised he had nothing to gain by staying and stormed out to his car.

'He'll be on his way to the solicitor's now, to find out if it's true,' said John.

'True?' I asked, kneeling down on the ground beside him. He was shaking with laughter. I was worried for him, had he had another breakdown?

'You need to lick some gold.' I looked down at where my watch strap should be and saw that I hadn't put it on. Time had meant nothing over the past few days and the watch had languished on my bedside table. I looked around for another source of gold. The carousel.

'Cath owns the pub.'

'Come over here, John,' I said, taking his arm and gently pushing him towards the carousel.

'Just lick the war horse's ear, there's plenty of gold leaf on it,' I said kindly.

He shook his head, but was still smiling.

'The vulture's beak?' I suggested, with a hint of desperation creeping in.

'No, Amanda, no need.'

'The goat's hoof – and that's my final offer!'

He shook his head again, so I jumped onto the carousel, stretched my arms around the horse's neck and let my tongue touch the inside of its ear. As my feet contacted the wooden floor of the carousel, it was as though I heard everything John had said, repeated very slowly.

'How can the pub be Gran's? It was vacant for almost 38 years and now Michael's got it.'

'All Michael has is a 12-month probationary period. He might have had a three-year lease after that, if things had been different.'

'How can Gran own the pub? It's owned by the Arlets, or was until they sold it, just like Michael said.'

'It hasn't been owned by the Arlet family since James Arlet owned it. James left the pub to your grandmother when he found out that she was pregnant with his child and he knew that he was dying.'

'I don't believe you. Why would he leave her an entire pub? He had a family and the living ones are in America now. He would have left it to them. And, if he loved her so much, why didn't he stop drinking? I think you should come inside, sit down and stop inventing stories.'

'I don't need to sit down. Cath and their baby were the only family he had left. Well, the only ones to whom he was speaking. He had been estranged from his own family for years. They contested the will, provoked into action by my father. It took five years to sort out.'

'I don't believe Gran wouldn't have told me if she owned it,' I said, my arms tightly folded.

'You never asked her.'

'Why would I ask her?' I thought it was a crazy thing for John to say. 'Should I have asked her randomly if she owned the Post Office, too?'

'She gave you enough hints over the years, why do you think she took you down there so often? I think she even tried to tell you on a couple of occasions.'

'Just because you take a child to a beauty spot repeatedly, doesn't mean you own it.'

'I can't say exactly what she was thinking of by not telling you clearly but, maybe, she thought it would be too much for you to take on, or that it would go to your head and you wouldn't keep your feet on the ground.' John disappeared for a minute and came back with my trainers. 'Put these on, let's go out for a run.'

We ran together but, at first, my feet wouldn't move. For at least 10 minutes, I struggled and the road felt too hard, the pounding of the concrete sending shock waves up my legs. I wanted to stop but John kept pushing me on. After 20 minutes, we had reached a comfortable pace and, after 40, he wanted to stop but I didn't. I wanted to be exhausted when I got home and, by the time we finally turned down the drive together an hour later, my legs were ready to buckle beneath me.

The following morning, Bill seemed very out of sorts. He came back home even though he was supposed to be working at the architect's office. He didn't want to discuss the pub. He couldn't even look at me. I was not surprised, it was just another thing that he had repressed, another annoyance to distract him from his buildings.

'That damned place, ugly and top heavy,' he said, before turning his attention to John, 'Your father has phoned my work number seven times this morning. How did he get hold of it?'

'I can't control what he does, Bill. Anyone can look up an architect's office. I expect he's heard about the pub.'

'Keep him away from The Tide,' was all he said. Then he walked away.

* * *

Coming back is supposed to be momentous. In films, it involves running towards people and, before the running, is the sharp intake of breath as you realise the most important person in your life has returned to you. But, going back to the pub, my grandmother's pub, was not at all notable. I walked along the river from the nearest village on the opposite bank so that I would remain unseen in the undergrowth. I wanted to creep up on the pub and view it through a stranger's eyes. As that was not possible, I thought seeing it from a distance might be useful. I was wearing my army uniform. I had even blackened my face with the river mud downstream.

I had skulked through the undergrowth and scratched my face and hands. Why was I cutting myself to pieces over Michael and Susan? Something told me I needed to face the situation and watch them together for as long as I could bear it. They were outside in the car park for a long time. Now that the truth about the ownership of the pub was revealed, it would have been offensive to Susan to be sheltered under a Furnish roof.

Susan didn't have much to move out as she had been there for only a few weeks. Even less time than me, but she still had an assurance about her walk that said that she and Michael were not about to split up. You could tell from her every movement that this was the last thing on her mind. I could see that she was wearing at least eight-centimetre heels because her foot slammed so hard on the ground, there was no rolling movement.

I saw Michael make several familiar gestures: running his hands through his hair, a certain lurching at people before he shook their hands (they were the removal men). I couldn't see the grin that accompanied the lurching, perhaps it wasn't there today. He stood with his legs quite far apart and I could see he was still delicious, even from this distance. I saw him give Susan one or two buoying up hugs and she responded with a lot of flapping like an exotic bird that had somehow failed to get off the ground, but still believed it could. That was her all over, extraordinary self-belief coupled with an unquestioning mind; it was all the power anyone needed. I didn't have it and never would; just an ability to overcomplicate things and allow them to go round and round in my head like a washing machine for ever stuck on spin.

* * *

I watched all afternoon, the removing of one piece of furniture after another. The clever way in which the shapes were loaded into the van to make the maximum use of space. I was mesmerised, almost daydreaming, and commending myself for feeling detached until I saw the wicker basket from the bathroom being loaded.

The wind changed, the tide came in and the faint smell of rotting animal in the woods was covered up by the smell of the mud with its mix of sea and river water; oysters and fish. Neither Susan nor Michael looked over to the riverbank once all afternoon or, if they did, it was a time in which I was trying to rub sticks together or poking at the ground with a branch. I lay down on the ground and smelt the earth but, the moment I did, a voice in my head said, 'Pull yourself together and don't be so melodramatic. There will be more opportunities for love and sex in the future.'

I couldn't even be miserable successfully. I was saving all my tears for when the van drove away and Susan and Michael followed in his car. But none came. That was the trouble with feelings, so unpredictable. It was never the thing that you thought would finish you off that did, never something obvious like a car disappearing with the man you loved in it. It was always something cheaper and more ridiculous – the way he brushed her shoulder on the night of the party. It was all in that movement, all foretold in one, lingering stroke.

Just as I was starting to feel a little ridiculous with the mud on my face and my combat gear, and wishing I were wearing something glamorous, I saw Gran on the quay, looking out towards me.

She waved quite casually and then disappeared, walking slowly towards the pub. I ran back down the rough path to the next village, each footfall was firm and deliberate. Then, stumbling, I crossed the river at the first point it narrowed enough to form mudbanks. I tried to dodge the really sloppy mud but I was still caked up to my calves. As I approached the pub, I saw her again, skulking round the outside of the building and looking in a dustbin.

'Good afternoon, love,' she said, as if anticipating my need to chop her up into little pieces on the spot and feed her to the fishes.

'Where on earth have you been when I needed you?' I demanded.

'I see that Michael and Susan have left with indecent haste. It's only taken them a day since hearing the news to organise a removal van. Mind you, all the pub furnishings are mine. I suppose I will have to reimburse Michael for the part of the lease he hasn't used. I knew Susan would find it intolerable to stay here once she had found out. She must have pressured Michael into a swift exit,' Gran said, thoughtfully.

'Where have you been?' I screamed.

'New Jersey, to thank James Arlet's brother.'

'For what?'

'When James left me the pub, it was contested. I lost it, but James' brother gave it straight back to me. No one knew locally, so I had the place to myself for 38 years with just your grandfather and I knowing.'

'Why did he give it back to you after taking you to court?'

'It was his family's doing. James and I were only together for seven months, not long enough, in their view, to give someone your life savings. But he knew that the pub was meant for me. Your father is on his way down with the key.'

'I didn't know if you would come back.'

'I said that I would.'

'Well, speaking to Arlet's brother didn't take you 30 days, where have you been for the rest of the time?'

'Walking about the earth, to and fro,' she laughed. 'That's what Satan said in *The Book of Job* when God asked him what he had been doing.'

I decided to go for another line of attack. Her dreadful treatment of Bill in all this. I hadn't worked up the courage to complain directly about her behaviour towards me, so I thought I would use Bill.

'I know Bill knew all the time that the baby was not his, but I don't understand why he stayed with you.'

'I expect he would justify it by saying that he was in love with me. Unfortunately, I was in love with somebody else.'

What could I say to that? Nothing much really. What can you say to someone who has devoted their life to loving a dead man and a dead child? Both noiseless, spotless, pristine ghosts. Gran, who was so good at telling other people how to run their lives and who was invariably right, regardless of the personality or circumstances of the person in question, had made such a mess of her own life.

Here was a woman in love with ghosts; ghosts who were perfect because they were dead; great, romantic swept you off your feet, whirled you round, always said the right thing ghosts. With the help of these spooks, she had subdued reality, made it roll over on command. When all the rest of us had was this muddy, stinking truth.

'Why don't you say something, Amanda?'

I quickly thought of one of her favourite sayings and uttered it flatly, 'Personal drama is delusion.'

'I know I must seem a hypocrite but you are not me.'

'I am you, that's the problem. I'm going to behave the same way with Michael that you have done with James Arlet, mourn for him for years.'

'It's hard for me to take the Michael thing seriously,' she said, dismissively.

'Why must you always be so insensitive?' I wept.

'Force of habit. I think of him as a mediocre town where you were temporarily waylaid. One of those towns where shopping centres are identical so it doesn't matter where you are, you can always find your overpriced clothing whose colours and cuts are dictated by a bunch of fools each season. A place where they have successfully banned drinkers from the town centre. Attractive, possibly, with a few Tudor buildings still standing but, ultimately, lacking in interest.'

I cried at Gran's demolition of my first love.

'He had an appealing thought pass through his head once, and it was you.'

'What if I turned on you about Arlet?' I asked her bitterly. She just smiled at me. 'Why did you help Michael if you had such a low opinion of him?'

'He was just there at the right time.'

'So, you used him to allow you to get back into the pub without causing a stir amongst the locals?'

'He was a foil for a while, I admit it. I could never find the right time to tell you about the pub.'

'And now Susan has reaped the benefits of your decorating for almost as long as I did and she had Michael, too.'

'For a while.'

'Do you think they won't stay together, then?'

It was always the same. Just as I thought I was making progress and the pain was easing, my mouth would betray me. I thought of something unintelligent and said it out loud, something that made my heart cartwheel. Like the thought of him coming back to me.

She smiled and I decided, for once, that I would ask her the questions I wanted. She had put herself in a position now where she would not be able to refuse to answer them.

'Why did you keep the pub? Why didn't you sell after all that had happened, Arlet dying and that girl drowning?'

'Doon would have loved that, to see me thoroughly defeated. I was always determined to hang onto the place for as long as it took.'

'Until what?'

'Until I had sufficiently recovered from having my life raked over in court. This was my space and I had the power to keep people away from it for as long as I chose. I owned a bit of land.'

'But you had six acres at home with a 13-metre carousel on it.'

'That was different. This was a public space, generally awash with people talking loudly, and I had the chance to silence them and keep it to myself. I could punish them for turning against me.'

'John said that you were vindicated, that nothing of which you were accused stood up in court. You had no part in the girl's drowning and the pub was eventually left to you legitimately.'

'The pub was rightfully mine. I had a child to bring up in it. But Doon stirred up Arlet's family, playing on all their greed and fears. He took the one place from me that was mine and my son's. But, after James and our baby had both died, I wanted James to have the run of the place until he was ready to leave. He stood for years in the bar touching those bottles but, far from being able to open them like the old days when he was alive, his fingers were unable to move even the dust on them. When he eventually accepted that, he left, taking our baby with him.'

I wasn't going to let her hijack the conversation with another flight of her imagination, 'Why did you decide to let the pub to Michael, of all people?'

'No reason, other than you were 18 and James had gone. I gave Michael a three-year lease, with a 12-month probationary period, to keep the place ticking over until you were old enough to have your own licence or sell it, if that's what you wanted to do. I didn't think for a second that you would fall for him.'

'That's why you were so obsessively interested in the place, the fixtures and fittings. You did the thing you said you'd never do, using me to relive your past.'

'The only reason I took such interest in the details is so that you would inherit a pristine building,' she said, neatly avoiding the other part of my sentence.

'But you left the place to fall apart for 37 years.'

'Yes, but once I had started renovating it, I wanted it done properly. No point in doing something half-heartedly.'

She had certainly done gloom wholeheartedly.

'You tricked me about the carousel,' I said.

'How so?'

'You set me up with that Chimes woman. You knew her, didn't you?'

'I met her years ago when your mother was a girl. I saw the way Sarah Chimes looked at the carousel so hungrily and knew she would always covet it.'

'That's why you left her details in that file so that I would find them?' She shrugged and looked bored. 'You knew that John would tell me the truth and it would put me in such a difficult position that I could never sell it.'

'I was prepared for you to sell the carousel.'

'What would you have done if I had sold it?'

'There's nothing underneath it now, just a few small bones.'

'But you knew I wouldn't sell it?'

'I gave you the opportunity to sell it and I meant it. But I suspected that you wouldn't. The carousel was never easy to live with.'

'Like you, then.'

'It's too complicated.'

'You didn't have to spend your life thinking about it.'

'Yes, I did.'

'So why did you offer it to me to sell?' I persisted.

'I wanted to stop thinking about it for a while, be like other people.'

'Other people?' I said incredulously. 'You *loathe* other people.'

'I had a moment of madness and indecision and I thought I envied them but, fortunately, it passed. Part of me thought that, if the carousel were sold, I would find a little bit more peace. I was temporarily taken in by your mother's Pollyanna propaganda but then I came to my senses and realised that peace isn't an option.'

'What do you mean?'

'I have peace in the garden, for which I am grateful, but I'm talking about an all-encompassing certainty that everything will work out all right.'

'Why didn't you move on from Arlet and the baby? Other people don't live like that. They get over things, move on and make choices.'

'Other people? Who cares about other people?' That was more like it, the old Gran was back.

'All I'm saying is, if a large group of people in society have suffered and moved on, that indicates it is possible to do so,' I said in a quiet but superior way.

But she would have none of it and swept me away with a shake of her head, 'People have a right to be miserable and remain so indefinitely if they choose, without the interference of other people suggesting they deal with it. There's no shame in misery, it's a natural reaction to the world.'

'I think it's cowardly and self-pitying to behave like that in the long term.'

'That's your opinion,' she sniffed.

'Some people don't want to spend a lifetime lonely and thinking about negative things.'

'That's up to them. I've never been a pedlar of happiness. If it's nonsense you are after, go and stay with your mother for a while. She can provide you with that handbook you were always looking for; the one with all the answers in it.'

I glared and she continued more gently, 'As a young girl, I let you play with matches and, apart from a few minor incidents including your eyelashes which grew back in profusion, and the time you set your dress on fire, you were responsible. That has always been the closest I go towards a child-rearing philosophy.'

I changed the conversation back to her mistreatment of my grandfather, 'What about Bill?'

'He can come or go as he's always been able to do.'

'What about love?'

'Mine for you?'

'For Bill.'

'Oh, we haven't time for that.'

'Do you love him?'

'There's a moment when he goes to sleep when his breathing changes, like a gear shifting down.'

'Is that love?'

'I doubt it.'

She reached into her pocket and threw a faded bit of half-folded plastic at me. It was an aggressive gesture and my first thought was that she had declared our straight talking over.

'It's the Rottweiler drawing,' I said, incredulously.

'Bill drew it after the court case was finally over and I had the pub back. I found it in the bin in his office. I had it laminated and put it up by the pub. Imagine that, the sum of Bill's anger at what life had thrown at him compared to mine. His, a small drawing of a dog and mine, a 13-metre fairground ride.'

'At least his came from him, you bought the carousel.'

'I willed it. It appeared when I needed it.'

'You didn't will it and, anyway, the carousel represents a lazy answer.' She started to speak, but I interrupted her, 'I'm not a child, I understand what it means. There is no vulture without corpses but I can't accept where that way of thinking ultimately leads. Complacency. I can't accept that you can hold the beauty of the world in one hand and the horror of it in the other and feel that this is a just balance. This is proclaimed as grown-up, unsentimental thinking when, in fact, it's simply indolence. It's exactly why nothing's done about nuclear threat and starvation.'

'That's just the tip of the meaning, like an iceberg.'

'So, why did you buy it?'

'Because I have a taste for imagery and the stomach for convoluted rhetoric. I never expected a quick, clear answer.'

'You can't really believe that, when we see God, we will be so awestruck that none of the questions will matter? We'll just roll over like dogs and say okay, fine, whatever suffering you've caused me in the past doesn't matter now?'

'Don't be ridiculous, Amanda, but one of the things the carousel represents is a place of acceptance. Now, people can find that any way they like. Mine is the garden, a shallow person's might be clothes,' she said, looking at my latest outfit.

'And, if they can't find it?'

'It's curtains.' She made a hand movement across her throat which sounded like tearing paper. Just as I threw my hands up in frustration, I saw John coming down the slope.

There was no point arguing with her. I couldn't make sense of the world any more than she could. I was defeated. The world seemed to be full of two types of people: those who never bothered asking questions and those who had asked – and then needed to spend the rest of their lives frantically searching for something to fill the terrifying hole that had come from daring to ask.

I thought about what a fantasy Michael had been. I found it impossible to separate my pedestal version of him from the reality of his flat feet and slightly high-pitched laugh. I couldn't explain logically why he still had a hold on me. Was it just about rejection, being overlooked for someone else whom I considered inferior? Was it nothing to do with Michael at all?

John approached us with his hands tight to his sides, 'I've got the key,' he said.

'Give it to Amanda.' I took it, the familiar key that I had held so often. 'Let's go in and have a look, then,' Gran said. 'See what needs to be done.'

'If you insist,' I said.

She blew sharply through her nose. 'Although Michael has cleared out of the pub today, you will have to see him. He's staying at Susan's house until they find somewhere else to live. She's putting it on the market.'

'It's taken you 12 years to get her out,' I said. 'To chase her out.'

'Rubbish,' said Gran. 'Enough about her. You should be the one who opens the door, Amanda. I signed the entire place over to you before I left.'

My hands flew to my face as I gazed at my grandmother to make sure she wasn't joking. She was serious, it was mine. I opened the door as I had done a hundred times before. The heavy lock and, with no window in the door, the familiar push into darkness. As we trudged up the stairs together, our footsteps were in time with one another. I switched the lights on in the main bar; something was wrong, the place didn't light up like it usually did. The sense of strangeness and comfort were gone. Then I saw what they had done. Painted over the yellow wall with a subtle brown. The kind of brown that is advertised as Mocha or Cappuccino; Pebble or Tranquil. Coming from a collection entitled Urban or having Modern somewhere in the title.

I turned, shaking and sobbing, to Gran, 'They've painted over your yellow.'

'Bastards!' growled John supportively.

'It doesn't matter, none of it matters,' Gran spoke quietly. She put her arms around me and I smelt the earthy, unfussy smell of her skin and was soothed by it. She whispered into my hair, 'Leave it.'

When I emerged from her arms, I felt strangely calm. 'How did you make that shade of yellow?' I asked.

'I can make it again. I can make it for you, Amanda.'

'What was in it?' I asked, hardly able to get the words out because she had shown me some warmth.

John broke the silence, 'Gold leaf, dog shit, banana skins, saffron, vomit.'

Gran thumped him affectionately.

'See, Doons and Furnishs *can* get on,' I said.

XVII

I Outwit my Grandmother

IT WAS now 38 years since my grandmother borrowed a table and chairs from the pub, carried them out into the river and set them up on a mudbank in the dark. My grandmother had sat on her seat with her knees drawn up and floated stubs of candles in foil pie dishes. She drank from a bottle of beer and cold-heartedly accepted my grandfather's proposal of marriage.

But now I was back at the same pub and my grandmother was looking at me with disdain because I had bought a box of doughnuts. Five for 99p.

'How is that possible?' she said.

'Spare me the doughnut/downfall of the world speech,' I replied.

'Who is suffering to enable you to eat doughnuts at 20p a go?'

Suffering was her thing.

I ran my nose around the ring of the doughnut, sniffing exaggeratedly, then I picked off single grains of sugar with my tongue. This would show her that I was in no mood for a lecture. Her eyes left the doughnut box and moved on to my legs.

'Where are those jeans from?' she asked.

'New,' I replied.

'They don't look new.'

'They're distressed.'

'*I* am distressed. As if I needed one final piece of evidence that life is absurd, it's you parading around as a pseudo-peasant.'

I did a provocative wiggle. She threw up her hands half-heartedly. 'So, we live in a society where shortening the life of clothes is not seen as perverse.'

'Call it secondhand without the smelliness,' I said.

'Nothing is without its stench.' Both of us stopped talking because we could hear a car slowly making its way down the narrow lanes.

'What time are you going to work?' she asked.

'In a bit.'

'The parasols will need putting up. People will burn in this sun.'

'Burn in hell?'

She laughed, and I was glad.

It had taken a while for us to return to this way of addressing one another and I was relieved that Gran had returned to normal after the difficult time we had been through. It felt good to have her back, belligerent as ever.

The car that we had heard moments ago, pulled into the car park, a few metres from us, and a tall man got out. Gran nodded to him. He hesitated about coming closer.

'I hear Bill will be back soon.' She nodded again. 'I'm sorry for what you've been through. I read it in the papers.'

'Extraordinary to be so interested in other people's lives,' said my grandmother when the man was out of earshot.

Regardless of what had happened, Bill was still my grandfather.

* * *

After I had found out about owning the pub and the news had settled in, we had a few nights of sitting about at home – growing fat on peace. I anticipated the future with hopefulness. I looked about my little family: Gran, Bill, John, and I. We were a strange lot but I saw us staying together; odder families had worked with compromise, understanding and time. Unfortunately, we didn't have any of those left.

One night, Bill seemed particularly agitated and asked John a favour, 'Can I borrow your car please?'

'I can drive you anywhere you need to go,' said John.

'Can I borrow the car or shall I call a taxi?'

John held out the keys, 'Of course, Bill. I'm sorry.'

Nobody spoke when he left. I tried to open my mouth a few times but heard nothing save for the faint popping of my lips parting. John read, going over the same page continually, unable to move on. Gran went out into the garden, only coming back in the moment Bill walked through the door, an hour and a half later. Bill stood on the lino in the hall in front of John and gave him back the keys, his feet were just big enough to obscure segments of the repeating pattern. I felt agitated, wanting him to stop shuffling. I just kept looking down at his feet and thinking, if I could just remember the repeating pattern before he moved again, everything would be all right.

Bill spoke, 'Your father is dead.'

John stood up unsteadily, dropping the keys. His head lurched forward as if to hear better, but his backside stuck out as if he'd rather sit back down again.

'For God's sake, Bill, tell me this is a wind-up!' John looked at my grandfather's face and saw that he wasn't joking.

'He came round when you three were last at The Tide. He was looking for you, John, screaming, "Give me back my son or I'll smash the place." He phoned today at the office, as he's done every day for weeks. He started his calls the day Cath left. I didn't think much of it to begin with but, last week, I started to jump whenever the phone rang and his voice genuinely unnerved me. This afternoon, just as I was about to leave work, he phoned and said that he would be down at the pub tonight at eight. By the time I got there, he had broken a window and got in.'

'Why didn't you just call the police?' John was frantic, pleading. We were all speechless.

'I hit him with one of those strange ornaments,' said Bill.

'Maybe he's just unconscious,' I sobbed.

Gran held out the keys to John, 'Get down there.' He snatched them and was gone, leaving the three of us together, numb. It was impossible to be further removed from my family fantasy of a few days ago.

'He pushed me against the shelves on what used to be the yellow wall and I just grabbed that thing by the neck and I hit him with it,' said Bill.

'The glass polar bear?' I asked.

Bill shrugged.

'Are you sure he's dead?' I repeated.

Gran shot me a look. 'It should have been me,' she said, 'I should have killed him.'

'Why the hell are we arguing about who killed him? I don't believe you two!' I shouted.

'I couldn't stop him phoning daily to say that he would make our lives hell for taking his son from him,' said Bill.

Bill looked at me and held out his palms, 'I've called the police.'

'Then we've got 20 minutes to tell Amanda the story.'

'You've had 19 years!' I shouted.

'Carry on, Bill,' Gran said quietly

'I should have thumped him years ago in the pub, should never have let him get to me. He was only telling the truth when he said you wouldn't have married me under any other circumstances.'

'He was an insane, egotistical maniac,' said Gran calmly.

I wondered at the ease in which she had just switched to 'was'.

'It was Cath he always wanted, though she never believed it. Something about her made him mad,' Bill was breathless, red in the face and more animated than I had ever seen him. 'How could she not see him clearly? How could she not be charmed? He was good looking, had every advantage in life and could have given her anything she wanted. He was obsessed with her but hated her at the same time, wanted to break her from the beginning. He could never believe that she was not interested in him, it made him want her all the more, although he was repulsed by her at the same time, by her behaviour,' he laughed.

'Were you never repulsed by my behaviour?' she asked him, smiling.

'I was mesmerised by you, same as every other sucker in the place.'

Buoyed up by this memory, Gran began to speak. 'Once, I was raucous and vibrant, and people lived through me. Dull people's mouths fell open at my flirting and sexually-repressed people were drawn to my antics as if I could heal them. But, after James' death, I retreated into my own head for a week. Seven days was all it took for Doon to contact the Arlet family and slither into their midst. In the meantime, during the build up to the funeral, Doon was at the pub daily. And, with each drink he ordered, he also gave away a free question, "Do you really think it was serious between James and Cath? I'm only asking. *You* know her past." The question that would lead to the greatest damage, he gave to that foolish girl, Josephine Flower, the one who drowned, to deliver, "How do we know that James is the father of Cath Furnish's baby?"

'Reputation always sits on a knife edge and, what can amuse one day, can repel the next. People are easily swayed in groups. Like skittles; when one falls, the other idiots will follow. So, one by one, the regulars withdrew into their moral shells. I had gone too far.

'I, of course, saw it differently. They had experienced their thrills and excitement through me and their small appetites were satiated. In the future, when their lives inevitably turned a little flat, I might crop up in the conversation at dinner parties, like a parable, showing them that their conservative choices had been the right ones all along. They might congratulate themselves on their maturity in discussing me more kindly but I'll have none of it because I own what I am. I have never lived through others nor looked for their approval.

'Doon thoughtfully introduced me to James' mother at the funeral. When she looked at me, I felt as though she were ploughing me into the ground as well as James. The service was a mockery. No one spoke a word about him that made me think they were speaking about the man I had known. The sweet, hapless man they conjured up was a mixture of propriety and wishful thinking.

'That night, back at the pub, I had a flash of inspiration. There were 18 regulars in and I suggested that we carry the tables and chairs from the pub out onto the mudbanks. We would bring all of the wine and beer, some candles and wait for the tide to come in. Then we could swim back to shore.

'Although there were 20 people in the room, only Doon and I spoke, 'He's had a good send off,' Doon argued.

'"This is one that better befits him," I had said, gathering bottles of beer in my arms and preparing to carry them outside.

'"The tables will be damaged in the water." Doon said.

'"They're my bloody tables."

'"Not yet, they're not."

'I put the bottles down. "What do you mean?"

'"Nothing."

'"No, come on, spit it out, you've seen his will. This place is mine."

'In front of everybody, he held out his hand to me as if to shake mine. I returned the squeeze.

'"Some people say that not *all* your muscles are as tight as that."

'The sniggering and downcast eyes told me that nobody else shared my vision for that night. So, I dragged a table and two chairs out by myself. It was a gargantuan effort, those things were solid pine and I was four months pregnant, but I got them onto a mudbank and went back to fetch the beer and the candles.

'I was pleased with my alternative funeral. The moon and the river were thoughtful mourners and the water rose around my chair legs. I let stubs of candles float downstream on foil pie dishes but I was not on my own for long. Bill waded out to join me, he took the spare seat that I had meant for James, I still felt him with me, and we sat on our chairs until they were almost submerged, then moved together onto the tabletop, from where we watched the chairs completely vanish. He asked me to marry him.

'I had barely accepted when we noticed Doon standing on the side of the bank and that girl pushing her way out towards us. She was screaming that Doon was in love with her and not me. Still, he stood there on the shore, listening to her yelling and all her accusations. I'd had enough. I told Bill to ignore her, leave her alone. He was all for carrying her back to the shore but I stopped him. Anyway, 10 minutes later, she was dead. It was the perfect opportunity for Doon who had been waiting to get me for two years. He just wanted my downfall, one way or another.

'So, naturally, the police were called and the investigation into her death became inextricably entangled with the pub being left to me. My relationships with James and a couple of others who were still around were examined in great detail. It took months to clear up and, during that time, every aspect of my life and my behaviour was raked up and raked over.'

'But you had done nothing wrong,' I said.

'I had transgressed unwritten rules. I had not behaved appropriately for a woman. That was enough.'

'But you had done nothing wrong!'

'Since when has life ever taken that into account?'

Gran and Bill both set off into the garden, as if they had all the time in the world, hand in hand, ambling towards the carousel. I followed, a one-woman audience. Gran sat on Leviathan the crocodile and Bill sat behind her with his arms around her waist and his head buried in her back. The machine was still.

'Get up, Amanda,' said Gran.

I jumped onto the carousel and sat down awkwardly on the floor beside them, holding onto one of the poles.

'Amanda,' Bill interrupted with some urgency. 'I want to tell you that your grandmother *was* The Tide, the reason everybody went there. It was always her place and Arlet's brother knew it, even when his family had won it back. It was always Cath's, it was destined to be Cath's. She never should have set up with me, not with someone else's child. She should have gone off and made her own way in life, but she was exhausted by the court case, repulsed by being looked

292

into like that and misjudged so cruelly. And she lost the place for a while, the very place she was going to bring up their baby, and finally, the child didn't survive.'

Gran moved herself slightly away from Bill. They stayed that way, her staring straight ahead. I wanted some show of affection between them. Now, and only now, there was a gap between them that could be bridged if only Gran would hold out a hand to Bill. This was their one and only moment, not 38 years ago when they sat together in a river, not their bungled relationship, but now. This was the time when, if one of them could just show enough courage or vulnerability, they could rise up together, strengthened by the experience. But, even with such a small gap between them physically, I knew it was never going to happen. I could no longer look. I went inside and sat on the sofa, waiting for the doorbell to ring. I jumped a few times, thinking I had heard the police car coming down our drive, before, finally, it arrived.

During Bill's court case, the dusty details of 38 years ago were brushed off and revealed in embarrassingly intimate detail. In all our minds, The Tide temporarily shed its new image like a coat and put on a pitiful, seedy look for the duration of the hearing. The trial included the details of the way in which Dr Charles Doon had died: bits of his broken skull had slashed into the tissue of his brain, causing a thousand tiny explosions as, piece by piece, his thoughts had shut down.

And the ludicrousness of the murder weapon: a transparent glass polar bear which had remained intact. The clear, glass bear was placed before us for everyone to see. There were so few details in the animal's form, I wondered what small changes to the shape would make it no longer recognisable as a bear. Maybe if it lost the indentations for the ears or the narrowness of the head. And then I looked at Gran. I didn't recognise her. It was as though someone had shifted a few of *her* lines, altered her shape imperceptibly and abandoned her, lumpen and defeated.

Of course, the court case involved hours and hours of talking, days upon days of cold, uncomfortable words which fell down our necks like drizzle. The words may have gone on and on, but the only ones that mattered were a handful – and they came from Susan Rink.

Susan became the narrator in the jury's eyes, the one who could make sense of the Furnishs. She was able to translate our lives for us, for she had an innate sense of what was needed to win people's trust and affection. I felt, even as she were performing, that people knew it was an act but they needed the show.

When asked by the prosecution about her relationship with my grandmother, Susan said, 'Cath Furnish and I have struggled to find common ground.'

'Come now, Mrs Rink, surely it's a little more than struggling to find common ground. You are neighbours and have cited seven incidents in the last 12 years, where you describe Cath Furnish's behaviour as obnoxious and deliberately obstructive. You go further in your statement, referring to her as self-pitying, an appalling guardian and a poor judge of character.'

Gran remained indifferent, her face passive apart from a mildly raised eyebrow, of which only those practiced at watching her might be aware.

And Susan on my grandfather, 'In all my dealings with him, I have found him completely placid, generous to a fault, quietly humorous and an excellent and devoted grandfather.'

And then came the words that saved Bill, it wasn't important which words went before or after, because these were the only ones that mattered.

'And can you enlighten us about Cath's relationship to Bill Furnish?'

'I never think of him as Bill Furnish, just Bill, because, of course, that was her surname. He agreed to change his name when they got married, just another concession to make her happy,' said Susan, aware that she now had the attention of the entire room.

'You have already extolled Bill Furnish's virtues but I need to ask you if you would consider him a violent man? Perhaps there were incidents over the years of which you were not aware? You were only a neighbour, after all.'

'Bill is not a fighter, he didn't have it in him. We have already heard how easily Doon knocked him to the floor in the fight leading up to the murder. He killed Doon for Cath, she goaded him into it.'

The court had to be silenced and Susan was told to answer the questions put to her, not deviate with her own theories.

So, that was him, neatly boxed up, hen-pecked and soft in the head to devote himself to such a woman for so many years. He had already suffered enough. What sort of man would not want to hang onto his own name and spread it about like seed? What sort of man would write-off the first 26 years of his life and start afresh with a new title? And his final mistake was to do his wife's bidding by murdering her nemesis. Of course, nobody admitted that Susan had changed the minds of the jury, they found a loophole for him instead. His sentence for manslaughter was reduced because of extreme provocation.

I continued to sell many a pint because of the pub's notoriety. Several deaths in one place, all connected to one another over 38 years. You could always tell them at the door, those who romanticised untimely ends, and I gave them the warm welcome on which my grandmother insisted. I offered no explanations or apologies for being related to any of my grandparents.

Now the pub was mine and I had stopped watching *Midlanders*. Recently, I'd had to fill in a form saying why I didn't possess a television licence: I had no television. I wrote that I could no longer believe in Maya, she was no longer credible to me. Somebody would have tried to destroy her by now if she were real. I could not bear to see her peddling her lies on the screen: that women can behave any way they liked these days without consequences. I expect they didn't read it, like Gran's political letters, mine were similarly destined for the bin.

As for Gran, whose side was I on: Marie or hers? I would always veer towards the Cath Furnish philosophy of life because she had instilled it in me so cleverly. She was a woman whose ideas were so out of kilter with the rest of society that she was difficult to be around but that didn't mean that she was wrong. I finally got her to talk to me about James Arlet.

'He was bored all the time, on edge.'

'Anxious you mean?' I asked.

'Yes.'

'Why couldn't he learn to relax?'

'How can you relax in this world?'

'I don't know. Yoga, *Scrabble*?' She shook her head at me. 'But why did he run a pub, of all things?' I asked.

'A stroke of genius, the perfect place for him. His very own pharmacy where he could self-medicate.'

'How can you say that?'

'You ask me now, after all these years, how I can speak the unpalatable?'

'Wouldn't you rather he'd been a postman or an accountant and survived?'

'There was no surviving to be done. Landlord was the sensible choice, it put him in control.'

'But he was out of control,' I argued.

'He was a man born without a skin. What can you do if you are born with no covering, no protection? You must make your own skin out of something. Alcohol gave James a skin.'

'But it was a false one.'

'It doesn't matter how you acquire a skin but you must have one. You have made yours from fashionable clothes, they serve to distract people, stop them seeing through to your bones.'

'Don't change the conversation,' I said, stroking my new scarf.

'And, with his skin on, he needed an audience, what better place than a pub? He could get on with what was left of his life and share what he had with everybody.'

'What was that?'

'Intelligence, radical ideas, humour, flights of fancy,' she seemed suddenly flattened by her own language. 'That's enough now, I have said enough.'

'I'm genuinely interested, I want to know all about him, what did he look like? Sound like?' I demanded.

'Those things are mine and I will not dilute or cheapen them with repetition.'

I shrugged and stormed out.

* * *

Gran confessed to my mother about forging the letter from John Doon, 20 years ago. My mother's face quivered for a moment in sorrow before she told us about the potential viewing figures for her latest pitch – *Celebrity Felons*.

We never heard from John again, he might have been estranged from his father but he wouldn't have wanted Bill to kill him. Briefly, I had a father, but he slipped away as neatly as he had stepped into our lives.

I was neither my grandmother nor my mother. I didn't necessarily believe in pot-scraping moments coming to all people; some of us might have had the ability to swerve and skirt doom indefinitely but, in that ability to turn at just the right moment, we might lose something.

I lived at the pub now, mostly alone. Sometimes, I invited the liquid-eyed decorator round. I didn't hear about Susan and Michael much but knew they were together and managing a place 30 miles away. After witnessing Susan's charismatic performance in court and how she had influenced the jury in the murder trial, getting Bill's sentence reduced, I finally forgave myself for falling under her spell when I was a child.

Bill ended up spending three years in prison for standing up for my grandmother. She said she never asked him to do it. 'He didn't do it for me. He thinks he did but, really, he was just salvaging his own pride. That's just the story he tells himself. We all have a tale. Yours is *The Red Shoes*,' she said.

'I know where you're going with this and I refuse to play.'

'Where am I going, Amanda?'

'Oh please, give me some credit, a tale about a young woman who chooses frivolous things over authenticity. A girl who leaves behind her worthy, homemade shoes and is distracted by a brighter, mass-produced pair. All because I disregard some of your teachings. You are giving me this as an example because you want to unsettle me, because I have finally escaped your gloom-ridden clutches.'

She laughed. But I was not going to let her get away with that, I wouldn't be diverted by an unexpected display of good humour, 'So, you get to choose your story and you have chosen *The Book of Job*, a myth about a man who loses everything and yet still remains dissatisfied with traditional answers to piety and suffering. How noble.'

She was looking uncomfortable, 'Get on with it.'

'The story of a man who won't shut up, won't tow the line. But doesn't Job, at the very end of his tether, say to his friends something like, "You are trying to rob me of my very character?"'

'Get to the point, Amanda.'

'Well, that line, it feels like you're always trying to do that to me.'

'I will never mention *The Red Shoes* again.'

'Good.'

There was an alliance between Doons and Furnishs, a walking, talking one: me. If, when Dr Doon were alive, Gran had held me by the feet and offered my arms to Doon as an olive branch, he would have grabbed me and broken every finger.

When Gran saw me flailing at the pub, she told me that, for a while, she lived through me. It was as though history were repeating itself and our lives were intertwined. She was paralysed with fear that the same things that had happened to her would happen to me. That was why she was unable to advise me, she felt helpless. If she implied that I were imagining things, then she wouldn't have to face her own past.

When I was called a slut, she had been called a lot worse. When people turned against me at Susan's party, the same thing had happened to her, in the same building. I looked roughly the same as she did at my age – but I was not her. I didn't have her charisma; I ran a pub and I was moderately popular but people came to see the river, not me. Or they came because they knew of her reputation. I needed people, she didn't seem to. I understood remorse, possibly falsely, but she had none whatsoever for anything she had ever done. I understood that anybody could be a victim but she thought that, once you were one, you could never return.

It was all about reputation with her; being cruelly misjudged, not being able to answer back. Just like Job was unable to make God hear him, so she had been unable to make people hear her. She didn't come down to the pub very often, it was my domain now. Working in the pub, watching some people drinking heavily, reminded me unnervingly of James Arlet. I didn't think that Gran should get away with what she had said about him self-medicating. I went to my mother for advice. She replied that Gran had idealised James' addiction, colluded with him, instead of seeing it for what it was. A man who wanted to scream like a baby every day but decided that he would be exposed if he did, so poured alcohol down his neck to suppress the cries.

'If she wants to venerate emotional cowardice that's up to her,' my mother said.

I paraphrased my mother's knowledge and threw it back at Gran, even though I thought it was harsh and simplistic.

Her answer was calm, 'James was certainly hiding something. Like a human pass the parcel, people would try to unwrap him and get closer to his core but he would distract them by giving out little prizes when he fell into their hands: warmth, jokes and stories. He was a man composed of so many layers and so much wrapping that there would never be enough music in the world to get to the heart of him.'

* * *

Living at the pub, I missed the carousel. I knew it would come to me in the end and I would never try to sell it again. There was something about that machine, in the staring and pondering over it that effected change inside a person.

Once, after closing time, when the moon was bright, I told everyone that they could go and I left the clearing up until the morning. I carried a plastic table and chair out into the water, not the heavy pub table and chairs that Gran had hauled. I sat roughly in the same place as my grandparents, on a mudbank in the middle of an estuary, and I wondered how many of the particles beneath me were the same. I wanted to experience what they had, but only fleetingly. I didn't want to remain there, so, after 10 minutes on my little island, I waded back to shore, leaving the table and chair behind for the river to sweep away.

Acknowledgements

I would like to thank Stephanie Forward, who encouraged my writing from the beginning, my Mum and Dad and Di Prentice, without whom this book would never have been written. Early readers of the novel, Sarah Astbury, Angel Stripe, Wendy Bicknell, Pearl Martin, Kathy Williams, Emma Bish and Kerry O'Grady proved extremely helpful. Also, my agent Isabel Atherton for initially spotting the book, and editor Fiona Shoop for her suggestions and masterful editing. Above all, I would like to thank my family – Pat, Dan and Vince.

Author's Note

For anybody who would like to look further into Job's story, Stephen Mitchell has made an extraordinary English poem out of the *Hebrew of Job*, packed with startling images and exquisite writing.

Mitchell, Stephen, *The Book of Job* (HarperCollins, New York, 1979).

The Exhibitionists by **Russell James**

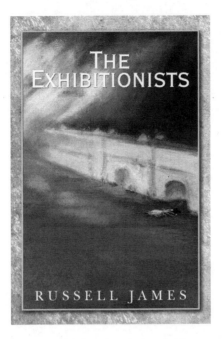

On the night Parliament burnt down, a child was conceived out of wedlock, a baby was abandoned, and another thrown into the Thames.

The lives of the three children interweave and mix with famous people of the Victorian era including Turner, Millais, Holman Hunt and the self-styled greatest historical artist of the time, Benjamin Haydon. Not to mention the intriguing He-Sing who conned the establishment into believing his colourful tales, even allowing him to meet Queen Victoria at the Great Exhibition of 1851.

Available from all good booksellers and as an eBook for all eReaders

ISBN 978-1-78095-004-4 (Hardback), £18.99
ISBN 978-1-78095-011-2 (Trade Paperback), £12.99

For more details and to see our other books, visit www.GoldenGuidesPress.com